The Heart Of Rachael

By

Kathleen Thompson Norris

Double 9
BOOKS

The Heart Of Rachael
by Kathleen Thompson Norris

Copyright © 2024

All Rights reserved.

ISBN: 978-93-61154-98-0

Published by

DOUBLE 9 BOOKS
2/13-B, Ansari Road
Daryaganj, New Delhi – 110002
info@double9books.com
www.double9books.com
Tel. 011-40042856

ABOUT THE AUTHOR

Kathleen Thompson Norris was an American novelist and newspaper columnist. Between 1911 and 1959, she was one of the most widely read and highest-paid female writers in the United States. Norris was a prolific writer, having written 93 novels, many of which were great sellers. Her stories were published often in the popular press of the time, including The Atlantic, The American Magazine, McClure's, Everybody's, Ladies' Home Journal, and Woman's Home Companion. Norris' novels promoted family and moralistic principles such as the sanctity of marriage, the dignity of motherhood, and the significance of service to others. Kathleen Thompson Norris was born in San Francisco, California, on July 16, 1880. Her parents were Josephine (née Moroney) and James Alden Thompson. When she was 19, both of her parents died. As the oldest sibling, she was essentially the head of a huge family and had to work. She first worked in a retail store, then in an accounting office, and last at the Mechanic's Institute Library. In 1905, she enrolled in the University of California, Berkeley's creative writing program and started creating short stories. In September 1906, the San Francisco Call, which had previously published several of her stories, engaged her to write a society column.

CONTENTS

BOOK I

CHAPTER I

The day had opened so brightly, in such a welcome wave of April sunshine, that by mid-afternoon there were two hundred players scattered over the links of the Long Island Country Club at Belvedere Bay; the men in thick plaid stockings and loose striped sweaters, the women's scarlet coats and white skirts making splashes of vivid color against the fresh green of grass and the thick powdering of dandelions. It was Saturday, and a half-holiday; it was that one day of all the year when the seasons change places, when winter is visibly worsted, and summer, with warmth and relaxation, bathing and tennis and motor trips in the moonlight, becomes again a reality.

There was a real warmth in the sunshine to-day, there was a fragrance of lilac and early roses in the idle breezes. "Hot!" shouted the players exultantly, as they passed each other in the green valleys and over the sunny mounds. "You bet it's hot!" agreed stout and glowing gentlemen, wiping wet foreheads before reaching for a particular club, and panting as they gazed about at the unbroken turf, melting a few miles away into the new green of maple and elm trees, and topped, where the slope rose, by the white columns and brick walls of the clubhouse.

Motor cars swept incessantly back and forth on the smooth roadway; a few riders, their horses wheeling and dancing, went down the bridle path, and there was a sprinkling of young men and women and some shouting and clapping on the tennis-courts. But golf was the order of the day. At the first tee at least two scores of impatient players waited their turn to drive off, and at the last green a group of twenty or thirty men and women, mostly women, were interestedly watching the putting.

Mrs. Archibald Buckney, a large, generously made woman of perhaps fifty, who stood a little apart from the group, with two young women and a mild-looking blond young man, suddenly interrupted a general discussion of scores and play with a personality.

"Is Clarence Breckenridge playing to-day, I wonder? Anybody seen him?"

"Must be," said the more definite of the two rather indefinite girls, with an assumption of bright interest. Leila Buckney, a few weeks ago, had announced her engagement to the mild-looking blond young man, Parker Hoyt, and she was just now attempting to hold him by a charm she suspected she did not possess for him, and at the same time to give her mother and sister the impression that Parker was so deeply in her toils that she need make no further effort to enslave him.

She had really nothing in common with Parker; their conversation was composed entirely of personalities about their various friends, and Leila felt it a great burden, and dreaded the hours she must perforce spend alone with her future husband. It would be much better when they were married, of course, but they could not even begin to talk wedding plans yet, because Parker lived in nervous terror of his aunt's disapproval, and Mrs. Watts Frothingham was just now in Europe, and had not yet seen fit to answer her nephew's dignified notification of his new plans, or the dutiful and gracious note with which Miss Leila had accompanied it.

The truth, though Leila did not know it, was that Mrs. Frothingham had a pretty social secretary named Margaret Clay, a strange, attractive little person, eighteen years old, whose mother had been the old lady's companion for many years. And to Magsie, as they all called her, young Mr. Hoyt had paid some decided attention not many months before. Mrs. Frothingham had seen fit to disapprove these advances then, but she was an extraordinarily erratic and cross-grained old lady, and her silence now had forced her nephew uncomfortably to suspect that she might have changed her mind.

"Darn it!" said the engaging youth to himself "It's none of her business, anyway, what I do!" But it made him acutely uneasy none the less. He was the possessor of a good income, as he stood there, this mild little blond; it came to him steadily and regularly, with no effort at all on his part, but, with his aunt's million--it must be at least that--he felt that he would have been much happier. There it was, safe in the family, and she was seventy-six, and without a direct heir. It would be too bad to miss it now!

He thought of it a great deal, was thinking of it this moment, in fact, and Leila suspected that he was. But Mrs. Buckney, aside from a half-formed wish that young persons were more demonstrative in these days, and that the wedding might be soon, had not a care in the world, and, after a moment's unresponsive silence, returned blithely to her query about Clarence Breckenridge.

"I haven't seen him," responded one of her daughters presently. "Funny, too! Last year he didn't miss a day."

"Of course he'll get the cup as usual, this year," Mrs. Buckney said brightly. "But I don't suppose young people with their heads full of wedding plans will care much about the golf!" she added courageously.

To this Miss Leila answered only with a weary shrug.

"Been drinking lately," Mr. Hoyt volunteered.

"You say he has?" Mrs. Buckney took him up promptly. "Is that so? I knew he did all the time, of course, but I hadn't heard lately. Well--! Pretty hard on Mrs. Breckenridge, isn't it?"

"Pretty hard on his daughter," Miss Leila drawled. "He has all kinds of money, hasn't he, Park?"

"Scads," said Mr. Hoyt succinctly. Conversation languished. Miss Leila presently said decidedly that unless her mother stood still, the sun, which was indeed sinking low in the western sky, got in everyone's eyes. Miss Edith said that she was dying for tea; Mr. Hoyt's watch was consulted. Four o'clock; it was a little too early for tea.

At about five o'clock the sunlight was softened by a steadily rising bank of fog, which drifted in from the east; a mist almost like a light rain beat upon the faces of the last golfers. There were no riders on the bridle path now, and the long line of motor cars parked by the clubhouse doors began to move and shift and lessen. People with dinner engagements melted mysteriously away, lights bloomed suddenly in the dining-room, shades were drawn and awnings furled.

But in the club's great central apartment--which was reception-room, lounging-room, and tea-room, and which, opened to the immense porches, was used for dances in summer, and closed and holly-trimmed, was the scene of many a winter dance as well--a dozen good friends and neighbors lingered for tea. The women, sunk in deep chairs about the blazing logs in the immense fireplace, gossiped in low tones together, punctuating their talk with an occasional burst of soft laughter. The men watched teacups, adding an occasional comment to the talk, but listening in silence for the most part, their amused eyes on the women's interested faces.

Here was a representative group, ranging in age from old Peter Pomeroy, who had been one of the club's founders twelve years ago, and at sixty was one of its prominent members to-day, to lovely Vivian Sartoris, a demure, baby-faced little blonde of eighteen, who might be confidently expected to make a brilliant match in a year or two. Peter, slim, hard, gray-haired and leaden-skinned, well-groomed and irreproachably dressed, was discussing a cotillion with Mrs. Sartoris, a stout, florid little woman who was only twice her daughter's age. Mrs. Sartoris really did look young to be the mother of a popular debutante; she rode and played golf and tennis as briskly as ever; it was her pose to bring up the subject of age at all times, and to threaten Vivian with terrible penalties if she dared marry before her mother was forty at least.

Old Peter Pomeroy, who had a shrewd and disillusioned gray eye, thought, as everyone else thought, that Mrs. Sartoris was an empty-headed little fool, but he rarely talked to a woman who was anything else, and no woman ever thought him anything but markedly courteous and gallant. He was old now, rich, unmarried, quite alone in the world. For forty years he had kept all the women of his acquaintance speculating as to his plans; marriageable women especially--perhaps fifty of them--had been able in all maidenliness to indicate to him that they might easily be persuaded to share the Pomeroy name and fortune. But Peter went on kissing their hands, and thrilling them with an intimate casual word now and then, and did no more.

Perhaps he smiled about it sometimes, in the privacy of his own apartments--apartments which were variously located in a great city hotel, an Adirondacks camp, a luxurious club, his own yacht, and the beautiful home he had built for himself within a mile of the spot where he was now having his tea. Sometimes it seemed amusing to him that so many traps were laid for him. He could appraise women quickly, and now and then he teased a woman of his acquaintance with a delightfully worded description of his ideal of a wife. If the woman thereafter carelessly indicated the possession of the desired qualities in herself, Peter saw that, too, but she never knew it, and never saw him laughing at her. She went on for a month or two dressing brilliantly for his carefully chaperoned little dinners, listening absorbed to his dissertations upon Japanese prints or draperies from Peshawar, until Peter grew tired and drew off, when she must put a brave face upon it and do her share to show that she realized that the little game was over.

He had not been entirely without feminine companionship, however, during the half-century of his life as a man. Everybody knew something--and suspected a great deal more--of various friendships of his. Even the girls knew that Peter Pomeroy was not over-cautious in the management of his affairs, but they did not like him the less, nor did their mothers find him less eligible, in a matrimonial sense. Sometimes he met the older women's hints quite seriously, with brief allusions to some "little girl" who was always as sweet and deserving and virtuous as his own fatherly interference in her affairs was disinterested and kind. "I did what I could for her--risking what might or might not be said," Mr. Pomeroy might add, with a hero's modest smile and shrug. And if nobody ever believed him, at least nobody ever challenged him.

Vivian Sartoris, girlishly perched on the great square leather fender that framed the fireplace, was merely a modern, a very modern, little girl, demurely dressed in the smartest of white taffeta ruffles, with her small feet in white silk stockings and shoes, a daring little black-and-white hat mashed down upon her soft, loose hair, and, slung about her shoulders, a woolly coat of clearest lemon yellow. Vivian gave the impression of a soft little watchful cat, unfriendly, alert, selfish. Her manner was studiedly rowdyish, her speech marred by slang; she loved only a few persons in the world besides herself. One of these few persons, however, was Clarence Breckenridge's daughter, Carol, affectionately known to all these persons as "Billy," and it was in Miss Breckenridge's defence that Vivian was speaking now. A general yet desultory discussion of the three Breckenridges had been going on for some moments. And some particular criticism of the man of the family had pierced Miss Sartoris' habitual attitude of bored silence.

"That's all true about him," she said, idly spreading a sturdy little hand to the blaze. "I have no use for Clarence Breckenridge, and I think Mrs. Breckenridge is absolutely the most cold-blooded woman I ever met! She always makes me feel as if she were waiting to see me make a fool of myself, so that she could smile that smooth superior smile at me. But Carol's different--she's square, she is; she's just top-hole--if you know what I mean--she's the finest ever," finished Miss Sartoris, with a carefully calculated boyishness, "and what I mean to say is, she's never had a fair deal!"

There was a little murmur of assent and admiration at this, and only one voice disputed it.

"You're not called upon to defend Billy Breckenridge, Vivian," said Elinor Vanderwall, in her cool, amused voice. "Nobody's blaming Billy, and Rachael Breckenridge can stand on her own feet. But what we're saying is that Clarence, in spite of what they do to protect him, will get himself dropped by decent people if he goes on as he IS going on! He was tennis champion four or five years ago; he played against an Englishman named Waters, who was about half his age; it was the most remarkable thing I ever saw--"

"Wonderful match!" said Peter Pomeroy, as she paused.

"Wonderful--I should say so!" Miss Vanderwall sighed admiringly at the memory. "Do you remember that one set went to nineteen--twenty-one? Each man won on his own service--'most remarkable match I ever saw! But Clarence Breckenridge couldn't hold a racket now, and his game of bridge is getting to be absolutely rotten. Crime, I call it!"

Vivian Sartoris offered no further remark. Indeed she had drifted into a low-toned conversation with a young man on the fender. Elinor Vanderwall was neither pretty nor rich, and she was unmarried at thirty-four, her social importance being further lessened by the fact that she had five sisters, all unmarried, too, except Anna, the oldest, whose son was in college. Anna was Mrs. Prince; her wedding was only a long-ago memory now. Georgiana, who came next, was a calm, plain woman of thirty-seven, interested in church work and organized charities. Alice was musical and delicate. Elinor was worldly, decisive, the social favorite among the sisters. Jeanette was boyish and brisk, a splendid sportswoman, and Phyllis, at twenty-six, was still babyish and appealing, tiny in build, and full of feminine charms.

All five were good dancers, good tennis and golf players, good horsewomen, and good managers. All five dressed well, talked well, and played excellent bridge. The fact of their not marrying was an eternal mystery to their friends, to their wiry, nervous little father, and their large, fat, serene mother; perhaps to themselves as well. They met life, as they saw it, with great cleverness, making it a rule to do little entertaining at home, where the preponderance of women was most notable, and refusing to accept invitations except singly. The Vanderwall girls were rarely seen together; each had her pose and kept to it, each helped the others to maintain theirs in turn. Alice's music, Georgiana's altruistic duties, these were matters of sacred family tradition, and if outsiders sometimes speculated as to the sisters' sincerity, at least no Vanderwall ever betrayed another. And despite their obvious handicaps, the five girls were regarded as social authorities, and their names were prominently displayed in newspaper accounts of all smart affairs. While making a fine art of feminine friendships, they yet diffused a general impression of being involved in endless affairs of the heart. They were much in demand to fill in bridge tables, to serve on club directorates, to amuse week-end parties, to be present at house weddings, and to remain with the family for the first blank day or two after the bride and groom were gone.

"Queer fellow, Breckenridge," said George Pomeroy, old Peter's nephew, a red-faced, florid, simple man of forty.

"Well, he never should have married as he did, it's all in a mess," a woman's voice said lazily. "Rachael's extraordinary of course--there's no one quite like her. But she wasn't the woman for him. Clarence wanted the little, clinging, adoring kind, who would put cracked ice on his forehead, and wish those bad saloonkeepers would stop drugging her dear big boy. Rachael looks right through him; she doesn't fight, she doesn't care enough to fight. She's just supremely bored by his weakness and stupidity. He isn't big enough for her, either in goodness or badness. I never knew what she married him for, and I don't believe anyone else ever did!"

"I did, for one," said Miss Vanderwall, flicking the ashes from her cigarette with a well-groomed fingertip. "Clarence Breckenridge never was in love but once in his life--no, I don't mean with Paula. I mean with Billy." And as a general nodding of heads confirmed this theory, the speaker went on decidedly: "Since that child was born she's been all the world to him. When he and Paula were divorced--she was the offender--he fretted himself sick for fear he'd done that precious five-year-old an injury. She didn't get on with her grandmother, she drove governesses insane, for two or three years there was simply no end of trouble. Finally he took her abroad, for the excellent reason that she wanted to go. In Paris they ran into Rachael Fairfax and her mother--let's see, that was seven years ago. Rachael was only about twenty-one or two then. But she'd been out since she was sixteen. She had the bel air, she was beautiful--not as pretty as she is now, perhaps--and of course her father was dead, and Rachael was absolutely on the make. She took both Clarence and Billy in hand. I understand the child was wearing jewelry and staying up until all hours every night. Rachael mothered her, and of course the child came to admire her. The funny thing is that Rachael and Billy hit it off very well to this day.

"She and Clarence were married quietly, and came home. And I don't think it was weeks, it was DAYS--and not many days--later, that Rachael realized what a fool she'd been. Clarence had eyes for no one but the girl, and of course she was a fascinating little creature, and she's more fascinating every year."

"She's not as attractive as Rachael at that," said Peter Pomeroy.

"I know, my dear Peter," Miss Vanderwall assented quickly. "But Billy's impulsive, and affectionate, at least, and Rachael is neither. Anyway, Billy's at the age now when she can't think of anything but herself. Her frocks, her parties, her friends--that's all Clarence cares about!"

"Selfish ass!" said a man's voice in the firelight.

"I KNOW Clarence takes Carol and her friends off on week-end trips," some woman said, "and leaves Rachael at home. If Rachael wants the car, she has to ask them their plans. If she accepts a dinner invitation, why, Clarence may drop out the last moment because Carol's going to dine alone at home and wants her Daddy."

"Rachael's terribly decent about it," said the deep voice of old Mrs. Torrence, who was chaperoning a grandson, glad of any excuse to be at the club. "Upon my word I wouldn't be! She will breakfast upstairs many a morning because Clarence likes Carol to pour his coffee. And when that feller comes home tipsy--"

"Five nights a week!" supplemented Peter Pomeroy.

"Five nights a week," the old lady agreed, nodding, "she makes him comfortable, quiets the house, and telephones around generally that Clarence has come home with a splitting headache, and they can't come--to dinner, or cards, or whatever it may be. But of course I don't claim that she loves him, nor pretends to. I can imagine the scornful look with which she goes about it."

"Well, why does she stand it?" said Mrs. Barker Emory, a handsome but somewhat hard-faced woman, with a manner curiously compounded of eagerness and uncertainty.

"Y'know, that's what I've been wondering," an Englishman added interestedly.

"Why, what else would she do?" Miss Vanderwall asked briskly.

"Rachael's a perfectly adorable and brilliant and delightful creature," summarized Peter Pomeroy, "but she's not got a penny nor a relative in the world that I've ever heard of! She's got no grounds for divorcing Clarence, and if she simply wanted to get out, why, now that she's brought Billy up, introduced her generally, whipped the girl into some sort of shape and got her the right sort of friends, I suppose she might get out and welcome!"

"No, Billy honestly likes her," objected Vivian Sartoris.

"She doesn't care for her enough to see that there's fair play," Elinor Vanderwall said quickly.

"Why doesn't she take a leaf from Paula's book," somebody suggested, "and marry again? She could go out West and get a divorce on any grounds she might choose to name."

"Well, Rachael's a cold woman, and a hard woman--in a way," Miss Vanderwall said musingly, after a pause, when the troubles of the Breckenridges kept the group silent for a moment. "But she's a good sport. She gets a home, and clothes, and the club, and a car and all the rest out of it, and she knows Billy and Clarence do need her, in a way, to run things, and to keep up the social end. More than that, Clarence can't keep up this pace long--he's going to pieces fast--and Billy may marry any day--"

"I understand Joe Pickering's a little bit touched in that quarter," said Mrs. Torrence.

"Yes--well, Clarence will never stand for THAT," somebody said.

Little Miss Sartoris neglected the Torrence grandson long enough to say decidedly:

"She wouldn't LOOK at Joe Pickering! Joe drinks, and Billy's had enough of that with her father. Besides, he has no money of his own! He's impossible!"

"Where's the mother all this time?" asked the Englishman. "I mean to say, she's living, isn't she, and all that?"

"Very much alive," Miss Vanderwall said. "Married to an Italian count--Countess Luca d' Asafo. His people have cut him off; they're Catholics. She has two little girls; there's an uncle who's obliged to leave property to a son, and it serves Paula quite right, I think. Where they live, or what on, I haven't the remotest idea. I saw her in a car on Fifth Avenue, not so long ago, with two heavy little black-haired girls; she looked sixty."

"Her sister, you know, was thick with my niece, Barbara Olliphant," said Peter Pomeroy. "And funny thing!--when Barbara was married..."

It was a long story, and fortunately moved away from the previous topic; so that when it was presently interrupted by the arrival of two women, everybody in the group had cause to feel gratitude for a merciful deliverance.

The two women were Rachael and Carol Breckenridge, who came in a little breathless, the throbbing engine of their motor car still sounding faintly from the direction of the club doorway. Carol, a slender, black-eyed, dusky-skinned girl of seventeen, took her place beside Miss Sartoris on the fender, granting a brief unsmiling nod to one or two friends, and eying the group between the loose locks of her smoky, cropped black hair with the inscrutable, almost brooding, expression that was her favorite affectation. Her lithe, loosely built little body was as flat as a boy's, she clasped her crossed knees with slender, satin-smooth little brown hands, exposing by her attitude a frill of embroidered petticoat, a transparent stretch of ash-gray silk stocking, and smart ash-gray buckskin slippers with silver buckles.

She was an effective little figure in the mingled twilight and firelight, but it was toward her beautiful stepmother that everybody looked as Rachael Breckenridge seated herself on the arm of old Mrs. Torrence's chair and sent a careless greeting about the circle.

"Hello, everybody!" she said, in a voice of extraordinary richness and sweetness, "Peter, Dolly, Vivian--HELLO, Elinor! How do you do, Mrs. Emory?" There was an aside when the newcomer said imperatively to a club attendant, "We'll have some light here, please!" Then she resumed easily: "I do beg your pardon, Mrs. Emory, I interrupted you--"

"I only said that you were a little late for tea," said Mrs. Emory, sweetly, wishing with a sort of futile rage that she could learn to say almost nothing when this other woman, with her insulting bright air of making one feel inferior, was about. The Emorys had lived in Belvedere Hills for two years, coming from Denver with much money and irrefutable credentials. They had been members of the club perhaps half that time, members in good standing. But Mrs. Emory would have paid a large sum to have Rachael Breckenridge call her "Belle," and Rachael Breckenridge knew it.

The lights, duly poured in a soft flood from all sides of the room, revealed in Mrs. Breckenridge one of those beauties that an older generation of diarists and letter writers frankly spelled with a capital letter as distinguishing her charms from those of a thousand of lesser degree. When such beauty is unaccompanied by intellect it is a royal dower, and its possessor may serenely command half a century of unquestioning adoration from the sons of men, and all the good things of life as well.

But when there is a soul behind the matchless eyes, and a keen wit animates the lovely mouth, and when the indication of the white forehead is not belied, it is a nice question whether great beauty be a gift of benign or malicious fairies. Not a woman in this room or in any room she entered could look at Rachael Breckenridge without a pang; her supremacy was beyond all argument or dispute. And yet there was neither complacency nor content in the lovely face; it wore its usual expression of arrogant amusement at a somewhat tiresome world.

Both in the instant impression it made, and under closest analysis, Rachael Breckenridge's beauty stood all tests. Her colorless skin was as pure as ivory, her dark-blue eyes, surrounded by that faint sooty color that only Irish eyes know, were set far apart and evenly arched by perfect brows. Her white forehead was low and broad, the lustreless black hair was swept back from it with almost startling simplicity, the line of her mouth was long, her lips a living red. Her figure, as she sat balancing carelessly on a chair-arm, showed the exquisite curves of a woman slow to develop, who is approaching the height of her beauty, and from the tip of her white shoe to the poppies on her soft straw hat there was that distinction in her clothing that betrayed her to be one of the few who may be always individual yet always in the fashion. She was a woman, quick, dynamic, impatient, who vitalized the very atmosphere in which she moved, challenging life by endless tests and measures, scornful of admiration, and ambitious, even in this recognized ambition of finding herself beautiful, prominent, and a rich man's wife, for something further and greater, she knew not what. She was an important figure in this world of hers; her word was authority, her decree law. Never was censure so quick as hers, never criticism so biting, or satire so witty. No human emotion was too sacred to form a target for her glancing arrows, nor was any affection deep enough to arouse in her anything but doubt and scorn.

"I don't want any tea, thank you, Peter," she said now, in the astonishingly rich voice that seemed to fill the words with new meaning. "And I won't allow the Infant to have any--no, Billy, you shall not. You've got a complexion, child; respect it. Besides, you've just had some. Besides, we're here for only two seconds--it's six o'clock. We're looking for Clarence--we seek a husband fond, a parent dear--"

"Clarence hasn't showed up here at all to-day," said Peter Pomeroy, stretching back comfortably in his chair, appreciative eyes upon Clarence's wife. "Shame, too, for we had some good golf. Course is in splendid condition. George beat me three up and two to play, but I don't bear any malice. Here I am signing for his highball."

"Well, then, we'll go on home," Mrs. Breckenridge said, without, however, changing her relaxed position. "Clarence is probably there; we've been playing cards at the Parmalees', or at least I have. Billy and Katrina were playing tennis with Kent and--who's the red-headed child you were enslaving this afternoon, Bill?"

"Porter Pinckard," Miss Breckenridge answered, indifferently, before entering into a confidential exchange of brevities with Miss Sartoris.

"I'll call him out, and run him through the liver," said Peter Pomeroy, "the miserable catiff! I'll brook no rivals, Billy."

Billy merely smiled lazily at this; her eyes were far more eloquent than her tongue, as she was well aware.

"Let her alone, Fascination Fledgerby!" said Mrs. Breckenridge briskly. "Why can't we take you home with us, Elinor? We go your way."

"You may," said Miss Vanderwall, rising. "You're dining at the Chases', aren't you, Billy? So am I. But I was going to change here. Where are you dining, Rachael?"

"Change at my house," Mrs. Breckenridge suggested, or rather commanded. "I'm dining in my room, I think. I'm all in." But the clear and candid eyes deceived no one. Clarence was misbehaving again, everybody decided, and poor Rachael could not bespeak five minutes of her own time until this particular period of intemperance was over. Miss Vanderwall, settling herself in the beautiful Breckenridge car five minutes later, faced the situation boldly.

"Where's Clarence, Rachael?"

"I haven't the remotest idea, my dear woman," said Mrs. Breckenridge frankly, yet with a warning glance at the back of her stepdaughter's head. Billy was at the wheel. "He didn't dine at home last night--"

"But we knew where he was," Billy said quickly, half turning.

"We knew where he was," agreed the older woman. "Watch where you're going, Bill! He told Alfred that he was dining in town, with a friend, talking business."

"I thought it was the night of Berry Stokes' dinner," suggested Miss Vanderwall.

"He wasn't there--I asked him not to go," said Billy.

"Oh--" Miss Vanderwall began and then abruptly stopped. "Oh!" said she mildly, in polite acquiescence.

They were sweeping through the April roadsides so swiftly that it was only a moment later when Rachael, reaching for the door, remarked cheerfully, "Here we are!"

The car had entered a white stone gateway, and was approaching a certain charming country mansion, one that was not conspicuous among a thousand others strewn over the neighboring hills and valleys, but a beautiful home nevertheless. Vines climbed the brick chimneys, and budding hydrangeas, in pots, topped the white balustrades of the porch. A hundred little details of perfect furnishing would have been taken for granted by the casual onlooker, yet without its lawns, its awnings, its window boxes and snowy curtaining, its glimpse of screened veranda and wicker chairs, its trim assembly of garage, stable, and servants' cottages, its porte-cochere, sleeping porches, and tennis court, it would have seemed incomplete and uncomfortable to its owners.

Rachael Breckenridge neither liked it nor disliked it. It had been her home for the seven years of her married life, except for the month or two she spent every winter in a New York hotel. She had never had any great happiness in it, to be sure, but then her life had been singularly lacking in moments of real happiness, and she had valued other elements, and desired other elements more. She had not expected to be happy in this house, she had expected to be rich and envied, and secure, and she was all of these things. That they were not worth attaining, no one knew better than Rachael now.

The house was of course a great care to her, the more so because Billy was in it so little, and was so frankly eager for the time when she should leave it and go to a house of her own, and because Clarence was absolutely indifferent to it in his better moods, and pleased with nothing when he was in the grip of his besetting sin. The Breckenridges did little formal entertaining, but the man of the house liked to bring men down from town for week-end visits, and Billy brought her young friends in and out with youthful indifference to domestic regulations, so that on Rachael, as housekeeper, there fell no light burden.

She carried it gracefully, knitting her handsome brows as the seasons brought about their endless problems, discussing bulbs with old Rafael in the garden when the snow melted, discussing paper and paint in the first glory of May, superintending the making of iced drinks on the hot summer afternoons, and in October filling her woodroom duly with the great logs that would blaze neglected in the drawing-room fireplace all winter long. The house was not large, as such houses go; too much room was wasted by a very modern architect in linen closets and coat closets, bathrooms and hall space, dressing-rooms, passages, and nooks and corners generally. Yet Rachael's guest-rooms were models in their way, and when she gave a luncheon the women who came were always ready to exclaim in despairing admiration over the beauty of the gardens, the flower-filled, airy rooms, the table appointments, and the hostess herself.

But when they said that she was "wonderful"--and it was the inevitable word for Rachael Breckenridge-the general meaning went deeper than this. She was wonderful in her pride, the dignity and the silence of her attitude toward her husband; she had been a wonderful mother to Clarence's daughter; not a loving mother, perhaps--she was not loving to anyone--but a miracle of determination and clearness of vision.

Who else, her friends wondered, could have cleared the social horizon for Paula Breckenridge's daughter so effectively? With what brisk resoluteness the new mother had cut short the aimless European wanderings, cropped the child's artificially curled hair, given away the unsuitable silk stockings and the ridiculous frocks and hats. Billy, shorn and bewildered, had been brought home; had entered Miss Proctor's select school, entered Miss Roger's select dancing class, entered Professor Darling's expensive riding classes. Billy, in dark-blue Peter Thompsons, in black stockings and laced boots, had been dropped in among other little girls in Peter Thompsons and laced boots, little girls with the approved names of Whittaker and Bowditch, Moran and Merridew and Parmalee.

Billy had never doubted her stepmother's judgment; like all of the new Mrs. Breckenridge's friends, she was deeply, dumbly impressed with that lady's amazing efficiency. She had been a spoiled and discontented little rowdy. She became an entirely self-satisfied little gentlewoman. Clarence, jealously watching her progress, knew that Rachael was doing for his daughter far more than he could ever do himself.

But Rachael, if she had expected reward, reaped none. Her husband was a supremely selfish man, and his daughter inherited his sublime ability to protect his own pleasure at any cost. Carol admired her step-mother, but she was an indolent and luxury-loving little soul, and even as early as her twelfth or fourteenth year she had been deeply flattered by the evidences of her own power over her father. Into her youthful training no reverence for parents--real or adopted--had been infused; she called her father "Clancy," as some of his intimate friends called him, and he delighted to take her orders and bow to her pretty tyranny.

Before she was sixteen he began to take her about with him: to dances, to the theatre, and for long trips in his car. He entered eagerly into her young friendships, frantic to prove himself as young at heart as she. He paid her the extravagant compliments of a lover, and gave her her grandmother's beautiful jewelry, as well as every trinket that caught her eye.

And Billy accepted his attentions with a finished coquetry that was far from childlike, a flush on her satin cheek, a dimple puckering the corner of her mouth, and silky lashes lowered over her satisfied eyes. She was inevitably precocious in many ways, but she was young enough still to fancy herself one of the irresistible beauties and belles of the world, and to flaunt a perfectly conscious arrogance in the eyes of all other women.

All this was bewildering and painful to Rachael. She had never loved her husband--love entered into none of her relationships--her marriage had been only a step in the steady progress of her life toward the position she desired in the world. But she had liked him. She had liked his child, and she had come into the new arrangement kindly and gallantly determined to make the venture at least as profitable to them both as it was to her.

To be ignored, to be deliberately set aside, to be insulted by a selfishness so calculating and so deliberate as to make her own attitude seem all warmth and generosity by comparison, genuinely astonished her. At first, indeed, a sort of magnificent impatience had prevented her from feeling any stronger emotion than astonishment. It was too ridiculous, said the bride to herself tolerantly; it could not go on, of course, this preposterous consideration of a child of ten, this belittling consideration of her own place in the scheme as less Clarence's wife than Billy's mother. It must adjust itself with every week that they three lived together, the child slipping back to her own life, the husband and wife sharing theirs. When Clarence's first fears for his daughter's comfort under the new rule were set at rest, when his confidence in the wisdom and efficiency of his wife was fully established, then a normal relationship must ensue. "Surely Clarence wouldn't ask a woman to marry him just to give Billy a home and social backing?" Rachael asked herself, in those first puzzled days in Paris.

That was seven years ago. She knew exactly that for truth now. Long ago she had learned that whatever impulse had moved Clarence Breckenridge to ask her to marry him was quickly displaced by his vision of Billy's need as being greater than his own.

It had been an unpalatable revelation, for Rachael was a woman proud as well as beautiful. But presently she had accepted the situation as it stood, somehow fighting her way, as the years went by, to fresh acceptances: the acceptance of Billy's ripening charms, the acceptance of Clarence's more and more frequent times of inebriated irresponsibility. Silently she made her mental adjustments, moving through her gay and empty life in an unsuspected bitterness of solitude, won to protest and rebellion only when the cold surface she presented to the world was threatened from within or without.

It was distinctly threatened now, she realized with a little sick twist of apprehension at heart, when her casual inquiry to a maid upon entering was answered by a discreet, "Yes, Mrs. Breckenridge, Mr. Breckenridge came home half an hour ago. Alfred is with him."

This was unexpected. Rachael did not glance either at her guest or her stepdaughter, but she disposed of them both in a breath.

"Someone wants you on the telephone, Billy," she repeated after the maid's information. "Take it in the library. Run right up to my room, Elinor, and I'll be there in two minutes. I'll send some one in with towels and brushes; you've time for a tub. Take these things, Helda, and give them to Annie, and tell her to lookout for Miss Vanderwall."

The square entrance hall was sweet with flowers in the early spring evening, Oriental rugs were spread on the dull mirror of the floor, opened doors gave glimpses of airy colonial interiors, English chintzes crowded with gay colored fruits and flowers, brick fireplaces framed in classic white and showing a brave gleam of brass firedogs in the soft lamplight. Not a book on the long tables, not an etching on the dull rich paper of the walls, struck a false note. It was all exquisitely in tone.

But Rachael Breckenridge, at best, saw less its positive perfections than the tiniest opening through which an imperfection might push its way, and in such an hour as this she saw it not at all. Her mouth a trifle firm in its outline, her face a little pale, she went quickly up the wide white stairway and along the open balcony above. There were several doors on this balcony, which was indeed the upper hall. Mrs. Breckenridge opened one of them without knocking, and closed it noiselessly behind her.

The room into which she admitted herself presented exactly the picture she had expected. The curtains, again of richly colored cretonne, were drawn, a softly toned lamp on the reading table, and another beside the bed, cast circles of pleasant light on the comfortable wicker chairs, the cream-colored woodwork, and the scattered books and magazines. Several photographs of Carol, beautifully framed, were on bookcase and dresser, and a fine oil painting of the child at fourteen looked down from the mantel. On the bed, a mahogany four-poster, with carved pineapples finishing the posts, the frilled cretonne cover had been flung back; Mr. Breckenridge had retired; his blond head was sunk in the pillows; he clutched the blankets about him with his arms, his face was not visible.

A quiet manservant, who was by turns butler, chauffeur, and valet, was stepping softly about the room. Rachael interrogated him in a low tone:

"Asleep, Alfred?"

"Oh, no, ma'am!" the man said quickly. "He's been feeling ill. He says he has a chill."

"When did he get home?" the wife asked.

"About half an hour ago, Mrs. Breckenridge. Mr. Butler telephoned me. Some of the gentlemen were going on--to one of the beach hotels for dinner, I believe, but Mr. Breckenridge felt himself too unwell to join them, so I went for him with the little car, and Mr. Joe Butler and Mr. Parks came home with him, Mrs. Breckenridge."

"Do you know if he went to bed last night at all?"

"No, ma'am, he said he did not. All the gentlemen looked as if they--looked as if they might have--" Alfred hesitated delicately. "It was Mr. Berry Stokes' bachelor dinner," he presently added.

At this moment there was a convulsion in the bed, and the red face of Clarence Breckenridge revealed itself. The eyes were bloodstained, the usually pale skin flushed and oily, the fair, thin hair tumbled across a high and well-developed forehead. Rachael knew every movement of the red and swollen lips, every tone of the querulous voice.

"Does Alfred have to stay up here doing a chambermaid's work?" demanded the man of the house fretfully. "My God! Can you or can't you manage--between your teas and card parties--to get someone else to put this room in order?" He ended in a long moan, and dropped his head again into the pillows.

"Do you know what he wants?" Rachael asked the man in a quick whisper. "Go down and get it, then!"

"I'm co-o-old!" said the man in the bed, going into a sudden and violent chill. "I've caught my death, I think. Joe made a punch--some sort of an eggnog--eggs were bad, I think. I'm poisoned. The stuff was rotten!" He sank mumbling back into the pillows.

Rachael, who had been hanging his coat carefully in the big closet adjoining his room, came to the bedside and laid her cool fingers on his burning forehead. If irrepressible distaste was visible in her face, it was only a faint reflection of the burning resentment in her heart.

"You've got a fever, Clarence," she announced quietly. The answer was only a furious and incoherent burst of denunciation; the patient was in utter physical discomfort, and could not choose his terms. Rachael--not for the first nor the hundredth time--felt within her an impulse to leave him here, leave him to outwear his miseries without her help. But this she could not do without throwing the house into an uproar. Clarence at these times had no consideration for public opinion, had no dignity, no self-control. Much better satisfy him, as she had done so many times before, and keep a brave face to the world.

So she placed a hot-water bag against his cold feet, went to her own room adjoining to borrow a fluffy satin comforter with which to augment his own bed covering, laid an icy towel upon his throbbing forehead, and when Alfred presently appeared with a decanter of whisky, Rachael watched her husband eagerly gulp down a glass of it without uttering one word of the bitter protest that rose to her lips.

She was not a prude, with the sublime inconsistency of most women whose lives are made the darker for drink; she did not identify herself with any movement toward prohibition, or refuse the cocktails, the claret, and the wine that were customarily served at her own and at other people's dinner-tables. But she hated coarseness in any form, she hated contact with the sodden, self-pitying, ugly animal that Clarence Breckenridge became under the influence of drink.

To-night, when he presently fell asleep, somewhat more comfortable in body, and soothed in spirit by the promise of a visit from the doctor, Rachael went into her own room and sinking into a deep chair sat staring stupidly at the floor. She did not think of the husband she had just left, nor of the formal dinner party being given, only half a mile away, to a great English novelist--a dinner to which the Breckenridges had of course been asked and upon which Rachael had weeks ago set her heart. She was tired, and her thoughts floated lazily about nothing at all, or into some opaque region of their own knowing, where the ills of the body might not follow.

Presently Miss Vanderwall, clothed in a trailing robe of soft Arabian cotton, came briskly out of the bathroom, her short dark hair hanging in a mane about her rosy face.

"Why so pensive, Rachael?" she asked cheerfully, pressing a button that lighted the circle of globes about the dressing-table mirror, and seating herself before it. But under her loose locks she sent a keen and concerned look at her hostess' thoughtful face.

"Tired," Rachael answered briefly, not changing her attitude, but with a fleeting shadow of a smile.

"How's Clancy?"

"Asleep. He's wretched, poor fellow! Berry Stokes' bachelor dinner, you know. That crowd is bad for him."

"I KNEW it must have been an orgy!" Miss Vanderwall declared vivaciously. "That was a silly slip of mine in the car. Billy doesn't know he went, I suppose?"

"No, he promised her he wouldn't. But everyone was at the dinner. Some of them came home early, I believe. But it was all kept quiet, because Aline Pearsall is such a little shrinking violet, I suppose," Mrs. Breckenridge said. "The Pearsalls are to think it was just an impromptu affair. Billy and Aline of course have no idea what a party it was. But Clarence says that poor Berry was worse than he, and a few of them are still keeping it up. It's a shame, of course--"

Her uninterested voice dropped into silence.

"Men are queer," Miss Vanderwall said profoundly, busy with ivory-backed brushes, powders, and pastes.

"The mystery to me--about men," mused Mrs. Breckenridge, her absent eyes upon the buckled slipper she held in her hand, "is not that they are as helpless as babies the moment anything goes wrong with their poor little heads or their poor little tummies, but that they work so hard, in spite of that, to increase the general discomfort of living. Women have a great deal of misery to bear, they are brave or cowardly about it as the case may be, but at least they endure and renounce and diet and keep early hours--or whatever's to be done--they TRY to lessen the sum of physical misery. But men go cheerily on--they smoke too much, and eat too much, and drink too much, and they bring the resulting misery sweetly and confidently to some woman to bear for them. It's hopeless!"

"H'm!" was Miss Vanderwall's thoughtful comment. Presently she added dubiously: "Did you ever think that another child might make a big difference to Clarence, Rachael? That he might come to care for a son as he does for Billy, don't you know--"

"Oh, I wasn't speaking of Clarence," Mrs. Breckenridge said coldly. And Elinor, recognizing a false step, winced inwardly.

"No, I didn't suppose you were!" she assented hastily.

"If there's one thing I AM thankful for," Rachael presently said moodily, "it's that I haven't a child. I'm rather fond of kiddies--nice kiddies, myself; and Clarence likes children, too. But things are quite bad enough now without that complication!" She brushed the loosened hair from her face restlessly, and sighed. "Sometimes, when I see the other girls," said she, "I think I'd make a rather good mother! However"--and getting suddenly to her feet, she flung up her head as if to be rid of the subject--"however, my dear, we shall never know! Don't mind me to-night, Elinor, I'm in a horrible mood, it will take nothing at all to set me off in what Bill used to call a regilyer tant'um!"

"Tantrum nothing," said Elinor, in eager sympathy, feeling with the greatest relief that she was reinstated in Rachael's good graces after her stupid blunder. "I don't see how you stand it at all!"

"It isn't the drinking and headaches and general stupidity in themselves, you know," Rachael said, reverting to her original argument, "but it's the atrocious UNNECESSITY of it! I don't mind Clarence's doing as other men do, I certainly don't mind his caring so much for his daughter"--her fine brows drew together--"but where do _I_ come in?" she demanded with a quizzical smile. "What's MY life? I ask only decency and civility, and I don't get it. The very servants in this house pity me--they see it all. When Clarence isn't himself, he needs me; when he is, he is all for Billy. I must apologize for breaking engagements; people don't ask us out any more, and no wonder! I have to coax money out of him for bills; Billy has her own check-book. I have to keep quiet when I'm boiling all over. I have to defend myself when I know I'm bitterly, cruelly wronged!"

Neither woman had any scruples about the subject under discussion, but even to Elinor Rachael had never spoken so freely before, and the guest, desperately attempting to remember every word for the delectation of her family and friends later on, felt herself at once honored and thrilled.

"Rachael--but why do you stand it?"

Mrs. Breckenridge threw her a look full of all conscious forbearance.

"Well, what would YOU do?"

"Well. I'd"--Miss Vanderwall arrested the hand with which she was carefully spreading her lips with red paste, to fling it, with a large gesture, into the air--"I'd--why don't you GET OUT? Simply drop it all?" she asked.

"For several reasons," the other woman returned promptly with a sort of hard, bright pride. "One very excellent one is that I haven't one penny. But I tell you, Elinor, if I knew how to put my hand on about a thousand dollars a year--there are little towns in France, I have friends in London--well"-- and with a sudden straightening of her whole body Rachael Breckenridge visibly rallied herself--"well, what's the use of talking?" she said. But, as she rose abruptly, Elinor saw the glint of tears on her lashes, and said to herself with a sort of pleased terror that things between Clarence and Rachael must be getting serious indeed.

She admired Mrs. Breckenridge deeply; more than that, the younger woman's friendship and patronage were valuable assets to Miss Vanderwall. But the social circle of Belvedere Hills was a small circle, and Elinor had spent every one of her thirty-five summers, or a part of every one, in just this limited group. There was little malice in her pleasure at getting this glimpse behind the scenes in Rachael's life; she would repeat her friend's confidence, later, with the calm of a person doing the accepted and expected thing, with the complacence of one who proves her right to other revelations from her listeners in turn. It was by such proof judiciously displayed that Elinor held her place in the front ranks of her own select little group of gossips and intimates. She wished the Breckenridges no harm, but if there were dark elements in their lives, Elinor enjoyed being the person to witness them. Thoughtfully adding a bloom to her cheeks with her friend's exquisite powder, Miss Vanderwall reflected sagely that, when one came to think of it, it must really be rather rotten to be married to Clarence Breckenridge.

Rachael presently came back, with the signs of her recent emotion entirely effaced, and her wonderful skin glowing faintly from a bath. Superbly independent of cosmetics, independent even of her mirror, she massed the thick short lengths of dark hair on the top of her head, thrust a jewelled pin through the coil, and began to hook herself into a lacy black evening gown that was loose and comfortable. Before this was finished her stepdaughter rapped on the door, and being invited, came in with the full self-consciousness of seventeen.

"All hooked up straight?" asked Rachael. "That gown looks rather well."

"Do you good women realize what time it is?" Miss Breckenridge asked, by way of reply.

"Has she got it a shade too short?" speculated Rachael, thoughtful eyes on the girl's dress.

"Well--I was wondering!" Carol said eagerly, flinging down her wrap, to turn and twist before a door that was a solid panel of mirror. "What do you think--we'll dance."

"Oh, not a bit," Rachael presently decided. "They're all up to the knees this year, anyway. Car come round?"

"Long ago," said Billy, and Elinor, reaching for her own wrap, declared herself ready. "I wish you were going, Rachael," the girl added as she turned to follow their guest from the room.

"Come back here a moment, Bill," Mrs. Breckenridge said casually, seating herself at the dressing-table without a glance at her stepdaughter. For a moment Miss Breckenridge stood irresolute in the doorway, then she reluctantly came in.

"You're just seventeen, Billy," said the older woman indifferently. "When you're eighteen, next March, I suppose you may do as you please. But until then--either see a little less of Joe Pickering, or else come right out in the open about it, and tell your father you want to see him here. This silly business of telephoning and writing and meeting him, here, there, and everywhere, has got to stop."

Billy stared steadily at her stepmother, her breath coming quick and high, her cheeks red.

"Who said I met him--places?" she said, in a seventeen-year-old-girl's idea of a tragic tone. Mrs. Breckenridge's answer to this was a shrug, a smile, and a motherly request not to be a fool.

There was silence for a moment. Then Billy said recklessly:

"I like him. And you can't make me deny it!"

"Like him if you want to," said Mrs. Breckenridge, "although what you can see in a man twice your age--with his particular history--However, it's your affair. But you'll have to tell your father."

Billy shut her lips mutinously, her cheeks still scarlet.

"I don't see why!" she burst forth proudly, at last.

To this Mrs. Breckenridge offered no argument. Carefully filing a polished fingertip she said quietly:

"I didn't suppose you would."

"And I think that if you tell him YOU interfere in a matter that doesn't in the LEAST concern you," Billy pursued hotly, uncomfortably eager to strike an answering spark, and reduce the conversation to a state where mutual concessions might be in order. "You have no BUSINESS to!"

Her stepmother was silent. She put on a ring, regarded it thoughtfully on her spread fingers, and took it off again.

"In the first place," Billy said sullenly, "you'll tell him a lot of things that aren't so!"

Silence. Outside the motor horn sounded impatiently. Billy suddenly came close to her stepmother, her dark, mobile little face quite transformed by anger.

"You can tell him what you please," she said in a cold fury, "but I'll know WHY you did it--it's because you're jealous, and you want everyone in the world to be in love with YOU! You hate me because my father loves me, and you would do anything in the world to make trouble between us! I've known it ever since I was a little girl, even if I never have said it before! I--" She choked, and tears of youthful rage came into her eyes.

"Don't be preposterous, Bill. You've said it before, every time you've been angry, in the last five years," the older woman said coolly. "This only means that you will feel that you have to wake me up, when you come in to-night, to say that you are sorry."

"I will not!" said the girl at white heat.

"Well, I hope you won't," Rachael Breckenridge said amiably, "for if there is one thing I loathe more than another, it is being waked up for theatricals in the middle of the night. Good-bye. Be sure to thank Mrs. Bowditch for chaperoning you."

"Are you going to speak to Clancy?" the girl demanded imperiously.

"Run along, Billy," Rachael said, with a faint show of impatience. "Nobody could speak to your father about anything to-night, as you ought to know."

For a moment Billy stood still, breathing hard and with tightly closed lips, her angry eyes on her step-mother. Then her breast rose on a childish, dry sob, she dropped her eyes, and moved a shining slipper-toe upon the rug with the immortal motion of embarrassed youth.

"You--you used to like Joe, Rachael," she said, after a moment, in a low tone.

"I don't dislike him now," Rachael said composedly.

"He's awfully kind--and--and good, and Lucy never understood him, or tried to understand him!" said Billy in a burst. The other woman smiled.

"If Joe Pickering told you any sentimental nonsense like that, kindly don't retail it to me," she said amusedly.

In a second Billy was roused to utter fury. Her cheeks blazed, her breath came short and deep. "I hate you!" she said passionately, and ran from the room.

Mrs. Breckenridge sat still for a few moments, but there was no emotion but utter weariness visible in her face. After a while she said, "Oh, Lord!" in a tone compounded of amusement and disgust, and rising, she took a new book from the table, and went slowly downstairs.

In the lower hall Alfred met her, his fat young face duly mysterious and important in expression.

"Mr. Breckenridge got a telephone message from Doctor Jordan, Mrs. Breckenridge; the doctor's been called into town to a patient, so he can't see Mr. Breckenridge to-night."

"Oh! Well, he'll probably be here in the morning," Rachael said carelessly.

"Excuse me, Mrs. Breckenridge, but Mr. Breckenridge seemed to be a good deal worried about himself, and he had me call Doctor Gregory," the man pursued respectfully.

"Doctor GREGORY!" echoed his mistress, with a laugh like a wail. "Alfred, what were you THINKING of! Why didn't you call me?"

"He wouldn't have me call you," Alfred said unhappily. "He spoke to the doctor himself. We got the housekeeper first, and she said Doctor Gregory was dressing. 'Tell him it's a matter of life and death,' says Mr. Breckenridge. Then we got him. 'I'm dining out,' he says, 'but I'll be there this evening.'"

"Oh, dear, dear, dear!" Mrs. Breckenridge said half to herself in serio-comic desperation. "Gregory--called in for a--for a--for this! If I could get hold of him! He didn't say where he was dining?"

"No, Mrs. Breckenridge," the man answered, with a great air of efficiency.

"Well, Alfred, I wish sometimes you knew a little more--or a little less!" Rachael said dispassionately. "Light a fire in the library, will you? I'll have my dinner there. Tell Ellie to send me up something broiled--nothing messy--and some strong coffee."

CHAPTER II

The coffee was strong. Mrs. Breckenridge found it soothing to rasped nerves and tired body, and after the dinner things had been cleared away she sat on beside the library fire, under the soft arc of light from the library lamp, sipping the stimulating fluid, and staring at the snapping and flashing logs.

A sense of merely physical well-being crept through her body, and for a little time even her active brain was quieter; she forgot the man now heavily sleeping upstairs, the pretty little tyrant who had rushed off to dinner at the Chases', and the many perplexing elements in her own immediate problem. She saw only the quiet changes in the fire as yellow flame turned to blue--sank, rose, and sank again.

The house was still. Kitchenward, to be sure, there was a great deal of cheerful laughter and chatter, as Ellie, sitting heavily ensconced in the largest rocker, embroidered a centrepiece for her sister's birthday, Annie read fortunes in the teacups, Alfred imitated the supercilious manner of a lady who had called that afternoon upon Mrs. Breckenridge, and Helda, a milk-blond Dane with pink-rimmed eyes, laughed with infantile indiscrimination at everything, blushing an agonized scarlet whenever Alfred's admiring eye met her own.

But the kitchen was not within hearing distance of the quiet room where Rachael sat alone, and as the soft spring night wore on no sound came to disturb her revery. It was not the first solitary evening she had had of late, for Clarence had been more than usually reckless, and was developing in his wife, although she did not realize it herself, a habit of introspection quite foreign to her real nature.

She had never been a thoughtful woman, her days for many years had run brilliantly on the surface of life, she knew not whence the current was flowing, nor why, nor where it led her; she did not naturally analyze, nor dispute events. Only a few years ago she would have said that to an extraordinary degree fortune had been kind to her. She had been born with an adventurous spirit, she had played her game well and boldly, and, according to all the standards of her type, she had won. But sitting before this quiet fire, perhaps it occurred to her to wonder how it happened that there were no more hazards, no more cards left to play. She was caught in a net of circumstances too tight for her unravelling. Truly it might be cut, but when she stood in the loose wreckage of it--how should she use her freedom? If it was a cage, at least it was a comfortable cage; at least it was better than the howling darkness of the unfamiliar desert beyond.

And yet she raged, and her hurt spirit flung itself again and again at the bars. Young and beautiful and clever, how had life tricked her into this deadlock, where had been the fault, and whose?

For some undefined reason Rachael rarely thought of the past. She did not care to bring its certainties, its panorama of blinded eyes and closed doors before her mental vision. But to-night she found herself walking again in those old avenues; her thoughts went back to the memories of her girlhood.

Girlhood? Her eyes smiled, but with the smile a little twinge of bitterness drew down her mouth. What a discontented, eager, restless girlhood it had been, after all. A girlhood eternally analyzing, comparing, resenting, envying. How she had secretly despised the other girls, typical of their class, the laughing, flirting, dress-possessed girls of a small California town. How she had despised her aunts, all comfortably married and prosperous, her aunts' husbands, her stodgy, noisy cousins! And, for that matter, there had never been much reverence in her regard for her mother, although Rachael loved that complaining little woman in her cool way.

But for her father, the tall, clever, unhappy girl had a genuine admiration. She did not love him, no one who knew Gerald Fairfax well could possibly have sustained a deep affection for him, but she believed him to be almost as remarkably educated and naturally gifted as he believed himself to be. Her uncles were simply country merchants, her mother's fat, cheerful father dealt in furniture, and, incidentally, coffins, but her father was an Englishman, and naturally held himself above the ordinary folk of Los Lobos.

Nobody knew much about him, when he first made his appearance in Los Lobos, this silky-haired, round-faced, supercilious stranger, in his smart, shabby Norfolk coat, which was perhaps one reason why every girl in the village was at once willing to marry him, no questions asked. His speech was almost a different tongue from theirs; he was thirty-five, he had dogs and a man-servant, instead of the usual equipment of mother, sisters, and "hired girl," and he seemed eternally bored and ungracious. This was enough for the Los Lobos girls, and for most of their mothers, too.

The newcomer bought a small ranch, three miles out of town, and lounged about it in a highly edifying condition of elegant idleness. He rode a good horse, drank a great deal, and strode out of the post-office once a week scattering monogrammed envelopes carelessly behind him. He had not been long in town before people began to say that his elder brother was a lord; a duke, Mrs. Chess Baxter, the postmistress said, because to her question regarding the rumor he had answered carelessly: "Something of that sort."

Thirty years ago there were a great many detached Englishmen in California, fourth and fifth sons, remittance men, family scapegraces who had been banished to the farthest frontier by relatives who regarded California as beyond the reach of gossip, and almost beyond the reach of letters. Checks, small but regular, arrived quarterly for these gentry, who had only to drink, sleep, play cards, and demoralize the girls of the country. Here and there among them, to be sure, were pink-skinned boys as fresh and sweet as the apple-blossoms under which they rode their horses, but for the most part the emigrants were dissipated, disenchanted, clinging loyally to the traditions of the older country that had discarded them, and scorning the fragrant and inexhaustible richness of the new land that had made them welcome. They were, as a class, silent, only voluble on the subject of the despised country of their adoption, and absolutely non-committal as to their own histories. But far from questioning their credentials, the women and girls everywhere accepted them eagerly, caught something of an English accent and something of an English arrogance.

So Clara Mumford, a rose of a girl, cream-skinned, blue-eyed, and innocent with the terrible innocence of the village girlhood that feels itself so wise--Clara, who knew, because her two older sisters were married, where babies come from, and knew, because of Alta Porter's experience, that girls--nice girls, who went with one through the high school--can yield to temptation and be ruined--Clara only felt, in shyly announcing her engagement to Gerald Fairfax, that Fate had been too kind.

That this glittering stranger twice her age--why, he was even a little bald--a man who had travelled, who knew people of title, knew books, and manners, and languages--that he should marry an undertaker's daughter in Los Lobos! It was unbelievable. Clara's only misgiving during her short engagement was that he would disappear like a dream. She agreed with everything he said; even carrying her new allegiance to the point of laughing a little at her own people: the layer cakes her mother made for the Sunday noonday dinner; the red-handed, freckled swain who called on her younger sister in the crisp, moonlighted winter evenings; and the fact that her father shaved in the kitchen.

A few weeks slipped by, and Clara duly confided her youth and her innocence and her roses to her English husband, a little ashamed of the wedding presents her friends sent her, even a little doubtful of her parents' handsome gift of a bird's-eye maple bedroom set and a parlor set in upholstered cherry.

On her side she accepted everything unquestionably: the shabby little ranch house that smelled of wood smoke, and tobacco smoke, and dogs; the easy scorn of her old friends on her husband's part that so soon alienated her from them; the drink that she quickly learned to regard with uneasiness and distrust. It was not that Jerry ever got really intoxicated, but he got ugly, excitable, irritable, even though quite in control of his actions and his senses.

Clara was a good cook, although not as expert as her fond mother's little substitutions and innocent manipulations during their engagement had led Gerald to believe. But she loved to please him, and when flushed and triumphant she put down some especially tempting dish before him, and felt his arm about her, tears of actual joy would stand in her bright eyes. They had some happy days, some happy hours, in the first newness of being together.

Gerald's man, Thomas, was an early cause of annoyance to Clara. She would not have objected to cooking for a farm "hand"; that was a matter of course with all good farmers' wives. But Thomas was more British, in all that makes the British objectionable, than his master, and Thomas was quite decidedly addicted to drink. He never thought of wiping a dish, or bringing Clara in a bucket of water from the well. He ate what she set out upon the kitchen table for him, three times a day, chatting pleasantly enough of the farm, the horses, chickens, and vegetable garden, if Clara was in an amiable mood, but if, busy at the sink, or clearing the dining-room table, she was inwardly fuming with resentment at his very existence, Thomas could be silent, too, and would presently saunter away, stuffing his pipe, without even the common courtesy of piling his dishes together for her washing. Thomas held long conversations with his master as they idled about the place; Clara would hear their laughter. The manservant slept in a small shed detached from the main house, and there were times when he did not appear in the morning. At such times Gerald with a pot of strong coffee likewise disappeared into the cabin.

"Pore old rotter!" the husband would say generously. "He's a decentish sort, don't you know? I meanter say, poor old Thomas did me an awfully good turn once--and that!"

Clara inferred from various hints that Gerald had once been in the English army, and had met Thomas, and befriended him, or been befriended by him, at that period of his existence. But, greatly to the little bride's disappointment, Gerald never spoke of his old home or his connections there. Clara had to draw what comfort she could from his intimation that all his relatives were unbelievably eminent and distinguished, the least of them superior in brain and achievement to any American who ever drew the breath of life.

And presently she forgot Thomas, forgot the petty annoyance of cooking and summer heat and dogs and physical discomfort, in the overwhelming prayer that the coming child, about whose advent Gerald, at first annoyed, had later been so generously good-natured, might prove a boy. Gerald, living uncomplainingly in this dreadful little country town, enduring Western conditions with such dignity, and loving his little wife despite her undertaker father, would be seriously disgusted, she knew, if she gave him a daughter.

"A--a girl?" Clara stammered, her wet eyes on the doctor's face, her panting little figure lost in the big outline of her mother's spare-room bed. She managed a brave smile, but there was a bitter lump in her throat.

A girl!

And she had been so brave, so sweet with Jerry, who had not enjoyed the three or four days of waiting at her mother's house; so strong in her agonies, as became the healthy, normal little country girl she was! Fate owed her a son, she had done her share, she had not flinched. And now--a girl! Fresh tears of disappointment came to take the place of tears of pain in her eyes. She remembered that Jerry had said, a few days before, "It'll be a boy, of course--all the old women about seem to have settled that--and I believe I'll cable Cousin Harold."

"Ma says it'll be a boy," Clara had submitted hopefully, longing to hear more of "Cousin Harold," to whom Gerald alluded at long intervals.

"Of course it will--good old girl!" Jerry had agreed. And that was only Thursday night, and this was in the late dawn of cold, wintry Saturday morning.

Her mother bent over her and kissed her wet forehead. Mrs. Mumford's big kind face was radiant; she had already four small grandsons; this was the first grand-daughter. More than that, the nurse was not here yet; she had been supreme through the ordeal; she had managed one more birth extremely well, and she rejoiced in the making of a nation.

"Such a nice baby, darling!" she whispered, "with her dear little head all covered with black hair! Neta's dressing her."

"Where's Gerald?" the young mother asked weakly.

"Right here! I'll let him in for a moment!" There was a satisfaction in Mrs. Mumford's voice; everything was proceeding absolutely by schedule. "And just as anxious to see you as you are to see him!" she added happily. These occasions were always the same, and always far more enjoyable to this practised parent than any pageant, any opera, any social distinction could have been. To comfortably, soothingly lead the trembling novice through the long experience, to whisk about the house capably and briskly busy with the familiar paraphernalia, to cry in sympathy with another's tears, to stand white-lipped, impotent, anguished through a few dreadful moments, and then to laugh, and rejoice, and reassure, before the happy hours of resting, and feeding, and cuddling began--this was the greatest satisfaction in her life.

Clara, afraid in this first moment to face his disappointment, felt in another the most delicious reassurance and comfort she had known in months. Jerry, taking the chair by the bedside, was so dear about it! The long night had much impressed the new-made father. They had had coffee at about two o'clock--Clara remembered wondering how they could sit enjoying it, instead of dashing the hideous cups to the floor, and rushing out of the horrible enclosure of walls and curtains--and as he bent over her she knew he had had something stronger since--but he was so dear!

"Well, we've had a night of it, eh?" he said kindly. "Funny how much one takes the little beggars for grawnted until it's one's own that kicks up the row? You've not seen her--she's a nice little beggar. You might get some sleep, I should think. I'm going to hang around until some sort of a family jamboree is over, at one o'clock--your mother insists that we have dinner--and then I'll go out to the rawnch. But I'll be in in the morning!"

"Girl!" said Clara, apologetically, whimsically, deprecatingly, her weak fingers clinging tightly to his.

"Ah, well, one carn't help that!" he answered philosophically. "We'll have a row of jolly little chaps yet!"

But there was never another child. Clara, having cast her fortunes in with her lord, was faithful to him through every breath she drew. But before Rachael's first crying, feverish little summer was over there had been some definite changes at the ranch. Thomas was gone, and Clara, pale and exhausted with the heat, engaged Ella, a young woman servant of her mother's selecting, to bake and wash and carry in stove-wood. Clara managed them all, Gerald, the baby, and the maid. Perhaps at first she was just a little astonished to find her husband as easily managed as Ella and far more easily managed than Rachael. Gerald Fairfax was surprised, too, lazily conceding his altered little wife her new and energetic way with a mental reservation that when she was strong and well again and the child less a care, things would be as they were. But Clara, once in power, never weakened for a moment again. Rachael grew up, a solitary and unfriendly, yet a tactful and diplomatic, little person on the ranch. She early developed a great admiration for her father, and a consequent regard for herself as superior to her associates. She ruled her mother absolutely from her fourth year, and remained her grandmother's great favorite among a constantly increasing flock of grandchildren. Some innate pride and scorn and dignity in the child won her her own way through school and school days; her young cousins were bewildered themselves by the respect and fealty they yielded her despite the contempt in which they held her affectations.

Clara had never been a religious woman and, married to an utter unbeliever, she had little enough to give a child of her own. But Clara's mother was a church woman, and her father a deeply religious man. It was his mother, "old lady Mumford"--Rachael's great-grandmother--who taught the child her catechism whenever she could get hold of that restless and lawless little girl.

Rachael had great fear and respect for her great-grandmother, and everything that was fine and good in the child instinctively responded to the atmosphere of her little home. It was an unpretentious home, even for Los Lobos: only a whitewashed California cabin with a dooryard full of wall flowers and geraniums, and pungent marigolds, and marguerites that were budding, blossoming, and gone to rusty decay on one and the same bush. The narrow paths were outlined with white stone ale-bottles, turned upside down and driven into the soft ground, and under the rustling tent of a lilac bush there were three or four clay pots filled with dry earth. There was a railed porch on the east side of the house, with vines climbing on strings about it, and here the old woman, clean with the wonderful, cool-fingered cleanness of frail yet energetic seventy-five, would sit reading in the afternoon shade that fell from the great shoulders of the blue mountains.

Inside were three rooms; there was no bathroom, no light but the kerosene lamps the old hands tended daily, no warmth but the small kitchen stove. All the furniture was old and shabby and cheap, and the antimacassars and pictures and teacups old Mrs. Mumford prized so dearly were of no value except for association's sake. Rachael's great-grandmother lived upon tea and toast and fruit sauce; sometimes she picked a dish of peas in her own garden and sometimes made herself a rice pudding, but if her children brought her in a chicken or a bowl of soup she always gave it away to some poorer neighbor who was ill, or who was "nursing that great strapping baby."

She read the Bible to Rachael and exhorted the half-believing, half-ashamed child to lay its lessons to heart.

"Your life will be full of change and of pleasure, there will be many temptations and much responsibility," said the sweet, stern, thin old voice. "Arm yourself against the wickedness of the world!"

Rachael, pulling the old collie's silky ears, thought nothing of the wickedness of the world but much of possible change and pleasure. She hoped her aged relative was right; certainly one would suppose Granny to be right in anything she said.

The time would have swiftly come when the child's changing heart would have found no room for this association, but before Rachael was twelve Granny was gone, the little house, with its few poor treasures shut inside it, was closed and empty. And only a year or two later a far more important change came into the girl's life. She had always disliked Los Lobos, had schemed and brooded and fretted incessantly through her childhood. It was with astonished delight that she heard that her parents, who had never, in a financial sense, drawn a free breath since their marriage, who had worried and contrived, who had tried indifference and bravado and strictest economy by turns, had sold their ranch for almost two thousand dollars more than its accumulated mortgages, and were going to England.

It was a glorious adventure for Rachael, even though she was too shrewd not to suspect the extreme hazard of the move. She talked in Los Lobos of her father's "people," hinted that "the family, you know, thinks we'd better be there," but she knew in her heart that a few months might find them all beggars.

Her father bought her a loose, big, soft blue coat in San Francisco, and a dashing little soft hat for the steamer. Rachael never forgot these garments throughout her entire life. It mattered not how countrified the gown under the coat, how plain the shoes on her slender feet. Their beauty, their becomingness, their comfort, actually colored her days. For twenty dollars she was transformed; she knew herself to be pretty and picturesque. "That charming little girl with the dark braids, going to England," she heard some man on the steamer say. The ranch, the chickens, weeds, and preserving, the dusty roads and shabby stores of Los Lobos were gone; she was no longer a gawky child; she was a young lady in a loose, soft, rough blue coat, with a black quill in her soft blue hat.

England received her wandering son coolly, but Rachael never knew it. Her radiant dream--or was it an awakening?--went on. Her mother, a neat, faded, querulous little woman, whose one great service was in sparing her husband any of the jars of life, was keyed to frantic anxiety lest Jerry be unappreciated, now that he had come back. Clara met the few men to whom her husband introduced her in London with feverish eagerness; afraid-- after fifteen years--to say one word that might suggest her own concern in Jerry's future, quivering to cross-examine him, when they were alone, as to what had been said, and implied, and suggested.

Nothing definite followed. They lived for a month or two at a delightful roomy boarding-house in London, where the modest meals Clara ordered appeared as if by magic, and where Miss Fairfax never sullied her pretty hands with dishwashing. Then they went to visit "Aunt Elsie" in a suburban villa for several weeks, a visit Rachael never thought of afterward without a memory of stuffy, neat, warm rooms, and a gushing of canaries' voices. Then they went down to Sussex, in the delicious fullness of spring, to live with several other persons in a dark country house, where "Cousin Harold" died, and there was much odorous crepe and a funeral. Cousin Harold evidently left something to Gerald. Rachael knew money was not an immediate problem. Hot weather came, and they went to the seaside with an efficient relative called Ethel, and Ethel's five children. Later, back in London, Gerald said, in his daughter's hearing, that he had made "rather a good thing of that little game of Bobbie's. Enough to tide us over--what? Especially if the Dickies ask us down for a bit," he had added. The Dickies did ask them down for a bit. They went other places. Gerald made a little money on the races, made "a good thing" of this, and "turned a bit over on that." Weeks made months and months years, and still they drifted cheerfully about, Gerald happier than he had ever been in exile, Clara fearful, admiring, ill at ease, Rachael in a girl's paradise.

She grew beautiful, with a fine and distinguished beauty definite in its appeal; before she was seven-teen she had her little reputation for it; she moved easily into a circle higher than even her father had ever known. She was witty, young, lovely, and in this happier atmosphere her natural gayety and generosity might well develop. She went about continually, and every year the circle of her friends was widened by more distinguished names.

At seventeen Mrs. Gouveneur Pomeroy of New York brought the young beauty back with her own daughter, Persis, for a winter in the great American city, and when Persis died Rachael indeed became almost as dear to the stricken parents. When she went back to London they gave her not only gifts but money, and for two years she returned to them for long visits.

So America had a chance to admire the ravishing Miss Fairfax, too, and Rachael had many conquests and one or two serious affairs. The girls had their first dances at the Belvedere Club; Rachael met them all, who were later to be her neighbors: the Morans and Parmalees, the Vanderwalls and the Torrences, and the Chases. She met Clarence Breckenridge and his wife, and the exquisitely dressed little girl who was Billy to-day.

And through all her adventures she looked calmly, confidently, and with conscious enjoyment for a husband. She flirted a little, and danced and swam and drove and played golf and tennis a great deal, but she never lost sight for an instant of the serious business of life. Money she must have--it was almost as essential to her as air--and money she could only secure through a marriage.

The young Englishman who was her first choice, in her twentieth year, had every qualification in the world. When he died, two or three months before the wedding-day, Rachael's mother was fond of saying in an aside to close friends that the girl's heart was broken. Rachael, lovely in her black, went down to stay with Stephen's mother, and for several weeks was that elderly lady's greatest comfort in life. Silent and serious, her manner the perfection of quiet grief, only Rachael herself knew how little the memory of Stephen interfered with her long reveries as she took his collies about in the soft autumn fogs. Only Rachael knew how the sight of Trecastle Hall, the horses, the servants, and the park filled her heart with despair. She might have been Lady Trecastle! All this might so easily have been her own!

She had loved Stephen, of course, she told herself; loving, with Rachael, simply meant a willingness to accept and to give. But love was of course a luxury; she was after the necessities of life. Well, she had played and lost, but she could play again. So she went to the Pomeroys' for the winter, and in the spring was brought back to London by her father's sudden death.

Gerald Fairfax's life insurance gave his widow a far more secured income than he had ever given his wife. It was microscopic, to be sure, but Clara Fairfax was a practised economist. The ladies settled in Paris, and Rachael was seriously considering a French marriage when, by the merest chance, in the street one day, a small homesick girl clutched at her thin black skirt, and sent her an imploring smile. Rachael, looking graciously down from under the shade of her frilly black parasol, recognized the little Breckenridge girl, obviously afflicted with a cold and lonesomeness and strangeness. Enslaving the French nurse with three perfectly pronounced sentences, Rachael went home with the clinging Carol, put her to bed, cheered her empty little interior with soup, soothed her off to sleep, and was ready to meet her crazed and terrified father with a long lecture on the care of young children, when, after an unavoidable afternoon of business, he came back to his hotel.

The rest followed. Rachael liked Clarence, finding it agreeable that he knew how to dress, how to order a dinner, tip servants, and take care of a woman in a crowd. His family was one of the oldest in America, and he was rich. She was sorry that Billy's mother was living, but then one couldn't have everything, and, after all, she was married again, which seemed to mitigate the annoyance. Rachael said to herself that this was a wiser marriage than the proposed one with poor Stephen: Stephen had been a wild, romantic boy, full of fresh passion and dazed with exultant dreams; Clarence was a man, longing less for moonshine and roses and the presence of his beloved one than for a gracious, distinguished woman who would take her place before the world as mistress of his home and guardian of his child.

She had sometimes doubted her power to make Stephen happy-- Stephen, who talked with all a boy's heavenly shyness of long days tramping the woods and long nights over the fire, of little sons and daughters romping in the Trecastle gardens; but she entered into her marriage with Clarence Breckenridge with entire self-confidence. She had been struggling more or less definitely all her life toward just such a position as this; it was a comparatively easy matter to fill it, now that she had got it.

Carol she considered a decided asset. The child adored her, and her services to Carol were so much good added to the beauty, charm, and wisdom that she brought into the bargain. That Clarence could ask more in the way of beauty, wisdom, and charm was not conceivable; Rachael knew her own value too well to have any doubts on that score.

And had her husband been a strong man, her dignified and ripened loveliness must inevitably have won him. She stood ready to be won. She held to her bond in all generosity. What heart and soul and body could do for him was his to claim. She did not love him, but she did not need love's glamour to show her what her exact value to him might be; what was her natural return for all her marriage gave her.

But quick-witted and cold-blooded as she was, she could not see that Clarence was actually a little afraid of her. He had been too rich all his life to count his money as an argument in his favor, and although he was not clever he knew Rachael did not love him, and hardly supposed that she ever could.

He felt with paternal blindness that she had married him partly for the child's sake, and returned to the companionship of his daughter with a real sense of relief.

Rachael, in turn, was puzzled. Carol was undeniably a pretty child, with all a spoiled child's confident charm, but in all good-natured generosity Rachael could not see in her the subtle and irresistible fascinations that her father so eagerly exploited. Surely no girl of ten, however gifted, could be reasonably supposed to eclipse completely the woman Rachael knew herself to be; surely no parental infatuation could extend itself to the point of a remarriage with the bettering of a small child's position alone the object.

Philosophy came promptly to the aid of the new-made wife. Billy was a child, and Clarence a greater child. The situation was annoying, was belittling to her own pride, but she would meet it with dignity nevertheless. After all, the visible benefits of the marriage were still hers: the new car, the new furs, the new and wonderful sense of financial ease, of social certainty.

She schooled herself to listen with an indulgent smile to her husband's fond rhapsodies about his daughter. She agreed amiably that Billy would be a great beauty, a heart-breaker, that "the little monkey had all the other women crazy with jealousy now, by Jove!" She selected the little gowns and hats in which the radiant Billy went off for long days alone with "Daddy," and she presently graciously consented to share the little girl's luxurious room because Billy sometimes awakened nervously at night. Rachael had been accustomed to difficulties in dealing with the persons nearest her; she met them resolutely. Sometimes a baffling sense of failure smote the surface of her life, like a cold wind that turns to white metal the smooth waters of a lake, but she held her head proudly above it, and even Clarence and his daughter never guessed what she endured. What did it matter? Rachael asked herself wearily. She had not asked for love. She had resolutely exchanged what she had to give for what she had determined to get; Clarence had made no blind protestations, had expected no golden romance. He admired her; she knew he thought it was splendid of her to manage the engagement and marriage with so little fuss; perhaps his jaded pulses fluttered a little when Rachael, exquisite in her bridal newness, stooped at the railway station to give the drooping Billy a good-bye kiss, and promise that in three days they would be back to rescue her from the hated governess; but paramount above all other emotions, she suspected, was the tremendous satisfaction of having gained just the right woman to straighten out his tangled domestic affairs, just the mother, as the years went by, to do the correct thing for Billy.

Of some of these things the woman who sat idly before the library fire was thinking, as the quiet evening wore on, and the purring of the flames and the ticking of the little mantel clock accented rather than disturbed the stillness. She was unhappy with a cold, dry wretchedness that was deeper than any pang of passion or of hate. The people she met, the books she read, the gowns she planned so carefully, and the social events that were her life, all--all--were dust and ashes. Clarence was less a disappointment and a shame to her than an annoyance; he neglected her, he humiliated her, true, but this meant infinitely less than that he bored her so mercilessly. Billy, with her youthful complacencies and arts, bored her; the sympathy of a few close friends bored her as much as the admiration and envy of the many who were not close. Cards, golf, dinners, and dances bored her. Rachael thought tonight of a woman she had known closely, a beautiful woman, too, and a rich and gifted woman, who, not many months ago, had quietly ended it all, had been found by horrified maids in her gray-and-silver boudoir lovelier than ever, in fixed and peaceful beauty, with the soft folds of her lacy gown spreading like the petals of a great flower about her and the little gleam of an empty bottle in her still, ringed hand...

A voice broke the library stillness. Rachael roused herself.

"What is it, Helda?" she asked. "Doctor Gregory? Ask him to come in. And ask Alfred--is Alfred still downstairs?--ask him to go up and see if Mr. Breckenridge is awake.

"This is very decent of you, Greg," she said, a moment later, as the doctor came into the room. "It doesn't seem right to interfere with your dinner for the same old stupid thing!"

"Great pleasure to do anything for you, Rachael," the newcomer said promptly and smilingly with the almost perfunctory courtesy that was a part of Warren Gregory's stock in trade. "You don't call on me often! I wish you did!"

She said to herself, as they both sat down before the fire, that it was probably true. Doctor Gregory was notoriously glad of an opportunity to serve his friends. He had not at all regretted the necessity of leaving his dinner partner at the salad for a professional call. He was quite ready to enjoy the Breckenridge sitting-room, the fire, the lamplight, the company of a beautiful woman. Rachael and he knew each other well, almost intimately; they had been friends for many years. She had often been his guest at the opera, had often chaperoned his dinner-parties at the club, for Warren Gregory's only woman relative was his old mother, who was neither of an age nor a type to take any part in his social life.

He was forty, handsome, dignified, with touches of gray in his close-clipped hair, but no other sign of years in his face or his big, well-built figure. He had clever, fine eyes behind black-rimmed glasses, a surgeon's clever hands, a pleasant voice. He lived with his mother in a fine old house on Washington Square, in New York City, and worked as tirelessly as if he were a penniless be ginner at his profession instead of a rich man, a rich woman's heir, and already recognized as a genius in his own line.

All women liked him, and he liked them all. He sent them books, marked essays in magazines for their individual consideration, took them to concerts, remembered their birthdays. But his only close friends were men, the men with whom he played tennis and golf, or with whom he was associated in his work.

With all his cleverness and all his charm, Warren Gregory was not a romantic figure in the eyes of most women. He had inherited from his old Irish mother a certain mildness, and a lenience, where they were concerned. He neither judged them nor idolized them. They belonged only to his leisure hours. His real life was in his club, in his books, and in the hospital world where there were children's tiny bones to set. He was conscious, as a man born in a different circle always is conscious, that he had, by a series of pleasant chances, been pushed straight into the inner heart of the social group whose doors are so resolutely closed to many men and women, and he liked it. His grand father had had blood but no money, his mother money but no social claim. He inherited, with the O'Connell millions, the Gregory name, and for perhaps ten years he had enjoyed an unchallenged popularity. He had inherited also, without knowing it, a definitely different standard from that held by all the men and women about him. In his simple, unobtrusive way he held aloof from much that they said and did. Greg, said the woman, was a regular Puritan about gossip, about drinking, about gambling.

They never suspected the truth: that he was shy. Sure of his touch as a surgeon, pleasantly definite about books and pictures, spontaneous and daring in the tennis court or on the links, under his friendly manner with women was the embarrassment of a young boy.

Before his tenth year his rigidly conscientious mother had instilled into the wondering little-boy mind certain mysterious yet positive moral laws. Purity and self-control were in the air he breathed while at her side, and although a few years later school and college had claimed him, the effect of those early lessons was definite upon his character. Diffidence and a sort of fear had protected him, far more effectually than any other means might have done, from the common vices of his age, and in those days a certain good-natured scorn from all his associates made him feel even more than his natural shyness, and marked him rather apart from other young men.

Keenly aware of this, it had been a tremendous surprise to the young physician, returning from post-graduate work in Germany a few years later, to find that what had once been considered a sort of laughable weakness in him was called strength of character now; that what had been a clumsy boy's inarticulateness was more charitably construed into the silence of a clever man who will not waste his words; and that mothers whose sons he had once envied for their worldly wisdom were turning to him for advice as to the extrication of these same sons from all sorts of difficulties.

Being no fool, he accepted the changed attitude with great readiness, devoting himself to his work and his mother, and pleasantly conscious that he was a success. He let women alone, except where music and art, golf and the club theatricals were the topic of interest, and, consequently, had come to his fortieth year with some little awe and diffidence still left for them in his secret heart. Rachael had told him, not long ago, that she believed he took no interest in women older than fourteen and younger than fifty, and there was some truth in the charge. But he was conscious to-night of taking a distinct interest in her as he sat down beside her fire.

He had never seen her so beautiful, he thought. She had dressed so hastily, so carelessly, that an utter simplicity enhanced the natural charm. Her dark hair was simply massed, her gown was devoid of ornament, her hands bare, except for her wedding-ring. On her earnest, exquisite face the occasion had stamped a certain soberness, she was neither hostess nor guest to-night; just a heartsick wife under the shadow of anger and shame.

"Well, what is it to-night?" Warren Gregory asked kindly.

"Oh, the same old thing, Greg. The Berry Stokes' dinner, you know!"

"Shame!" the doctor said warmly, touched by her obvious depression. "I'll go up. I can give him some pills. But you know, he can't keep this up forever, Rachael. He's killing himself!"

In her sensitive mood the mildly reproachful tone was too much. Rachael's breast rose, her eyes brightened angrily.

"Perhaps you'll tell me what more I can do, Greg!"

He looked at her in surprise; the shell of Mrs. Breckenridge's cool reserve was not often pierced.

"My dear girl--" he stammered. "Why, Rachael--!"

For battling with a moment of emotion she had flung her beautiful head back against the brilliant cretonne of the chair, her eyes closed, her hands grasping the chair-arms. A tear slipped from under her lids.

"I didn't for one second mean--" he began again uncomfortably.

Suddenly she straightened herself in her chair, and opened her eyes widely. He saw her lovely breast, under its filmy black chiffon, rise stormily. Her voice was rich with protest.

"No, you didn't mean anything, Greg, nobody means anything! Nobody is anything but sorry for me: you, Billy, Elinor, the woman who expected us at dinner to-night, the servants at the club!" she said hotly. "Nobody blames me, and yet every one wonders how it happens! Nobody thinks it anything but a little amusing, a little shocking. I am to write the notes, and make the excuses, and be shamed--and shamed--shamed--"

Her voice broke. She rose to her feet, and rested an elbow on the mantel, and stared moodily at the fire. There was a silence.

"Rachael, I'm sorry!" Gregory said presently, impulsively.

Instantly her April smile rewarded him.

"I know you are, Greg!" she answered gratefully. "And I know," she added, in a low tone, "that you are one of the persons who will understand--when I end it all!"

"End it all!" he echoed sharply.

"Not suicide," she reassured him smilingly. She flung herself back in her chair again, holding her white hand, with its ring, between her face and the fire. "No," she said thoughtfully, "I mean divorce."

There eyes met; both were pale, serious.

"Divorce!" he echoed, after a pause. "I never thought of it--for you!

"I haven't thought of it myself, much," Rachael admitted, with a troubled smile.

As a matter of fact she had thought of it, since the early days of her marriage, but never as an actual possibility. She had preferred bondage and social position to freedom and the uncomfortable status of the divorced woman. She realized now that she might think of it in a slightly different way. She had been a penniless nobody seven years ago; she was a personage now. The mere fact that he was a Breckenridge would win some sympathy for Clarence, but she would have her faction, too.

More than that, she would never be younger, never handsomer, never better able to take the plunge, and face the consequences.

"I'm twenty-eight, Greg," she said reasonably, "I'm not stupid, I'm not plain--don't interrupt me! Is this to be my fate? I'm capable of loving--of living--I don't want to be bored--bored--bored for the rest of my life!"

Warren Gregory, stunned and surprised, eyed her sympathetically.

"Belvedere Bay bore you?" he asked, smiling a little uneasily.

"No--it's not that. I don't want more dinners and dances and jewels and gowns!" Rachael answered musingly. She stared sombrely at the fire, and there was a moment's silence.

Suddenly her mood changed. She smiled, and locking her hands together, as she leaned far forward in her chair, she looked straight into his eyes.

"Greg," she said, "do you know what I'd like to be? I'd like to be far away from cities and people, a fisherman's wife on an ocean shore, with a baby coming every year, and just the delicious sea to watch! I could be a good wife, Greg, if anybody really--loved me!"

Laughing as she looked at him, she did not disguise the fact that tears misted her lashes. Warren Gregory felt himself stirred as he had not been before in his life.

"Well," he said, with an unsteady laugh, "you could be anything! With you for his wife, what couldn't a man do!"

Hardly conscious of what he did or said, he got to his feet, and she stood, too, smiling up at him. Both were breathing hard.

"To think," he said, with a sort of repressed violence, "that you, of all women, should be Clarence Breckenridge's wife!"

"Not long!" she answered, in a whisper.

"You mean that you are really going to leave him, Rachael?"

"I mean that I must, Greg, if I am not to go mad!"

"And where will you go?" she asked.

"Oh--to Vera, to Elinor." She paused, frowning. "Or away by myself," she decided suddenly. "Away from them all!"

"Rachael," he said quickly, "will you come to my mother?"

Rachael smiled. "To your mother!"

He read her incredulity in her voice.

"But she loves you," he said eagerly. "And she'd be--we'd both be so proud to show people--to prove--that we knew where the right lay!"

"My dear Don Quixote," she answered affectionately, "I love you for asking me! But I will be better alone. I must think, and plan. I've made a mess of my life so far, Greg; I must take the next step carefully!"

He was clinging to her hands as she stood, in all her grave beauty, before him.

"If I hadn't been such a bat, Rachael, all those eleven years ago!" he said, daringly, breathlessly.

"Have we known each other so long, Greg?"

"Ever since that first visit of yours with little Persis Pomeroy! And I remember you so well, Rachael. I remember that Bobby Governeur was enslaved!"

"Dear old Bobby! But I don't remember you, Greg!"

"Because I was thirty then, my dear, and you were seventeen! I was just home from four years' work in Germany; I was afraid of girls your age!"

"Afraid--of ME?" The three words were like a caress, like holding her in his arms.

"I'm afraid so!" he said, not quite steadily. "I'm afraid I've always liked you too well. I--I CARE--that you're unhappy, that you're unkindly treated. I--I--wish I could do something, Rachael."

"You DO do something," she said, deeply stirred in her turn. "I'm--you don't know how fond I am of you, Greg!"

For answer she felt his arms about her, and for a throbbing minute they stood so; Rachael braced lightly, her beautiful breast rising and falling, her breath coming quickly. Her magnificent eyes, wide-open, like a frightened child's, were fixed steadily upon him. He caught the fragrance of her hair, of her fresh skin; he felt the softness and firmness of her slender arms.

"Rachael!" he said, in a sharp whisper. "Don't--don't say that--if you don't--mean it!"

"Greg!" she answered, in the same tone. "Don't--frighten me!"

Instantly she was free, and he was standing by the fire with folded arms, looking at her.

"You have missed love, and I have missed it," Warren Gregory said presently. "We'll be patient, Rachael. I'll wait; we'll both wait--"

"Greg!" she could only answer still in that stricken whisper, still pale. She stood just as he had left her.

A silence fell between them. The physician took out a cigarette from his gold case with trembling ringers.

"I'm a little giddy, Rachael," he said after a moment. "I--on my honor I don't know what's happened to me! You're the most wonderful woman in the world--I've always thought that--but it never occurred to me--the possibility--"

He paused, confused, unable to find the right words.

"You've been facing this all alone," he continued presently. "Poor Rachael! You've been splendid--wonderfully brave! You have me beside you now; I'll help you if I may. Some day we may find a way out! Well," he finished abruptly, "suppose I go up and see Clarence?"

For answer she rose, and without speaking again went ahead of him up the stairway and left him at the door of her husband's room. He did not see her again that night.

Half an hour later he came down, dismissed his car, and walked home under the spring stars. In his veins, like a fire, still ran the excited, glorious consciousness of his madness. In his ears still echoed the wonderful golden voice; he could hear her very words, and he took certain phrases from his memory, and gloated over them as another man might have gloated over strings of pearls: "I'd like to be far away from cities and people, a fisherman's wife on an ocean shore with a baby coming every year and just the delicious sea to watch!" "Greg--don't frighten me!"

Exquisite, desirable, enchanting--every inch of her--her voice, her eyes, her slender hand with its gold circle. What a woman! What a wife! What radiant youth and beauty and charm--and all trampled in the mire by Clarence Breckenridge, of all insensate brutes! How could laughter and courage and beauty survive it?

He was going to the club, a mile away from the Breckenridge house, but long before the visions born that evening were exhausted, he saw the familiar lights, and the awninged porches, and heard the faint echoes of the orchestra. They were dancing.

Warren Gregory turned away again, and plunged into the darkness of the roadside afresh. "My dear Don Quixote!" With what a look of motherly amusement and tenderness she had said it. What a woman! He had never kissed her. He had never even thought of kissing Clarence Breckenridge's wife.

He thought of his mother, tried to forget her with a philosophical shrug, and found that the slender, black-clad, quiet-voiced vision was not to be so easily dismissed. It was said of old Madam Gregory that she had never been heard to raise her voice in the course of her sixty honored years. Of the four sons she had borne, three were dead, and the husband she had loved so faithfully lay beside them. She was slightly crippled, her outings confined to a slow drive every day. She was solitary in a retinue of servants.

But that modulated voice and those cool, temperate eyes were still a power. His mother's displeasure was a very real thing to Warren Gregory, and the thought of adding another sorrow to the weight on those thin shoulders was not an easy one for him to entertain.

It would be a sorrow. Mrs. Gregory was a rigid Catholic, her life's one prayer nowadays was that her beloved son might become one, too. Her marriage at seventeen to a non-Catholic had been undertaken in the firm conviction that faith like hers must win the conversion of her beloved James, the best, the most honorable of men. When her oldest son was born, and given his father's name, she saw, in her husband's willingness to further plans for the baptism, definite cause for hope. Another son was born, there was another christening; it was the father's own hand that gave the third baby lay-baptism only a few moments before the tiny life slipped back into the eternity from which it had so lately come.

A year or two later a fourth son was born. Presently the dignified Mrs. Gregory was taking a trio of small, sleek-headed boys to Sunday-school, watching every phase in the development of their awakening souls with terror and with hope. What fears she suffered in spirit during those years no one but herself knew. Outwardly, the hospitable, gracious life of the great house went on; the Gregorys were prominent in charities, they opened their mountain camp for the summer, they travelled abroad, they had an audience with the Pope. Time went on, and the twelve-year-old George was taken from them, breaking the father's heart, said the watching world. But there was a strange calm in the mother's eyes as they rested on the dead child's serene face: Heaven had her free offering, now she must have her reward.

A few months later James Gregory became a convert to her religion. Charles, the second son, had never wavered from his mother's faith, and rejoiced with her in this great event. But the first-born, Warren, as all but his mother called him, to avoid confusion with his father, was a junior in college when these changes took place, and when he came home for the long vacation his mother knew what her cross must be for the years to come. He listened to her with the appalling silence of the nineteen-year-old male, he kissed her, he returned gruff, embarrassed answers to her searching questions of his soul, and he escaped from her with visibly expanding lungs and averted eyes. She knew that she had lost him.

Men called him a good man, and she assented with dry lips and heavy eyelids. Charles died, leaving a young widow and an infant son, the father shortly followed, and Warren came home from his interne year, and was a good son to her in her dark hour. When they began to say of him that he would be great, she smiled sadly. "My father was a doctor," she said once to an old friend, "and James inherits it!" But at a memory of her own father, erect and rosy among his girls and boys in the family pew, she burst into tears. "I would rather have him with his father, with George and Charles, and with my angel Francis, than have him the greatest man that ever lived!" she said.

But if she had not made him a good Catholic she had made him a good man, and it was a fair and honorable record that Warren Gregory could offer to the woman he loved. Love--it had come to him at last. His thoughts went back to Rachael. It seemed to him that he had always known how deeply, how recklessly he loved her.

He had a thrilling memory of her as Persis Pomeroy's guest, years ago, an awkward, delightful seventeen-year-old, with her hair in two thick braids, looped up at the neck, and tied with a flaring black bow. He remembered watching her, hearing for the first time the delicious voice with its English accent: "Well, I should say it was indeed!"

"Well, I should say it was indeed!" Across more than ten years he recalled the careless, crisp little answer to some comment from Persis, his first precious memory of Rachael. The girls, he remembered, were supposedly too young for a certain dance that was imminent, they were opposing their youthful petulance--baffled roses and sunshine--to Mrs. Pomeroy's big, placid negatives. Gregory could still see the matron's comfortably shaking head, see Persis attacking again and again like a frantic butterfly, and see "the little English girl," perched on the porch rail, looking from mother to daughter smilingly, with her blue, serious eyes.

Why had he never thought of her again until Clarence Breckenridge brought her back with him, a bride, six years later? Or, rather, having thought of her, as he undoubtedly had, why had he not found the time to cross the water and go to see her? Nothing might have come of it, true. But she might have yielded to him as readily as to Clarence Breckenridge!

"I love her!" he said to himself, and it seemed wonderful, sad, and sweet, joyous and terrible to admit it. "I love her. But she doesn't love me or anyone, poor Rachael! She's forgotten me already!"

CHAPTER III

As a matter of fact, Rachael thought about him very often during the course of the next two or three days, and after he had left her that night she could think of nothing else. To the admiration of men she was cheerfully accustomed; perhaps it would be safe to say that not in the course of the past ten years had she ever found herself alone in a man's company without evoking a more or less definite declaration of his admiration for her. But to-night's affair was a little distinctive for several reasons. Warren Gregory was a most exceptional man, for one thing; he was reputedly a coldblooded man, for another; and for a third, he had been extraordinarily in earnest. There had been no hesitation, he had committed himself wholeheartedly. She was conscious of a pleasurable thrill. However gracious, however gallant Warren was, there had been no social pretence in his attitude to-night.

And for a few moments she let her imagination play pleasantly with the situation. It was at least a new thought, and life had run in a groove for a long, long time. Granted the preliminaries safely managed, it would be a great triumph for the woman whom Clarence Breckenridge had ignored to come back into this group as Warren Gregory's wife.

Rachael got into bed, flinging two or three books down beside her pillow and lighting the shaded lamp that stood at the bedside. She found herself unable to read.

"Wouldn't Florence and Gardner buzz!" she thought with a smile. "And if they buzzed at the divorce, what WOULDN'T they say if I really did remarry? But the worst of it is"--and Rachael reaching for The Way of All Flesh sighed wearily--"the worst of it is that one never DOES carry out plans, or _I_ never do, any more. I used to feel equal to any situation, now I don't--getting old, perhaps. I wonder"--she stared dreamily at the soft shadows in the big room--"I wonder if things are as queer to most people as they are to me? I don't get much joy out of life, as it is, and yet I don't DARE cut loose and go away. No maid, no club, living at some cheap hotel--no, I couldn't do that! I wish there was someone who could advise me--some disinterested person, someone who--well, who loved me, and who knew that I've always tried to be decent, always tried to play the game. All I want is to be reasonably well treated; to have a good time and be among pleasant people--"

Her thoughts wandered about among the various friends whose judgment might serve at this crisis to clear her own thoughts and simplify the road before her. Strangely enough, Warren Gregory's own mother was the first of whom she thought; that pure and austere and uncompromising heart would certainly find the way. Whether Rachael had the courage to follow it was another question. She loved old Mrs. Gregory; they were good friends. But Rachael dismissed her with a little shudder, as from the spatter of icy water against her bared breast. The bishop? Rachael and Clarence duly kept a pew in one of the city's fashionable churches; it was the Breckenridge family pew, rented by the family for a hundred years. But they never sat in it, although Rachael felt vaguely sometimes that for reasons undefined they should, and Clarence was apt in moments of sentiment to reproach his wife with the statement that his grandmother had been a faithful church woman, and his mother had always attended church on pleasant mornings in winter.

But the bishop called on Rachael once a year, and Rachael liked him, and mingled an air of pretty penitence for past negligences with a gracious promise of better conduct in future. His Grace was a fine, breezy, broadminded man, polished in manner, sympathetic, and tolerant. He had not risen to his present eminence by too harsh a rebuke of the sinner.

His handsome young assistant, Father Graves, as he liked to be called, was far more radical. But a great deal was forgiven this attractive boyish celibate by the women of the Episcopal parish. They enjoyed his scoldings, gave him their confidences, and asked his advice, though they never followed it. His slender, black-clad figure, with the Roman collar, was admired by many bright eyes at receptions and church bazaars.

Still, Rachael could not somehow consider herself as seriously asking either of these two clergymen for advice. She could see the bishop, fitting finely groomed fingers together, pursing his lips for a judicial reply.

"My dear Mrs. Breckenridge, that Clarence is now passing through a most unfortunate, most lamentable, period in his life is, alas, perfectly true. His mother--a lovely woman--was one of my wife's dearest friends, one of my own. His first marriage was much against her wishes, poor dear lady, and--as my wife was saying the other day--had she lived to see him happily married again, and her grandchild in such good hands, it could not but have been a great joy to her. Yes. ... Now, you and I know Clarence--know his good points, and know his faults. That's one of the sad things about us poor human beings, we get to know each other so well! And isn't it equally true that we're not patient enough with each other?--oh, yes, I know we try. But do we try HARD enough? Isn't there generally some fault on both sides, quick words, angry, hasty actions, argument and blame, when we say things we don't mean and that we are sure to regret, eh? We all get tired of the stupid round of daily duty, and of the people we are nearest to--that's a sad thing, too. We'd all like a change, like to see if we couldn't do something else better! And so comes the break, and the cloud on a fine old name, and all because we aren't better soldiers--we don't want to march in line! Bless me, don't I know the feeling myself? Why, that good little wife of mine could tell you some tales of discouragement and disenchantment that would make you open your eyes! But she braces me up, she puts heart into me--and the first thing I know I'm marching again!"

And having comfortably shifted the entire trend of the conversation from his parishioner to himself and found nothing insurmountable in his own problem, the good bishop would chuckle mischievously at finding his eminent self quite human after all, and would suggest their going in to find Mrs. Bishop, and having a cup of tea. These women, always restless and dissatisfied, were a part of his work; he prided himself upon the swiftness and tact with which he disposed of them.

Rachael's mouth twisted wryly at the thought of him. No, she could not bare her soul to the bishop.

Nor could she approach Father Graves with any real hope of a helping word. To seek him out in his study--that esthetically bare and yet beautiful room, with its tobacco-brown hangings and monastic furnishing in black oak--would be to invite mischief. To sit there, with her eloquent eyes fixed upon his, her haunting voice wrapping itself about his senses, would be a genuine cruelty toward a harmless, well-intentioned youth whose heroism in abjuring the world, the flesh, and the devil had not yet been great enough to combat his superb and dignified egotism. At best, he would be won by Rachael's revelation of her soul to a long and frankly indiscreet talk of his own; at worst, he would construe her confidences in an entirely personal sense, and feel that she came not at all to the priest and all to the man.

Dismissing him from her councils, Rachael thought of Florence Haviland, the good and kind-hearted and capable matron who was Clarence's sister and only near relative. She and Florence had always been good friends, had often discussed Clarence of late. What sort of advice would Florence's forty-five years be apt to give to Rachael's twenty-eight? "Don't be so absurd, Rachael, half the men in our set drink as much as Clarence does. Don't jump from the frying-pan into the fire. Remember Elsie Rowland and Marian Cowles when you talk so lightly of divorce!"

That would be Florence's probable attitude. Still, it was a bracing attitude, heartily positive, like everything Florence did and said. And Florence was above everything else a church member, a prominent Christian in her self-sacrificing wifehood and motherhood, her social and charitable and civic work. She might be unflattering, but she would be right. Rachael's last conscious thought, as she went off to sleep, was that she would take the earliest possible moment to extract a verdict from Florence.

She went into her husband's room at ten o'clock the next morning to find Billy radiantly presiding over a loaded breakfast tray, and the invalid, pale and pasty, and with no particular interest in food evinced by the twitching muscles of his face, nevertheless neatly brushed and shaved, propped up in pillows, and making a visible effort to appear convalescent.

"How are you this morning?" Rachael asked perfunctorily, with her quick glance moving from the books on the table to the wood fire burning lazily behind brass firedogs. Everything was in perfect order, Helda's touch visible everywhere.

"Fine," Clarence answered, also perfunctorily. His coffee was untouched, and the cigarette in his long holder had gone out, but Billy was disposing of eggs, toast, bacon, and cream with youthful zest. Clarence's hot, sick gaze rested almost with hostility upon his wife's cool beauty; in a gray linen gown, with a transparent white ruffle turned back from her white throat, she looked as fresh as the fresh spring morning.

"Headache?" said the nicely modulated, indifferent voice.

To this solicitude Clarence made no answer. A dark, ugly look came into his face, and he turned his eyes sullenly and wearily away.

"How was the Chase dinner, Bill?" pursued the cheerful visitor, unabashed.

"Same old thing," Carol answered briefly.

"You're not up to the Perrys' lunch to-day, are you, Clancy?"

"Oh, my God, no!" burst from the sufferer.

"Well, I'll telephone them. If Florence comes in this morning I'm going to say you're asleep, so keep quiet up here. Do you want to see Greg again?"

"No, I don't!" said Clarence, with unexpected vigor. "Steer him off if you can. Preaching at me last night as if he'd never touched anything stronger than malted milk!"

"I don't imagine I'll have much trouble steering him off," Rachael said coldly. "His Sundays are pretty well occupied without--sick calls!"

There was a delicate and scornful emphasis on the word "sick" that brought the blood to Clarence Breckenridge's face. Billy flushed, too, and an angry light flamed into her eyes.

"That's not fair, Rachael!" the girl said hotly, "and you know it's not!"

The glances of the three crossed. Billy was breathing hard; Clarence, shakily holding a fresh match to his cold cigarette, sent a lowering look from daughter to wife. Rachael shrugged her shoulders.

"Well, I'll have my breakfast," she said, and turning she went from the room and downstairs to the sunshiny breakfast porch. There were flowers on the little round table, a bright glitter was struck from silver and glass, an icy grapefruit, brimming with juice, stood at her place. The little room was all windows, and to-day the cretonne curtains had been pushed back to show the garden brave in new spring green, the exquisite freshness of elm and locust trees that bordered it, and far away the slopes of the golf green, with the scarlet and white dots that were early players moving over it. Sunshine flooded the world, great plumes of white and purple lilac rustled in their tents of green leaves, a bee blundered from the blossoming wistaria vine into the room, and blundered out again. Far off Rachael heard a cock breaking the Sabbath stillness with a prolonged crow, and as the clock in the dining-room chimed one silver note for the half-hour, the bells of the church in the little village of Belvedere Bay began to ring.

Of the comfort, the beauty, and the harmony of all this, however, Rachael saw and felt nothing. Her brief interview with her husband had left a bitter taste in her mouth. She felt neither courage nor appetite for the new day. Annie carried away the blue bowl of porridge untouched, reporting to Ellie: "She don't want no eggs, nor sausage, nor waffles--nothing more!"

Ellie, the cook, who boarded a four-year-old daughter with the gardener and his wife, at the gate-lodge, was deep in the robust charms of this young person, and not sorry to be uninterrupted.

"Thank goodness she don't," she said. "Do you want a little waffle all for yourself, Lovey? Do you want to pour the batter into Ma's iron yourself? Pin a napkin round her, Annie! An' then you can eat it out on the steps, darlin', because it just seems to be a shame to spend a minute indoors when God sends us a mornin' like this!"

"It must have been grand, walking to church this morning, all right," said Alfred, who was busy with golf sticks and emery on the vine-shaded porch.

"It was!" said Ellie and Annie together, and Annie added: "Rose from Bowditch's was there, and she says she can't get away but about once a month. She always has to wait on the children's breakfast at eight, and then down comes the others at half-past nine, or later, the way she never has a moment until it's too late for High! I told her she had a right to look for another place!"

"There's worse places than this," Ellie said, watching her small daughter begin on her waffle. A general nodding of heads in a contented silence indicated that there was some happiness in the Breckenridge household even though it was below stairs.

Rachael's sombre revery was presently interrupted by the smooth crushing of wheels on the pebbled drive and the announcement of Mrs. Haviland, who followed her name promptly into the breakfast-room. A fine, large, beautifully gowned woman, with a prayer book in her white-gloved hand, and a veil holding her close, handsome spring hat in place, she glanced at the coffee and hot bread with superiority only possible to a person whose own breakfast is several hours past.

"Rachael, you lazy woman!" said Florence Haviland lightly, breathing deep, as a heavy woman in tight corsets must perforce breathe on a warm spring morning. "Do you realize that it's almost eleven o'clock?"

"Perfectly!" Mrs. Breckenridge said. "I slept until nine, and felt quite proud of myself to think that I had got through so much of the day!"

Mrs. Haviland gave her a sharp look in answer, not quite disapproving, yet far from pleased.

"I started the girlies off to eight o'clock service," she said capably. "Fraulien went with them, and that leaves the maids free to go when they please." This was one of Mrs. Haviland's favorite illusions. "Gardner begged off this morning, he's been so good about going lately that I couldn't very well refuse, so I started early and have just dropped him at the club."

"Was Gardner at the Berry Stokes bachelor dinner on Friday night?" asked Rachael. Mrs. Haviland was all comprehension at once.

"No, he couldn't. Mr. Payne of the London branch was here you know, and Gardner's been terribly tied. He left yesterday, thank goodness. Clarence went of course? Oh, dear, dear, dear!"

The last three words came on a gentle sigh. Clarence's sister compressed her lips and shook her handsome head.

"Is he very bad?" she asked reluctantly.

"Pretty much as usual," Rachael answered philosophically. "I had Greg in." And suddenly, unexpectedly, she felt a quick happy flutter at her heart, and a roseate mist drifted before her eyes.

"It's disgraceful!" Mrs. Haviland said, eying Rachael hopefully for a wifely denial. As this was not forthcoming, she went on briskly: "However, my dear, Clarence isn't the only one! They say Fred Bowditch is actually"-- her voice sank to a discreet undertone as she added the word--"violent; and poor Lucy Pickering needed a rest cure the moment she got her divorce, she was in such a nervous state. I'm not defending Clarence--"

"What are you doing, then?" Rachael asked, with her cool smile.

"Well, I--" Mrs. Haviland, who had been drifting comfortably along on a tide of words, stopped, a little at a loss. "I hope I don't have to defend your own husband to you, Rachael," she said reproachfully.

"I'm getting pretty tired of it," said Rachael moodily.

Mrs. Haviland watched the downcast beautiful face opposite her with a sense of growing alarm.

"My dear," she said impressively, "of course it's hard for you; we all know that. But just at this time, Rachael, it would be absolutely FATAL to have any open break with Clarence--"

Rachael flung up her head impatiently, then dropped her face in her hands.

"I don't want any open break," she muttered.

"You do? Oh, you DON'T?" Mrs. Haviland questioned anxiously. "No, of course you don't. He's not himself now, for several reasons. For one-- and that's what I specially came to speak to you about--for one thing, he's terribly worried about Carol. Carol," repeated Mrs. Haviland significantly, "and Joe Pickering."

Rachael raised sombre eyes, but did not speak.

"Is Carol here?" her aunt asked delicately.

"Dressing," Rachael answered briefly.

"Do you realize," Mrs. Haviland said, "that everyone is beginning to talk?"

"Perfectly," Rachael admitted. "But what do you expect me to do?"

"SOMETHING must be done," said the other woman firmly.

"By whom?" Rachael countered lightly.

"Well--by Clarence, I suppose," Mrs. Haviland suggested discontentedly.

"Clarence!" Rachael's tone was but a scornful breath. Her glance toward the ceiling evoked more clearly than any words a vision of Clarence's condition at the moment.

"Well, I suppose he can't do anything just now, anyway," his sister conceded ruefully. "Can't you--couldn't you talk to her, Rachael?"

"Talk to her?" Mrs. Breckenridge smiled at some memory. "My dear Florence, you don't suppose I haven't talked to her!"

"Well, I suppose of course you have," Mrs. Haviland said hastily. "But my dear, it's dreadful! People are beginning to ask questions; a reporter-- we don't know who he was--telephoned Gardner. Of course Gardner hung up--"

"I can say no more than I have said," Rachael observed thoughtfully. "What authority have I? Clarence could influence her, I think, but she lies simply and flatly to Clarence."

Mrs. Haviland winced at the ugly word.

"Joe drinks," Rachael went on, "but he doesn't drink as much as her adored Daddy does. Joe is thirty-nine and Billy is seventeen--well, that's not his fault. Joe is divorced--well, but Carol's mother is living, and Clarence's second wife isn't exactly ostracised by society! A clergyman of your own church married Clarence and me--" The little scornful twist of the beautiful mouth stung a church woman conscious of personal integrity, and Mrs. Haviland said:

"A great many of them won't! The church is going to take a stand in the matter. The bishops are considering a canon. ..."

Mrs. Breckenridge shrugged her shoulders indifferently. Theology did not interest her.

"And as Billy is too young and too blind to see that Joe isn't a gentleman," she continued, "or to realize that Lucy got her divorce against his will, to believe that her money might well influence a gentleman of Joe's luxurious tastes and dislike for office work--why, I suppose they will be married!"

"Never!" said Florence Haviland, with some heat, "DON'T!"

"Unless Clarence shoots him," submitted Rachael. A look of intense anxiety clouded Mrs. Haviland's eyes.

"I believe he would," she said, in a wretched whisper, with a cautious glance about.

"He might," his wife said seriously. "If ever it comes to that, we shall simply have to keep them apart. You see Billy--the clever little devil--"

"Oh, Rachael, DON'T use such words!" said the church woman. "Father Graves was saying only the other day that one's speech should be 'yea, yea' and--"

"I daresay!" Mrs. Breckenridge's smile was indulgent. It had been many years since Florence had succeeded in ruffling her. "Billy, then," she resumed, "keeps her father happy in the thought that he is all the world to her, and that her occasional chats with Joe are of an entirely uplifting and impersonal character."

"Impersonal! Uplifting!" Mrs. Haviland repeated indignantly. "There wasn't very much uplift about them the other night. Gardner and I stopped in to see if we couldn't take you to the Hoyts', but you'd gone. Carol had on that flame-colored dress of hers, her hair was fluffed all over her ears in that silly way the girls do now; Joe couldn't take his eyes off her. The only light they had in the drawing-room was the yellow lamp and the fire; it was the coziest thing I ever saw!"

"Vivvy Sartoris was here!" Rachael said quickly.

"Don't you believe it, my dear!" Mrs. Haviland returned triumphantly. "Carol was very demure, 'Tante' this and 'Tante' that, but I knew right away that something was amiss! 'Oh,' I said right out flatly, 'are you alone here, Carol?' and she answered very prettily: 'Vivian was to be here, but she hasn't come yet!' This was after half-past seven."

"I understood Vivian WAS here," said Rachael, flushing darkly. "Let me see--the next morning--where was I? Oh, yes, it was your luncheon, and Billy had gone out for some tennis when I came downstairs. I supposed of course--but I didn't ask. I DID ask Helda what time she had let the gentleman out and she said before eleven--not much after half-past ten, in fact."

"You see, we mustn't go on suppositions and halftruths any more," said Mrs. Haviland in delicate reproach. "When we have that wonderful and delicate thing, a girl's soul, to deal with, we must be SURE."

"I suppose I'd better tell Clarence that--about Wednesday night," Rachael said, downing with some effort an impulse to ask Florence not to be so smug.

"Well, I think you had," the other agreed, with visible relief.

"As for me," Mrs. Breckenridge said, nettled by her sister-in-law's attitude, and mischievously interested in the effect of her thunderbolt, "I'm just desperately tired of it. I can't see that I'm doing Clarence, or Billy, or myself, any good! I'd like to resign, and let somebody else try for a while!"

Steel leaped into Mrs. Haviland's light-blue eyes. She felt the shock in every fibre of body and soul, but she flung herself gallantly into the charge. Her large form straightened, her expression achieved a certain remoteness.

"What do you mean by that?" she asked sharply.

"The usual thing, I suppose," Rachael answered indifferently.

The older woman, watching her closely, essayed a brief, dry laugh.

"Don't talk absurdities," she said boldly. But Rachael saw the uneasiness under the assured manner, and smiled to herself.

"It's not absurd at all," she protested, still with her smiling, half-negligent air; "I've put it off years longer than most women would; now I'm getting rather tired."

"It's a great mistake to talk that way, whether you mean it or not," Mrs. Haviland said, after an uncomfortable moment, during which her face flushed, and her breath began to come rather fast. "But you're joking, of course; you're too sensible to take any step that would only plunge you into fresh difficulties. Clarence is very trying, I know--we all know that--but let's try to face the situation sensibly, and not fly off the handle like this! Why, Rachael dear, I can hardly believe it's your cool-headed, reasonable self talking," she went on more quietly. "Don't--don't even think about it! In the first place, you couldn't get it!"

"Oh, yes, I could. Clarence wouldn't contest it," Rachael said. "He'd agree to anything to be rid of me. If not--if he wouldn't agree to my filing suit under the New York law, I could establish my residence in California or Nevada, and bring suit there. ..."

Mrs. Haviland gasped.

"Give up your home and your car and your maids for some small hotel?" she questioned, with her favorite air of neatly placing her fingertip upon the weak spot in her opponent's armor. "No clubs, no dinners, none of your old friends--have you thought of that?"

"You may imagine that I've thought of it from a good many angles, Florence," Rachael said coldly, finding that what had been a mere drifting idea was beginning to take rather definite form in her mind. It was delightful to see the usually complacent and domineering Florence so agitated and at a loss.

"I never dreamed--" Mrs. Haviland mused dazedly. "How long, in Heaven's name, have you been thinking about it?"

"Oh, quite some time," said Rachael.

"Well, it's awful!" the other woman said. "It'll make the most awful--and as if poor Clarence hadn't been all through it all once! I declare it makes me sick! But I can't believe you're serious. Rachael, think--think what it means!"

"It's a very serious thing," the other assented placidly. "But Clarence has no one but himself to blame."

"Only Clarence won't BE blamed, my dear; men never are!" Mrs. Haviland suggested unkindly. Rachael reddened.

"_I_ don't care what they say or whom they blame!" she answered proudly.

"Ah, well, my dear, we aren't any of us really indifferent to criticism," the older woman said, watching closely the effect of her words. "People are censorious--it's too bad, it's a pity--but there you are. 'There must have been something we didn't understand,' they say, 'there must be another man!'"

Rachael raised her head a little, and managed a smile.

"That's what they say," Mrs. Haviland went on, mildly triumphant. "And no matter how brave or how independent a woman is, she doesn't like THAT." There came to the speaker suddenly, under her smooth flow of words, a sickening shock of realization: it was of Rachael and Clarence she was speaking, her nearest relatives; it was one of the bulwarks of her world that was threatened! Without her knowledge her tone became less sure and more sincere. "For God's sake, think what you are doing, dear," she said pleadingly; "think of Carol and of us all! Don't drag us all through the papers again! I know what Clarence is, poor wretched boy; he's always had too much money, he's always had his own way. I know what you put up with week in and week out--"

Mrs. Haviland's usual attitude of assured superiority never impressed her sister-in-law. Her pompous magnificence was a source of unmitigated amusement to Rachael. But now the older woman's emotion had carried her on to genuine and honest expression in spite of herself, and listening, Rachael found herself curiously stirred. She looked down, conscious of a sudden melting in her heart, a thickening in her throat.

"I've always been so fond of you, Rachael," Florence went on. "I've always stood your friend--you know that--"

"I know," Rachael said huskily, her lashes dropped.

"Long before I knew how much you would be liked, Rachael, and what a fuss people were going to make over you, I made you welcome," continued Florence simply, with tears in her eyes. "I thanked God that Clarence had married a good woman, and that Carol would have a refined and a--I may say a Christian home. Isn't that true?"

"I know," Rachael said again with an effort, as she paused.

"Then think it over," besought the other woman eagerly. "Think that Carol will marry, and that Clarence--" Her ardent tone dropped suddenly. There was a moment's pause. Then she added dryly, "How do, dear?"

"How do, Tante Firenze!" said Carol, who had come abruptly into the room. "How are the girls? Say, listen! Is Isabelle going to the Bowditches'?"

"I don't even know that Charlotte is going," Mrs. Haviland said, with an aunty smile of baffling sweetness that yet contained a subtle reproof. "Uncle Gardner and I haven't made up our minds. Isabelle in any case would only go to look on, so she is not so much interested, but poor Charlotte is simply on tenterhooks to know whether it's to be yes or no. Girls' first parties"--her indulgent smile included Rachael--"dear me, how important they seem!"

"I should think you'd have to answer Mrs. Bowditch," said Carol in plain disgust at this maternal vacillation.

"Mrs. Bowditch is fortunately an old enough friend, dear, to waive the usual formalities," her aunt answered sweetly.

"But, my gracious--Charlotte's two months older than I am, and she won't know any of the men!" Carol protested.

"Don't speak in that precocious way, Bill," Rachael said sharply. "You went to your first dances last winter!"

Carol gave her stepmother a look conspicuously devoid of affection, and turned to adjust her smart little hat with the aid of a narrow mirror hanging between the glass dining-room doors.

"You couldn't drop me at the club, on your way to church, Tante?" she presently inquired. And to Rachael she added, with youthful impatience, "I told Dad where I was going!"

Mrs. Haviland rose somewhat heavily.

"Glad to. Any chance of you coming to lunch, Rachael? What are your plans?"

"Thank you, no, woman dear! I may go over to Gertrude's for tea."

The little group broke up. Mrs. Haviland and her niece went out to the waiting motor car purring on the pebbled drive. Rachael idly watched them out of sight, sighed at the thought of wasting so beautiful a day indoors, and went slowly upstairs. Her husband, comfortably propped in pillows, looked better.

"Clarence," said she, depositing several pounds of morning papers upon the foot of his bed, "who's Billy lunching with at the club?"

Clarence picked up the uppermost paper, fixed his eyes attentively upon it, and puffed upon his cigarette for reply.

"Do you know?" Rachael asked vigorously.

No answer. Mr. Breckenridge, his eyes still intent upon what he was reading, held his cigarette at arm's length over the brass bowl on the table beside the bed, and dislodged a quarter-inch of ash with his little finger.

Rachael, briskly setting his cluttered table to rights, gave him an angry glance that, so far as any effect upon him was concerned, was thrown away.

"Don't be so rude, Clarence," she said, in annoyance. "Billy said you agreed to her going to the club for golf. Who's she with?"

At last Mr. Breckenridge raised sodden and redshot eyes to his wife's face, moistening his dark and swollen lips carefully with his tongue before he spoke. He was a fat-faced man, who, despite evidences of dissipation, did not look his more than forty years. There was no gray in his thin, silky hair, and there still lingered an air of youth and innocence in his round face. This morning he was in a bad temper because his whole body was still upset from the Friday night dinner and drinking party, and in his soul he knew that he had cut rather a poor figure before Billy, and that the little minx had taken instant advantage of the situation.

"I just want to say this, Rachael," Clarence said, with an icy dignity only slightly impaired by the lingering influences of drink. "I'm Billy's father, and I understand her, and she understands me. That's all that's necessary; do you get me?" He put his cigarette holder back in his mouth, gripped it firmly between his teeth, and turned again to his paper. "If some of you damned jealous women who are always running around trying to make trouble would let her ALONE" he went on sulkily, "I'd be obliged to you--that's all!"

Rachael settled her ruffles in a big wing-chair with the innocent expression of a casual caller. She took a book from the reading table, and fluttered a few pages indifferently.

"Listen, Clancy," said she placatingly. "Florence was just here, and she says--and I agree--that there is no question that Joe Pickering is devoted to Bill. Now, I don't say that Billy is equally devoted--"

"Ha! Better not!" said Clarence at white heat, one eye watchful over the top of the paper.

"But I DO say," pursued Rachael steadily, "that she is with him a good deal more than she will admit. Yesterday, for instance, when she was playing tennis with the Parmalees and the Pinckard boy, Kent came up to the house to get some ginger ale. I happened to be dummy, and I went out on the terrace. Joe's horse was down near the courts, and Joe and Billy were sitting there on one of the benches--where the others were I don't know. When Kent went down with the ginger ale, Joe got on his horse and went off. Of course it was only for a few minutes, but Billy didn't say anything about it--"

Her voice, with a tentative question in it, rested in air. Clarence turned a page with some rustling of paper.

"Then Florence says," Rachael went on after a moment, "that when she and Gardner stopped here Wednesday night Joe was here, and Vivvie Sartoris wasn't here. Now, of course, I don't KNOW, for I didn't ask Alfred---"

"There you go," said the sick man witheringly. "That's right--ask the maids, and get all the servants talking; all come down on the heels of a poor little girl like a pack of yapping wolves! I suppose if she was plain and unattractive--I should think you'd be ashamed," he went on, changing his high and querulous key to one of almost priestly authority and reproof, "Upon my word, it's beneath your dignity. My little girl comes to me, and she explains the whole matter. Pickering admires her--she can't help that-- and she has an influence over him. She tells me he hasn't touched a thing but beer for six weeks, just because she asked him to give up heavy drinking. He told her the other day that if he had met her a few years ago, Lucy never would have left him. She's wakened the boy up, he's a different fellow--"

"All that may be true," Rachael said quickly, the color that his preposterous rebuke had summoned to her cheeks still flushing them, "still, you don't want Billy to marry Joe Pickering! You know that sort of pity, and that business of reforming a man--" She paused, but Clarence did not speak. "Not that Billy herself realizes it, I daresay," Rachael added presently, watching the reader's absorbed face for an answering look.

Silence.

"Clarence!" she began imperatively.

Clarence withdrew his attention from the paper with an obvious effort, and spoke in a laboriously polite tone.

"I don't care to discuss it, Rachael."

"But--" Rachael stopped short on the word. Silence reigned in the big, bright room except for the occasional rustle of Clarence's newspaper. His wife sat idle, her eyes roving indifferently from the gayly papered walls to the gayly flowered hangings, the great bowl of daffodils on the bookcase, the portrait of Carol that, youthful and self-conscious, looked down from the mantel. On the desk a later photograph of Carol, in a silver frame, was duly flanked by one of Rachael, the girl in the gown she had worn for her first big dance, the woman looking out from under the narrow brim of a snug winter hat, great furs framing her beautiful face, and her slender figure wrapped in furs. Here also was a picture of Florence Haviland, her handsome face self-satisfied, her trio of homely, distinguished-looking girls about her, and a small picture of Gardner, and two of Clarence's dead mother: one, as they all remembered her, a prim-looking woman with gray hair and magnificent lace on her unfashionable gown, the other, taken thirty years before, showing her as cheerful and youthful, a cascade of ringlets falling over her shoulder, the arm that coquettishly supported her head resting upon an upholstered pedestal, a voluminous striped silk gown sweeping away from her in rich folds. There was even a picture of Clarence and Florence when they were respectively eight and twelve, Clarence in a buttoned serge kilt and plaid stockings, his fat, gentle little face framed in damp careful curls, Florence also with plaid stockings and a scalloped frock. Clarence sat in a swing; Florence, just behind him, leaned on an open gate, her legs crossed carelessly as she rested on her elbows. And there was a picture of their father, a simple-faced man in an ample beard, taken at that period when photographs were highly glazed, and raised in bas relief. Least conspicuous of all was a snapshot framed in a circle of battered blue-enamel daisies, the picture of a baby girl laughing against a background of dandelions and meadow grass. And Rachael knew that this was Clarence's greatest treasure, that it went wherever he went, and that it was worn shabby and tarnished from his hands and his lips.

Sometimes she looked at it and wondered. What a bright-faced, gay little thing Billy had been! Who had set her down in that field, and quieted the rioting eyes and curls and dimples, and anchored the restless little feet, while Baby watched Dad and the black box with the birdie in it? Paula? Once, idly interested in those old days before she had known him, she had asked about the picture. But Clarence, glad to talk of it, had not mentioned his wife.

"It was before my father died; we were up in the old Maine place," he had said. "Gosh, Bill was cute that day! We went on a drive--no motor cars then--and took our lunch, and after lunch the kid comes and settles herself in my arms--for a nap, if you please! 'Say, look-a-here,' I said, 'what do you think I am--a Pullman?' I wanted a smoke, by George! She wasn't two, you know. Her fat little legs were bare, we'd put her into socks, and her face was flushed, and she just looked up at me through her hair and said, 'Hing!'

Well, it was good-bye smoke for me! I sang all right, and she cuddled down as pleased as a kitten, and off she went!"

To-day Rachael's eyes wandered from the picture to Clarence's face. She tried to study it dispassionately, but, still shaken by their recent conversation, and sitting there, as she knew she was sitting there, merely to prove that it had had no effect upon her, she felt this to be a little difficult.

What sort of a little boy had he been? A fat little boy, of course. She disliked fat little boys. A spoiled little boy, never crossed in any way. His mother made him go to Sunday-school, and dancing school, and to Miss Nesmith's private academy, where he was coaxed and praised and indulged even more than at home. And old Fanny, who was still with Florence, superintended his baths and took care of his clothes, and ran her finger over the bristles of his toothbrush every morning, to see if he had told her the truth. He rarely did; they used to laugh about those old deceptions. Clarence used to laugh as violently as the old woman when she accused him of occasional kicking and biting.

Other boys came in to play with him. Was it because of his magic lantern and his velocipede, his unending supply of cream puffs and licorice sticks, or because they liked him? Rachael knew only a detail here and there: that he had danced a fancy dance with Anna Vanderwall when he was a fat sixteen, at a Kermess, and that he had given a stag dinner to twenty youths of his own age a few days before he went off to college, and that they had drunk a hundred and fifty dollars' worth of champagne. She knew that his allowance at college was three hundred dollars a month, and that he never stayed within it, and it was old Fanny's boast that every stitch the boy ever wore from the day he was born came from London or Paris. His underwear was as dainty as a bride's; he had his first dress suit at fifteen; at college he had his suite of three big rooms furnished like showrooms, his monogrammed cigarettes, his boat, and his horse.

The thought of all these things used to distress his mother when she was old and much alone. She attempted to belittle the luxury of Clarence's boyhood. She told Rachael that he was treated just as the other boys were. Her conscience was never quite easy about his upbringing.

"You can't hold a boy too tight, you know, or else he'll break away altogether," old lady Breckenridge would say to Rachael, sitting before a coal fire in the gloomy magnificence of her old-fashioned drawingroom and pressing the white fingers of one hand against the agonized joints of the other. "I was often severe with Clarence, and he was a good boy until he got with other boys; he was always loving to me. He never should have married Paula Verlaine," she would add fretfully. "A good woman would have overlooked his faults and made a fine man of him, but she was always an empty-headed little thing! Ah, well"--and the poor old woman would sigh as she drew her fluffy shawl about her shoulders--"I cannot blame myself, that's my great consolation now, Rachael, when I think of facing my Master and rendering an account. I have been heavily afflicted, but I am not the first God-fearing woman who has been visited with sorrow through her children!"

Clarence had visited his mother often in the weeks that preceded her death, but she did not take much heed of his somewhat embarrassed presence, nor, to Rachael's surprise, did her last hours contain any of those heroic joys that are supposedly the reward of long suffering and virtue. An unexpressed terror seemed to linger in her sickroom, indeed to pervade the whole house; the invalid lay staring drearily at the heavy furnishings of her immense dark room, a nurse slipped in and out; the bloody light of the westering sun, falling through stairway windows of colored glass, blazed in the great hallway all through the chilly October afternoons. Callers came and went, there were subdued voices and soft footsteps; flowers came, their wet fragrance breaking from oiled paper and soaked cardboard boxes, the cards that were wired to them resisting all attempts at detachment. Clergymen came, and Rachael imitated their manner afterward, to the general delight.

On the day before she died Mrs. Breckenridge caught her son's plump cool hand in her own hot one, and made him promise to stop drinking, and to go to church, and to have Carol confirmed. Clarence promised everything.

But he did not keep his promises. Rachael had not thought he would; perhaps the old lady herself had not thought he would. He was sobered at the funeral, but not sober. Six weeks later all the bills against the estate were in. Florence had some of the family jewels and the family silver, Rachael had some, some was put away for Billy; the furniture was sold, the house rented for a men's club, and a nondescript man, calling upon young Mrs. Breckenridge, notified her that the stone had been set in place as ordered. They never saw it; they paid a small sum annually for keeping the plot in order, and the episode of Ada Martin Langhorne Breckenridge's life was over.

Clarence drank so heavily after that, and squandered his magnificent heritage so recklessly, that people began to say that he would soon follow his mother. But that was four years ago, and Rachael looking dispassionately at him, where he lay dozing in his pillows, had to admit that he had shown no change in the past four--or eight, or twelve--years. Like many a better woman, and many a better wife, she wondered if she would outlive him, vaguely saw herself, correct and remote, in her new black.

Involuntarily she sighed. How free she would be! She wished Clarence no ill, but the fact remained that, loose as was the bond between them, it galled and checked them both at every step. Their conversations were embittered by a thousand personalities, they instinctively knew how to hurt each other; a look from Clarence could crush his poised and accomplished wife into a mere sullen shrew, and she knew that it took less than a look from her--it took the mere existence of her youth and health and freshness--to infuriate him sometimes. At best, their relationship consciously avoided hostility. Rachael was silent, fuming; Clarence fumed and was silent; they sank to light monosyllables; they parted as quickly as possible. Would Clarence like to dine with this friend or that? Rachael didn't think he would, but might as well ask him. No, thank you! he wouldn't be found dead in that bunch. Did Rachael want to go with the Smiths and the Joneses to dine at the Highway, and dance afterward? Oh, horrors! no, thank you!

It was only when she spoke of Billy that Rachael was sure of his interest and attention, and of late she perforce had for Billy only criticism and disapproval. Rachael read the girl's vain and shallow and pleasure-loving little heart far more truly than her father could, and she was conscious of a genuine fear lest Billy bring sorrow to them all. Society was indulgent, yes, but an insolent and undeveloped little girl like Billy could not snap her fingers at the law without suffering the full penalty. Rachael would suffer, too. Florence and her girls would suffer, and Clarence--well, Clarence would not bear it. "What an awful mix-up it is!" Rachael thought wearily. "And what a sickening, tiresome place this world is!"

And then suddenly the thought of Warren Gregory came back, and the new curious sensation of warmth tugged at her heart.

CHAPTER IV

Mrs. Gardner Haviland, whirling home in her big car, after church, was hardly more pleased with life than was her beautiful sister-in-law, although she was not quite as conscious of dissatisfaction as was Rachael. Her position as a successful mother, wife, housekeeper, and member of society was theoretically so perfect that she derived from it, necessarily, an enormous amount of theoretical satisfaction. She could find no fault with herself or her environment; she was pleasantly ready with advice or with an opinion or with a verdict in every contingency that might arise in human affairs, as a Christian woman of unimpeachable moral standing. She knew her value in a hectic and reckless world. She did not approve of women smoking, or of suffrage, but she played a brilliant game of bridge, and did not object to an infinitesimal stake. She belonged to clubs and to their directorates, yet it was her boast that she knew every thought in her children's hearts, and the personal lives and hopes and ambitions of her maids were as an open book to her.

Still, she had her moments of weakness, and on this warm day of the spring she felt vaguely disappointed with life. Rachael's hints of divorce had filled her with a real apprehension; she felt a good aunt's concern at Billy's reckless course, and a good sister's disapproval of Clarence and his besetting sin.

But it was not these considerations that darkened her full handsome face as she went up the steps of her big, widespread country mansion; it was some vaguer, more subtle discontent. She had not dressed herself for the sudden warmth of the day, and her heavy flowered hat and trim veil had given her a headache. The blazing sunlight on white steps and blooming flowers blinded her, and when she stepped into the dark, cool hall she could hardly see.

The three girls were there, well-bred, homely girls, in their simple linens: Charlotte, a rather severe type, eyeglassed at eighteen, her thick, light-brown hair plainly brushed off her face and knotted on her neck, was obviously the opposite of everything Billy was; conscientious, intellectual, and conscious of her own righteousness, she could not compete with her cousin in Billy's field; she very sensibly made the best of her own field. Isabelle was a stout, clumsy girl of sixteen, with a metal bar across her large white teeth, red hair, and a creamy skin. Little Florence was only nine, a thin, freckled, sensitive child, with a shy, unsmiling passion for dogs and horses, and little in common with the rest of the world.

Their mother had expected sons in every case, and still felt a little baffled by the fact of her children's sex. Charlotte proving a girl, she had said gallantly that she must have a little brother "to play with Charlotte." Isabelle, duly arriving, probably played with Charlotte much more amiably than a brother would have done, and Mrs. Haviland blandly accepted her existence, but in her heart she was far from feeling satisfied. She was, of course, an absolutely competent mother to girls, but she felt that she would have been a more capable and wonderful mother to boys.

More than six years after Isabelle's birth Florence Haviland began to talk smilingly of "my boy." "Gardner worships the girls," she said, with wifely indulgence, "but I know he wants a son--and the girlies need a brother!" A resigned shrug ended the sentence with: "So I'm in for the whole thing again!"

It was said that Mrs. Haviland greeted the news that the third child was a daughter with a mechanically bright smile, as one puzzled beyond all words by perverse event, and that her spoken comment was the single mild ejaculation: "Extraordinary!"

Now the two older Haviland girls, following their mother into her bedroom, seated themselves there while she changed her dress. Florence junior, in passionate argument with the butler over the death of one of the drawing-room goldfish, remained downstairs. Mrs. Haviland, casting the hot, high-collared silk upon the bed, took a new embroidered pongee from a box, and busied herself with its unfamiliar hooks and straps. Charlotte and Isabelle were never quite spontaneous in their conversations with their mother, their attitude in talking with her being one of alert and cautious self-consciousness; they did not breathe quite naturally, and they laughed constantly. Yet they both loved this big, firm, omnipotent being, and believed in her utterly and completely.

"We met Doctor Gregory and Charlie near the club this morning, M'ma," volunteered Isabelle.

"And they asked about Mrs. Bowditch's dance," Charlotte added with a little innocent craft. "But I said that M'ma had been unable to decide. Of course I said that we would LIKE to go, and that you knew that, and would allow it if you possibly could."

"That was quite right, dear," Mrs. Haviland said to her oldest daughter, calmly ignoring the implied question, and to Isabelle she added kindly:

"M'ma doesn't quite like to hear you calling a young man you hardly know by his first name, Isabelle. Of course, there's no harm in it, but it cheapens a girl just a LITTLE. While Charlotte might do it because she is older, and has seen Charlie Gregory at some of the little informal affairs last winter, you are younger, and haven't really seen much of him since he went to college. Don't let M'ma hear you do that again."

Isabelle turned a lively scarlet, and even Charlotte colored and was silent. The younger girl's shamed eyes met her mother's, and she nodded in quick embarrassment. But this tacit consent did not satisfy Mrs. Haviland.

"You understand M'ma, don't you, dear?" she asked. Isabelle murmured something indistinguishable.

"Yes, M'ma!" said that lady herself, encouragingly and briskly. Isabelle duly echoed a husky "Yes, M'ma!"

"Did you give my message to Miss Roper, Charlotte?" pursued the matron.

"She wasn't at church, M'ma," said Charlotte, taken unawares and instinctively uneasy. "Mrs. Roper said she had a heavy cold; she said she'd been sleeping on the sleeping porch."

"So M'ma's message was forgotten?" the mother asked pleasantly.

Charlotte perceived herself to be in an extremely dangerous position. Long ago both girls had lost, under this close surveillance and skilful system of cross-examination, their original regard for truth as truth. That they usually said what was true was because policy and self-protection suggested it. Charlotte had time now for a flying survey of the situation and its possibilities before she answered, somewhat uncertainly:

"I asked Mrs. Roper to deliver it, M'ma. Wasn't that--" Her voice faltered nervously. "Was it something you would have rather telephoned about?"

"Would rather have telephoned about?" Mrs. Haviland corrected automatically. "Well, M'ma would rather FEEL that when she sends a message it is given to JUST the person to whom she sent it, in JUST the way she sent it. However, in this case no harm was done. Don't hook your heel over the rung of your chair, dear! Ring the bell, Isabelle, I want Alice."

"I'll hook you, M'ma!" volunteered Charlotte.

"Thank you, dear, but I want to speak to Alice. And now you girls might run along. I'll be down directly."

A moment later she submitted herself patiently to the maid's hands. Florence was a conscientious woman, and she felt that she owed Alice as well as herself this little office. Charlotte might have hooked her gown for her; indeed, she might with a small effort have done it herself, but it was Alice's duty, and nothing could be worse for Alice, or any servant, than to have her duties erratically assumed by others on one day and left to her on the next. This was the quickest way to spoil servants, and Florence never spoiled her servants.

"They have a pleasant day for their picnic," she observed now, kindly. Alice was on her knees, her face puckered as she busied herself with the hooks of a girdle, but she smiled gratefully. Her two brothers had borrowed their employer's coal barge to-day, and with a score of cherished associates, several hundred sandwiches, sardines, camp-chairs, and bottles of root beer, with a smaller number of chaperoning mothers and concertinas, and the inevitable baby or two, were making a day of it on the river. Alice had timidly asked, a few days before, for a holiday to-day, that she might join them, but Mrs. Haviland had pointed out to her reasonably that she, Alice, had been at home, unexpectedly, because of her mother's illness, not only the previous Sunday, but the Saturday, too, and had got half-a-day's leave of absence for her cousin's wedding only the week before that. Alice was only eighteen, and her little spurt of bravery had been entirely exhausted long before her mistress's pleasant voice had stopped. Nothing more was said of the excursion until to-day.

"I guess they'll be eating their lunch, now, at Old Dock Point," said Alice, rising from her knees.

"Well, I hope they'll be careful; one hears of so many accidents among foolish young people there!" Mrs. Haviland answered, going downstairs to join her daughters in the hall, and, surrounded by them, proceeding to her own lunch.

For a while she was thoughtfully silent, and the conversation was maintained between the older girls and their governess. Charlotte and Isabelle chatted both German and French charmingly. Little Florence presently began to talk of her goldfish, meanwhile cutting a channel across her timbale through which the gravy ran in a stream.

Usually their mother listened to them with a quiet smile; they were well-educated girls, and any mother's heart must have been proud of them. But to-day she felt herself singularly dissatisfied with them. She said to herself that she hated Sundays, of all the days of the week. Other days had their duties: music, studies, riding, tennis, or walks, but on Sundays the girls were a dead weight upon her. Somehow, they were not in the current of good times that the other girls and boys of their ages were having. If she suggested brightly that they go over to the Parmalees' or the Morans' and see if the young people were playing tennis, she knew that Charlotte would delicately negative the idea: "They've got their sets all made up, M'ma, and one hates to, unless they specially ask one, don't you know?" They might go, of course, and greet their friends decorously, and watch the game smilingly for a while. Then they would come home with Fraulein, not forgetting to say good-bye to their hostess. But, although Charlotte played a better game than many of the other girls, and Isabelle played a good game, too, there were always gay little creatures in dashing costumes who monopolized the courts and the young men, and made the Haviland girls feel hopelessly heavy and dull. They would come home and tell their mother that Vivian Sartoris let two of the boys jump her over the net, and that Cousin Carol wore Kent Parmalee's panama all afternoon, and called out to him, right across the court, "Come on down to the boathouse, Kent, and let's have a smoke!"

"Poor Vivian--poor Billy!" Mrs. Haviland would say. "Men don't really admire girls who allow them such familiarities, although the silly girls may think they do! But when it comes to marrying, it is the sweet, womanly girls to whom the men turn!"

She did not believe this herself, nor did the girls believe it, but, if they discussed it when they were alone together, before Mamma, they were always decorously impressed.

"Any plans for the afternoon, girlies?" she asked now, when the forced strawberries were on the table, and little Florence was trying to eat the nuts out of her cake, and at the same time carefully avoid the cake itself and the frosting.

"What's Carol doing, M'ma?"

"When M'ma asks you a question, Isabelle, do not answer with another question, dear. I dropped Carol at the club, but I think Aunt Rachael means to pick her up there later, and go on to Mrs. Whittaker's for tea."

"We met Mrs. Whittaker in the Exchange yesterday, M'ma, and she very sweetly said that you were to--that is, that she hoped you would bring us in for a little while this afternoon. Didn't she, Isabelle?"

"I don't want to go!" Isabelle grumbled. But her mother ignored her.

"That was very sweet of Aunt Gertrude. I think I will go over to the club and see what Papa is planning and how his game is going, and then I could pick you girls up here."

"I'm going over to play with Georgie and Robbie Royce!" shrilled Florence. "They're mean to me, but I don't care! I hit George in the stomach---"

Mrs. Haviland looked as pained as if the reported blow had fallen upon her own person, but she was strangely indulgent to her youngest born, and now did no more than signal to the nurse, old Fanny, who stood grinning behind the child's chair, that Miss Florence might be excused. Florence was accordingly borne off, and the girls drifted idly upstairs, Isabelle confiding to her sister as she dutifully brushed her teeth that she wished "something" would happen! Alice muttered to Sally, another maid, over her strong hot tea, that you might as well be dead as never do a thing in God's world you wanted to do, but the rest of the large staff enjoyed a hearty meal, and when Percival brought the car around at three o'clock, Mrs. Haviland, magnificent in a change of costume, spent the entire trip to the club in the resentful reflection that the man had obviously had coffee and cream and mutton for his lunch--disgusting of him to come straight to his car and his mistress still redolent of his meal, but what could one do? In Mrs. Haviland's upper rear hall was a framed and typewritten list of rules for the maids, conspicuous upon which were those for daily baths and regular use of toothbrushes. But Percival never had seen this list, and he was a wonderful driver and a special favorite with her husband. She decided that there was nothing to be done, unless of course the thing recurred, although the moment's talk with Percival haunted and distressed her all day.

She duly returned to the house for her daughters a little after four o'clock, and in amicable conversation they went together to the tea, a crowded, informal affair, in another large house full of rugs and flowers, rooms dark and rich with expensive tapestries and mahogany, rooms bright and gay with white enamel and chintz and wicker furniture.

Everybody was here. Jeanette and Phyllis, as well as Elinor Vanderwall, Peter Pomeroy and George, the Buckneys and Parker Hoyt, the Emorys, the Chases, Mrs. Sartoris and old Mrs. Torrence and Jack, all jumbled a greeting to the Havilands. Of Carol they presently caught a glimpse standing on a sheltered little porch with Joe Pickering's sleek head beside her. They were apparently not talking, just staring quietly down at the green terraces of the garden. Rachael was pouring tea, her face radiant under a narrowbrimmed, close hat loaded with cherries, her gown of narrow green and white stripes the target for every pair of female eyes in the room.

Charlotte Haviland, in her mother's wake, chanced to encounter Kenneth Moran, a red-faced, well-dressed and blushing youth of her own age. Her complacent mother was witness to the blameless conversation between them.

"How do you do, Kenneth? I didn't know you were here!"

"Oh, how do you do, Charlotte? How do you do, Isabelle? I didn't know you were here!"

Isabelle grinned silently in horrible embarrassment but Charlotte said, quick-wittedly:

"How is your mother, Kenneth, and Dorothy?"

"She's well--they're well, thank you. They're here somewhere--at least Mother is. I think Dorothy's still over at the Clays', playing tennis!"

He laughed violently at this admission, and Charlotte laughed, too.

"It's lovely weather for tennis," she said encouragingly. "We--"

"You--" Mr. Moran began. "I beg your pardon!"

"No, I interrupted you!"

"No, that was my fault. I was only going to say that we ought to have a game some morning. Going to have your courts in order this year?"

"Yes, indeed," Charlotte said, with what was great vivacity for her. "Papa has had them all rolled; some men came down from town--we had it all sodded, you know, last year."

"Is that right?" asked Mr. Moran, as one deeply impressed. "We must go to it--what?"

"We must!" Charlotte said happily. "Any morning, Kenneth!"

"Sure, I'll telephone!" agreed the youth enthusiastically. "I'm trying to find Kent Parmalee; his aunt wants him!" he added mumblingly, as he began to vaguely shoulder his way through the crowd again.

"You'd better take a microscope!" said Charlotte wittily. And Mr. Moran's burst of laughter and his "That's right, too!" came back to them as he went away.

"Dear fellow!" Mrs. Haviland said warmly.

"Isn't he nice!" Charlotte said, fluttered and glowing. She hoped in her heart that she would meet him again, but although the Havilands stayed until nearly six o'clock they did not do so; perhaps because shortly after this conversation Kenneth Moran met Miss Vivian Sartoris, and they took a plateful of rich, crushy little cakes and went and sat under the stairs, where they took alternate bites of each other's mocha and chocolate confections, and where Vivian told Kenneth all about a complicated and thrilling love affair between herself and one of the popular actors of the day. This narrative reflected more credit upon the young woman's imagination than upon her charms had the listener but suspected it, but Kenneth was not a brilliant boy, and they had a lovely time over their confidences.

Charlotte's romantic encounter with the gentleman, however, made her happy for several hours, and colored her cheeks rosily.

"You're getting pretty, Carlotta!" said her Aunt Rachael, observing this. "Don't drink tea, that's a good child! You can stuff on cakes and chocolate of course, Isabelle," she added, "but Charlotte's complexion ought to be her FIRST THOUGHT for the next five years!"

"I don't really want any," asserted Charlotte, feeling wonderfully grown-up and superior to the claims of a nursery appetite. "But can't I help you, Aunt Rachael?"

"No, my dear, you can't! I'm through the worst of it, and being bored slowly but firmly to death! Gertrude, I'm just saying that your party bores me."

"So sorry about you, Rachael!" said the slim, laceclad hostess calmly. "Here's Judy Moran! Nearly six, Judy, and we dine at seven on Sundays. But never mind, eat and drink your fill, my child."

"Billy's flirtin' her head off out there!" wheezed stout Mrs. Moran, dropping into a chair. "Joe and Kent and young Gregory and half a dozen others are out there with her."

Mrs. Breckenridge, who had begun to frown, relaxed in her chair.

"Ah, well, there's safety in numbers!" she said, reassured. "You take cream, Judy, and two lumps? Give Mrs. Moran some of those little damp, brown sandwiches, Isabelle. A minute ago she had some of the most heavenly hot toast here, but she's taken it away again! I wish I could get some tea myself, but I've tried three times and I can't!"

She busied herself resignedly with tongs and teapot, and as Mrs. Moran bit into her first sandwiches, and the Haviland girls moved away at a word from their mother, Rachael raised her eyes and met Warren Gregory's look.

He was standing, ten feet away, in a doorway, his eyelids half dropped over amused eyes, his hands sunk in his coat pockets. Rachael knew that he had been there for some moments, and her heart struggled and fluttered like a bird in a snare, and with a thrill as girlish as Charlotte's own she felt the color rise in her cheeks.

"Come have some tea, Greg," she said, indicating the empty chair beside her.

"Thank you, dear," he answered, his head close to hers for a moment as he sat down. The little word set Rachael's heart to hammering again. She glanced quickly to see if Mrs. Moran had overheard, but that lady had at last caught sight of the maid with the hot toast, and her ample back was turned toward the teatable.

Indeed, in the noisy, disordered room, which was beginning to be deserted by straggling groups of guests, they were quite unobserved. To both it was a delicious moment, this little domestic interlude of tea and talk in the curved window of the dining-room, lighted by the last light of a spring day, and sweet with the scent of wilting spring flowers.

"You make my heart behave in a manner not to be described in words!" said Rachael, her fingers touching his as she handed him his tea.

"It must be mine you feel," suggested Warren Gregory; "you haven't one--by all accounts!"

"I thought I hadn't, Greg, but, upon my word---" She puckered her lips and raised her eyebrows whimsically, and gave her head a little shake. Doctor Gregory gave her a shrewdly appraising look, sighed, and stirred his tea.

"If ever you discover yourself to be the possessor of such an organ, Rachael," said he dispassionately, "you won't joke about it over a tea-table! You'll wake up, my friend; we'll see something besides laughter in those eyes of yours, and hear something besides cool reason in your voice! I may not be the man to do it, but some man will, some day, and--when John Gilpin rides--"

The eyes to which he referred had been fixed in serene confidence upon his as he began to speak. But a second later Rachael dropped them, and they rested upon her own slender hand, lying idle upon the teatable, with its plain gold ring guarded by a dozen blazing stones. Had he really stirred her, Warren Gregory wondered, as he watched the thoughtful face under the bright, cherry-loaded hat.

"You know how often there is neither cool reason nor any cause for laughter in my life, Greg," she said, after a moment. "As for love--I don't think I know what love is! I am an absolutely calculating woman, and my first, last, and only view of anything is just how much it affects me and my comfort."

"I don't believe it!" said the doctor.

"It's true. And why shouldn't it be?" Rachael gave him a grave smile. "No one," said she seriously, "ever--ever--EVER suggested to me that there was anything amiss in that point of view! Why is there?"

"I don't understand you," said the doctor simply.

"One doesn't often talk this way, I suppose," she said slowly. "But there is a funny streak of--what shall I call it?--conscience, or soul, or whatever you like, in me. Whether I get it from my mother's Irish father or my father's clergyman grandfather, I don't know, but I'm eternally defending myself. I have long sessions with myself, when I'm judge and jury, and invariably I find 'Not Guilty!'"

"Not guilty of what?" the man asked, stirring his untasted cup.

"Not guilty of anything!" she answered, with a child's puzzled laugh. "I stick to my bond, I dress and talk and eat and go about--" Her voice dropped; she stared absently at the table.

"But--" the doctor prompted.

"But--that's just it--but I'm so UNHAPPY all the time!" Rachael confessed. "We all seem like a lot of puppets, to me--like Bander-log! What are we all going round and round in circles for, and who gets any fun out of it? What's YOUR answer, Greg--what makes the wheels go round?"

"'Tis love--'tis love--that makes--etcetera, etcetera," supplied the doctor, his tone less flippant than his words.

"Oh--love!" Rachael's voice was full of delicate scorn. "I've seen a great deal of all sorts and kinds of love," she went on, "and I must say that I consider love a very much overrated article! You're laughing at me, you bold gossoon, but I mean it. Clarence loved Paula madly, kidnapped her from a boarding-school and all that, but I don't know how much THEIR seven years together helped the world go round. He never loved me, never once said he did, but I've made him a better wife than she did. He loves Bill, now, and it's the worst thing in the world for her!"

"THERE'S some love for you," said Doctor Gregory, glancing across the room to the figures of Miss Leila Buckney and Mr. Parker Hoyt, who were laughing over a cabinet full of ivories.

"I wonder just what would happen there if Parker lost his money to-morrow--if Aunt Frothy died and left it all to Magsie Clay?" Rachael suggested, smiling.

The doctor answered only with a shrug.

"More than that," pursued Rachael, "suppose that Parker woke up tomorrow morning and found his engagement was all a dream, found that he really hadn't asked Leila to marry him, and that he was as free as air. Do you suppose that the minute he'd had his breakfast he would go straight over to Leila's house and make his dream a heavenly reality? Or would he decide that there was no hurry about it, and that he might as well rather keep away from the Buckney house until he'd made up his mind?"

"I suppose he might convince himself that an hour or two's delay wouldn't matter!" said the doctor, laughing.

"If you talk to me of clothes, or of jewelry, or of what one ought to send a bride, and what to say in a letter of condolence, I know where I am," said Rachael, "but love, I freely confess, is something else again!"

"I suppose my mother has known great love," said the man, after a pause. "She spends her days in that quiet old house dreaming about my father, and my brothers, looking at their pictures, and reading their letters--"

"But, Greg, she's so unhappy!" Rachael objected briskly. "And love-- surely the contention is that love ought to make one happy?"

"Well, I think her memories DO make her happy, in a way. Although my mother is really too conscientious a woman to be happy, she worries about events that are dead issues these twenty years. She wonders if my brother George might have been saved if she had noticed his cough before she did; there was a child who died at birth, and then there are all the memories of my father's death--the time he wanted ice water and the doctors forbade it, and he looked at her reproachfully. Poor Mother!"

"You're a joy to her anyway, Greg," Rachael said, as he paused.

"Charley is," he conceded thoughtfully, "and in a way I know I am! But not in every way, of course," Warren Gregory smiled a little ruefully.

"So the case for love is far from proved," Rachael summarized cheerfully. "There's no such thing!"

"On the contrary, there isn't anything else, REALLY, in the world," smiled the man. "I've seen it shining here and there; we get away from it here, somewhat, I'll admit"--his glance and gesture indicated the other occupants of the room--"and, like you, I don't quite know where we miss it, and what it's all about, but there have been cases in our wards, for instance: girls whose husbands have been brought in all smashed up--"

"Girls who saw themselves worried about rent and bread and butter!" suggested Rachael in delicate irony.

"No, I don't think so. And mothers--mothers hanging over sick children--"

The women nodded quickly.

"Yes, I know, Greg. There's something very appealing about a sick kiddie. Bill was ill once, just after we were married, such a little thing she looked, with her hair all cut! And that DID--now that I remember it--it really did bring Clarence and me tremendously close. We'd sit and wait for news, and slip out for little meals, and I'd make him coffee late at night. I remember thinking then that I never wanted a child, to make me suffer as we suffered then!"

"Mother love, then, we concede," Doctor Gregory said, smiling.

"Well, yes, I suppose so. Some mothers. I don't believe a mother like Florence ever was really made to suffer through loving. However, there IS mother love!"

"And married love."

"No, there I don't agree. While the novelty lasts, while the passion lasts--not more than a year or two. Then there's just civility--opening the city house, opening the country house, entertaining, going about, liking some things about each other, loathing others, keeping off the dangerous places until the crash comes, or, perhaps, for some lucky ones, doesn't come!"

"What a mushy little sentimentalist you are, Rachael!" Gregory said with a rather uncomfortable laugh. "You're too dear and sweet to talk that way! It's too bad--it's too bad to have you feel so! I wish that I could carry you away from all these people here--just for a while! I'd like to prescribe that sea beach you spoke about last night! Wouldn't we love our desert island! Would you help me build a thatched hut, and a mud oven, and string shells in your hair, and swim way out in the green breakers with me?"

"And what makes you think that there would be some saving element in our relationship?" Rachael asked in a low voice. "What makes you think that our love would survive the--the dry-rot of life? People would send us silver and rugs, and there would be a lot of engraving, and barrels of champagne, and newspaper men trying to cross-examine the maids, and caterers all over the place, but a few years later, wouldn't it be the same old story? You talk of a desert island, and swimming, and seaweed, Greg! But my ideas of a desert island isn't Palm Beach with commercial photographers snapping at whoever sits down in the sand! Look about us, Greg--who's happy? Who isn't watching the future for just this or just that to happen before she can really feel content? Young girls all want to be older and more experienced, older girls want to be young; this one is waiting for the new house to be ready, that one--like Florence--is worrying a little for fear the girls won't quite make a hit! Clarence worries about Billy, I worry about Clarence--"

"I worry about you!" said Doctor Gregory as she paused.

"Of course you do, bless your heart!" Rachael laughed. "So here we are, the rich and fashionable and fortunate people of the world, having a cloudless good time!"

"You know, it's a shame to eat this way--ruin our dinners!" said Mrs. Moran, suddenly entering the conversation. "Stop flirting with Greg, Rachael, and give me some more tea. One lump, and only about half a cup, dear. Tell me a good way to get thin, Greg! Agnes Chase says her doctor has a diet--you eat all you want, and you get thin. Agnes says Lou has a friend who has taken off forty-eight pounds. Do you believe it, Greg? I'm too fat, you know--"

"You carry it well, Judy," said Rachael, still a little shaken by the abruptly closed conversation, as the doctor, with a conscious thrill, perceived.

"Thank you, my dear, that's what they all say. But I'd just as soon somebody else should carry it for awhile!"

"Listen, Rachael," said their hostess, coming up suddenly, and speaking quickly and lightly, "Clarence is here. Where in the name of everything sensible is Billy?"

"Clarence!" said Rachael, uncomfortable premonition clutching at her heart.

"Yes; you come and talk to him, Rachael," Mrs. Whittaker said, in the same quick undertone. "He's all right, of course, but he's just a little fussy--"

"Oh, if he wouldn't DO these things!" Rachael said apprehensively as she rose. "I left him all comfortable--Joe Butler was coming in to see him! It does EXASPERATE me so! However!"

"Of course it does, but we all know Clarence!" Mrs. Whittaker said soothingly. "He seems to have got it into his head that Billy--You go talk to him, Rachael, and I'll send her in."

"Billy's doing no harm! What did he say?" Rachael asked impatiently.

"Oh, nothing definite, of course. But as soon as I said that Billy was here--he'd asked if she was--he said, 'Then I suppose Mr. Pickering is here, too!'"

"He's the one person in the world afraid of talk about Billy, yet if he starts it, he can blame no one but himself!" Rachael said, as she turned toward the adjoining room. An unexpected ordeal like this always annoyed her. She was equal to it, of course; she could smooth Clarence's ruffled feelings, keep a serene front to the world, and get her family safely home before the storm; she had done it many times before. But it was so unnecessary! It was so unnecessary to exhibit the Breckenridge weaknesses before the observant Emorys, before that unconscionable old gossip Peter Pomeroy, and to the cool, pitying gaze of all her world!

She found Clarence the centre of a small group in the long drawing-room. He and Frank Whittaker were drinking cocktails; the others--Jeanette Vanderwall, Vera Villalonga, a flushed, excitable woman older than Rachael, and Jimmy and Estelle Hoyt--had refused the drink, but were adding much noise and laughter to the newcomer's welcome.

"Hello, Clarence" Rachael said, appraising the situation rapidly as she came up. "I would have waited for you if I had thought you would come!"

"I just--just thought I would--look in," Clarence said slowly but steadily. "Didn't want to miss anything. You all seem to be having--having a pretty good time!"

"It's been a lovely tea," Rachael assured him enthusiastically. "But I'm just going. Billy's out here on the porch with a bunch of youngsters; I was just going after her. Don't let Frank give you any more of that stuff, Clancy. Stop it, Frank! It always gives him a splitting headache!"

The tone was irreproachably casual and cheerful, but Clarence scowled at his wife significantly. His dignity, as he answered, was tremendous.

"I can judge pretty well of what hurts me and what doesn't, thank you, Rachael," he said coldly, with a look ominous with warning.

"That's just what you can't, dear," Mrs. Whittaker, who had joined the group, said pleasantly. "Take that stuff away, Frank, and don't be so silly! If Frank," she added to the group, "hadn't been at it all afternoon himself he wouldn't be such an idiot."

"Greg says he'll take us home, Clarence," Rachael said, in a matter-of-fact tone. "It's a shame to carry you off when you've just got here, but I'm going."

"Where's Billy?" Clarence asked stubbornly.

"Right here!" his wife answered reassuringly. And to her great relief Billy substantiated the statement by coming up to them, a little uneasy, as her stepmother was, over her father's appearance, yet confident that there was no real cause for a scene. To get him home as fast as possible, and let the trouble, whatever it might be, break there, was the thought in both their minds.

"Had enough tea, Monkey?" said Rachael pleasantly, aware of her husband's sulphurous gaze, but carefully ignoring it. "Then say day-day to Aunt Gertrude!"

"If Greg takes you home, send Alfred back with the runabout for me," Billy suggested.

"So that you can stay a little longer, eh?" said Clarence, in so ugly a tone and with so leering a look for his daughter that Rachael's heart for a moment failed her. "That's a very nice little plan, my dear, but, as it happens, I came over in the runabout! I'm a fool, you know," said Clarence sullenly. "I can be hoodwinked and deceived and made a fool of--oh, sure! But there's a limit! There's a limit," he said in stupid anger to his wife. "And if I say that I don't like certain friendships for my daughter, it means that _I_ DON'T LIKE CERTAIN FRIENDSHIPS FOR MY DAUGHTER, do you get me? That's clear enough, isn't it, Gertrude?"

"It's perfectly clear that you're acting like an idiot, Clancy," Mrs. Whittaker said briskly. "Nobody's trying to hoodwink you; it isn't being done this year! You've got an awful katzenjammer from the Stokes' dinner, and all you men ought to be horsewhipped for letting yourselves in for such a party. Now if you and Rachael want to go home in the runabout, I'll send Billy straight after you with Kenneth or Kent--"

"I'll take Billy home," Clarence said heavily.

By this time Rachael was so exquisitely conscious of watching eyes and listening ears, so agonized over the realization that the fuss Clarence Breckenridge made at the Whittakers' over Joe Pickering would be handed down, a precious tradition, over every tea and dinner table for weeks to come, so miserably aware that a dozen persons, at least, among the audience were finding in this scene welcome confirmation of all the odds and ends of gossip that were floating about concerning Billy, that she would have consented blindly to any arrangement that might terminate the episode.

It was not the first time that Clarence had made himself ridiculous and his family conspicuous when not quite himself. At almost every tea party and at every dance and dinner at least one of the guests similarly distinguished himself. Rachael knew that there would be no blame in her friends' minds, but she hated their laughter.

"Do that, then," she agreed quickly. "Greg, will bring me!"

"By George," said Clarence darkly to his hostess, "I'd be a long time doing that to you, Gertrude! If you had a daughter--"

"My dear Clarence, your daughter is old enough to know her own mind!" Mrs. Whittaker said impatiently.

"And you're only making me conspicuous for something that's ENTIRELY in your own brain!" blazed Billy. As usual, her influence over her father was instantaneous.

"Because I love you, you know that," he said meekly. "I--I may be TOO careful, Billy. But--"

"Nonsense!" said Billy in a nervous undertone close to tears. "If you loved me you'd have some consideration for me!"

"When I say a thing, don't you say it's nonsense," Clarence said with heavy fatherly dignity. "I'll tell you why--because I won't stand for it!"

"Oh, aren't they hopeless!" Mrs. Whittaker asked with an indulgent laugh and a glance for Rachael.

"Well, I won't be taken home like a bad child!" flamed Billy.

"I'd like to bump both your silly heads together," Rachael exclaimed, steering them toward the porch. "Yes, you bring the car around, Kent," she added to one of the onlookers in an urgent aside. "Come on, Bill? get in. Get in, Clarence! Don't be an utter fool--"

In another moment it was settled. Billy, looking fretty and sulky, said: "Good-bye, Aunt Gertrude! I'm sorry for this, but it's not my fault!" Frank Whittaker almost bodily lifted his somewhat befuddled guest into the car, the door of the runabout went home with a bang. Billy snatched the wheel, and Clarence, with an attempt at a martyred expression, sank back in his seat. The car rocked out of sight, and was gone.

Rachael, in silent dignity, turned about on the wide brick steps to reenter the house. Where there had been a dozen interested faces a moment ago there was no one now except Gertrude Whittaker, whose expression betrayed her as tactfully divided between unconcern and sympathy, and Frank Whittaker, who was looking thoughtfully at the cloudless spring sky as one anticipating a change of weather.

Rachael caught Mrs. Whittaker's eye and shrugged her shoulders wearily. She began slowly to mount the steps.

"It was nothing at all!" said the hostess cheerfully, adding immediately, "You poor thing!"

"All in the day's work!" Rachael said, on a long sigh. And turning to the man who stood silently in the doorway she asked, with all the confidence of a weary child, "Will you take me home, Greg?"

Her glance and the doctor's met. In the last soft, brilliant light of the afternoon long shadows fell from the great trees nearby. Rachael's green and white gown was dappled with blots of golden light, her troubled, glowing eyes were of an almost unearthly beauty, and her slender figure, against the background of colonial white paint and red brick, had all the tremulous, reedy grace of a young girl's figure. In the long look the two exchanged there was some new element born of this wonderful hour of spring, and of the woman's need, and the man's nearness. Both knew it, although Rachael did not speak again, and, also in silence, the doctor nodded, and went past her down the steps for his car.

"Too bad!" Mrs. Whittaker said, coming back from a brief disappearance beyond the doorway. "But such things will happen! It's too bad, Rachael, but what can one do? Are you going to be warm enough? Sure? Don't give it another thought, dear, nobody noticed it, anyway. And listen--any chance of a game tonight? I could send over for you. Marian's with me, you know, and we could get Peter or Greg for a fourth."

"No chance at all," Rachael said bitterly. She had always loved to play bridge with Greg; under the circumstances it would be a delicious experience. She layed brilliantly, and Greg, when he was matched by partner and opponents, became absorbed in the game with absolutely fanatic fervor. Rachael had a vision of her own white hand spreading out the cards, of the nod and glance that said clearly: "Great bidding, Rachael; we're as safe as a church!"

Clarence did not play bridge, he did not care for music, for books, for pictures. He played poker, and sometimes tennis, and often golf; a selfish, solitary game of golf, in which he cared only for his own play and his own score, and paid no attention to anyone else.

Gregory's great car came round the drive. "Good-bye, Gertrude," said Rachael with an unsmiling nod of farewell, and Mrs. Whittaker thought, as Elinor Vanderwall had thought the night before, that she had never seen Rachael look so serious before, and that things in the Breckenridge family must be coming rapidly to a crisis.

Doctor Gregory, as the lovely Mrs. Breckenridge packed her striped green and white ruffles trimly beside him, turned upon her a quick and affectionate smile. It asked no confidence, it expressed no sympathy, it was simply the satisfied glance of a man pleased with the moment and with the company in which he found himself. To Rachael, overwrought, nervous, and ashamed, no mood could have been more delicately tuned. She sank back against the deep upholstery luxuriously, and drew a long breath, inhaling the delicious air of early summer twilight. What a sweet, clean, solid sort of friend Greg was, thought Rachael, noticing the clever, well-groomed hands on the wheel, the kindly earnestness of the handsome, sun-browned face, the little wrinkle between the dark eyes that meant that Doctor Gregory was thinking.

"Straight home?" said he, giving her a smiling glance.

"If you please, Greg," Rachael answered, a sudden vision of the probable state of affairs at home causing her to end the words with a quick sigh.

Silence. They were running smoothly along the lovely country roads that were bowered so generously in fresh green that great feathery boughs of maple and locust brushed against the car. The birds were still now, and the sunlight gone, although all the world was still flooded with a soft golden light. The first dew had fallen, bringing forth from the dust a sweet and pungent odor.

"Thinking about what I said to you last night?" asked the doctor suddenly.

"I am afraid I am--a little," Rachael answered, meeting his quick side glance with another as fleet.

"And what do you think about it?" he asked. For answer Rachael only sighed wearily, and for a while they went on in silence. But when they had almost reached the Breckenridge gateway Doctor Gregory spoke again.

"Do you often have a scene like that one just now to get through?"

The color rushed into Rachael's face at his friendly, not too sympathetic, tone. She was still shaken from the encounter with Clarence, and still thrilling to the memory of her talk with Warren Gregory last night, and it was with some new quality of hesitation, almost of bewilderment, that she said:

"That--that wasn't anything unusual, Greg."

Doctor Gregory stopped the car at the foot of her own steps, the noise of the engine suddenly ceased, and they faced each other, their heads close together.

"But since last night," Rachael added, smiling after a moment's thought, "I know I have a friend. I believe now, when the crash comes, and the whole world begins to talk, that one person will not misjudge me, and one person will not misunderstand."

"Only that?" he asked. She raised her glorious eyes quickly, trying to smile, and it brought his heart to a quick stop to see that they were brimming with tears.

"Only that?" she echoed. "My dear Greg, after seven such years as I have had as Clarence's wife, that is not a small thing!"

Their hands were together now, and he felt hers cling suddenly as she said:

"Don't--don't let me drag you into this, Greg!"

"This is what I want you to believe," Warren Gregory told her, "that you are not his wife, you are nothing to him any more. And some day, some day, you're going to be happy again!"

A wonderful color flooded her face; she gave him a look half-frightened, half-won. Then with an almost inaudible "Good-night," she was gone.

Warren Gregory stood watching the slender figure mount the steps. She did not turn to nod him a fare-well, but vanished like a shadow into the soft shadows of the doorway. Yet he was enough a lover to find consolation in that. Rachael Breckenridge was not flirting now, forces far greater than any she had ever known were threatening the shallow waters of her life, and she might well be troubled and afraid.

"She is not his wife any more," Warren Gregory said, half aloud, as he turned back to his car. "From now on she belongs to me! She SHALL be mine!"

CHAPTER V

From that day on a bright undercurrent made bearable the trying monotony of her life. Rachael did not at once recognize the rapid change that began to take place in her own feelings, but she did realize that Warren Gregory's attitude had altered everything in her world. He was flirting, of course, he was only half in earnest; but it was such delicious flirting, it was a half-earnestness so wonderfully satisfying and sweet.

She did not see him every day, sometimes she did not see him for two or three days, but no twenty-four hours went by without a message from him. A day or two after the troubled Sunday on which he had driven her home she stood silent a moment, in the lower hall, one hand resting on the little box of damp, delicious Freesia lilies, the fingers of the other twisting his card. The little message scribbled on the card meant nothing to other eyes, just the two words "Good morning!" but in some subtle way they signified to her a morning in a wider sense, a dawning of love and joy and peace in her life. The next day they met--and how wonderful these casual meetings among a hundred gay, unseeing folk, had suddenly become!--and on the following day he came to tea with her, a little hour whose dramatic and emotional beauty was enhanced rather than spoiled for them both when Clarence and Billy and some friends came in to end it.

On Thursday the doctor's man delivered into Mrs. Breckenridge's hand a package which proved to be a little book on Browning of which he had spoken to her. On the fly leaf was written in the donor's small, fine handwriting, "R. from G. The way WAS Caponsacchi." Rachael put the book on her bedside table, and wore June colors all day for the giver's sake. Greg, she thought with a fluttering heart, was certainly taking things with rather a high hand. Could it be possible, could it be POSSIBLE, that he cared for a woman at last, and was she, Rachael Breckenridge, a neglected wife, a penniless dependent upon an unloving husband, that woman?

Half-forgotten emotions of girlhood began to stir within her; she flushed, smiled, sighed at her own thoughts, she dreamed, and came bewildered out of her dreams, like a child. What Clarence did, what Carol did, mattered no longer; she, Rachael, again had the centre of the stage.

Weeks flew by. The question of summer plans arose: the Villalongas wanted all the Breckenridges in their Canadian camp for as much as possible of July and August. Clarence regarded the project with the embittered eye of utter boredom, Billy was far from enthusiastic, Rachael made no comment. She stood, like a diver, ready for the chilling plunge from which she might never rise, yet, after which, there was one glorious chance: she might find herself swimming strongly to freedom. The sunny, safe meadows and the warm, blue sky were there in sight, there was only that dark and menacing stretch of waters to breast, that black, smothering descent to endure.

Now was the time. The pretence that was her married life must end, she must be free. In her thought she went no farther. Rachael outwardly was no better than the other women of her world; inwardly there was in her nature an instinctive niceness, a hatred for what was coarse or base. For years the bond between her and Clarence Breckenridge had been only an empty word. But it was there, none the less, and before she could put any new plan into definite form, even in her own heart, it must be broken.

Many of the women she knew would not have been so fine. For more than one of them no tie was sacred, and no principle as strong as their own desire for pleasure. But she was different, as all the world should see. No carefully chaperoned girl could be more carefully guarded than Rachael would be guarded by herself until that time--the thought of it put her senses to utter rout--until such time as she might put her hand boldly in Gregory's, and take her place honorably by his side.

The taste of freedom already began to intoxicate her even while she still went about Clarence's house, bore his moods in silence, and imparted to Billy that half scornful, half humorous advice that alone seemed to penetrate the younger woman's shell of utter perversity. Mrs. Breckenridge, as usual followed by admiring and envious and curious eyes, walked in a world of her own, entirely oblivious of the persons and events about her, wrapped in a breathless dream too exquisitely bright to be real.

It was a dream still so simple and vague that she was not conscious of wishing for Warren Gregory's presence, or of being much happier when they were together than when she was deliciously alone with her thoughts of him.

About a month after the Whittaker tea Rachael found herself seated in the tile-floored tea-room at the country club with Florence. There had been others in the group, theoretically for tea, but these were scattered now, and among the various bottles and glasses on the table there was no sign of a teacup.

"So glad to see you alone a moment, Rachael--one never does," said Florence. "Tell me, do you go to the Villalongas'?"

The Heart Of Rachael | 89

"Clarence and Billy will, I suppose," the other woman said with an enigmatic smile.

"But not you?"

"Perhaps; I don't know, Florence." Rachael's serene eyes roved the summer landscape contentedly. Mrs. Haviland looked a little puzzled. "Things are better, aren't they, dear?" she asked delicately.

"Things?"

"Between you and Clarence, I mean."

"Oh! Yes, perhaps they are. Changed, perhaps."

"How do you mean changed?" Florence was instantly in arms.

"Well, it couldn't go on that way forever, Florence," Rachael said pleasantly.

Rendered profoundly uneasy by her tone, the other woman was silent for a moment.

"Perhaps it is just as well to make different plans for the summer," she said presently. "We all get on each other's nerves sometimes, and change or separation does us a world of good."

"Doctor Gregory! Doctor Gregory! At the telephone!" chanted a club attendant, passing through the tea-room.

"On the tennis courts," Mrs. Breckenridge said, without turning her head. "You had better make it a message: explain that he's playing!"

"I didn't see him go down," remarked Florence, diverted.

"His car came in about half an hour ago; he and Joe Butler went down to the courts without coming into the club at all," Rachael said.

"I wonder what he's doing this summer?" mused the older lady.

"I believe he's going to take his mother abroad with him," said the well-informed Rachael. "She'll visit some friends in England and Ireland, and then join him. He's to do the Alps with someone, and meet her in Rome."

"She tell you?" asked Mrs. Haviland, interested.

"He did," the other said briefly.

"I didn't know she had any friends," was Florence's next comment. "I don't see her visiting, somehow!"

"Oh, my dear. Old Catholic families with chapels in their houses, and nuns, and Mother Superiors!" Rachael's tone was light, but as she spoke a cold premonition seized her heart. She fell silent.

A moment later Charlotte, who had been hovering uncertain the doorway of the room, came out to join her mother with a bri spontaneous air.

"Oh, here you are, M'ma!" said Charlotte. "Are you ready to go?"

"Been having a nice time, dear?" her mother asked fondly.

"Very," Charlotte said. "I've been looking over old magazines in i library--SO interesting!"

This literary enthusiasm struck no answering spark from the matron.

"In the library!" said Florence quickly. "Why, I thought you were witl Charley!"

"Oh, no, M'ma," answered Charlotte, with her little air that was not quite prim and not quite mincing, and that yet suggested both. "Charley left me just after you did; he had an engagement with Straker." She reached for a macaroon, and ate it with a brightly disengaged air, her eyes, behind their not unbecoming glasses, studying the golf links with absorbed interest.

"Anyone else in the library?" Florence asked in a dissatisfied tone.

"No. I had it all to myself!" the girl answered pleasantly.

"Why didn't you go down to the courts, dear? I think Papa is playing!"

"I didn't think of it, M'ma," said Charlotte lucidly.

"What a dreadful age it is," mused Rachael. "I wonder which phase is hardest to deal with: Billy or poor little Carlotta?" Aloud, from the fulness of her own happiness, she said: "Suppose you walk down to the courts with me, Infant, and we will see what's going on?"

"If M'ma doesn't object," said the dutiful daughter.

"No, go along," Florence said with vague discontent. "I've got to do some telephoning, anyway."

Charlotte, being eighteen, could think of nothing but herself, and Rachael, wrapped in her own romance, was amused, as they walked along, to see how different her display of youthful egotism was from Billy's, and yet how typical of all adolescence.

"Isn't it a wonderful afternoon, Aunt Rachael?" Charlotte said, as one in duty bound to be entertaining. "I do think they've picked out such a charming site for the club!" And then, as Rachael did not answer, being indeed content to drink in the last of the long summer day in silence, Charlotte went on, with an air blended of comprehension and amusement: "Poor M'ma, she would so like me to be a little, fluffy, empty-headed

butterfly of a girl, and I know I disappoint her! It isn't that I don't like boys," pursued Charlotte, the smooth and even stream of her words beginning to remind Rachael of Florence, "or that they don't like me; they're always coming to me with their confidences and asking my advice, but it's just that I can't take them seriously. If a boy wants to kiss me, why, I say to him in perfect good faith, 'Why shouldn't you kiss me, John? When I'm fond of a person I always like to kiss him, and I'm sure I'm fond of you!'" Charlotte stopped for a short laugh full of relish. "Of course that takes the wind out of their sails completely," she went on, "and we have a good laugh over it, and are all the better friends! That is," said Charlotte, thoroughly enjoying herself, "I treat my men friends exactly as I do my girl friends. Do you think that's so extraordinary, Aunt Rachael? Because I can't do anything different, you know--really I can't!"

"Just be natural--that's the best way," said Rachael from the depths of an icy boredom.

"Of course, some day I shall marry," the girl added in brisk decision, "because I love a home, and I love children, and I think I would be a good mother to children. But meanwhile, my books and my friends mean a thousand times more to me than all these stupid boys! Why is it other girls are so crazy about boys, Aunt Rachael?" asked Charlotte, brightly sensible. "Of course I like them, and all that, but I can't see the sense of all these notes and telephones and flirtations. I told Vivvie Sartoris that I was afraid I knew all these boys too well; of course Jack and Kent and Charley are just like brothers! It all"--Charlotte smiled, signed, shook her disillusioned young head--"it all seems so awfully SILLY to me!" she said, and before Rachael could speak she had caught breath again and added laughingly: "Of course I know Billy doesn't agree with me, and Billy has plenty of admiration of a sort, and I suppose that satisfies her! But, in short," finished Charlotte, giving Rachael's arm a squeeze as they came out upon the tennis courts, "in short, you have an exacting little niece, Auntie dear, and I'm afraid the man who is going to make her happy must be out of the ordinary!"

Rachael sighed a long deep sigh, but no other answer was demanded, for the knot of onlookers welcomed them eagerly to the benches beside the courts, and even the players--Gardner Haviland, Louis Chase, a fat young man in an irreproachable tennis costume; Warren Gregory and Joe Butler found time for a shouted "Hello!"

"How do you do, Kent?" said Charlotte to a young man who was sprawling on the sloping grass between the benches and the court. The young man blinked, sat up, and snatched off his hat.

"Oh, how do you do, Charlotte? I didn't know you were here," he said enthusiastically. "Some game--what?"

"It SEEMS to be," said Charlotte with smiling, deep significance. Both young persons laughed heartily at this spirited exchange. A silence fell. Then Mr. Parmalee turned back to watch the players, and Charlotte, who had seated herself, leaned back in her seat and gave a devoted attention to the game.

Gregory came to Rachael the instant the game was over; she had known, since the first triumphant instant when his eyes fell upon her, that he would. She had seen the color rush under his brown skin, and, alone among all the onlookers, had known why Greg put three balls into the net, and why he laughed so inexplicably as he did so. And Rachael thought, for the first time, how sweet it would be to be his wife, to sit here lovely in lavender stripes and loose white coat: Warren Gregory's wife.

"You mustn't do that," he said, sitting down on the bench beside her, and wiping his hot face.

"Mustn't do what?" she asked.

"Mustn't turn up suddenly when I don't expect you. It makes me dizzy. Look here--what are you doing? I'm going up to the pool. I've got to get back into town to-night. When can I see you?"

"Why"--Rachael rose slowly, and slowly unfurled her parasol--"why, suppose we walk up together?"

They strolled away from the courts deliberately, openly. Several persons remembered weeks later that they went slowly, stopped now and then. No one thought much of it at the time, for only a week later Doctor Gregory took his mother to England, and during that week it was ascertained that he and Mrs. Breckenridge saw each other only once, and then were in the presence of his mother and of Carol Breckenridge and young Charles Gregory as well. There was no tiniest peg for gossip to hang scandal upon, for where old Mrs. James Gregory was, decorum of an absolutely puritanic order prevailed.

Yet that stroll across the grass of the golf links was a milestone in Rachael Breckenridge's life, and every word that passed between Gregory and herself was graven upon her heart for all time. The aspect of laughter, of flirtation, was utterly absent to-day. His tone was crisp and serious, he spoke almost before they were out of the hearing of the group on the courts.

"I've been wanting to talk to you, Rachael; in fact"--he laughed briefly--"in fact, I am talking to you all day long, these days," he said, "arguing and consulting and advising and planning. But before we can talk, there's Clarence. What about Clarence?"

Something in the gravity of his expression as their eyes met impressed Rachael as she had rarely been impressed in her life before. He was in deadly earnest, he had planned his campaign, and he must take the first step by clearing the way. How sure he was, how wonderfully, quietly certain of his course.

"We are facing a miserable situation, but it's a commonplace one, after all," said Warren Gregory, as she did not speak. "I--you can see the position I'm in. I have to ask you to be free before I can move. I can't go to Breckenridge's wife---"

The color burned in both their faces as they looked at each other.

"It IS a miserable position, Greg," Rachael said, after a moment's silence. "And although, as you say, it's commonplace enough, somehow I never thought before just what this sort of thing involves! However, the future must take care of itself. For the present there's only this. I'm going to leave Clarence."

Warren Gregory drew a long breath.

"He won't fight it?"

"I don't think he will." Rachael frowned. "I think he'll be willing to furnish--the evidence. Especially if he has no reason to suspect that I have any other plans," she added thoughtfully.

"Then he mustn't suspect," the doctor said instantly.

"Nor anyone," she finished, with a look of alarm.

"Nor anyone, of course," he repeated.

"I don't know that I HAVE any other plans," Rachael said sadly. "I won't think beyond that one thing. Our marriage has been an utter and absolute failure, we are both wretched. It must end. I hate the fuss, of course--"

He was watching her closely, too keenly tuned to her mood to disquiet her with any hint of the lover's attitude now.

"And just how will you go about it?" he asked.

"I shall slip off to some quiet place, I think. I'll tell him before he goes away. My attorneys will handle the matter for me--it's a sickening business!" Rachael's beautiful face expressed distaste.

"It's done every day," Warren Gregory said.

"Of course divorce is not a new idea to me" Rachael presently pursued. "But it is only in the last two or three days--for a week, perhaps--that it has seemed to have that inevitable quality--that the-sooner-over-the-better sort of urgency. I wonder why I didn't do it years ago. I shall"--she laughed sadly--"I shall hate myself as a divorced woman," she said. "It's a survival of some old instinct, I suppose, but it doesn't seem RIGHT."

"It's done all the time," was the doctor's simple defence. "And oh, my dear," he added, "you will know--and I will know--we can't keep knowing--"

She stopped short, her lovely face serious in the shade of her parasol, her dark-blue eyes burning with a sort of noble shame.

"Greg!" she said quickly and breathlessly. "Please---Let's not--let's not say it. Let me feel, all this summer, that it wasn't said. Let me feel that while I was living under one man's roof, and spending his money, that I didn't even THINK of another man. It's done all the time, you say, that's true. But I HATE it. Whether I leave Clarence, and make my own life under new conditions, and never remarry, or whether, in a year or two--but I won't think of that!" And to his surprise and concern, as she stopped short on the grassy path, the eyes that Rachael turned toward him were brimming with tears. "You s-see what a baby I am becoming, Greg," she said unsteadily. "It's all your doing, I'm afraid! I haven't cried for years--loneliness and injustice and unhappiness don't make me cry! But just lately I've known what it was to dream of--of joy, Greg. And if that joy is ever really coming to us, I want to be worthy of it. I want to start RIGHT this time. I want to spend the summer quietly somewhere, thinking and reading. I'm going to give up cards and even cocktails. You smile, Greg, but I truly am! Just for this time, I mean. And it's come to me, just lately, that I wouldn't leave Clarence if he really needed me, or if it would make him unhappy. I'm going to be different--everything SEEMS different already--"

"Don't you know why?" he said with his grave smile, as she paused. It was enchanting to him to see the color flood her face, to see her shy eyes suddenly averted. She did not answer, and they walked slowly toward the clubhouse steps.

"There's only one thing more to say," Warren Gregory said, arresting her for one more moment. "It's this: as soon as you're free, I'm coming for you. You may not have made up your mind by that time, Rachael. My mind will never change."

Shaken beyond all control by his tone, Rachael did not even raise her eyes. Her flush died away, leaving her face pale. He saw her breast rise on a quick breath.

"Will you write me?" he asked, after a moment.

"Oh, yes, Greg!" she answered quickly, in a voice hardly above a whisper. "When do you go?"

"On Wednesday--a week from to-day, in fact. And that reminds me, Billy says you are coming into town early next week?"

"Monday, probably." Rachael was coming back to the normal. "She needs things for camp, and I've got a little shopping to do."

"Then could you lunch with Mother? Little Charley'll be there: no one else. Bring Billy. Mother'd love it. You're a great favorite there, you know."

"I may not always be a favorite there," Rachael said with a rueful smile.

"Don't worry about Mother," Warren Gregory said with a confidence that in this moment of excitement and exhilaration he almost felt was justified. "Mother's a dear!"

That was all their conversation. When they entered the clubhouse Doctor Gregory turned toward the swimming pool and Rachael was instantly drawn into a game of bridge. She played like a woman in a dream, was joined by Billy, went home in a dream, and presently found herself and her husband fellow guests at a dreamlike dinner-party.

Why not?--why not?--why not? The question drummed in head and heart day and night. Why not end bondage, and taste freedom? Why not end unhappiness, and try joy? She had done her best to make her first marriage a success, and she had failed. Why not, with all kindness, with all generous good wishes, end the long experiment? Who, in all her wide range of acquaintances, would think the less of her for the obviously sensible step? The world recognized divorce as an indispensable institution: one marriage in every twelve was dissolved.

And remarriage, a brilliant second marriage, was universally approved. Even such a stern old judge as Warren's mother counted among her acquaintances the divorced and remarried. To reappear, triumphant, beloved, beautiful, before one's old world--

But no--of this Rachael would not permit herself to think. Time alone could tell what her next step must be. The only consideration now must be that, even if Warren Gregory had never existed, even if there were no other man than Clarence Breckenridge in the world, she must take the step. Better poverty, and work, and obscurity, if need be, with freedom, than all Clarence could offer her in this absurd and empty bondage.

Once firmly decided, she began to chafe against the delays that made an immediate announcement of her intentions unwise. If a thing was to be done, as well do it quickly, thought Rachael, as she listened patiently to the vacillating decisions of Carol and her father in regard to the Villalonga camping plan. At one time Clarence completely abandoned the idea, throwing the watchful and silent Rachael into utter consternation. Carol was alternately bored by the plan and wearily interested in it. Their characteristic absorption in their own comfort was a great advantage to Rachael at this particular juncture; she had been included in Mrs. Villalonga's invitation as a matter of course, but such was the life of the big, luxurious establishment known as the "camp" that all three of the Breckenridges, and three more of them had there been so many, might easily have spent six weeks therein without crossing each other's paths more than once or twice a week. It never occurred to either Carol or her father to question Rachael closely as to her pleasure in the matter. They took it for granted that she would be there if no pleasanter invitation interfered exactly as they themselves would.

An enormous income enabled the sprightly Mrs. Villalonga to conduct her midsummer residence in the Canadian forests upon a scale that may only be compared to a hotel. She usually asked about one hundred friends to visit her for an indefinite time, and of this number perhaps half availed themselves of the privilege, drifting in upon her at any time, remaining only while the spirit moved, and departing unceremoniously, perhaps, if the hostess chanced to be away at the moment, with no farewells at all, when any pleasanter prospect offered.

Mrs. Villalonga was a large, coarse-voiced woman, with a heart of gold, and the facial characteristics that in certain unfortunate persons suggest nothing so much as a horse. She sent a troop of servants up to the woods every year, following them in a week or two with her first detachment of guests. She paid her chef six thousand dollars a year, and would have paid more for a better chef, if there had been one. She expected three formal meals every day, including in their scope every delicacy that could be procured at any city hotel, and also an indefinite number of lesser meals, to be served in tennis pavilion, or after cards at night, or whenever a guest arrived.

By the time she reached the camp everything must be complete for another summer, awnings flapping gently outside the striped canvas "tents" that were really roomy cabins provided with shower baths and wide piazzas. The great cement-walled swimming pool must be cleaned, the courts rolled, the cars all in order, the boats and bath-houses in readiness. A miniature grocery and drug store must be established in the building especially designed for this use; the little laundry concealed far up in the woods must be operating briskly.

Then, from the middle of June to the first of September, the camp was in full swing. There were dances and campfires and theatricals and fancy-dress affairs innumerable. Ice and champagne and California peaches and avocados from Hawaii poured from the housekeeping department in an unending stream; there were new toothbrushes and new pajamas for the unexpected guest, there were new bathing suits in boxes for the girls who had driven over from Taramac House and who wanted a swim, there were new packs of cards and new boxes of cigars, and there were maids--maids--maids to run for these things when they were wanted, and carry them away when their brief use was over.

Then it would be September, and everything would end as suddenly as it began. The Villalongas would go to Europe, or to Newport, Vera loudly, joyously, insistently urging everyone to visit them there if it were the latter. In November they would be in their town house with new paintings and new rugs to show their guests: a portrait of Vera, a rug stolen from a Sultan's palace.

Everybody said that Vera Villalonga did this sort of thing extremely well; indeed she had no rival in her own particular field. The weekly society journals depended upon her to supply them with spectacular pictures of a Chinese ball every November and a Micareme dance every spring; they sent photographers all the way up to her camp that their readers might not miss a yearly glimpse of the way Mrs. Villalonga entertained.

But Rachael, who had spent a portion of six summers with the Villalongas, found herself, in her newly analytical mood, wondering just who got any particular pleasure out of it all. Vera herself, perhaps. Certainly her husband, who would spend all his time playing poker and tennis, would have been as happy elsewhere. Her two sons, tall, dark young men, in connection with whose characters the world in general contented itself merely with the word "wild," would be there only for a week or two at most. Billy would wait for Joe Pickering's letters, Clarence would drink, and watch Billy. Little Mina Villalonga, who had a minor nervous ailment, would wander about after Billy. The Parmalees would come up for a visit, and the Morans would come. Jack Torrence, spoiled out of all reason, would promise a week and come for two days; Porter Pinckard would compromise upon a mere hour or two, charging into the camp in his racing car, introducing hilarious friends, accepting a sandwich and a bottle of beer, and then tearing off again. Straker Thomas, silent, mysterious, ill, would drift about for a week or two; Peter Pomeroy would go up late in July, and be adored by everyone, and take charge of the theatricals.

"The maids probably get any amount of fun out of it," mused Rachael. Vera was notably generous to her servants: a certain pool was reserved for them, and their numbers formed a most congenial society every summer. "I don't believe I'll go to Vera's this year," Mrs. Breckenridge said aloud to her husband and stepdaughter.

"I'm not crazy about it," Billy agreed fretfully.

"Might as well," was the man's enthusiastic contribution.

"Oh, I'm GOING!" Billy said discontentedly. "But I don't see why you and Rachael have to go."

"Don't you?" her father said significantly.

"Joe Pickering's going to be in Texas this whole summer, if that's what you mean!" flamed Billy.

"I'm glad to hear it," Clarence commented.

"Anyway, you might depend upon Vera to take absolute good care of Bill," Rachael said soothingly. "It's time you both got away to some cooler place, if you are going to fight so about nothing! Why do you do it? Billy can't marry anyone for eleven months, and if she wants to marry the man in the moon then you can't stop her. So there you are!"

"And I'm capable of running my own affairs," finished Billy with a look far from filial.

"You only waste your breath arguing with Clarence when he's got one of his headaches," Rachael said to her stepdaughter an hour or two later when they were spinning smoothly into the city for the planned shopping. "Of course he'll go to Vera's, and of course you'll go, too! Just don't tease him when he's all upset."

"Well, what does he drink and smoke so much, and get this way for?" Billy demanded sullenly.

"What does anybody do it for?" Rachael countered. And a second later her singing heart was with Gregory again. He did not do it!

She entered into Billy's purchasing perplexities with great sympathy; a successful hat was found, several deliciously extravagant and fragile dresses for camping.

"You're awfully decent about all this, Rachael." Billy said once; "it must be a sweet life we lead you sometimes!"

Something in the girl's young glance touched Rachael strangely. They were in the car again now, going toward Mrs. Gregory's handsome, old-fashioned house on Washington Square. Rachael was inspired to seize the propitious second.

"Listen, Bill," she said, and paused. Billy eyed her curiously. Obtuse as she was, a certain change in Rachael had not entirely escaped the younger woman.

"Well?" she asked, on guard.

"Well--" Rachael faltered. Motherly advice was not much in her line. "It's just this, Bill," she resumed slowly, "when you think of marriage, don't think of just a few weeks or a few months; think of all the time. Think of other things than just--that sort of--love. Children, you know, and--and books, don't you know? Things that count. Be--I don't say be guided entirely by what your father and lots of other persons think, but be influenced by it! Realize that we have no motive but--but affection, in advising you to be sure."

The stumbling, uncertain words were unlike Mrs. Breckenridge's usual certain flow of reasoning. But in spite of this, or because of it, Billy was somewhat impressed.

"I had an aunt in California," Rachael continued, "who cried, and got whipped and locked up, and all the rest of it, and she carried her point. But she was unhappy. ..."

"You mean because Joe is divorced?" Billy asked in a somewhat troubled voice.

The scarlet rushed to Rachael's face.

"N--not entirely," she answered in some confusion.

"That is, you don't think divorced people ought to remarry, even if the divorce is fair enough?" Billy pursued, determined to be clear.

"Well, I suppose every case is different, Bill."

"That's what you've always SAID!" Billy accused her vivaciously. "You said, time and time again, that if people can't live together in peace they OUGHT to separate, but that it was another thing if they married again!"

"Did I?" Rachael asked weakly, adding a moment later, with obvious relief in her tone: "Here we are! It's only this, Bill," she finished, as they mounted the brownstone steps, "be sure. You can do anything, I suppose. Only be sure!"

Mrs. Gregory would be down in a few minutes, old Dennison said. Rachael murmured something amiable, and the two went into the dark, handsome parlors; the house was full of parlors; on both sides of the hall stately, crowded rooms could be glimpsed through open doors.

"Isn't it fierce?" Billy said with a helpless shrug. Rachael smiled and shook her head slowly in puzzled consent. "Don't you suppose they ever AIR it?" pursued the younger woman in a low tone. The air had a peculiarly close, dry smell.

"It wouldn't seem so," Rachael said, looking at the life-size statues of Moorish and Neopolitan girls, the mantel clock representing a Dutch windmill, the mantel itself, of black marble, gilded and columned, with a mirror in a carved walnut frame stretching ten feet above it, the beaded fire screen, the voluminous window curtains of tasselled rep, and the ornate walnut table across whose marble top a strip of lace had been laid. Everything was ugly and expensive and almost everything was old-fashioned, all the level surfaces of tables, mantel, and piano top were filled with small articles, bits of ivory carving from China, leather boxes, majolica jars, photographs in heavy frames, enormous illustrated books, candlesticks, and odd teacups and trays.

Smiling down--how Rachael knew that smile, half-quizzical and half-tender--from a corner of the room was a beautiful oil portrait of Warren Gregory, the one really fine thing in the room. By some chance the painter had caught on his face the very look with which he might, in the flesh, have studied this dreadful room. Rachael felt a thrill go to her heels as she looked back at the canvas, and far down in the deeps of her being the thought stirred that some day her hand might be the one to change all this--to make the woodwork colonial white, and the paper rich with color, to have the black marble changed to creamy tiles, and the rep curtains torn away. Then how charming the place would be when visitors came in from the hot street!

"A million apologies--all my fault!" said Doctor Gregory in the doorway. His mother, in rustling black silk, was on his arm. She had given up her cane to-day to use the living support, and no lover could have wished to appear more charming in his lady's eyes than did Warren Gregory appear to Rachael as he lowered the frail old figure to a chair and neglected his guests while he made his mother comfortable.

"He would have you think, now, that I was the cause of the delay," said the old lady in a sweet voice that betrayed curiously the weakness of the flesh and the strength of the spirit. "But I assure you my beauty is no longer a matter of great importance to me!"

"So it was Greg who was curling his hair?" Rachael asked, with one swift and eloquent glance for him before she drew a much-fringed hassock to his mother's knee and seated herself there with the confidence of a captivating child. "I always thought he was rather vain! But let's not talk about him, we only make him worse. Tell me about yourself?"

Mrs. Gregory was a rather spirited old lady, and liked to fancy, with the pathetic complacency of the passing generation, that her sense of humor quite kept up with the times. Rachael knew her well, and knew all her stories, but this only made her the pleasanter companion. She quickly carried the conversation into the past, and was content to be a listener; indeed, with a hostess far removed in type from herself it was the only safe role to play. The conversation was full of pitfalls for this charming and dutiful worldling, and Rachael was too clever to risk a fall.

She was afraid of the crippled little gentlewoman in the big chair, and Warren Gregory was afraid, too. Some mysterious element in her regard for them made luncheon an ordeal for them both, although Billy's healthy young eyes saw only an old woman, impotent and alone; the maids were respectful and pitying, and young Charles Gregory, who joined them at luncheon, Was obviously unimpressed by his grandmother's power, but was smitten red and inarticulate at the first glimpse of Billy.

This youth, after silently disposing of several courses, finally asked in a husky voice for Miss Charlotte Haviland, and relapsed into silence again. Billy flirted youthfully with her host, Rachael devoted herself to the old lady.

She had always been happy here, a marked favorite with old Mrs. Gregory to whom her audacious nonsense had always seemed a great delight before. But to-day she was conscious of a change, she could not control the conversation with her usual sure touch, she floundered and contradicted herself like a schoolgirl. One of her brilliant stories fell rather flat because its humor was largely supplied by an intoxicated man--"of course it was dreadful, but then it was funny, too!" Rachael finished lamely. Another flashing account won from the old hostess the single words "On Sunday?"

"Well, yes. It was on Sunday. I am afraid we are absolute pagans; we don't always remember to go to church, by any means!" Rachael began to feel that a cloud of midges were buzzing about her face. Every topic led her deeper into the quicksand. There was a definite touch of resentment under the gracious manner in which she presently said her good-bye, and they were no sooner in the motor car than she exclaimed to Billy:

"Didn't Mrs. Gregory seem horribly cross to you to-day? She made me feel as if I'd broken all the Commandments and was dancing on the pieces!"

"What do you know about Charles asking for Charlotte?" was Billy's only answer. "Isn't he just the sort of mutt who would ask for Charlotte!"

"Isn't she quite lovely?" said Mrs. Gregory from over the fleecy yarn she was knitting, when the guests had gone.

"Carol?" the doctor countered.

"Yes, Carol, too. But I was thinking of Mrs. Breckenridge. Do you see her very often, James?"

"Quite a bit. Do you mind my smoking?"

"I often wonder," pursued the old lady innocently, "what such a sweet, gay, lovely girl could see in a fellow like poor Clarence Breckenridge!"

"Great marvel she doesn't throw him over!" Warren said casually.

"It distresses me to hear you talk so recklessly, my son," Mrs. Gregory said after a brief pause,

"Lord, Mother," her son presently observed impatiently, "is it reasonable to expect that because a girl like that makes a mistake when she is twenty or twenty-one, that she shall pay for it for the rest of her life?"

"Unfortunately, we are not left in any doubt about it," the old lady said dryly. And as Warren was silent she went on with quavering vigor: "It is not for us to judge her husband's infirmities. She is his wife."

"Oh, well, there's no use arguing it," the man said pleasantly after a sulphurous interval. "Fortunately for her, most people don't feel as you do."

"You surely don't think that _I_ originated this theory?" his mother asked quietly after a silence, during which her long needles moved a little more swiftly than was natural.

"I don't think anything about it. I KNOW that you're much, much narrower about such things than your religion or any religion gives you any right to be," Warren asserted hotly. "It is nothing to me, but I hate this smug parcelling out of other people's affairs," he went on. "Mrs. Breckenridge is a very wonderful and a most unfortunate woman; her husband isn't fit to lace her shoes--"

"All that may be true," his mother interrupted with some agitation.

"All that may be true, you say! And yet if Rachael left him, and tried to find happiness somewhere else--"

"The law is not of MY making, James," the old lady intervened mildly, noting his use of the discussed woman's name with a pang.

"But it IS of your making--you people who sit around and say what's respectable and what's not respectable! Who are you to judge?"

"I try not to judge," Mrs. Gregory said so simply that the man's anger cooled in spite of himself. "And perhaps I am foolish, James, all mothers are. But you are the last of my four sons, and I am a widow in my old age, and I tremble for you. When a woman with beauty as great as that confides in you, my child, when she turns to you, your soul is in danger, and your mother sees it. I cannot--I cannot be silent--"

Rachael herself, an hour ago, had not used her youth and beauty with more definite design than was this other woman using her age and infirmity now. Warren Gregory was almost as readily affected.

"My dear Mother," he said sensibly and charmingly, "don't think for one instant that I do not appreciate your devotion to me. What has suddenly put into your head this concern about Mrs. Breckenridge, I can't imagine. I know that if she were ever in any trouble or need you would be the first to defend her. She is in a peculiarly difficult position, and in a professional way I am somewhat in her confidence, that's all!"

"I should think she could do something with Clarence," the old lady said, somewhat mollified. "Interest him in something new; lead him away from bad influences."

"Clarence is rather a hopeless problem," Warren Gregory said. The talk drifted away to other persons and affairs, but when they presently parted, with great amiability on both sides, Warren Gregory knew that his mother's suspicions had in some mysterious way been aroused, and old Mrs. Gregory, sitting alone in the heat of the afternoon, writhed in the grip of a definite apprehension. Absurd--absurd--to interpret that married woman's brightly innocent glances into a declaration of love, absurd to find passion concealed in Warren's cheerfully hospitable manner. But she could not shake off the terrified conviction that it was so.

"Mr. and Mrs. Theodore Moulton of England have rented for the season the house of Mr. and Mrs. Clarence Breckenridge, at Belvedere Bay," stated the social columns authoritatively. "Mr. Breckenridge and Miss Carol Breckenridge will leave at once for the summer camp of Mrs. Booth Villalonga, at Elks Leap, where Mrs. Breckenridge will join them after spending a few weeks with friends."

Rachael saw the notice on the morning of the last day that she and Clarence were together. In the afternoon Billy and Clarence were to leave for the north, and Rachael was to go to Florence for a day or two. She had been unusually indefinite about her plans for the summer, but in the general confusion of all plans this had not been noticed. She had superintended the packing and assorting and storing of silver and linen, as a matter of course, and it was easy to see that certain things indisputably her own went into certain crates. Nobody questioned her authority, and Clarence and Billy paid no attention whatever to the stupid proceeding of getting the house in order for tenants.

On this last morning she sat at the breakfast table studying these two who had been her companions for seven years, and who suspected so little that this companionship was not to last for another seven years, for an indefinite time. Billy was in a bad temper because her father was not taking Alfred and the car with them to the camp, as he had done for the two previous years. Clarence, sullen as always under Billy's disapproval, was pretending to read his paper. He had a severe headache this morning, his face looked flushed and swollen. He was dreading the twenty-four hours in a hot train, even though the Bowditches, going up in their own car to their own camp, had offered the Breckenridges its comparative comfort and coolness for the entire trip.

"Makes me so sick," grumbled Billy, who looked extremely pretty in a Chinese coat of blue and purple embroideries; "every time I want to move I'll have to ask Aunt Vera if I may have a car! No fun at all!"

"Loads of horses and cars up there, my dear," Rachael said pacifically. She was quivering from head to foot with nervous excitement; the next few hours were all-important to her. And, under the pressure of her own great emotions, Billy seemed only rather pitiful and young to-day, and even Clarence less a conscious tyrant, and more a blundering boy, than he had seemed. She bore them no ill will after these seven hard years; indeed a great peace and kindliness pervaded her spirit and softened her manner toward them both. Her marriage had been a great disappointment, composed of a thousand small disappointments, but she was surprised to find that some intangible and elementary emotion was about to make this parting strangely hard.

"Yes, but it's not the same thing," Billy raged. Rachael began a low-voiced reassurance to which the younger woman listened reluctantly, scowling over her omelette, and interposing an occasional protest.

"Oh, yap--yap--yap! My God, I do get tired of hearing you two go on and on and on!" Clarence presently burst out angrily. "If you don't want to go, Billy, say so. I'm sick of the whole thing, anyway!"

"You know very well I never wanted to go," Billy answered. And because, being now committed to the Villalonga visit, she perversely dreaded it, she pursued aggrievedly, "I'd EVER so much rather have gone to California, Dad!"

How sure the youngster was of her power, Rachael thought, watching him instantly soften under his daughter's skilful touch.

"For five cents," he said eagerly, "I'd wire Vera, and you and I'd beat it to Santa Barbara! What do you say?"

"And if Rachael promised to be awfully good, she could come, too!" Billy laughed. But the girl's gay patronage was never again to be extended to Rachael Breckenridge.

"You couldn't disappoint Vera now," she protested.

"Oh, Lord! make some objections!" Clarence growled.

"My dear boy, it's nothing to me, whatever you do," Rachael said quickly. "But Vera Villalonga is a very important friend for Bill. There's no sense in antagonizing her--"

"No, I suppose there isn't," Billy said slowly. "But I wish she'd not ask us every summer. I suppose we shall be doing this for the rest of our lives!"

She trailed slowly from the room, and Clarence took one or two fretful glances at his paper.

"Gosh, how you do love to spoil things!" he said bitterly to his wife in a sudden burst.

Rachael did not answer. She rose after a few moments, and carried her letters into the adjoining room. When Clarence presently passed the door she called him in.

"Now or never--now or never!" said Rachael's fast-beating heart. She was pale and breathing quickly as he came in. But Clarence, sick and headachy, did not notice these signs of strong emotion.

"Clarence, I need some money," Rachael said simply.

"What for?" he asked unencouragingly.

The color came into his wife's face. She did not ask often for money, although he was rich, and she had been his wife for seven years. It was a continual humiliation to Rachael that she must ask him at all for the little actual money she spent, and tell him what she did with it when she got it. Clarence might lose more money at poker in a single night than Rachael touched in a month; it had come to him without effort, and of the two, she was the one who made a real effort to hold the home together. Yet she was a pensioner on his bounty, obliged to wait for the propitious mood and moment. Under her hand at this moment was Mary Moulton's check for one thousand dollars, more than she had ever had at one time in her life. She could not touch it, but Clarence would turn it into bills, and stuff them carelessly into his pocket, to be scattered in the next week or two wherever his idle fancy saw fit.

"Why, for living, and travelling expenses," she answered, with what dignity she could muster.

"Thought you had some money," he grumbled in evident distaste.

"Come in here a moment," Rachael said in a voice that rather to his surprise he obeyed. "Sit down there," she went on, and Clarence, staring at her a little stupidly, duly seated himself. His wife twisted about in her desk chair so that she could rest an arm upon the back of it, and faced him seriously across that arm.

"Clarence," said she, conscious of a certain dryness in her mouth, and a sick quivering and weakness through-out her whole body, "I want to end this."

"What?" asked Clarence, puzzled and dull, as she paused.

"I want to be free," Rachael said, stumbling awkwardly over the phrase that sounded so artificial and dramatic. They looked at each other, Clarence's bewildered look slowly changing to one of comprehension under his wife's significant expression. There was a silence.

"Well?" Clarence said, ending it with an indifferent shrug.

"Our marriage has been a farce for years--almost from the beginning," Rachael asserted eagerly. "You know it, and I know it--everyone does. You're not happy, and I'm wretched. I'm sick of excuses, and pretending, and prevaricating. There isn't a thing in the world we feel alike about; our life has become an absolute sham. It isn't as if I could have any real influence over you--you go your way, and do as you please, and I take the consequences. I realize now that every word I say jars on you. Why, sometimes when you come into a room and find me there I can tell by the expression on your face that you're angry just at that! I've too much self-respect, I've too much pride, to go on this way. You know how I hate divorce--no woman in the world hates it more--but tell me, honestly, what do we gain by keeping up a life like this? I used to be happy and confident and full of energy a few years ago; now I'm bored all the time. What's the use, what's the use--that's the way I feel about everything--"

"You're not any more tired of it than I am!" Clarence interrupted sullenly.

"Then why keep it up?" she asked urgently. "You've Billy, and your clubs, and your car, to fill your time. There'll be a fuss, of course, and I hate that, but we'll both be away. We've given it a fair trial, but we simply aren't meant for each other. Good heavens! it isn't as if we were the first man and woman who--"

"Don't talk as if I were opposing you," Clarence said with a weary frown.

Rachael, snubbed, instantly fell silent.

"I've got my side in all this dissatisfied business, too," the man presently said with unsteady dignity. "You never cared a damn for me, or what became of me! I've had you ding-donging your troubles at me day and night; it never occurs to you what I'm up against." He looked at his watch. "You want some money?" he asked.

"If you please," Rachael answered, scarlet-cheeked.

"Well, I can write a check--" he began.

"Here's this check of Mary Moulton's for July," Rachael said, nervously adding: "She wants to pay month by month, because I think she hopes you'll rent after August. I believe she'd keep the place indefinitely, on account of being near her mother, and for the boys."

Clarence took the check, and, hardly glancing at it, scrawled his slovenly "C. L. Breckenridge" across the back with a gold-mounted fountain pen. Rachael, whose face was burning, received it back from his hand with a husky "Thank you. You'll have to furnish the grounds, I presume--there will be a referee--nothing need get out beyond the fact that I am the complainant. You--won't contest? You--won't oppose anything?" She hated herself for the question, but it had to be asked.

"Nope," the man said impatiently.

"And"--Rachael hesitated--"and you won't say anything, Clarence," she suggested, "because the papers will get hold of it fast enough!"

"You can't tell me anything about that," he said sullenly. Then there came a silence. Rachael, looking at him, wished that she could hate him a little more, wished that his neglects and faults had made a little deeper impression. For a minute or two neither spoke. Then Clarence got up and left the room, and Rachael sat still, the little slip held lightly between her fingers. The color ebbed slowly from her face, her heart resumed its normal beat, moments went by, the little clock on her desk ticked on and on. It was all over; she was free. She felt strangely shaken and cold, and desolately lonely.

He loved her as little as she loved him. They had never needed each other, yet there was in this severance of the bond between them a strange and unexpected pain. It was as if Rachael's heart yearned over the wasted years, the love and happiness that might have been. Not even the thought of Warren Gregory seemed warm or real to-day; a great void surrounded her spirit; she felt a chilled weariness with the world, with all men--she was sick of life.

On the following day she gave Florence a hint of the situation. It was only fair to warn the important, bustling matron a trifle in advance of the rest of the world. Rachael had had a long night's sleep; she already began to feel deliciously young and free. She was to spend a few nights at the Havilands', and the next week supposedly go to the Princes' at Bar Harbor; really she planned to disappear for a time from her world. She must go up to town for a consultation with her lawyer, and then, when the storm broke, she would slip away to little Quaker Bridge, the tiny village far down on Long Island upon which, quite by chance, she had stumbled two years before. No one would recognize her there, no one of her old world could find her, and there for a month or two she could walk and bathe and dream in wonderful solitude. Then--then Greg would be home again.

"I want to tell you something, Florence," Rachael said to her sister-in-law when she was stretched upon the wide couch in Florence's room, watching with the placidity of a good baby that lady's process of dressing for an afternoon of bridge, or rather the operations with cold cream, rubber face brush, hair tonic, eyebrow stick, powder, rouge, and lip paste that preceded the process of dressing. Mrs. Haviland, even with this assistance, would never be beautiful; in justice it must be admitted that she never thought herself beautiful. But she thought rouge and powder and paste improved her appearance, and if through fatigue or haste she was ever led to omit any or all of these embellishments, she presented herself to the eyes of her family and friends with a genuine sensation of guilt. Perhaps three hours out of all her days were spent in some such occupation; between bathing, manicuring, hair-dressing, and intervals with her dressmaker and her corset woman it is improbable that the subject of her appearance was long out of the lady's mind. Yet she was not vain, nor was she particularly well satisfied with herself when it was done. That about one-fifth of her waking time--something more than two months out of the year--was spent in an unprofitable effort to make herself, not beautiful nor attractive, but something only a little nearer than was natural to a vague standard of beauty and attractiveness, never occurred, and never would occur, to Florence Haviland.

"What is it?" she asked now sharply, pausing with one eyebrow beautifully pencilled and the other less definite than ever by contrast.

"I don't suppose it will surprise you to hear that Clarence and I have decided to try a change," Rachael said slowly.

"How do you mean a change?" the other woman said, instantly alert and suspicious.

"The usual thing," Rachael smiled.

"What madness has got hold of that boy now?" his sister exclaimed aghast.

"It's not entirely Clarence," Rachael explained with a touch of pride.

"Well, then, YOU'RE mad!" the older woman said shortly.

"Not necessarily, my dear," Rachael answered, resolutely serene.

"Go talk to someone who's been through it," Florence warned her. "You don't know what it is! It's bad enough for him, but it's simple suicide for you!"

"Well, I wanted you to hear it from me," Rachael submitted mildly.

"Do you mean to say you've decided, seriously, to do it?"

"Very seriously, I assure you!"

"How do you propose to do it?" Florence asked after a pause, during which she stared with growing discomfort at her sister-in-law.

"The way other people do it," Rachael said with assumed lightness. "Clarence agrees. There will be evidence."

Mrs. Haviland flushed.

"You think that's fair to Clarence?" she asked presently.

"I think that in any question of fairness between Clarence and me the balance is decidedly in my favor!" Rachael said crisply. "Personally, I shall have nothing to do with it, and Clarence very little. Charlie Sturgis will represent me. I suppose Coates and Crandall will take care of Clarence--I don't know. That's all there is to it!"

Her placid gaze roved about the ceiling. Mrs. Haviland gazed at her in silence.

"Rachael," she said desperately, "will you TALK to someone--will you talk to Gardner?"

"Why should I?" Rachael sat up on the couch, the loosened mass of her beautiful hair falling about her shoulders. "What has Gardner or anyone else to do with it? It's Clarence's business, and my business, and it concerns nobody else!" she said warmly. "You look on from the outside. I've borne it for seven years! I'm young, I'm only twenty-eight, and what is my life? Keeping house for a man who insults me, and ignores me, who puts me second to his daughter, and has put me second since our wedding day-- making excuses for him to his friends, giving up what I want to do, never knowing from day to day what his mood will be, never having one cent of money to call my own! I tell you there are days and days when I'm too sick at heart to read, too sick at heart to think! Last summer, for instance, when we were down at Easthampton with the Parmalees, when everyone was so wild over bathing, and tennis, and dancing, Clarence wasn't sober ONE MOMENT of the time, not one! One night, when we were dancing--but I won't go into it!"

"I know," Florence said hastily, rather frightened at this magnificent fury. "I know, dear, it's too bad--it's dreadful--it's a great shame. But men are like that! Now Gardner--"

"All men aren't like that! Gardner does that sort of thing now and then, I know," Rachael rushed on, "but Gardner is always sorry. Gardner takes his place as a man of dignity in the world. I am nothing to Clarence; I have never been to him one-tenth of what Billy is! I have borne it, and borne it, and now I just can't--bear it--any longer!"

And Rachael, to her own surprise and disgust, burst into bitter crying, and, stammering some incoherency about an aching head, she went to her own room and flung herself across the bed. The suppressed excitement of the last few days found relief in a long fit of sobbing; Florence did not dare go near her. The older woman tried to persuade herself that the resentment and bitterness of this unusual mood would be washed away, and that Rachael, after a nap and a bath, would feel more like herself, but nevertheless she went off to her game in a rather worried frame of mind, and gave but an imperfect attention to the question of hearts or lilies.

Rachael, heartily ashamed of what she would have termed her schoolgirlish display of emotion, came slowly to herself, dozed over a magazine, plunged into a cold bath, and at four o'clock dressed herself exquisitely for Mrs. Whittaker's informal dinner. Glowing like a rose in her artfully simple gown of pink and white checks, she went downstairs.

Florence had come in late, bearing a beautiful bit of pottery, the first prize, and was again in the throes of dressing, but Gardner was downstairs restlessly wandering about the dimly lighted rooms and halls. He was fond of Rachael, and as they walked up and down the lawn together he tried, in a blunt and clumsy way, to show her his sympathy.

"Floss tells me you're about at the end of your rope--what?" said Gardner. "Clarence is the limit, of course, but don't be too much in a hurry, old girl. We'd be--we'd be awfully sorry to have you come to a smash, don't you know--now!"

Thus Gardner. Rachael gave him a glimmering smile in the early dusk.

"Not much fun for me, Gardner," she said gravely.

"Sure it's not," Gardner answered, clearing his throat tremendously. Neither spoke again until Florence came down, but later, in all honesty, he told his wife that he had pitched into Rachael no end, and she had agreed to go slow.

Florence, however, was not satisfied with so brief a campaign. She and Rachael did not speak of the topic again until the last afternoon of Rachael's stay. Then the visitor, coming innocently downstairs at tea time, was a little confused to see that besides Mrs. Bowditch and her oldest daughter, and old Mrs. Torrence, the Bishop and Mrs. Thomas were calling. Instantly she suspected a trap.

"Rachael, dear," Florence said sweetly, when the greetings were over, "will you take the bishop down to look at the sundial? I've been boasting about it."

"You sound like a play, Florence," her sister-in-law said with a little nervous laugh. "'Exit Rachael and Bishop, L.' Surely you've seen the sundial, Bishop?"

"I had such a brief glimpse of it on the day of the tea," Bishop Thomas said pleasantly, "that I feel as if I must have another look at that inscription!" Smiling and benign, rather impressive in his clerical black, the clergyman got to his feet, and turned an inviting smile to Rachael.

"Shall I take you down, Bishop?" Charlotte asked, her eagerness to be socially useful fading into sick apprehension at her mother's look.

"No, I'll go!" Rachael ended the little scene by catching up her wide hat. "Come on, Bishop," she said courageously, adding, as soon as they were out of hearing, "and if you're going to be dreadful, begin this moment!"

"And why, pray, should I be dreadful?" the bishop asked, smiling reproachfully. "Am I usually so dreadful? I don't believe it would be possible, among these lovely roses"--he drew in a great breath of the sweet afternoon air--"and with such a wonderful sunset telling us to lift up our hearts." And sauntering contentedly along, the bishop gave her an encouraging smile, but as Rachael continued to walk beside him without raising her eyes, presently he added, whimsically: "Would it be dreadful, Mrs. Breckenridge, if one saw a heedless little child--oh, a sweet and dear, but a heedless little child--going too near the cliffs--would it be dreadful to say: 'Look out, little child! There's a terrible fall there, and the water's cold and dark. Be careful!'" The bishop sat down on the carved stone bench that had been set in the circle of shrubs that surrounded the sundial, and Rachael sat down, too.

"Well, what about the child?" he persisted, when there had been a silence.

Rachael raised sombre eyes, her breast rose on a long sigh.

"I am not a child," she said slowly.

"Aren't we all children?" asked the bishop, mildly triumphant.

Rachael, sitting there in Florence's garden, looking down at the white roofs of the village and the smooth sheet of blue that was Belvedere Bay, felt a burning resentment enter her heart. How calm and smug and sure of themselves they were, these bishops and Florences and old lady Gregorys! How easy for them to advise and admonish, to bottle her up with their little laws and platitudes, these good people married to other good people, and wrapped in the warmth of mutual approval and admiration! The bishop was talking--

"Children, yes, the best and wisest of us is no more than that," he was saying dreamily, "and we must bear and forbear with each other. Not easy? Of course it's not easy! But no cross no crown, you know. I have known Clarence a great many years--"

"I am sorry to hurt Florence--God knows I'm sorry for the whole thing!" Rachael said, "but you must admit that I am the best judge of this matter. I've borne it long enough. My mind is made up. You and I have always been good friends, Bishop Thomas"--she laid a beautiful hand impulsively on his arm--"and you know that what you say has weight with me. But believe me, I'm not jumping hastily into this: it's come after long, serious thought. Clarence wants to be free as well--"

"Clarence does?" the clergyman asked, with a disapproving shake of his head.

"He has said so," Rachael answered briefly.

"And what will your life be after this, my child?"

To this she responded merely with a shrug. Perhaps the bishop suspected that such a calm confidence in the future indicated more or less definite plans, for he gave her a shrewd and searching look, but there was nothing to be said. The lovely lady continued to stare at the soft turf with unsmiling eyes, and the clergyman could only watch her in puzzled silence.

"After all," Rachael said presently, giving him a rueful glance, "what are the statistics? One marriage in twelve fails--fails openly, I mean--for of course there are hundreds that don't get that far. Sixty thousand last year!"

"If those ARE the statistics," said the bishop warmly, "it is a disgrace to a Christian country!"

"But you don't call this a Christian country?" Rachael said perversely.

"It is SUPPOSEDLY so," the clergyman asserted.

"Supposedly Christian," she mused, "and yet one marriage out of every twelve ends in divorce, and you Christians--well, you don't CUT us! We may not keep holy the Sabbath day, we may not honor our fathers and mothers, we may envy our neighbor's goods, yes, and his wife, if we like, but still--you don't refuse to come to our houses!"

"I don't know you in this mood," said Bishop Thomas coldly.

"Call it Neroism, or Commonsensism, or Modernism, or anything you like," Rachael said with sudden fire, "but while you go on calling what you profess Christianity, Bishop, you simply subscribe to an untruth. You know what our lives are, myself and Florence and Gardner and Clarence; is there a Commandment we don't break all day long and every day? Do we give our coats away, do we possess neither silver nor gold in our purses, do we love our neighbors? Why don't you denounce us? Why don't you shun the women in your parish who won't have children as murderers? Why don't you brand some of the men who come to your church--men whose business methods you know, and I know, and all the world knows--as thieves!"

"And what would my branding them as murderers and thieves avail?" asked the bishop, actually a little pale now, and rising to face her as she rose. "Are we to judge our fellowmen?"

"I'm not," Rachael said, suddenly weary, "but I should think you might. It would be at least refreshing to have you, or someone, demonstrate what Christianity is. It would be good for our souls. Instead," she added bitterly, "instead, you select one little thing here, and one little thing there, and putter, and tinker, and temporize, and gloss over, and build big churches, with mortgages and taxes and insurance to pay, in the name of Christianity! If I were little Annie Smith, down in the village here, I could get a divorce for twenty-five dollars, and you would never hear of it. But Clarence Breckenridge is a millionaire, and the Breckenridges have gone to your church for a hundred years, and so it's a scandal that must be averted if possible!"

"The church frowns on divorce," said the bishop sternly. "At the very present moment the House of Bishops, to which I have the distinguished honor to belong, is considering taking a decided stand in the matter. Divorce is a sin--a sin against one of God's institutions. But when I find a lady in this mood," he continued, with a sort of magnificent forbearance, "I never attempt to combat her views, no matter how extraordinarily jumbled and--and childish they are. As a clergyman, and as an old friend, I am grieved when I see a hasty and an undisciplined nature about to do that which will wreck its own happiness, but I can only give a friendly warning, and pass on. I do not propose to defend the institution to which I have dedicated my life before you or before anyone. Shall we go back to the house?"

"Perhaps we had better," Rachael agreed. And as they went slowly along the wide brick walk she added in a softened tone: "I do appreciate your affectionate interest in--in us, Bishop. But--but it does exasperate me, when so many strange things are done in the name of Christianity, to have--well, Florence for instance--calmly decreeing that just these other certain things shall NOT be done!"

"Then, because we can't all be perfect, it would be better not to try to be good at all?" the bishop asked, restored to equanimity by what he chose to consider an unqualified apology, and resuming his favorite attitude of benignant adviser.

Rachael sighed wearily in the depth of her soul. She knew that kindly admonitory tone, that complacent misconception of her meaning. She said to herself that in a moment he would begin to ask himself questions, and answer them himself.

"We are not perfect ourselves," said the clergyman benevolently, "yet we expect perfection in others. Before we will even change our own lives we like to look around and see what other people are doing. Perfectly natural? Of course it's perfectly natural, but at the same time it's one of the things we must fight. I shall have to tell you a little story of our Rose, as I sometimes tell some of my boys at the College of Divinity," continued the good man. Rose, an exemplary unmarried woman of thirty, was the bishop's daughter. "Rose," resumed her father, "wanted to study the violin when she was about twelve, and her peculiar old pater decided that first she must learn to cook. Her mother quite agreed with me, and the young lady was accordingly taken out to the kitchen and introduced to some pots and pans. I also got her some book, I've forgotten its name--her mother would remember; 'Complete Manual of Cookery'--something of that sort. A day or two later I asked her mother how the cooking went. 'Oh,' she said, 'Rose has been reading that book, and she knows more than all the rest of us!'"

Rachael laughed generously. They had reached the house again now, and Florence, glancing eagerly toward them, was charmed to see both smiling. She felt that the bishop must have influenced Rachael, and indeed the clergyman himself was sure that her mood was softer, and found opportunity before he departed to say to his hostess in a low tone that he fancied that they would hear no more of the whole miserable business.

"Oh, Bishop, how wonderful of you!" said Florence thankfully.

CHAPTER VI

Two weeks later the news of the Breckenridge divorce burst like a bomb in the social sky. Immediately pictures of the lovely wife, of Clarence, of the town house and the country house began to flood the evening papers, and even the morning journals found room for a column or two of the affair on inside pages. Clarence was tracked to his mountain retreat, and as much as possible was made of his refusal to be interviewed. Mrs. Breckenridge was nowhere to be found.

The cold wind of publicity could not indeed reach her in the quiet lanes and along the sandy shore of Quaker Bridge. Rachael, known to everyone but her kind old landlady as "Mrs. Prescott," could even glance interestedly at the papers now and then. Her identity, in three long and peaceful months, was not even so much as suspected. She did not mind the plain country table, the inconvenient old farmhouse; she loved her new solitude. Unquestioned, she dreamed through the idle days, reading, thinking, sleeping like a child. She spent long hours on the seashore watching the lazy, punctual flow and tumble of the waves that were never hurried, never delayed; her eyes followed the flashing wings of the gulls, the even, steady upward beat of strong pinions, the downward drifting through blue air that was of all motion the most perfect.

And sometimes in those hours it seemed to Rachael that she was no more in the great scheme of things than one of these myriad gulls, than one of the grains of sand through which she ran her white, unringed fingers. Clarence was a dream, Belvedere Bay was a dream; it was all a hazy, dim memory now: the cards and the cocktails, the dancing and tennis, the powder and lip-red in hot rooms and about glittering dinner tables. What a hurry and bustle and rush it all was--for nothing. The only actualities were the white sand and the cool green water, and the summer sun beating down warmly upon her bare head.

She awakened every morning in a large, bright, bare room whose three big windows looked into rustling maple boughs. The steady rushing of surf could be heard just beyond the maples. Sometimes a soft fog wrapped the trees and the lawn in its pale folds, and the bell down at the lighthouse ding-donged through the whole warm, silent morning, but more often there was sunshine, and Rachael took her book to the beach, got into her stiff, dry bathing suit, in a small, hot bathhouse furnished only by a plank bench and a few rusty nails, and plunged into the delicious breakers she loved so well. Busy babies, digging on the beach, befriended her, and she grew to love their sudden tears and more sudden laughter, their stammered confidences, and the touch of their warm, sandy little hands. She became an adept at pinning up their tiny bagging undergarments, and at disentangling hat elastics from the soft hair at the back of moist little necks. If a mother occasionally showed signs of friendliness, Rachael accepted the overture pleasantly, but managed to wander next day to some other part of the beach, and so evade the definite beginning of a friendship.

The warm sunshine, flavored by the salty sea, soaked into her very bones. Everything about Quaker Bridge was bare, and worn, and clean; nothing was crowded, or hurried, or false. Barren dunes, and white, bleaching sand, colorless little houses facing the elm-lined main street, colorless planks outlining the road to the water; the monotonous austerity, the pure severity of the little ocean village was full of satisfying charm for her. If she climbed a sandy rise beyond Mrs. Dimmick's cottage, and faced the north, she could see the white roadway, winding down to Clark's Bar, where the ocean fretted year after year to free the waters of the bay only twelve feet away. Beyond on the slope, was the village known as Clark's Hills, a smother of great trees with a weather-whipped spire and an occasional bit of roof or fence in evidence, to show the habitation of man.

In other directions, facing east or west or south, there was nothing but the sand, and the coarse straggling bushes that rooted in the sand, and the clear blue dome of the sky. Rachael, whose life had been too crowded, gloried in the honey-scented emptiness of the sand hills, the measureless, heaving surface of the ocean, the dizzying breadth and space in which, an infinitesimal speck, she moved.

She had sensibly taken her landlady, old Mrs. Dimmick, into her confidence, and pleased to be part of the little intrigue, and perhaps pleased as well to rent her two best rooms to this charming stranger, the old lady protected the secret gallantly. It was all much more simple than Rachael had feared it would be. Nobody questioned her, nobody indeed paid attention to her; she wandered about in a blissful isolation as good for her tired soul as was the primitive life she led for her tired body.

Yet every one of the idle days left its mark upon her spirit; gradually a great many things that had seemed worth while in the old life showed their true and petty and sordid natures now; gradually the purifying waters of solitude washed her soul clean. She began to plan for the future--a future so different from the crowded and hurried past!

Warren Gregory's letters came regularly, postmarked London, Paris, Rome. They were utterly and wholly satisfying to Rachael, and they went far to make these days the happiest in her life. Her heart would throb like a girl's when she saw, on the little drop-leaf table in the hallway, the big square envelope addressed in the doctor's fine hand; sometimes--again like a girl--she carried it down to the beach before breaking the seal, thrilled with a thousand hopes, unready to put them to the test. Yesterday's letter had said: "My dearest,"--had said: "Do you realize that I will see you in five weeks?" Could to-day's be half as sweet?

She was never disappointed. The strong tide of his devotion for her rose steadily through letter after letter; in August the glowing letters of July seemed cold by contrast, in September every envelope brought her a flaming brand to add to the fires that were beginning to blaze within her. In late September there was an interval; and Rachael told herself that now he was on the ocean--now he was on the ocean--

By this time the digging babies were gone, the beach was almost deserted. Little office clerks, men and women, coming down for the two weeks of rest that break the fifty of work, still arrived on the late train Saturday, and went away on the last train two weeks from the following Sunday, but there were no more dances at the one big hotel, and some of the smaller hotels were closed. The tall, plain, attractive woman--with the three children and the baby, who drove over from Clark's Hills every day, and, who, for all her graying hair and sun-bleached linens, seemed to be of Rachael's own world--still brought her shrieking and splashing trio to the beach, but she had confided to Mrs. Dimmick, who had known her for many summers, that even her long holiday was drawing to a close. Mrs. Dimmick brought extra blankets down from the attic, and began to talk of seeing her daughter in California. Rachael, drinking in the glory of the dying summer, found each day more exquisite than the last, and gratified her old hostess by expressing her desire to spend all the rest of her life in Quaker Bridge.

She had, indeed, come to like the villagers thoroughly; not the summer population, for the guests at all summer hotels are alike uninteresting, but for the quiet life that went on year in and year out in the little side streets: the women who washed clothes and swept porches, who gardened with tow-headed babies tumbling around them, who went on Sundays to the little bald-faced church at ten o'clock. Rachael got into talk with them, trying to realize what it must be to walk a hot mile for the small transaction of selling a dozen eggs for thirty cents, to spend a long morning carefully darning an old, clean Nottingham lace curtain that could be replaced for three dollars. She read their lives as if they had been an absorbing book laid open for her eyes. The coming of the Holladay baby, the decline and death of old Mrs. Bird, the narrow escape of Sammy Tew from drowning, and the thorough old-fashioned thrashing that Mary Trimble gave her oldest son for taking a little boy like Sammy out beyond the "heads,"--all these things sank deep into the consciousness of the new Rachael. She liked the whitewashed cottages with their blazing geraniums and climbing honeysuckle, and the back-door yards, with chickens fluffing in the dust, and old men, seated on upturned old boats, smoking and whittling as they watched the babies "while Lou gets her work caught up".

October came in on a storm, the most terrifying storm Rachael had ever seen. Late in the afternoon of September's last golden day a wind began to rise among the dunes, and Rachael, who, wrapped in a white wooly coat and deep in a book, had been lying for an hour or two on the beach, was suddenly roused by a shower of sand, and sat up to look at the sky. Clouds, low and gray, were moving rapidly overhead, and although the tide was only making, and high water would not be due for another hour, the waves, emerald green, swift, and capped with white, were already touching the landmost water-mark.

Quickly getting to her feet, she started briskly for home, following the broken line of kelp and weeds, grasses, driftwood, and cocoanut shells that fringed the tide-mark, and rather fascinated by the sudden ominous change in sea and sky. In the little village there was great clapping of shutters and straining of clotheslines, distracted, bareheaded women ran about their dooryards, doors banged, everywhere was rush and flutter.

"D'clare if don't think th' folks at Clark's Hills going to be shut of completely," said Mrs. Dimmick, bustling about with housewifely activity, and evidently, like all the village and like Rachael herself, a little exhilarated by the oncoming siege.

"What will they do?" Rachael demanded, unhooking a writhing hammock from the porch as the old woman briskly dragged the big cane rockers indoors.

"Oh, ther' wunt no hurt come t'um," Mrs. Dimmick said. "But--come an awful mean tide, Clark's Bar is under water. They'll jest have to wait until she goes down, that's all."

"Shell I bring up some candles from suller; we ain't got much karosene!" Florrie, the one maid, demanded excitedly. Chess, the hired man, who was Florrie's "steady," began to bring wood in by the armful, and fling it down by the airtight stove that had been set up only a few days before.

The wind began to howl about the roof; trees in the dooryard rocked and arched. Darkness fell at four o'clock, and the deafening roar of the ocean seemed an actual menace as the night came down. Chess and Florrie, after supper, frankly joined the family group in the sitting-room, a group composed only of Rachael and Mrs. Dimmick and two rather terrified young stenographers from the city.

These two did not go to bed, but Rachael went upstairs as usual at ten o'clock, and drifted to sleep in a world of creaking, banging, and roaring. A confusion and excited voices below stairs brought her down again rather pale, in her long wrapper, at three. The Barwicks, mother, father, and three babies, had left their beach cottage in the night and the storm to seek safer shelter and the welcome sound of other voices than their own.

After that there was little sleep for anyone. Still in the roaring darkness the clocks presently announced morning, and a neighbor's boy, breathless, dripping in tarpaulins, was blown against the door, and burst in to say with youthful relish that the porches of the Holcomb house were under water, and the boardwalk washed away, and folks said that the road was all gone betwixt here and the lighthouse. Rain was still falling in sheets, and the wind was still high. Rachael braved it, late in the afternoon, to go out and see with her own eyes that the surf was foaming and frothing over the deserted bandstand at the end of the main street, and got back to the shelter of the house wet and gasping, and with the first little twist of personal fear at her heart. Suppose that limitless raging green wall down there rose another ten--another twenty--feet, swept deep and roaring and resistless over little Quaker Bridge, plunged them all for a few struggling, hopeless moments into its emerald depths, and then washed the little loosely drifting bodies that had been men and women far out to sea again?

What could one do? No trains came into Quaker Bridge to-day; it was understood that there were washouts all along the line. Rachael sat in the dark, stuffy little sitting-room with the placid Barwick baby drowsing in her lap, and at last her face reflected the nervous uneasiness of the other women. Every time an especially heavy rush of rain or wind struck the unsubstantial little house, Mrs. Barwick said, "Oh, my!" in patient, hopeless terror, and the two young women looked at each other with a quick hissing breath of fear.

The night was long with horror. There were other refugees in Mrs. Dimmick's house now; there were in all fifteen people sitting around her little stove listening to the wind and the ocean. The old lady herself was the most cheerful of the group, although Rachael and one or two of the others managed an appearance at least of calm.

"Declare," said the hostess, more than once, "dunt see what we's all thinkin' of not to git over to Clark's Hills 'fore the bar was under water! They've got sixty-foot elevation there!"

"I'd just as soon try to get there now," said Miss Stokes of New York eagerly.

"There's waves eight feet high washin' over that bar," Ernest Barwick said, and something in the simple words made little Miss Stokes look sick for a moment.

"What's our elevation?" Rachael asked.

"'Bout--" Mr. Barwick paused. "But you can't tell nothing by that," he contented himself with remarking after a moment's thought.

"But I never heard--I never HEARD of the sea coming right over a whole village!" Rachael hated herself for the fear that dragged the words out, and the white lips that spoke them.

"Neither did I!" said half a dozen voices. There was silence while the old clock on the mantel wheezed out a lugubrious eight strokes. "LORD, how it rains!" muttered Emily Barwick.

Nine o'clock--ten o'clock. The young women, the old woman, the maid and man who would be married some day if they lived, the husband and wife who had been lovers like them only a few years ago, and who now had these three little lives to guard, all sat wrapped in their own thoughts. Rachael sat staring at the stove's red eye, thinking, thinking, thinking. She thought of Warren Gregory; his steamer must be in now, he must be with his mother in the old house, and planning to see her any day. To-morrow--if there was a to-morrow--might bring his telegram. What would his life be if he might never see her again? She could not even leave him a note, or a word; on this eve of their meeting, were they to be parted forever? Should she never tell him how dearly--how dearly--she loved him? Tears came to her eyes, her heart was wrung with exquisite sorrow.

She thought of Billy--poor little Billy--who had never had a mother, who needed a mother so sadly, and of her own mother, dead now, and of the old blue coat of thirteen years ago, and the rough blue hat. She thought of her great-grandmother in the little whitewashed California cottage under the shadow of the blue mountains, with the lilacs and marigolds in the yard. And colored by her new great love, and by the solemn fears of this endless night, Rachael found a tenderness in her heart for all those shadowy figures that had played a part in her life.

At midnight there came a thundering crash on the ocean side of the house.

"Oh, God, IT'S THE SEA!" screamed Emily Barwick. They all rushed to the door and flung it open, and in a second were out in the wild blackness of the night. Still the roaring and howling and shrieking of the elements, still the infuriated booming of the surf, but--thank God--no new sound. There was no break in the flying darkness above them; the street was a running sheet of water in the dark.

Yet strangely they all went back into the house vaguely quieted. Rachael presently said that no matter what was going to happen, she was too cold and tired to stay up any longer, and went upstairs to bed. Miss Stokes and Miss McKim settled themselves in their chairs; Emily Barwick went to sleep with her head against her husband's thin young shoulder. Somebody suggested coffee, and there was a general move toward the kitchen.

Rachael, a little bewildered, woke in heavenly sunlight in exactly the position she had taken when she crept into bed the night before. For a few minutes she lay staring at the bright old homely room, and at the clock ticking briskly toward nine.

"Dear Lord, what a thing sunshine is?" she said then slowly. No need to ask of the storm with this celestial reassurance flooding the room. But after a few moments she got up and went to the window. The trees, battered and torn, were ruffling such leaves as were left them gallantly in the wind, the paths still ran yellow water, the roadway was a muddy waste, eaves were still gurgling, and everywhere was the drip and splash of water. But the sky was clear and blue, and the air as soft as milk.

As eager as a child Rachael dressed and ran downstairs, and was out in the new world. The fresh wind whipped a glorious color into her face; the whole of sea and sky and earth seemed to be singing.

Trees were down, fences were down, autumn gardens were all a wreck; and the ocean, when she came to the shore, was still rolling wild and high. But it was blue now, and the pure sky above it was blue, and there was utter protection and peace in the sunny air. Landmarks all along the shore were washed away, and beyond the first line of dunes were pools left by the great tide, scummy and sinking fast into the sand, to leave only a fringe of bubbles behind. Minor wreckages of all sorts lay scattered all along the beach: poles and ropes, boxes and barrels.

Rachael walked on and on, breathing deep, swept out of herself by the fresh glory of the singing morning. Presently she would go back, and there would be Warren's letter, or his telegram, or perhaps himself, and then their golden days would begin--their happy time! But even Warren to-day could not intrude upon her mood of utter gratitude and joy in just living--just being young and alive in a world that could hold such a sea and such a sky.

A full mile from the village, along the ocean shore, a stream came down from under a cliff, a stream, as Rachael and investigating children had often proved to their own satisfaction, that rose in a small but eminently satisfactory cave. The storm had washed several great smooth logs of driftwood into the cave, and beyond them to-day there was such a gurgling and churning going on that Rachael, eager not to miss any effect of the storm, stepped cautiously inside.

The augmented little river was three times its usual size, and was further made unmanageable by the impeding logs swept in by the high tide. Straw and weeds and rubbish of every description choked its course, and little foaming currents and backwaters almost filled the cave with their bubbling and swirling.

Rachael, with a few casual pushes of a sturdy little shoe, accomplished such surprising results in freeing and directing the stream that she fell upon it in sudden serious earnest, grasping a long pole the better to push obstructing matters aside, and growing rosy and breathless over her self-imposed and senseless undertaking.

She had just loosened a whole tangle of wreckage, and had straightened herself up with a long, triumphant "Ah-h!" of relief, as the current rushed it away, when a shadow fell over the mouth of the cave. Looking about in quick, instinctive fear, she saw Warren Gregory smiling at her.

For only one second she hesitated, all girlhood's radiant shyness in her face. Then she was in his arms, and clinging to him, and for a few minutes they did not speak, eyes and lips together in the wild rapture of meeting.

"Oh, Greg--Greg--Greg!" Rachael laughed and cried and sang the words together. "When did you come, and how did you get here? Tell me--tell me all about it!" But before he could begin to answer her their eager joy carried them both far away from all the conversational landmarks, and again they had breath only for monosyllables, instinct only to cling to each other.

"My girl, my own girl!" Warren Gregory said. "Oh, how I've missed you--and you're more beautiful than ever--did you know it? More beautiful even than I remembered you to be, and that was beautiful enough!"

"Oh, hush!" she said, laughing, her fingers over the mouth that praised her, his arm still holding her tight.

"I'll never hush again, my darling! Never, never in all the years we spend together! I am going to tell you a hundred times a day that you are the most beautiful, and the dearest--Oh, Rachael, Rachael, shall I tell you something? It's October! Do you know what that means?"

"Yes, I suppose I do!" She laughed, and colored exquisitely, drawing herself back the length of their linked arms.

"Do you know what you're going to BE in about thirty-six hours?"

"Now--you embarrass me! Was--was anything settled?"

"Shall you like being Mrs. Gregory?"

"Greg--" Tears came to her eyes. "You don't know how much!" she said in a whisper.

They sat down on a great log, washed silver white with long years of riding unguided through the seas, and all the wonderful world of blue sky and white sand might have been made for them. Rachael's hand lay in her lover's, her glorious eyes rarely left his face. Browned by his summer of travel, she found him better than ever to look upon; hungry after these waiting months, every tone of his voice held for her a separate delight.

"Did you ever dream of happiness like this, Rachael?"

"Never--never in my wildest flights. Not even in the past few months!"

"What--didn't trust me?"

"No, not that. But I've been rebuilding, body and soul. I didn't think of the future or the past. It was all present."

"With me," he said, "it was all future. I've been counting the days. I've not done that since I was at school! Rachael, do you remember our talk the night after the Berry Stokes' dinner?"

"Do I remember it?"

"Ah, my dear, if anyone had said that night that in six months we would be sitting here, and that you would have promised yourself to me! You don't know what my wife is going to mean to me, my dearest. I can't believe it yet!"

"It is going to mean everything in life to me," she said seriously. "I mean to be the best wife a man ever had. If loving counts--"

"Do you mean that?" he said eagerly. "Say it--do you mean that you love me?"

"Love you?" She stood up, pressing both hands over her heart as if there were real pain there. For a few paces she walked away from him, and, as he followed her, she turned upon him the extraordinary beauty of her face transfigured with strong emotion.

"Greg," she said quietly, "I didn't know there was such love! I've heard it called fire and pain and restlessness, but this thing is ME! It is burning in me like flame, it is consuming me. To be with you"--she caught his wrist with one hand, and with her free hand pointed out across the smiling ocean--"to be with you and KNOW you were mine, I could walk straight out into that water, and end it all, and be glad--glad--glad of the chance! I loved you yesterday, but what is this to-day, when you have kissed me, and held me in your arms!" Her voice broke on something like a sob, but her eyes were smiling. "All my life I've been asleep," said Rachael. "I'm awake now--I'm awake now! I begin to realize how helpless one is--to realize what I should have done if you hadn't come--"

"My darling," Gregory said, his arms about her "what else--feeling as we feel--could I have done?"

Held in his embrace, she rested her hands upon his shoulders, and looked wistfully into his eyes.

"It is as WE feel, isn't it?" she said. "I mean, it isn't only me? You--you love me?"

Looking down at her dropped, velvety lashes, feeling the warm strong beat of her heart against his, holding close as he did all her glowing and fragrant beauty, Warren Gregory felt it the most exquisite moment of his life. Her youth, her history, her wonderful poise and sureness so intoxicatingly linked with all a girl's unexpected shyness and adorable uncertainties, all these combined to enthrall the man who had admired her for many years and loved her for more than one.

"Love you?" he asked, claiming again the lips she yielded with such a delicious widening of her eyes and quickening of breath.

"You see, Warren," she said presently, "I'm not a girl. I give myself to you with a knowledge and a joy no girl could possibly have. I don't want to coquette and delay. I want to be your wife, and to learn your faults, and have you learn mine, and settle down into harness--one year, five years--ten years married! Oh, you don't know how I LONG to be ten years married. I shan't mind a bit being nearly forty. Forty--doesn't it sound SETTLED, and sedate--and that's what I want. I--I shall love getting gray, and feeling that you and I don't care so much about going places, don't you know? We'll like better just being home together, won't we? We're older than most people now, aren't we?"

He laughed aloud at the bright face so enchantingly young in its restored beauty. He had expected to find her charming, but in this new phase of girlishness, of happiness, she was a thousand times more charming than he had dreamed. It was hard to believe that this eager girl in a striped blue and yellow and purple skirt, and rough white crash hat, was the bored, the remote, the much-feared Mrs. Clarence Breckenridge. Something free and sweet and virginal had come back to her, or been born in her. She was like no phase of the many phases in which he had known her; she was a Rachael who had never known the sordid, the disillusioning side of life. Even her seriousness had the confident, eager quality of youth, and her gayety was as pure as a child's. She had cast off the old sophistication, the old recklessness of speech; she was not even interested in the old associates. The world for her was all in him and their love for each other, and she walked back to Quaker Bridge, at his side, too wholly swept away from all self-consciousness to know or to care that they were at once the target for all eyes.

A wonderful day followed, many wonderful days. Doctor Gregory's great touring car and his livened man were at Mrs. Dimmick's door when they got back, an incongruous note in little Quaker Bridge, still gasping from the great storm.

"Your car?" Rachael said. "You drove down?"

"Yesterday. I put up at Valentine's--George Valentine's, you know, at Clark's Hills."

"Oh, that's my nice lady--gray haired, and with three children?" Rachael said eagerly. "Do you know her?"

"Know her? Valentine is my closest associate. They meet us in town to-morrow: he's to be best man. You'll have to have them to dinner once a month for the rest of your life!"

The picture brought her happy color, the shy look he loved.

"I'm glad, Greg. I like her immensely!"

They were at the car; she must flush again at the chauffeur's greeting, finding a certain grave significance, a certain acceptance, in his manner.

"Wife and baby well, Martin?"

"Very well, thank you, Mrs. Breckenridge."

"Still in Belvedere Hills?"

"Well, just at present, yes, Madam."

"You see, I am looking for suitable quarters for all hands," Doctor Gregory said, his laugh drowning hers, his eyes feasting on her delicious confusion. She was aware that feminine eyes from the house were watching her. Presently she had kissed Mrs. Dimmick good-bye. Warren had put his man in the tonneau; he would take the wheel himself for the three hours' run into town.

"Good-bye, my dear!" said the old lady, adding with an innocent vacuity of manner quite characteristic of Quaker Bridge. "Let me know when the weddin's goin' to be!"

"I'll let you know right now," said Doctor Gregory, who, gloved and coated, was bustling about the car, deep in the mysterious rites incidental to starting. "It's going to be to-morrow!"

"Good grief!" exclaimed Mrs. Dimmick delightedly. "Well," she added, "folks down here think you've got an awfully pretty bride!"

"I'm glad she's up to the standard down here," Warren Gregory observed. "Nobody seems to think much of her looks up in the city!"

Rachael laughed and leaned from her place beside the driver to kiss the old lady again and to wave a general good-bye to Florrie and Chess and the group on the porch. As smoothly as if she were launched in air the great car sprang into motion; the storm-blown cottages, the battered dooryards, the great shabby trees over the little post office all swept by. They passed the turning that led to Clark's Bar, and a weather-worn sign-post that read "Quaker Bridge, 1 mile." It was not a dream, it was all wonderfully true: this was Greg beside her, and they were going to be married!

Rachael settled back against the deep, soft cushions in utter content. To be flying through the soft Indian summer sunshine, alone with Greg, to actually touch his big shoulder with her own, to command his interest, his laughter, his tenderness, at will--after these lonely months it was a memorable and an enchanting experience. Their talk drifted about uncontrolled, as talk after long silence must: now it was a waiter on the ocean liner of whom Gregory spoke, or perhaps the story of a small child's rescue from the waves, from Rachael. They spoke of the roads, splendidly hard and clean after the rain, and of the villages through which they rushed.

But over their late luncheon, in a roadside inn, the talk fell into deeper grooves, their letters, their loneliness, and their new plans, and when the car at last reached the traffic of the big bridge, and Rachael caught her first glimpse of the city under its thousand smoking chimneys, there had entered into their relationship a new sacred element, something infinitely tender and almost sad, a dependence upon each other, a oneness in which Rachael could get a foretaste of the exquisite communion so soon to be.

They were spinning up the avenue, through a city humming with the first reviving breath of winter. They were at the great hotel, and Rachael was laughing in Elinor Vanderwall's embrace. The linen shop, the milliner, a dinner absurdly happy, and one of the new plays--a sunshiny morning when she and Elinor breakfasted in their rooms, and opened box after box of gowns and hats--the hours fled by like a dream.

"Nervous, Rachael?" asked Miss Vanderwall of the vision that looked out from Rachael's mirror.

"Not a bit!" the wife-to-be answered, feeling as she said it that her hands, busy with long gloves, were shaking, and her knees almost unready to support her.

"It must be wonderful to marry a man like Greg," said the bridesmaid thoughtfully. "He simply IS everything and HAS everything--"

"Ah, Elinor, it's wonderful to marry the man you love!" Rachael turned from the mirror, her blue eyes misted with tears under the brim of her wedding hat.

"YOU!" Elinor smiled. "That I should live to see it! You--in love!"

"And unashamed, and proud of it!" Rachael said with a tremulous laugh. "Are you all ready? Shall we go down?" She turned at the door and put one arm about her friend. "Kiss me, Elinor, and wish me joy," said she.

"I don't have to!" asserted Miss Vanderwall, with a hearty kiss nevertheless, "for it will be your own fault entirely if there's ever the littlest, teeniest cloud in the sky!"

BOOK II

CHAPTER I

Yet, even then, as Rachael Gregory admitted to herself months later, there had been a cloud in the sky--a cloud so tiny and so vague that for many days she had been able to banish it in the flooding sunshine all about her whenever it crossed her vision.

But it was there, and after a while other tiny clouds came to bear it company, and to make a formidable shadow that all her philosophy could not drive away. Philosophy is not the bride's natural right; the honeymoon is a time of unreason; a crumpled rose-leaf in those first uncertain weeks may loom larger than all the far more serious storms of the years to come.

Rachael, loving at last, was overwhelmed, intoxicated, carried beyond all sanity by the passion that possessed her.

When Warren Gregory came to find her at Quaker Bridge on that unforgettable morning after the storm, a chance allusion to Mrs. Valentine, the charming unknown lady with the gray hair, had distracted Rachael's thoughts from the point at issue. But later on, during the long drive, she had remembered it again.

"But Greg, dear, did you tell me that you and Doctor Valentine drove down yesterday in all that frightful storm?"

"No, no, of course not, my child; we came down late the night before-- why, yesterday we couldn't get as far as the gate! Mrs. Valentine's brother was there, and we played thirty-two rubbers of bridge! Sweet situation, you two miles away, and me held up after three months of waiting!"

She said to herself, with a little pain at her heart, that she didn't understand it. It was all right, of course, whatever Greg did was all right, but she did not understand it. To be so near, to have that hideous war of wind and water raging over the world, and not to come somehow--to swim or row or ride to her, to bring her delicious companionship and reassurance out of the storm! Why, had she known that Greg was so near no elements that ever raged could have held her--

But of course, she was reminding herself presently, Greg had never been to Quaker Bridge, he had no reason to suppose her in actual danger; indeed, perhaps the danger had always been more imagined than real. If his hosts had been merely bored by the weather, merely driven to cards, how should he be alarmed?

"Did the Valentines know what a tide we were having in Quaker Bridge?" she asked, after a while.

"Never dreamed it; didn't know we'd been cut off until it was all over!" That was reassuring, at least. "And, you see, I couldn't say much about our plans. Alice Valentine's all wool, of course, but she's anything but a yard wide! She wouldn't have understood--not that it matters, but it was easier not! She was sweet to you at the wedding, and she'll ask us to dinner, and you two will get along splendidly. But she's not as--big as George."

"You mean, she doesn't like the--divorce part of it?"

"Or words to that effect," the doctor answered comfortably. "Of course, she'd never have said a word. But they are sort of simple and old-fashioned. George understands--that's all I care about. Do you see?"

"I see," she answered slowly. But when he spoke again the sunshine came back to her heart; he had planned this, he had planned that, he had wired Elinor, the power boat was ready. She was a woman, after all, and young, and the bright hours of shopping, of being admired and envied, and, above all, of being so newly loved and protected, were opening before her. What woman in the world had more than she, what woman indeed, she asked herself, as he turned toward her his keen, smiling look of solicitude and devotion, had one-tenth as much?

Later on, in that same day, there was another tiny shadow. Rachael, however, had foreseen this moment, and met it bravely.

"How's your mother, Greg?" she asked suddenly.

"Fine," he answered, and with a swift smile for her he added, "and furious!"

"No--is she really furious?" Rachael asked, paling.

"Now, my dearest heart," Warren Gregory said with an air of authority that she found strangely thrilling and sweet, "from this moment on make up your mind that what my good mother does and says is absolutely unimportant to you and me! She has lived her life, she is old, and sick, and unreasonable, and whatever we did wouldn't please her, and whatever anyone does, doesn't satisfy her anyway! In forty years--in less than that, as far as I'm concerned--you and I'll be just as bad. My mother acted like a martyr on the steamer; she was about as gay with her old friends in London as you or I'd be at a funeral; she had an air of lofty endurance and forbearance all the way, and, as I said to Margaret Clay in Paris, the only time I really thought she was enjoying herself was when she had to be hustled into a hospital, and for a day or two there we really thought she was going to have pneumonia!"

Rachael's delightful laugh rang out spontaneously from utter relief of heart.

"Oh, Greg, you're delicious! Tell me about old Lady Frothingham, is she difficult, too? And how's pretty Magsie Clay?"

"Now, if we're married to-morrow," the doctor Went on, too much absorbed in his topic to be lightly distracted. "But do you hear me, Ma'am? How does it sound?"

"It sounds delicious! Go on!"

"If we're married to-morrow, I say--it could be to-day just as well, but I suppose you girls have to buy clothes, and have your hands manicured, and so on--"

"You know we do, to say nothing of lying awake all night talking about our beaux!"

"Well"--he conceded it somewhat reluctantly--"then, to-morrow, some time before I go with Valentine to call for you, I'll go down to see my mother. She'll kiss me, and sigh, and feel martyred. In a month or two she'll call on me at the office. 'Why don't you and your wife come to see me, James?' 'Would you like us to, Mother? We fancied you were angry at us.' 'I am sorry, my son, of course, but I have never been angry. Will you come to-morrow night?' And when we go, my dear, you'd never dream that there was anything amiss, I assure you!"

"I'll make her love me!" said Rachael, smiling tenderly.

"Perhaps some day you'll have a very powerful argument," he said with a significant glance that brought the quick blood to her face. "Mother couldn't resist that!"

She did not answer. It was a part of this new freshness and purity of aspect that she could not answer.

"You asked about Margaret Clay," the doctor remembered presently. "She was the same old sixpence, only growing up now; she owns to nineteen--isn't she more than that? She always did romance and yarn so much about herself that you can't believe anything."

"She's about twenty-one, perhaps no more than twenty," Rachael said, after some thought. "Did they say anything about Parker and Leila?"

"No, but the old lady can't do much harm there. She'll not last another six months. She may leave Margaret a slice, but it won't be much of a slice, for Parker could fight if it was. Leila's pretty safe. We'll have to go to that wedding, by the way!"

"Oh, Greg, the fun of going places together!" She was her happiest self again. His mother and Alice Valentine and everything else but their great joy was forgotten as they lingered over their luncheon and planned for their wedding day.

If they could only have been alone together, always, thought the new-made wife, when two perfect weeks on the powerful motor boat were over, and all the society editors were busily announcing that Doctor and Mrs. James Warren Gregory were furnishing their luxurious apartment in the Rotterdam, where they would spend the winter. They were so happy together; there was never enough time to talk and to be silent, never enough of their little luncheons all by themselves, their theatre trips, their afternoon drives through the sweet, clear early winter sunshine on the Park.

Always in the later years Rachael could feel the joy of these days again when she caught the scent of fresh violets. Never a day passed that Warren did not send her or bring her a fragrant boxful. They quivered on the breast of her gown, and on her dressing-table they made her bedroom sweet. Now and then when she and Warren were to be alone she braided her dark hair and wound it about her head, tucking a few violets against the rich plaits, conscious that the classic simplicity of the arrangement enhanced her beauty, and was pleased in his pleasure.

It suited her whim to carry out the little affectation in her soaps and toilet waters; he could not pick up her handkerchief or hold her wrap for her without freeing the delicate faint odor of her favorite flower. When they met downtown for dinner there was always the little ceremony of finding the florist, and all the operas this winter were mingled for Rachael with the most exquisite fragrance in the world.

These days were perfect. It was only when the outside world entered their paradise that anything less than perfect happiness entered, too. Rachael's old friends--Judy Moran, Elinor, and the Villalongas--said, and said with truth, that she had changed. She had not tried to change, but it was hard for her to get the old point of view now, to laugh at the old jokes, to listen to the old gossip. She had been cold and wretched only a year before, but she had had the confident self-sufficiency of a gypsy who walks bareheaded and irresponsible through a world whose treasure will never come her way. Now Rachael, tremulous and afraid, was the guardian of the great treasure, she knew now what love meant, and she could no longer face even the thought of a life without love.

Tirelessly, and with increasing satisfaction, she studied her husband's character, finding, like all new wives, that almost all her preconceived ideas of him had been wrong. Like all the world, she had always fancied Greg something of an autocrat, positive almost to stubbornness in his views.

Now it was amusing to discover that he was really a rather mild person, except where his work was concerned, rarely taking the initiative in either praising or blaming anybody or anything, deeply influenced by the views of other persons, and content to be rather a listener and onlooker than an active participant in what did not immediately concern him. Rachael found this, for some subtle reasons of her own, highly pleasing. It made her less afraid of her husband's criticism, and spared her many of those tremors common to the first months of married life. Also, it gave her an occasional chance to influence him, even to protect him from his own indifference to this issue or that.

She laughed at him, accusing him of being an impostor. Why, everyone thought Dr. Warren Gregory, with his big scowl and his firm-set jaw, was an absolute Tartar, she exulted, when as a matter of fact he was only a little boy afraid of his wife! He hated, she learned, to be uncertain as to just the degree of dressing expected of him on different occasions, he hated to enter hotels by the wrong doors, to hear her dispraise an opera generally approved, or find good in a book branded by the critics as worthless. With all his pride in her beauty, he could not bear to have her conspicuous; if her laughter or her unusual voice attracted any attention in a public place, she could see that it made him uncomfortable. These things Rachael might have considered flaws in another man. In Warren they were only deliciously amusing, and his reliance upon her, where she had expected only absolute self-possession from him, seemed to make him more her own.

Rachael, daughter of wandering adventurers, had a thousand times more assurance than he. In her secret heart she had no regard for any social law; society was a tool to be used, not a weight under which one struggled helplessly. She dictated where he followed precedent; she laughed where he was filled with apprehension. Seriously, she set her wits and her love to the task of accustoming him to joy, and day by day he flung off the old, half-defined reluctances that still bound him, and entered more fully into the delights of the care-free, radiant hours that lay before them.

His wife saw the change in him, and rejoiced. But what she did not see, as the months went on, was the no less marked change in herself. As Warren's nature expanded, and as he began to reach quite naturally for the various pleasures all about him, Rachael's soul experienced an alteration almost directly opposed.

She became thoughtful, almost reserved, she began to show a certain respect for convention--not for the social conventions at which she had always laughed, and still laughed, but for the fundamental laws of truth, simplicity, and cleanness, upon which the ideal of civilization, at least, is based. She noticed that she was beginning to like "good" persons, even homely, dowdy, good persons, like Alice and George Valentine. She lost her old appetite for scandal, for ugly stories, for reckless speech.

Warren, freed once and for all from his old prejudice, found nothing troublesome now in the thought that she had been another man's wife; it was a common situation, it was generally approved. As in other things, he had had stupidly conventional ideas about it once--that was all. But Rachael winced at the sound of the word "divorce," not because of her own divorce, but at the thought that some other man and woman had promised in their first love what later they could not fulfil, and hated each other now where they had loved each other once, at the thought that perhaps--perhaps one of them loved the other still!

"Divorce is--monstrous," she said soberly to her husband in one of their hours of perfect confidence.

"How can we say it, of all persons, my darling? Don't be hidebound!"

"No," she smiled reluctantly, "I suppose we can't. But--but I never feel like a divorced woman, Warren, I feel like a different woman, but not as if that term fitted me. It sounds so--coarse. Don't you think it does?"

"No, I never thought of it quite that way. Everyone makes mistakes," he answered cheerfully.

"Don't you care--that it's true of me?" she asked.

"Are you trying to make me jealous, you gypsy!" he laughed. But there was no answering laughter in her face.

"Yes, perhaps I am," she admitted, as if she were a little surprised that it was so. And in her next slowly worded sentence she discovered for herself another truth. "I mind it, Warren!" she said. "I wish, with all my heart, that it wasn't so!"

"That isn't very consistent, sweet. Your life made you what you were, the one woman in the world I could ever have loved. Why quarrel with the process?"

"I wish you cared!" she said wistfully.

"Cared?"

"Yes--suffered over it--objected. Then I could keep proving to you that I never in my life loved anyone, man, woman, or child, until now!"

"But I believe that, my darling!"

She smiled at his wide, innocent look, a mother's amused yet hopeless smile, and as they rose from their late luncheon he put his arm about her and tipped her beautiful face up toward his own.

"Don't you realize, my darling, that just as you are, you are perfect to me--not nearly perfect, or ninety-nine per cent. perfect, but pressed down and running over, a thousand per cent., a million per cent.?" he asked.

Her dark beauty glowed; she was more lovely than ever in her exquisite content.

"Oh, Warren, if you'd only say that to me over and over!" she begged.

"Dear Heaven, hear the woman! What else DO I do?"

"Oh, I don't mean now. I mean always, all through our lives. It's ALL I want to hear!"

"Do you realize that you are an absolute--little--tyrant?" he asked, laughing. Radiantly she laughed back.

"I only realize one thing in these days," she answered; "I only live for one thing!"

It was true. The world for her now was all in her husband, his smile was her light, and she lived almost perpetually in the sunshine. When they were parted--and they were never long parted--the memory of this glance or that tone, this eager phrase or that sudden laugh, was enough to keep her happy. When they met again, whether she came to meet him in his own hallway, or rose, lovely in her furs, and walked toward him in some restaurant or hotel, joy lent her a new and almost fearful beauty. To dress for him, to make him laugh, to hold his interest, this was all that interested her, and for the world outside of their own house she cared not at all. They had their own vocabulary, their own phrases for moments of mirth or tenderness; among her gowns he had his favorites. among the many expressions of his sensitive face there were some that it was her whimsical pleasure always to commend. Their conversation, as is the way with lovers, was all of themselves, and all of praise.

Long before they were ready for the world it began to make its demands. Rachael loved her own home--they had chosen a large duplex apartment on Riverside Drive--loved the memorable little meals they had before the fire, the lazy, enchanting hours of reading or of music in the big studio that united the two large floors, the scent of her husband's cigar, the rustle of her own gown, the snow slipping and lisping against the window, and it was with great reluctance that she surrendered even one evening. But there was hospitable Vera Villalonga and her dreadful New Year's dance, and there were the Bowditch dinner and the Hoyt dinner and the Parmalee's dance for Katrina. Unwillingly the beautiful Mrs. Gregory yielded to the swift current, and presently they were caught in the rush of the season, and could not have withdrawn themselves except for serious cause.

Rachael smiled a little wryly one morning over Mrs. George Valentine's cordially worded invitation to an informal dinner, but she accepted it as a matter of course, and wore her most beautiful gown. She deliberately set out to capture her hostess' friendship, and simple, sweet Mrs. Valentine could not long resist her guest's beauty and charm--such a young, fresh creature as she was, not a bit one's idea of an adventuress, so genuinely interested in the children, so obviously devoted to Warren.

Rachael, on her side, contemplated the Valentines with deep interest. She found them a rather puzzling study, unlike any married couple that she had ever chanced to know. Alice was one of those good, homely, unfashionable women who seem utterly devoid of the instinct for dressing properly. Her masses of dull brown hair she wore strained from her high forehead and wound round her head in a fashion hopelessly obsolete. Her evening gown, of handsome gray silk, was ruined by those little fussy touches of lace and ruffling that brand a garment instantly as "homemade."

George was one of the plainest of men, shy, awkward, insignificant looking, with a long-featured, pleasant face, and red hair. Warren had told his wife at various times that George was "a prince," and physically, at least, Rachael found him disappointing, especially beside her own handsome husband. She knew he was clever, with a large practice besides his work as head surgeon at one of the big hospitals, but Warren had added to this the information that George was a poor business man, and ill qualified to protect his own interests.

Yet, in his own home--a handsome and yet shabby brownstone house in the West Fifties--he appeared to better advantage. There was a brightness in his plain face when he looked at his wife, and an adoring response in her glance that after twelve years of married life seemed admirable to Rachael. "Alice" was a word continually on his lips; what Alice said and thought and did was evidently perfection. Before the Gregorys had been ten minutes in the house on their first visit he had gone downstairs to inspect the furnace, wound and set a stopped clock, answered the telephone twice, and fondly carried upstairs a refractory four-year-old girl, who came boldly down in her nightgown, with reproaches and requests. On his return from this trip he brought down the one-year-old baby, another girl, delicious in the placid hour between supper and bed, and he and his wife and Warren Gregory exchanged admiring glances as the beautiful Mrs. Gregory took the child delightedly in her arms, contrasting her own dark and glowing loveliness with the tiny Katharine's gold and roses.

It was a quiet evening, but Rachael liked it. She liked their simple, affectionate talk, their reminiscences, the serenity of the large, plainly furnished rooms, the glowing of coal fires in the old-fashioned steel-barred grates. She liked Alice Valentine's placidity, the sureness of herself that marked this woman as more highly civilized than so many of the other women Rachael knew. There was none of Judy's and Gertrude's and Vera's excitability and restlessness here. Alice was concerned neither with her own appearance nor her own wants; she was free to comment with amusement or wonder or admiration upon larger affairs. Rachael wondered, as beautiful women have wondered since time began, what held this man so tightly to this mild, plain woman, and by what special gift of the gods Alice Valentine might know herself secure beyond all question in a world of beauty and charm and youth.

"Well, what d'you think of her, Alice?" Doctor Gregory had asked proudly when his wife was on his arm and leave-taking was in order.

"Think you're lucky, Greg," Mrs. Valentine answered earnestly. "You've got a dear, good, lovely wife!"

"And you are going to let me come and make friends with the boy and the girls some afternoon?" Rachael asked.

"If you WILL," their mother said, and she and Rachael kissed each other. Gregory chuckled, in high feather, all the way home.

"You're a wonder, Ladybird! I have NEVER seen you sweeter nor prettier than you were to-night!"

Rachael leaned back in the car with a long, contented sigh.

"One can see that she was all ready to hate me, Greg; a woman who had been married, and who snapped up her favorite bachelor--"

He laughed triumphantly. "She doesn't hate you now!"

"No, and I'll see to it that she never does. She's my sort of woman, and the children are absolute loves! I like that sort of old-fashioned prejudice-

-honestly I do--that honor-thy-father-and-thy-mother-and-keep holy-the-sabbath-day sort of person. Don't you, Greg?"

"We--ll, I don't like narrowness, sweet."

"No." Rachael pondered in the dark. "Yet if you're not narrow you seem to be--really the only word for it is--loose," she submitted. "Somehow lately, a great many persons--the girls I know--do seem to be a little bit that way."

"You don't find THEM judging you!" her husband said. Rachael answered only by a rather faint negative; she would not elucidate further. This was one of the things she could never tell Warren, a thing indeed that she would hardly admit to her own soul.

But she said to herself that she knew now the worst evil of divorce. She knew that it coarsened whomever it touched, that it irresistibly degraded, that it lowered all the human standard of goodness and endurance, and self-sacrifice. However justified, it was an evil; however properly consummated, it soiled the little group it affected. The disinclination of a good woman like Alice Valentine to enter into a close friendship with a younger and richer and more beautiful woman whose history was the history of Rachael Gregory was no mere prejudice. It was the feeling of a restrained and disciplined nature for an unchecked and ill-regulated one; it was the feeling of a woman who, at any cost, had kept her solemn marriage vow toward a woman who had broken her word.

Rachael was beginning to find it more comprehensible, even more acceptable, than the attitude of her own old world. Fresh from the Eden that was her life with Warren, she had turned back to the friends whose viewpoint had been hers a few months ago.

Were they changed, or was she? Both were changed, she decided. She had been a cold queen among them once, flattered by their praise and laughter, reckless in speech, and almost as reckless in action. But now her only kingdom was in Warren Gregory's heart. She had no largesse for these outsiders; she could not answer them with her old quick wit now; indeed she hardly heard them. And on their side, where once there had been that certain deference due to the woman who, however wretched and neglected, was still Clarence Breckenridge's wife, now she noticed, with quick shame, a familiarity, a carelessness, that indicated plainly exactly the fine claim to delicacy that she had forfeited. Her position in every way was better now than it had been then. But in some subtle personal sense she had lost caste. A story was ventured when she chanced to be alone with Frank Whittaker and George Pomeroy that her presence would have forbidden in the old days, and Allen Parmalee gave her a sensation of absolute sickness by merrily introducing her to his sister from Kentucky with the words: "Don't stare at her so hard, Bess! Of course you remember her: she was Mrs. Breckenridge last year, but now she's making a much better record as Mrs. Gregory!"

The women were even more frank; Clarence's name was often mentioned in her presence; she was quite simply congratulated and envied.

"My dear," said Mrs. Cowles, at a women's luncheon, "you were extraordinarily clever, of course, but don't forget that you were extremely lucky, too. Clarence making no fuss, taking all the trouble to provide the evidence, and Greg being only too anxious to step into his shoes, made it easy for you!"

"I'm no prude," Rachael smiled, over a raging heart. "But I couldn't see this coming, nobody did. All I could do was to break free before my self-respect was absolutely gone!"

"Go tell that to the White Wings, darling," laughed Mrs. Villalonga, lazily blowing smoke into rings and spirals.

"Seriously, Vera, I mean it!"

"Seriously, Rachael, do you mean to tell me that you hadn't the SLIGHTEST idea--" Mrs. Villalonga roused herself, to smilingly study the other woman's face as she asked the question. "Not a word--not a HINT?"

"Ah, well--" Rachael's face was flaming. She would have put her hand in the fire to be able to say "No." The others laughed cheerfully.

"Nobody misunderstands you, dear: you were in a rotten fix and you got out of it nicely," said fat Mrs. Moran, and Mrs. Villalonga added consolingly: "Why, my heavens, Rachael, I'd leave Booth to-morrow for anyone half as handsome as Warren Gregory!"

In March the Gregorys sent out cards for their first really large entertainment, a Mardi-Gras ball. Rachael and Warren spent many happy hours planning it: the studio was to be cleared, two other big rooms turned into one for the supper, music for dancing, musical numbers for the entertainment; it would be perfect in every detail, one of the notable affairs of the winter. Rachael hailed it as the end of the season. They were to make a flying trip to the Bermudas in April, and after that Rachael happily planned a month or two in the almost deserted city before Warren would be free to get away to the mountains or the boat. It was with a delightful sense of freedom that she realized that her first winter in her new role was nearly over. Next winter her divorce and remarriage would be an old story, there would be other gossip more fascinating and more new, she would be taken quite for granted. Again, she might more easily evade the social demand next winter without exposing herself to the charge of being fickle or changed. This year her brave and dignified facing of the world had been a part of the price she paid for her new happiness. Now it was paid.

And for another reason, half-defined, Rachael was glad to see the months go by. She had been Warren Gregory's wife for nearly six months now, and the rapture of being together was still as great for them both as it had been in the first radiant days of their marriage. For herself, indeed, she knew that the joy was constantly deepening, and even the wild hunger and passion of her heart could find no flaw in his devotion. Her surrender to him was with a glorious and unashamed completeness, the tones of her extraordinary voice deepened when she spoke to him, and in her eyes all who looked might read the story of insatiable and yet satisfied love.

CHAPTER II

Plans for the big dance presently began to move briskly, and there was much talk of the affair. As hostess, Rachael would not mask, nor would Warren, but they were already amusing themselves with the details of elaborate costumes. Warren's rather stern and classic beauty was to be enhanced by the blue and buff of an officer of the Revolution, fine ruffles falling at wrist and throat, wide silver buckles on square-toed shoes, and satin ribbon tying his white wig. Rachael, separately tempted by the thought of Dutch wooden shoes and of the always delightful hoop skirts, eventually abandoned both because it was not possible historically to connect either costume with the one upon which Warren had decided. She eventually determined to be the most picturesque of Indian maidens, with brown silk stockings disappearing into moccasins, exquisite beadwork upon her fringed and slashed skirt, feathers in her loosened hair, and a small but matchless tiger skin, strapped closely across her back, to lend a touch of distinction to the costume.

On the Monday evening before the dance she tried on her regalia and appeared before her husband and three or four waiting dinner guests, so exquisite a vision of glowing and radiant beauty that their admiration was almost a little awed. Her cheeks were crimson between her loosened rich braids of hair; her eyes shone deeply blue, and the fantastic costume, with its fluttering strips of leather and richly colored wampum, gave an extraordinary quality of youth and almost of frailty to her whole aspect.

"The woman just sent this home. I couldn't resist showing you!" said Rachael, in a shower of compliments. "Isn't my tiger a darling? Warren went six hundred and seventy-two places to catch him. Of course there never was a stripey tiger like this in North America but what care I? I'm only a poor little redskin; a trifling inconsistency like that doesn't worry ME!"

"Me taky you my wikiup-HUH!" said Frank Whittaker invitingly. "You my squaw?"

"Come here, Hattie Fishboy," said her husband, catching her by the arm. His face showed no more than an amused indulgence to her caprice, but Rachael knew he was pleased. "Well, when you first planned this outfit I thought it was going to be an awful mess," said he, turning her slowly about. "But it isn't so bad!"

"Isn't so bad!" Mrs. Bowditch said scornfully; "it's the loveliest thing I ever saw. I'll tell you what, Rachael, if you come down to Easthampton this summer we'll have a play, and you can be an Indian--"

"I'd love it," Rachael said, and making a deep bow before her husband she added: "I'll be Squaw-Afraid-of-Her-Man!"

She heard them laughing as she ran upstairs to change to a more conventional dress.

"Etta," said she, consigning the Indian costume to her maid, "I'm too happy to live!"

Etta, one of those homely, conscientious women who extract in some mysterious way an actual pride and pleasure from the beauty of the women whom they serve, smiled faintly and dully.

"The weather's getting real nice now," she submitted, as one who will not discourage a worthy emotion.

Rachael laughed out joyously. The next instant she had flung up a window and leaned out in the spring darkness. Trees on the drive were rustling over pools of light, a lighted steamboat went slowly up the river, the brilliant eyes of motor cars curved swiftly through the blackness. A hurdy-gurdy, guarded by two shadowy forms, was pouring out a wild jangle of sound from the curb. When the window was shut, a moment later, the old Italian man and woman who owned the musical instrument decided that they must mark this apartment house for many a future visit, and, chattering hopefully, went upon their way. The belladonna in the spangled gown, who had looked down upon them for a brief interval, meanwhile ran down to her guests.

She was in wild spirits, inspired with her most enchanting mood; for an hour or two there was no resisting her. Mrs. Whittaker and Mrs. Bowditch fell as certainly under her spell as did the three men. "She really HAS changed since she married Greg," said Louise Bowditch to Mrs. Whittaker; "but it's all nonsense--this talk about her being no more fun! She's more fun than ever!"

"She's prettier than ever," Gertrude Whittaker said with a sigh.

The next afternoon, a dreary, wet afternoon, at about four o'clock, Warren Gregory stepped out of the elevator, and quietly admitted himself to his own hallway with a latchkey. It was an unusual hour for the doctor to come home, and in the butler's carefully commonplace tone as he answered a few questions Warren knew that he knew.

The awning had been stretched across the sidewalk, caterers' men were in possession, the lovely spacious rooms were full of flowers; the big studio had been emptied of furniture, there were great palms massed in the musicians' corner; maids were quietly busy everywhere; no eye met the glance of the man of the house as he went upstairs.

He found Mrs. Gregory alone in her own luxurious room. No one who had seen her in the excited beauty of the night before would have been likely to recognize her now. She was pale, tense, and visibly nervous, wrapped in a great woolly robe, as if she were cold, and with her hair bound carelessly and tightly back as a woman binds it for bathing.

"You've seen it?" she said instantly, as her husband came in.

"George called my attention to it; I came straight home. I knew"--he was kneeling beside her, one arm about her, all his tenderness and devotion in his face--"I knew you'd need me."

She laid an arm about his neck, sighed deeply, but continued to stare distractedly beyond him.

"Warren, what shall we do?" she said with a certain vagueness and brokenness in her manner that he found very disquieting.

"Do, sweetheart?" he echoed at a loss.

"With all those people coming to-night," she added, mildly impatient.

"Why, what CAN we do, dear?"

"You don't mean," Rachael said incredulously, "that we shall have to GO ON with it?"

"Think a minute, dearest. Why shouldn't we?"

"But"--her color, better since his entrance, was waning again--"with Clarence Breckenridge dying while we dance!" she shuddered.

"Could anything be more preposterous than your letting anything that concerns Clarence Breckenridge affect what you do now?" he asked with kindly patience.

"No, it's not that!" she answered feverishly. "But--but for any old friend one would--would make a difference, and surely--surely he was more than that!"

"He WAS more than that, of course, but he has been less than nothing to you for a long time!"

"Yes, legally--technically, of course," Rachael agreed nervously. She sat silent for a moment, frowning over some sombre thought. "But, Warren, they'll all know of it, they'll all be THINKING of it," she said presently. "I--really I don't think I can go through it!"

"It's too bad, of course," Warren Gregory said with his arm still about her. "I'd give ten thousand dollars to have had the poor fellow select some other time. But you've had nothing to do with it, and you simply must put it out of your mind!"

"It was Billy's marriage, of course!"

"Of course. She was married yesterday, you see, the day she came of age. Poor kid--it's rather a sad start for her, especially with no one but Joe Pickering to console her!"

"She was mad about her father," Rachael said in a preoccupied whisper. "Poor Billy--poor Billy! She never crossed him in anything but this. What did you see it in?"

"The World. How did you hear it?"

"Etta brought up the paper." She closed her eyes and leaned back in her chair. "It seemed to jump at me--his picture and the name. Is he living--where is he?"

"At St. Mark's. He won't live. Poor fellow!" Warren Gregory scowled thoughtfully as he gave a moment's thought to the other man's situation, and then smiled sunnily at his wife with a brisk change of topic. "Well," he said cheerfully, "is anyone in this place glad to see me, or not, or what?"

"It just seems to me that I CANNOT face all those people to-night!" Rachael said, giving him a quick, unthinking kiss before she gently put him away from her, and got to her feet. "It seems so wrong--so coarse--to be utterly and totally indifferent to the man who was my husband a year ago. I don't love him, he is nothing to me, but it's all wrong, this way. If it was Peter Pomeroy or Joe Butler, of COURSE we'd put off our dance--Warren," she turned to him with sudden hope in her eyes, "do you suppose anybody'll come?"

"My dear girl," he said, displeased, "why are you working yourself into a fever over this? It's most unfortunate, but as far as you're concerned, it's unavoidable, and you'll simply have to put a brave face on it, and get through it SOMEHOW! I am absolutely confident that when you've pulled yourself together you'll come through with flying colors. Of course everyone'll come; this is their chance to show you exactly how little they ever think of you as Breckenridge's wife! And this is your chance, too, to act as if you'd never heard of him. Dash it! it does spoil our little party, but it can't be helped!"

"Do you suppose Billy's with him?" Rachael asked, her absent, glittering eyes fixed upon her own person as she sat before her mirror.

"Oh, no--she and Pickering sailed yesterday for England--that's the dreadful thing for her. Clarence evidently spent the whole night at the club, sitting in the library, thinking. Berry Stokes went in for his mail after the theatre, and they had a little talk. He promised to dine there to-night. At about ten this morning Billings, the steward there, saw old Maynard going out--Maynard's one of the directors--and asked him if he wouldn't please go and speak to Mr. Breckenridge. Mayn went over to him, and Clarence said, 'Anything you say--'"

Rachael gave a gasp that was like a shriek, and put her two elbows on the dressing-table, and her face in her hands. It was Clarence's familiar phrase.

"Oh, don't--don't--don't--Greg!"

"Well, that was all there was to it," her husband said, watching her anxiously. "He had the thing in his pocket. He stood up--everybody heard it. Fellows came rushing in from everywhere. They got him to a hospital."

"Florence is with him, of course?"

"Florence is at Palm Beach."

"Then who IS with him, Greg?"

"My dear girl, how do I know? It's none of my affair!"

Rachael sat still for perhaps two minutes, while her husband, ostentatiously cheerful, moved about the room selecting a change of clothes.

"To-morrow you can take it as hard as you like, sweet," said he. "But to-night you'll have to face the music! Now get into something warm--it's a little cool out--and I'll take you for a spin, and we'll have dinner somewhere. Then we'll get back here about eight o'clock, and take our time dressing."

"Yes, I'll do that," Rachael agreed automatically. A moment later she said urgently: "Warren, isn't there a chance that I'm right about this? Mightn't it be better simply to telephone everyone that the dance is postponed? Make it next week, or Mi-Careme--anything. If they talk--let them! I don't care what they say. They'll talk anyway. But every fibre of my being, every delicate or decent instinct I ever had, rebels against this. Say I'm not well, and let them buzz! I know what you are going to say--I know that it would SEEM less sensitive, less fine, to mourn for one man while I'm another man's wife, than to absolutely ignore what happens to him, but you know what's the truth! I never loved him, and I love every hair of your head--you know that. Only--"

She stopped short, baffled by the difficulty of expressing herself accurately.

"If you really love me, do what I ask you to-night," Warren Gregory said firmly.

His wife sat as if turned to stone for only a few seconds. When she spoke it was naturally and cheerfully.

"I'll be ready in no time, dear. Where are we to dine?" She glanced at her little crystal clock as she spoke, as if she were computing casually the length of the drive before dinner. But what she said in her heart was, "At this time to-morrow it will all have been over for many hours!"

A few days later the Gregorys sailed for Bermuda, Rachael with a sense of whipped and smarting shame that was all the more acute because she could not share it with this dearest comrade and confidant. Warren thought indeed that the miserable episode of the past week had been dismissed from her mind, and delighting like a boy in the little holiday, and proud of his beautiful wife, he found their hours at sea cloudless. With two men, whose acquaintance was made on the steamer, they played bridge, and Rachael's game drew other players from all sides to watch her leads and grin over her bidding. They walked up and down the deck for hours together, they lay side by side in deck chairs lazily watching the blue water creep up and down the painted white ropes of the rail; but they never spoke of Clarence Breckenridge.

The Mardi-Gras dance had been like a hideous dream to Rachael. She had known that it would be hard from the first sick moment in which the significance of Clarence's suicide had rushed upon her. She had known that her arriving guests would be gay and conversational, that the dance and the supper would go with a dash and swing which no other circumstance could more certainly have assured for them; and she knew that in every heart would be the knowledge that Clarence Breckenridge was dying by his own hand, and his daughter on the ocean, and that this woman in the Indian dress, with painted lips and a tiger skin outlining her beautiful figure, had been his wife.

This she had expected, and this was as she had expected. But there were other circumstances that made her feel even more acutely the turn of the screw. Joe Butler, always Clarence's closest friend, did not come to the dance, and at about twelve o'clock an innocent maid delivered to Warren a message that several persons besides Warren heard: "Mr. Butler to speak to you on the telephone, Doctor Gregory."

Everyone could surmise where Joe Butler was, but no one voiced the supposition. Warren, handsome in his skirted coat, knee breeches, and ruffles, disappeared from the room, and the dancing went on. The scene was unbelievably brilliant, the hot, bright air sweet with flowers and perfume, and the more subtle odors of silk and fine linen and powder on delicate skin. Warren was presently among them again, and there was a supper, the hostess' lovely face showing no more strain or concern than was natural to a woman eager to make comfortable nearly a hundred guests.

After supper there was more dancing, and an augmented gayety. There were no more telephone messages, nor was there any definite foundation for the rumor that was presently stealthily circulating. Women, powdering their noses as they waited for their wraps, murmured it in the dressing-rooms; a clown, smoking in the hall, confided it to a Mephistopheles; a pastry cook, after his effusive good-nights, confirmed it as he climbed into the motorcar that held the Pierrette who was his wife: "Dead, poor fellow!"

"Dead, poor Clarence!" said Mrs. Prince, magnificent as Queen Elizabeth, as she and Elinor Vanderwall went downstairs. She had once danced a fancy dance with him more than twenty years ago. "Awful!" said Elinor, shuddering.

After the last guest was gone Warren telephoned to the hospital, Rachael, a little tired and pale in the Indian costume, watching and listening tensely. She was sick at heart. Even into the library, where they stood, the Mardi-Gras disorder had penetrated: a blue silk mask was lying across Warren's blotter, a spatter of confetti lay on the polished floor, and on the reading table was a tray on which were two glasses through whose amber contents a lazy bubble still occasionally rose. The logs that had snapped in the fireplace were gone, only gray ashes remained, and to Rachael, at least, the room's desolation and disorder seemed to typify her own state of mind.

She could tell from Warren's look that he found the whole matter painful and distasteful to an almost unbearable degree; on his handsome serious face was an expression of grim endurance, of hurt yet dignified protest against events. He did not blame her, how could he blame her? But he was suffering in every fibre of his sensitive soul at this sordid notoriety, at this blatant voicing of a hundred ugly whispers in a matter so closely touching the woman he loved.

"Dead?" Rachael said quietly, when his brief conversation was over.

Warren Gregory, setting the telephone back upon the desk, nodded gravely.

Rachael made no comment. For a moment her eyes widened nervously, and a little shudder rippled through her. Then silently she gathered up the leather belt and chains of beads that she had been loosening as she listened, and slowly went toward the door.

They did not speak again of Clarence that night, although they chatted easily for the next hour on other topics, even laughing a little as the various episodes of the evening were passed in review.

But Rachael did not sleep, nor did she sleep during the long hours of the following night. On the third night she wakened her husband suddenly from his sleep.

"Greg--Greg! Won't you talk to me a little? I'm going mad, I think!"

"Rachael! What is it?" stammered the doctor, blinking in the dim light of Rachael's bedside lamp. His wife, haggard, with her rich hair falling in two long braids over her shoulders, was sitting on the side of his bed. "What is it, darling--hear something?" he asked, more naturally, putting his arm about her.

"I've been lying awake--and lying awake!" said Rachael, panting. "I haven't shut my eyes--it's nearly three. Greg, I keep seeing it--Clarence's face, you know, with that horrible scar! What shall I do?"

Shivering, gasping, wild-eyed, she clung to him, and for a long hour he soothed her as if she had been an hysterical child. He put her into a comfortable chair, mixed her a sedative, and knelt beside her, slowly winning her back to calm and sanity again. It was terrible, of course, but no one but Clarence himself was to blame, unless it was poor Billy--

"Yes, I must see Billy when she comes back!" Rachael said quickly, when the tranquillizing voice reached this point. If Warren Gregory's quiet mouth registered any opposition, she did not see it, and he did not express it. She was presently sound asleep, still catching a long childish breath as she slept. But she woke smiling, with all the horrid visions of the past few days apparently blotted out, and she and Warren went gayly downtown to get steamer tickets, and buy appropriate frocks and hats for the spring heat of Bermuda.

In midsummer came the inevitable invitation to visit old friends at Belvedere Bay. Rachael was pleased to accept Mrs. Moran's hospitality for a glorious July week. Warren, to her delight, took an eightdays' holiday, and while he looked to his racquet and golf irons she packed her prettiest gowns. Belvedere Bay welcomed them rapturously, and beautiful Mrs. Gregory was the idol of the hour. Mrs. Moulton, giving a tennis tea during this week, duly sent Mrs. Gregory a card. But when society wondering whether Rachael would really be a guest in her own old home, had duly gathered at the Breckenridge house, young Dicky Moran was so considerate as to be flung from his riding-horse. Neither the Gregorys nor the Morans consequently appeared at the tea, but Rachael, meeting all inquirers on the Moran terrace, late in the afternoon, with the news that Dicky was quite all right, no harm done, asked prettily for details of the affair they had missed.

She told herself that the past really made no difference in the radiant present, but she knew it was not so. In a thousand little ways she had lost caste, and she saw it, if Warren did not. A certain bloom was gone. Girls were not quite as deferentially adoring, women were a little less impressed. The old prestige was somehow lessened. She knew that newcomers at the club, struck by her beauty, were a little chilled by her history. She felt the difference in the very air.

In her musings she went over the old arguments hotly. Why was she merely the "divorced Mrs. Gregory?" Why were these casual inquirers not told of Clarence, of her long endurance of neglect and shame? More than once the thought came to her, that if other, events had been as they were, and only the facts of her divorce and remarriage lacking, she would have been Clarence's widow now.

"What's the difference? It all comes out the same!" commented Warren, to whom she confided this thought.

"Then you and I would have been only engaged now," said Rachael, smiling. "And I would like that!"

"You mean you regret your marriage?" he laughed, his arms about her.

"I'd like to live the first days over and over and over again, Greg!" she answered passionately.

"You are an insatiable creature!" he said. But her earnestness was beginning to puzzle him a little. She was too deeply wrapped in her love for her own happiness or his. There was something almost startling in her intensity. She was jealous of every minute that they were apart; she made no secret of her blind adoration.

Warren had at first found this touching; it had humbled him. Later, in the first months of their marriage, he had shared it, and their mutual passion had seemed to them both a source of inexhaustible delight. But now, even while he smiled at her, his keen sensitiveness where her dignity was concerned had shown him that there was in her attitude something a little pitiful, something even a little absurd.

Judy and Gertrude and little Mrs. Sartoris listened interestedly when Rachael talked of Greg, of his likes, his dislikes, his favorite words, his old-maidish way of arranging his ties, his marvellous latest operation. But Warren, watching his wife's flushed, lovely face, wondered if they were laughing at her. He smiled uncomfortably when she interrupted her bridge game to come across the club porch to him, to ask him if the tennis had been good, to warn him that he would catch cold if he did not instantly get out of those wet flannels, to ask Frank Whittaker what he meant by beating her big boy three sets in succession?

"Rachael, I'm dealing for you--come back here!" Gertrude might call.

"Deal away!" Rachael, one hand on Warren's arm, would look saucily at the others over his shoulder. "I like my beau," she would assert brazenly, "and if you say a word more, I'll kiss him here and now!"

They all shrieked derisively when the kiss was duly delivered and Gregory Warren with a self-conscious laugh had escaped to his shower. But Rachael saw nothing absurd; she told Warren that she loved him, and let them laugh if they liked!

"Listen, dearest!" he said on the last night of their stay. "Will you be a darling, and not trail round the links if we play to-morrow?"

"Why not?" asked Rachael absently, fluffing his hair from her point of vantage on the arm of his chair.

"Well, wouldn't you rather stay up on the porch with the girls?"

"If you men want to swear at your strokes, I decline to be a party to it!" Rachael said maternally.

"I know. But, darling, it does rather affect our game," Warren said uncertainly; "that is, you don't play, you see! And it only gets you hot and mussy, and I love my wife to be waiting when we come up. It isn't that I don't think you're a darling to want to do it," he added in hasty concern.

No use. She was deeply hurt. She went to her dressing-table and began her preparations for the night with a downcast face. Certainly she wouldn't bother Warren. She only did it because she loved him so. A tear splashed down on her white hand.

Next day she triumphantly accompanied the golfers. Warren had petted and coaxed her out of her sulks, and she was radiant again. When they had said their good-byes to Judy, and were spinning into town in the car that afternoon, she made him confess that she had not spoiled the game at all; he couldn't make her believe that Frank and Tom and Peter had been pretending their pleasure at having her go along!

But later in the summer she realized that Belvedere Bay was smiling quietly at her bride-like infatuation, and she resented it deeply. The discovery came about on a lazy summer afternoon when several women, Rachael among them, were enjoying gossip and iced drinks on the Parmalees' porch. Rachael had been talking of the emeralds that Warren was having reset for her, and chanced to observe that Tiffany's man had said that Warren's taste in jewelry was astonishing.

"Rachael," yawned little Vivian Sartoris, "for heaven's sake talk about something else than Warren?"

"I talk about him because I like him!" Rachael said. "Better than anybody else in the world."

"And he likes you better than anybody else in the world, I suppose?" Vivian said idly.

"He says so," Rachael answered with a demure smile. "Then that settles it!" Vivian laughed. But she and several of her intimates fell into low conversation, and the older women were presently interrupted by Vivian's voice again. "Rachael!" she challenged, "Katrina says that SHE knows somebody Warren likes as well as he does you!"

"I did not!" protested Katrina, scarlet-cheeked and giggling, giving Vivian, who sat next her on the wide tiled steps, a violent push.

"Oh, you did, too!" one of the group exclaimed.

Katrina murmured something unintelligible.

"Well, that's the same thing!" Vivian assured her promptly. "She says now that Warren DID like her as well, Rachael!"

"Well, don't tell me who it is, and break my heart!" Rachael warned them. But her old sense of humor so far failed her that she could not help adding curiously, "If Warren ever cared for anybody else, he'll tell me!"

There was a general burst of laughter, and Rachael colored.

"No, it's nobody," Katrina said hastily. "It's only idiocy!" She and the other girls laughed in a suppressed fashion for some time. Finally, to Rachael's secret relief, Gertrude Whittaker energetically demanded the secret. More giggling ensued. Then Katrina agreed that she would whisper it in Mrs. Whittaker's ear, which she did. Rachael saw Gertrude color and look puzzled for a second, then she laughed scornfully.

"What geese girls are! I never heard anything so silly!" Gertrude said. Several hours later she told Rachael.

She did not tell her without some hesitation. It was so silly--it was just like that scatter-brained Katrina, she said. Rachael, proudly asserting that nothing Katrina said would make any difference to her, nevertheless urged the confidence.

"Well, it's nothing," Gertrude said at last. "This is what Katrina said: she said that Warren Gregory had liked Rachael Breckenridge as well as he liked Rachael Gregory! That was all."

Rachael looked puzzled in turn for a minute. Then she smiled proudly, and colored.

"But that's not true," she said presently. "For I have never seen a man change as much since marriage as Warren! It's still a perfect miracle to him. He says himself that he gets happier and happier--"

"Oh, Rachael, you're hopeless!" Gertrude laughed, and Rachael colored again. She flushed whenever she thought of this particular visit.

Far happier were the days they spent with the Valentines at Clark's Bar. Rachael loved them all dearly, from little Katharine to the big quiet doctor; she was not misunderstood nor laughed at here.

They swam, tramped, played cards, and talked tirelessly. Rachael slept like a child on the wide, windbathed porch. To the great satisfaction of both doctors she and Alice grew to be devoted friends, and when Warren's holiday was over, Rachael stayed on, for a longer visit, and the men came down in the car on Fridays.

On her birthday this year her husband gave Rachael Gregory, and her heirs and assigns forever, a roomy, plain old colonial farmhouse that stood near Alice's house, in a ring of great elms, looking down on the green level surface of the sea. Rachael accepted it with wild delight. She loved the big, homelike halls, the simple fireplaces, the green blinds that shut a sweet twilight into the empty rooms. Her own barns, her own strip of beach, her own side yard where she and Alice could sit and talk, she took eager possession of them all.

She went into town for chintzes, papers, wicker tables and chairs. She brought old Mrs. Gregory down for the housewarming, and had all the Valentines to dinner on the August evening when the Gregorys moved in. And late that same evening, when Warren's arms were about her, she told him her great news. There were to be little feet running about Home Dunes, and a little voice echoing through the new home. "Shall you be glad, Greg?" she asked, with tears in her eyes; "shall you be just a little jealous?"

"Rachael!" he said in a quick, tense whisper, afraid to believe her. And Rachael, caught in his dear arms, and with his cheek against her wet lashes, felt a triumph and a confidence rise within her, and a glorious content that it was so.

When the happy suspicion was a happy certainty she told his mother, and entered at once into the world of advice and reassurance, planning and speculation that belongs to women alone. Mrs. Valentine was also full of eager interest and counsel, and Rachael enjoyed their solicitude and affection as she had enjoyed few things in life. This was a perfectly natural symptom, that was a perfectly natural phase, she must do this thing, get that, and avoid a third.

The fact that she was not quite herself in soul or body, that she must be careful, must be guarded and saved, was a source of strange and mysterious satisfaction to her as the quick months slipped by. Her increasing helplessness shut her quite naturally away into a world that contained only her husband and herself and a few intimate friends, and Rachael found this absolutely satisfying, and did not miss the social world that hummed on as busily and gayly as ever without her.

Her baby was born in March, a beautiful boy, like his father even in the first few moments of his life. Rachael, whose experience had been, to her astonishment, described complacently by physician and nurses as "perfectly normal," was slow to recover from the experience in body; perhaps never quite recovered in soul. It changed all her values of life--this knowledge of what the coming of a child costs; she told Alice that she was glad of the change.

"What a fool I've been about the shadows," she said. "This is the reality! This counts, as it seems to me that nothing else I ever did in my life counts."

She felt nearer than ever to Warren now, and more dependent upon him. But a new dignity came into her relationship with him: husband and wife, father and mother, they wore the great titles of the world, now!

He found her more beautiful than ever, and as the baby was the centre of her universe, and all her hopes and fears and thoughts for the child, the old bridal attitude toward him vanished forever, and she was the more fascinating for that. His love for her rose like a great flame, and the passionate devotion for which she had been wistfully waiting for months enveloped her now, when, shaken in body and soul, she wished only to devote herself to the miracle that was her child.

When he was but six weeks old James Warren Gregory Third terrified the little circle of his family and friends with a severe touch of summer sickness. The weather, in late April, was untimely--hot and humid--and the baby seemed to suffer from it, even in his airy nursery. There were two hideous days in which he would take no food, and when Rachael heard nothing but the little wailing voice through the long hours. All night she sat beside him, hearing Warren's affectionate protests as little as she heard the dignified remonstrance of the nurse. When day came she was haggard and exhausted, but still she would not leave her baby. She knelt at the crib, impressing the tiny countenance upon mind and heart--her first-born baby, upon whose little features the wisdom of another world still lingered like a light!

Only a few weeks old, and thousands of them older than he died every year! Fear in another form had come to Rachael now--life seemed all fear.

"Oh, Warren, is he very ill?"

"Pretty sick, dear little chap!"

"But, Warren, you don't think--"

"My darling, I don't know!"

She turned desperately to George Valentine when that good friend came in his professional capacity at five o'clock.

"George, there's been a change--I'm sure of it. Look at him!"

"You ought to take better care of your wife, Greg," was Doctor Valentine's quiet almost smiling answer to this. "You'll have her sick next!"

"How is he?" Rachael whispered, as the newcomer bent over the baby. There was a silence.

"Well, my dear," said Doctor Valentine, as he straightened himself, "I believe this little chap has decided to remain with us a little while. Very--much--better!"

Rachael tried to smile, but burst out crying instead, and clung to her husband's shoulder.

"Let him have his sleep out, Miss Snow," said the doctor, "and then sponge him off and try him with food!"

"Oh--yes--yes--yes!" the baby's mother said eagerly, drying her eyes. "And you'll be back later, George?"

"Not unless you telephone me, and I don't think you'll have to," George Valentine said. Rachael's face grew radiant with joy.

"Oh, George, then he is better!" She was breathing like a runner.

"Better! I think he'll be himself to-morrow. Console yourself, my dear Rachael, with the thought that you'll go through this a hundred times with every one of your children!"

"Oh, what a world!" Rachael said, half laughing and half sighing. But later she said to Warren, "Yet isn't it deliciously worth while!"

He had persuaded her to have some supper, and then they had come back to the nursery, to see if the baby really would eat. He had awakened, and had had his bath, and was crying again, but, as Rachael eagerly said, it was a healthy cry. Trembling and smiling, she took the little creature in her arms, and when the busy little lips found her breast, Rachael felt as if she could hardly bear the exquisite incoming rush of joy again.

Warren, watching her, smiled in deep satisfaction, and Miss Snow smiled, too. But before she gave herself up to the luxury of possession the mother's tears fell hot on the baby's delicate gown and tiny face, and from that hour Rachael loved her son with the passionate and intense devotion she felt for his father.

Years later, looking at the pictures they took of him that summer, or perhaps stopped by the sight of some white-coated baby in the street, she would say to herself,--with that little heartache all mothers know, "Ah, but Jim was the darling baby!" After the first scare he bloomed like a rose, a splendid, square, royal boy who laughed joyously when admitted to the company of his family and friends, and lay contentedly dozing and smiling when it seemed good to them to ignore him. Rachael found him the most delightfully amusing and absorbing element her life had ever known; she would break into ecstatic laughter at his simplest feat--when he yawned, or pressed his little downy head against the bars of his crib and stared unsmilingly at her. She would run to the nursery the instant she arrived home, her eager, "How's my boy?" making the baby crow, and struggle to reach her, and it was an event to her to meet his coach in the park, and give him her purse or parasol handle with which to play. Often old Mary, the nurse, would see Mrs. Gregory pick up a pair of tiny white shoes that still bore the imprint of the fat little feet, and touch them to her lips, or catch a crumpled little linen coat from the drawer, and bury her face in it for a moment.

Even in his tiny babyhood he was companionable to his mother, Rachael even consenting to the plan of taking him to Home Dunes in June, although by this arrangement she saw Warren only at week-end intervals until the doctor's vacation came in August. When he came down, and the big car honked at the gate, she invariably had the baby in her arms when she came to meet him.

"Hello, Daddy. Here we are! How are you, dearest?" Rachael would say, adding, before he could answer her: "We want you to notice our chic Italian socks, Doctor Gregory; how's that for five months? Take him, Greg! Go to Daddy, Little Mister!"

"All very well, but how's my wife?" Warren Gregory might ask, kissing her over the baby's bobbing head.

"Lovely! Do you know that your son weighs fifteen pounds--isn't that amazing?" Rachael would hang on his free arm, in happy wifely fashion, as they went back to the house.

"Want to go with me to London?" he asked her one day in the late fall when they were back in town.

"Why not Mars?" she asked placidly, putting a fresh, stiff dress over Jimmy's head.

"No, but I'm serious, my dear girl," Warren Gregory said surprised. "But--I don't understand you. What about Jim?"

"Why, leave him here with Mary. We won't be gone four weeks."

Rachael smiled, but it was an uneasy, almost an affronted, smile.

"Oh, Warren, we couldn't! I couldn't! I would simply worry myself sick!"

"I don't see why. The child would be perfectly safe. George is right here if anything happened!"

"George--but George isn't his mother!" Rachael fell silent, biting her lip, a little shadow between her brows. "What is it--the convention?" she presently asked. "Do you HAVE to go?"

"It isn't absolutely necessary," Warren said dryly. But this was enough for Rachael, who opened the subject that evening when George and Alice Valentine were there.

"George, DOES Warren have to go to this London convention, or whatever it is?"

"Not necessarily," smiled Doctor Valentine. "Why, doesn't he want to go?"

"I don't want him to go!" Rachael asserted.

"It would be a senseless risk to take that baby across the ocean," Alice contributed, and no more was said of the possibility then or at any other time, to Rachael's great content.

But when the winter season was well begun, and Jimmy delicious in his diminutive furs, Doctor Gregory and his wife had a serious talk, late on a snowy afternoon, and Rachael realized then that her husband had been carrying a slight sense of grievance over this matter for many weeks.

He had come in at six o'clock, and was changing his clothes for dinner, half an hour later, when Rachael came into his dressing-room. Her hair had been dressed, and under her white silk wrapper her gold slippers and stockings were visible, but she seemed disinclined to finish her toilette.

"Awful bore!" she said, smiling, as she sat down to watch him.

"What--the Hoyts? Oh, I don't think so!" he answered in surprise.

"They all bore me to death," Rachael said idly. "I'd rather have a chop here with you, and then trot off somewhere all by ourselves! Why don't they leave us alone?"

"My dear girl, that isn't life," Warren Gregory said firmly. His tone chilled her a little, and she looked up in quick penitence. But before she could speak he antagonized her by adding disapprovingly: "I must say I don't like your attitude of criticism and ungraciousness, my dear girl! These people are all our good friends; I personally can find no fault with them. You may feel that you would rather spend all of your time hanging over Jim's crib--I suppose all young mothers do, and to a certain extent all mothers ought to--but don't, for heaven's sake, let everything else slip out of your life!"

"I know, I know!" Rachael said breathlessly and quickly, finding his disapproval almost unendurable. Warren did not often complain; he had never spoken to her in this way before. Her face was scarlet, and she knew that she wanted to cry. "I know, dear," she added more composedly; "I am afraid I do think too much about Jim; I am afraid"--and Rachael smiled a little pitifully--"that I would never want anyone but you and the boy if I had my own way! Sometimes I wish that we could just slip away from everybody and everything, and never see these people again!"

If she had expected him to endorse this radical hope she was disappointed, for Warren responded briskly: "Yes, and we would bore each other to death in two months!"

Rachael was silent, but over the sinking discouragement of her heart she was gallantly forming new resolutions. She would think more of her clothes, she would make a special study of dinners and theatre parties, she would be seen at the opera at least every other week.

"I gave up the London trip just because you weren't enthusiastic," Warren was saying, with the unmistakable readiness of one whose grievances have long been classified in his mind. "It's baby--baby--baby! I don't say much--"

"Indeed you don't!" Rachael conceded gratefully.

"But I think you overdo it, my dear!" finished her husband kindly. Clarence Breckenridge's wife would have assumed a different attitude during this little talk, but Rachael Gregory felt every word like a blow upon her quivering heart. She could not protest, she could not ignore. Her love for him made this moment one of absolute agony, and it was with the humility of great love that she met him more than halfway.

"You're right, of course, Greg, and it must have been stupid for you!" Stupid! It seemed even in this moment treason, it seemed desecration, to use this word of their quiet, wonderful summer together!

"Well," he said, mollified, "don't take what I say too much to heart. It's only that I love my wife, and am proud of her, and I don't want to cut out everything else but Jim's shoes and Mary's day off!" He came over and kissed her, and Rachael clung to him.

"Greg, as if I could be angry with you for being jealous of your son!"

"Trust a woman to put that construction on it," he said, laughing. "You like to think I'm jealous, don't you?"

"I like anything that makes you seem my devoted adorer," Rachael answered wistfully, and smiling whimsically she added, "and I am going to get some new frocks, and give a series of dinners, and win you all over again!"

"Bully!" approved Doctor Gregory, cheerfully going on with his dressing. Rachael watched him thoughtfully for a moment before she went on to her own dressing-room.

Long afterward she remembered that this conversation marked a certain change in her life; it was never quite glad, confident morning again, although for many months no definite element seemed altered. Alice and old Mrs. Gregory had told her, and all the world agreed, that the coming of her child would draw her husband and herself more closely together, but, as Rachael expressed it to herself, it was if she alone moved--moved infinitely nearer to her husband truly, came to depend upon him, to need him as she had never needed him in her life before. But there was always the feeling that Warren had not moved. He stood where he had always been, an eager sympathizer in these new and intense experiences, but untouched and unaltered himself.

For her pain, for her responsibility, for her physical limitations, he had the most intense tenderness and pity, but the fact remained that he might sleep through the nights, enjoy his meals, and play with his baby, when the mood decreed, untroubled by personal handicap.

Rachael, like all women, thought of these things seriously during the first year of her child's life, and in February, when Jimmy was beginning to utter his first delicious, stammering monosyllables, it was with great gravity that she realized that motherhood was approaching her again, that at Thanksgiving she would have a second child. She was wretchedly languid and ill during the entire spring, and found her mother-in-law's and Alice Valentine's calm acceptance of the situation bewildering and discouraging.

"My dear, I don't eat a meal in comfort, the entire time!" Alice said cheerfully. "I mind that more than any other phase!"

"But I am such a broken reed!" Rachael smiled ruefully. "I have no energy!"

The older woman laughed.

"I know, my dear--haven't I been through it all? Just don't worry, and spare Greg what you can--"

Rachael could do neither. She wanted Warren every minute, and she wanted nobody else. Her favorite hours were when she lay on the couch, near the fire, playing with his free hand, while he read to her or talked to her. She wanted to hear, over and over again, that he loved no one else; and sometimes she declined invitations without even consulting him, "because we're happier by our own fire than anywhere else, aren't we, dearest?" "Don't tell me about your stupid operations!" she would smile at him, "talk about--US!"

She went over and over the details of her old life with a certain morbid satisfaction in his constant reassurance. Her marriage had not been the cause of Clarence's suicide, nor of Billy's elopement; she had done her share for them both, more than her share!

Summer came, and she and the baby were comfortably established at Home Dunes. Warren came when he could, perhaps twice a month, and usually without warning. If he promised her the week-ends, she felt aggrieved to have him miss one, so he wired her every day, and sent her books and fruit, letters and magazines every week, and came at irregular intervals. Alice and George Valentine and their children, her garden, her baby, and the ocean she loved so well must fill this summer for Rachael.

CHAPTER III

The beautiful Mrs. Gregory made her first appearance in society, after the birth of her second son, on the occasion of Miss Leila Buckney's marriage to Mr. Parker Hoyt. The continual postponement of this event had been a standing joke among their friends for two or three years; it took place in early December, at the most fashionable of all the churches, with a reception and supper to follow at the most fashionable of all the hotels. Leila naturally looked tired and excited; she had made a gallant fight for her lover, for long years, and she had won, but as yet the returning tide of comfort and satisfaction had not begun in her life. Parker had been a trying fiance; he was a cool-blooded, fishlike little man; there had been other complications: her father's heavy financial losses, her mother's discontent in the lingering engagement, her sister's persisting state of unmarriedness.

However, the old aunt was at last dead. Parker had dutifully gone to her side toward the end, and had returned again, duly, bringing the casket, and escorting Miss Clay. And now Mamma was dressed, and Edith was in a hideously unbecoming green and silver gown, and the five bridesmaids were duly hatted and frocked in green and silver, and she was dressed, too, realizing that her new corsets were a trifle small, and her lace veil too heavy.

And the disgusting caterer had come to some last-moment agreement with Papa whereby they were to have the supper without protest, and the florist's insolent man had consented to send the bouquets at last. The fifteen hundred dreadful envelopes were all addressed, the back-breaking trying-on of gowns was over, the three hundred and seventy-one gifts were arranged in two big rooms at the hotel, duly ticketed, and the three hundred and seventy-one dreadful personal notes of thanks had been somehow scribbled off and dispatched. Leila was absolutely exhausted, and felt as pale and pasty as she looked. People were all so stupid and tiresome and inconsiderate, she said wearily to herself, and the awful breakfast would be so long and dull, with everybody saying the same thing to her, and Parker trying to be funny and simply making himself ridiculous! The barbarity of the modern wedding impressed itself vaguely upon the bride as she laughed and talked in a strained and mechanical manner, and whatever they said to her and to her parents, the guests were afterward unanimous in deciding that poor Leila had been an absolute fright.

But Mrs. Gregory, in her dark blue suit and her new sables, won everybody's eyes as she came down the church aisle with her husband beside her. Her son was not quite a month old, and if she had not recovered her usual wholesome bloom, there was a refined, almost a spiritual, element in her beauty now that more than made up for the loss. She wore a fragrant great bunch of violets at her breast, and under the sweeping brim of her hat her beautiful eyes were as deeply blue as the flowers. She seemed full of a new wifely and matronly charm to-day, and it was quite in key with the pose that old Mrs. Gregory and young Charles should be constantly in her neighborhood. Her relatives with her, her babies safe at home, young Mrs. Gregory was the personification of domestic dignity and decorum.

At the hotel, after the wedding, she was the centre of an admiring group, and conscious of her husband's approving eyes, full of her old brilliant charm. All the old friends rallied about her--they had not seen much of her since her marriage--and found her more magnetic than ever. The circumstances of her marriage were blotted out by more recent events now: there was the Chase divorce to discuss; the Villalonga motor-car accident; Elinor Vanderwall had astonished everybody a few weeks before by her sudden marriage to millions in the person of old Peter Pomeroy; now people were beginning to say that Jeanette Vanderwall might soon be expected to follow suit with Peter's nephew George. The big, beautifully decorated reception-room hummed with gay gossip, with the tinkling laughter of women and the deeper tones of men.

Caterers' men began to work their way through the crush, bearing indiscriminately trays of bouillon, sandwiches, salads, and ices. The bride, with her surrounding bridesmaids, was still standing at the far end of the room mechanically shaking hands, and smilingly saying something dazed and inappropriate to her friends as they filed by; but now various groups, scattered about the room, began to interest themselves in the food. Elderly persons, after looking vaguely about for seats, disposed of their coffee and salad while standing, and soon there was a general breaking-up; the Buckney-Hoyt wedding was almost a thing of the past.

Rachael, thinking of the impending dinner-hour of little Gerald Fairfax Gregory, began to watch the swirling groups for Warren. They could slip away now, surely; several persons had already gone. Her heart was in her nursery, where Jim was toddling back and forth tirelessly in the firelight, and where, between the white bars of the new crib, was the tiny roll of snowy blankets that enclosed the new baby.

"That's a pretty girl," she found herself saying involuntarily as her absent eyes were suddenly arrested by the face and figure of one of the guests. "I wonder who that is?"

The brown eyes she was watching met hers at the same second, and smiling a little question, their owner came toward her.

"Hello, Rachael," the girl said. "How are you after all these years?"

"Magsie Clay!" Rachael exclaimed, the look of uncertainty on her face changing to one of pleasure and welcome. "Well, you dear child, you! How are you? I knew you were here, and yet I couldn't place you. You've changed--you're thinner."

"Oh, much thinner, but then I was an absolute butterball!" Miss Clay said. "Tell me about yourself. I hear that you're having a baby every ten minutes!"

"Not quite!" Rachael said, laughing, but a little discomposed by the girl's coolness. "But I have two mighty nice boys, as I'll prove to you if you'll come see me!"

"Don't expect me to rave over babies, because I don't know anything about them," said Magsie Clay, with a slow, drawling manner that was, Rachael decided, effective. "Do they like toys?"

"Jimmy does, the baby is rather young for tastes of any description," Rachael answered with an odd, new sense of being somehow sedate and old-fashioned beside this composed young woman. Miss Clay was not listening. Her brown eyes were moving idly over the room, and now she suddenly bowed and smiled.

"There's Greg!" she said. "What a comfort it is to see a man dress as that man dresses!"

"I've been looking for you," Warren Gregory said, coming up to his wife, and, noticing the other woman, he added enthusiastically: "Well, Margaret! I didn't know you! Bless my life and heart, how you children grow up!"

"Children! I'm twenty-two!" Miss Clay said, pouting, with her round brown eyes fixed in childish reproach upon his face. They had been great friends when Warren was with his mother in Paris, nearly four years ago, and now they fell into an animated recollection of some of their experiences there with the two old ladies. While they talked Rachael watched Magsie Clay with admiration and surprise.

She knew all the girl's history, as indeed everybody in the room knew it, but to-day it was a little hard to identify the poised and beautiful young woman who was looking so demurely up from under her dark lashes at Warren with the "little Clay girl" of a few years ago.

Parker Hoyt's aunt, the magnificent old Lady Frothingham, had been just enough of an invalid for the twenty years preceding her death to need a nurse or a companion, or a social secretary, or someone who was a little of all three. The great problem was to find the right person, and for a period that actually extended itself over years the right person was not to be found, and the old lady was consequently miserable and unmanageable.

Then came the advent of Mrs. Clay, a dark, silent, dignified widow, who more than met all requirements, and who became a companion figure to the little, fussing, over-dressed old lady. From the day she first arrived at the Frothingham mansion Mrs. Clay never failed her old employer for so much as a single hour. For fifteen years she managed the house, the maids, and, if the truth were known, the old lady herself, with a quiet, irresistible efficiency. But it was early remarked that she did not manage her small daughter with her usual success. Magsie was a fascinating baby, and a beautiful child, quicker of speech than thought, with a lovely little heart-shaped face framed in flying locks of tawny hair. But she was unmanageable and strong-willed, and possessed of a winning and insolent charm hard to refuse.

Her mother in her silent, repressed way realized that Magsie was not having the proper upbringing, but her own youth had been hard and dark, and it was perhaps the closest approach to joy that she ever knew when Magsie glowing under her wide summer hats, or radiant in new furs, rushed up to demand something preposterous and extravagant of her mother, and was not denied.

She was a stout, conceited sixteen-year-old when her mother died, so spoiled and so self-centred that old Lady Frothingham had been heard more than once to mutter that the young lady could get down from her high horse and make herself useful, or she could march. But that was six years ago. And now--this! Magsie had evidently decided to make herself useful, but she had managed to make herself beautiful and fascinating as well. She was in mourning now for the good-hearted old benefactress who had left her a nest-egg of some fifteen thousand dollars, and Rachael noticed with approval that it was correct mourning: simple, severe, Parisian. Nothing could have been more becoming to the exquisite bloom of the young face than the soft, clear folds of filmy veiling; under the small, close-set hat there showed a ripple of rich golden hair. The watching woman thought that she had never seen such self-possession; at twenty-two it was almost uncanny. The modulated, bored young voice, the lazily lifted, indifferent young eyes, the general air of requesting an appreciative world to be amusing and interesting, or to expect nothing of Miss Magsie Clay, these things caused Rachael a deep, hidden chuckle of amusement. Little Magsie had turned out to be something of a personality! Why, she was even employing a distinct and youthfully insolent air of keeping Warren by her side merely on sufferance--Warren, the cleverest and finest man in the room, who was more than twice her age!

"To think that she is younger than Charlotte!" Rachael ejaculated to herself, catching a glimpse of Charlotte, towed by her mother, uncomfortable, ignored, blinking through her glasses. And when she and Warren were in the car homeward bound, she spoke admiringly of Magsie. "Did you ever see any one so improved, Warren? Really, she's quite extraordinary!"

Warren smiled absently.

"She's a terribly spoiled little thing," he remarked. "She's out for a rich man, and she'll get him!"

"I suppose so," Rachael agreed, casting about among the men she knew for an appropriate partner for Miss Clay.

"Suppose so!" he echoed in good-humored scorn. "Don't you fool yourself, she'll get what she's after! There isn't a man alive that wouldn't fall for that particular type!"

"Warren, do you suppose so?" his wife asked in surprise.

"Well, watch and see!"

"Perhaps--" Rachael's interest wandered. "What time have you?" she asked.

He glanced at his watch. "Six-ten."

"Six-TEN! Oh, my poor abused baby--and I should have been here at quarter before six!" She was all mother as she ran upstairs. Had he been crying? Oh, he had been crying! Poor little old duck of a hungry boy, did he have a bad, wicked mother that never remembered him! He was in her arms in an instant, and the laughing maid carried away her hat and wrap without disturbing his meal. Rachael leaned back in the big chair, panting comfortably, as much relieved over his relief as he was. The wedding was forgotten. She was at home again; she could presently put this baby down and have a little interval of hugging and 'tories with Jimmy.

"You'll get your lovely dress all mussed," said old Mary in high approval.

"Never mind, Mary!" her mistress said in luxurious ease before the fire, "there are plenty of dresses!"

A week later Warren came in, in the late afternoon, to say that he had met Miss Clay downtown, and they had had tea together. She suggested tea, and he couldn't well get out of it. He would have telephoned Rachael had he fancied she would care to come. She had been out? That was what he thought. But how about a little dinner for Magsie? Did she think it would be awfully stupid?

"No, she's not stupid," Rachael said cordially. "Let's do it!"

"Oh, I don't mean stupid for us," Warren hastened to explain. "I mean stupid for her!"

"Why should it be stupid for her?" Rachael looked at him in surprise.

"Well, she's awfully young, and she's getting a lot of attention, and perhaps she'd think it a bore!"

"I don't imagine Magsie Clay would find a dinner here in her honor a bore," Rachael said in delicate scorn. "Why, think who she is, Warren--a nurse's daughter! Her father was--I don't know what--an enlisted man, who rose to be a sergeant!"

"I don't believe it!" he said flatly.

"It's true, Warren. I've known that for years--everybody knows it!"

"Well," Warren Gregory said stubbornly, "she's making a great hit just the same. She's going up to the Royces' next week for the Bowditch theatricals, and she's asked to the Pinckard dinner dance. She may not go on account of her mourning."

"Her mourning is rather absurd under the circumstances," Rachael said vaguely, antagonized against anyone he chose to defend. "And if people choose to treat her as if she were Mrs. Frothingham's daughter instead of what she really is, it's nice for Magsie! But I don't see why we should."

"We might because she is such a nice, simple girl," Warren suggested, "and because we like her! I'm not trying to keep in the current; I've no social axe to grind; I merely suggested it, and if you don't want to--"

"Oh, of course, if you put it that way!" Rachael said with a faint shrug.. "I'll get hold of some eligibles--we'll have Charlie, and have rather a youthful dinner!"

Warren, who was shaving, was silent for a few minutes, then he said thoughtfully:

"I don't imagine that Charlie is the sort of person who will interest her. She may be only twenty-two, but she is older than most girls in things like that. She's had more offers now than you could shake a stick at--"

"She told you about them?"

"Well, in a general way, yes--that is, she doesn't want to marry, and she hates the usual attitude, that a lot of college kids have to be trotted out for her benefit!"

This having been her own exact attitude a few seconds before, Rachael flushed a little resentfully.

"What DOES she want to do?"

Warren shaved on for a moment in silence, then with a rather important air he said impulsively:

"Well, I'll tell you, although she told me in confidence, and of course nothing may come of it. You won't say anything about it, of course? She wants to go on the stage."

"Really!" said Rachael, who, for some reason she could not at this moment define, was finding the conversation extraordinarily distasteful.

"Yes, she's had it in mind for years," Warren pursued with simplicity. "And she's had some good offers, too. You can see that she's the kind of girl that would make an immediate hit, that would get across the footlights, as it were. Of course, it all depends upon how hard she's willing to work, but I believe she's got a big future before her!"

There was a short silence while he finished the operation of shaving, and Rachael, who was busy with the defective clasp of a string of pearls, bent absorbedly over the microscopic ring and swivel.

"Let's think about the dinner," she said presently. She found that he had already planned almost all the details.

When it took place, about ten days later, she resolutely steeled herself for an experience that promised to hold no special enjoyment for her. Her love for her husband made her find in his enthusiasm for Magsie something a little pitiful and absurd. Magsie was only a girl, a rather shallow and stupid girl at that, yet Warren was as excited over the arrangements for the dinner as if she had been the most important of personages. If it had been some other dinner--the affair for the English ambassador, or the great London novelist, or the fascinating Frenchman who had painted Jimmy--she told herself, it would have been comprehensible! But Warren, like all great men, had his simple, almost childish, phases, and this was one of them!

She watched her guest of honor, when the evening came, with a puzzled intensity. Magsie was in her glory, sparkling, chattering, almost noisy. Her exquisite little white silk gown was so low in the waist, and so short in the skirt, that it was almost no gown at all, yet it was amazingly smart. She had touched her lips with red, and her eyelids were cunningly given just a hint of elongation with a black pencil. Her bright hair was pushed severely from her face, and so trimly massed and netted as not to show its beautiful quantity, and yet, somehow, one knew the quantity was there in all its gold glory.

Rachael, magnificent in black-and-white, was ashamed of herself for the instinctive antagonism that she began to feel toward this young creature. It was not the fact of Magsie's undeniable youth and beauty that she resented, but it was her affectations, her full, pouting lips, her dimples, her reproachful upward glances. Even these, perhaps, in themselves, she did not resent, she mused; it was their instant effect upon Warren and, to a greater or lesser degree, upon all the other men present, that filled her with a sort of patient scorn. Rachael wondered what Warren's feeling would have been had his wife suddenly picked out some callow youth still in college for her admiring laughter and earnest consideration.

It was sacrilege to think it. It was always absurd, an older man's kindly interest in, and affection for, a pretty young girl, but what harm? He thought her beautiful, and charming, and talented--well, she was those things. It was January now, in March they were going to California, then would come dear Home Dunes, and before the summer was over Magsie would be safely launched, or married, and the whole thing but an episode! Warren was her husband and the father of her two splendid boys; there was tremendous reassurance in the thought.

But that evening, and throughout the weeks that followed, Rachael mused somewhat sadly upon the extraordinary susceptibility of the human male. Magsie's methods were those of a high-school belle. She pouted, she dimpled, she dispensed babyish slaps, she lapsed into rather poorly imitated baby talk. She was sometimes mysterious and tragic, according to her own lights, her voice deep, her eyes sombre; at other times she was all girl, wild for dancing and gossip and matinees. She would widen her eyes demurely at some older woman, plaintively demanding a chaperon, all these bad men were worrying her to death; she had nicknames for all the men, and liked to ask their wives if there was any harm in that? Like Billy, and like Charlotte, she never spoke of anyone but herself, but Billy was a mere beginner beside Magsie, and poor Charlotte like a denizen of another world.

Magsie always scored. There was an air of refinement and propriety about the little gypsy that saved her most daring venture, and in a society bored to death with its own sameness she became an instant favorite. Everyone said that "there was no harm in Magsie," she was the eagerly heralded and loudly welcomed cap-and-bells wherever she went.

Early in March there was an entertainment given in one of the big hotels for some charity, and Miss Clay, who appeared in a dainty little French comedy, the last number on the program, captured all the honors. Her companion player, Dr. Warren Gregory, who in the play had taken the part of her guardian, and, with his temples touched with gray, his peruke, and his satin coat and breeches, had been a handsome foil for her beauty, was declared excellent, but the captivating, piquant, enchanting Magsie was the favorite of the hour. Before the hot, exciting, memorable evening was over the rumor flew about that she had signed a contract to appear with Bowman, the great manager, in the fall.

The whole experience was difficult for Rachael, but no one suspected it, and she would have given her life cheerfully to keep her world from suspecting. Long before the rehearsals for the little play were over she knew the name of that new passion that was tearing and gnawing at her heart. No use to tell herself that if Magsie WAS deeply admired by Warren, if Magsie WAS beautiful, if Magsie WAS constantly in his thoughts, way, she, Rachael, was still his wife; his home, his sons, his name were hers! She was jealous--jealous--jealous of Magsie Clay.

She could not bear even the smothering thought of a divided kingdom. Professionally, socially, the world might claim him; but no one but herself should ever claim even one one-hundredth of that innermost heart of his that had been all her own! The thought pierced her vitally, and she felt in sick discouragement that she could not fight, she could not meet his cruelty with new cruelty. Her very beauty grew dimmed, and the old flashing wit and radiant self-confidence were clouded for a time. When she was alone with her husband she felt constrained and serious, her heart a smouldering furnace of resentment and pain.

"What do you think of this, dearie?" he asked eagerly one afternoon. "We got talking about California at the Princes' last night, and it seems that Peter and Elinor plan to go; only not before the first week in April. Now, that would suit me as well as next week, if it wouldn't put you out. Could you manage it? The Pomeroys take their car, and an awfully nice crowd; just you and I--if we'll go--Peter and Elinor, and perhaps the Oliphants, and a beau for Magsie!"

Rachael had been waiting for Magsie's name. But there seemed to be nothing to say. She rose to the situation gallantly. She put the boys in the care of their grandmother and the faithful Mary, with Doctor Valentine's telephone number pasted prominently on the nursery wall. She bought herself charming gowns and hats, she made herself the most delightful travelling companion that ever seven hot and spoiled men and women were fortunate enough to find. When everyone, even Magsie, was bored and cross, upset by close air, by late hours, by unlimited candy and cocktails, Mrs. Gregory would appear from her stateroom, dainty, interested, ready for bridge or gossip, full of enthusiasm for the scenery and for the company in which she found herself. When she and Warren were alone she often tried to fancy herself merely an acquaintance again, with an acquaintance's anxiety to meet his mood and interest him. She made no claims, she resented nothing, and she schooled herself to praise Magsie, to quote her, and to discuss her.

The result was all that she could have hoped. After the five weeks' trip Warren was heard to make the astonishing comment that Magsie was a shallow little thing, and Rachael, hungrily kissing her boys' sweet, bewildered faces, and laughing and crying together as Mary gave her an account of every hour of her absence, felt more than rewarded for the somewhat sordid scheme and the humiliating effort. Little Gerald was in short clothes now, a rose of a baby, and Jimmy at the irresistible age when every stammered word and every changing expression had new charm.

CHAPTER IV

Ten days later, in the midst of her preparations to leave the city for Clark's Hills, Rachael was summoned to the telephone by the news of a serious change in young Charlie Gregory's condition. Charlie had been ill for perhaps a week; kept at home and babied by his grandmother and Miss Cannon, the nurse, visited daily by his adored Aunt Rachael, and nearly as often by the uproarious young Gregorys, and duly spoiled by every maid in the house. Warren went in to see him often in the evenings, for trivial as his illness was, all the members of his immediate family agreed later that there had been in it, from the beginning, something vaguely alarming and menacing.

He was a quiet, peculiar, rather friendless youth at twenty-six; he had never had "girls," like the other boys, and, while he read books incessantly, Rachael knew it to be rather from loneliness than any other motive, as his silence was from shyness rather than reserve. His dying was as quiet as his living, between a silent luncheon in the gloomy old dining-room when nobody seemed able either to eat or speak, and a dreadful dinner hour when Miss Cannon sobbed unobtrusively, Warren and Rachael talked in low tones, and the chairs at the head and foot of the table were untenanted.

Only a day or two later his grandmother followed him, and Rachael and her husband went through the sombre days like two persons in an oppressive dream. Great grief they did not naturally feel, for Warren's curious self-absorption extended even to his relationship with his mother, and Charlie had always been one of the unnecessary, unimportant figures of which there are a few in every family. But the events left a lasting mark upon Rachael's life. She had grown really to love the old woman, and had felt a certain pitying affection for Charlie, too. He had been a good, gentle, considerate boy always, and it was hard to think of him as going before life had really begun for him.

On the morning of the day he died an incident had occurred, or rather two had occurred, that even then filled her with vague discomfort, and that she was to remember for many days to come.

She had been crossing the great, dark entrance hall, late in the morning, on some errand to the telephone, or to the service department of the house, her heart burdened by the sombre shadow of death that already lay upon them all, when the muffled street-door bell had rung, and the butler, red eyed, had admitted two women. Rachael, caught and reluctantly glancing toward them, had been surprised to recognize Charlotte Haviland and old Fanny.

"Charlotte!" she said, coming toward the girl. And at her low, tense tone, Charlotte had begun to cry.

"Aunt Rachael"--the old name came naturally after seven years--"you'll think I'm quite crazy coming here this way"--Charlotte, as always, was justifying her shy little efforts at living--"but M'ma was busy, and"--the old, nervous gasp--"and it seemed only friendly to come and--and inquire--"

"Don't cry, dear!" said Rachael's rich, kind voice. She put a hand upon Charlotte's shoulder. "Did you want to ask for Charlie?"

"I know how odd, how very odd it must look," said Charlotte, managing a wet smile, "and my crying--perfectly absurd--I can't think why I'm so silly!"

"We've all been pretty near crying, ourselves, this morning," Rachael said, not looking at her, but rather seeming to explain to the sympathetic yet pleasurably thrilled Fanny. "Dear boy, he is very ill. Doctor Hamilton has just been here; and he tells us frankly that it is only a question of a few hours now--"

At this poor Charlotte tried to compose her face to the merely sorrowful and shocked expression of a person justified in her friendly concern, but succeeded only in giving Mrs. Gregory a quivering look of mortal hurt.

"I was afraid so," she stammered huskily. "Elfrida Hamilton told me. I was so--sorry--"

Rachael began to perceive that this was a great adventure, a tragic and heroic initiative for Charlotte. Poor Charlotte, red-eyed behind her strong glasses, the bloom of youth gone from her face, was perhaps touching this morning, the pinnacle of the few strong emotions her life was to know.

"How well did you know Charlie, dear?" asked Rachael when Fanny was for the moment out of hearing and they were in the dark, rep-draped reception-room. She had asked Charlotte to sit down, but Charlotte nervously had said that she could stay but another minute.

"Oh, n-n-not very well, Aunt Rachael--that is, we didn't see each other often, since"--Rachael knew since when, and liked Charlotte for the clumsy substitute--"since Billy was married. I know Charlie called, but M'ma didn't tell me until weeks later, and then we were on the ocean. We met now and then, and once he telephoned, and I think he would have liked to see me, but M'ma felt so strongly--there was no way. And then last summer--we h-h-happened to meet, he and I, at Jane Cook's wedding, and we had quite a talk. I knew M'ma would be angry, but it just seemed as if I couldn't think of it then. And we talked of the things we liked, you know, the sort of house we both liked--not like other people's houses!" Charlotte's plain young face had grown bright with the recollection, but now her voice sank lifelessly again. "But M'ma made me promise never to speak to him again, and of course I promised," she said dully.

"I see." Rachael was silent. There seemed to be nothing to say.

"I suppose I couldn't--speak to him a moment, Aunt Rachael?" Charlotte was scarlet, but she got the words out bravely.

"Oh, my dear, he wouldn't know you. He doesn't know any of us now. He just lies there, sometimes sighing a little--"

Charlotte was as pale now as she had been rosy before, her lip trembled, and her whole face seemed to be suffused with tears.

"I see," she said in turn. "Thank you, Aunt Rachael, thanks ever so much. I--I wish you'd tell his grandmother how sorry I am. I--suppose Fanny and I had better go now."

But before she went Rachael opened her arms, and Charlotte came into them, and cried bitterly for a few minutes.

"Poor little girl!" said the older woman tenderly. "Poor little girl!"

"I always loved you," gulped Charlotte, "and I would have come to see you, if M'ma--And of course it was nothing but the merest friendship b-between Charlie and me, only we--we always seemed to like each other."

And Charlotte, her romance ended, wiped her eyes and blew her nose, and went away. Rachael went slowly upstairs.

Late that same afternoon, as she and the trained nurse were dreamily keeping one of the long sick-watches, she looked at the patient, and was surprised to see his rather insignificant eyes fixed earnestly upon her. Instantly she went to the bedside and knelt down.

"What is it, Charlie-boy?" she asked, in the merest rich, tender essence of a tone. The sick eyes broke over her distressedly. She could see the fine dew of perspiration at his waxen temples, and the lean hand over which she laid her own was cool after all these feverish days, unwholesomely cool.

"Aunt Rachael--" The customs of earth were still strong when he could waste so much precious breath upon the unnecessary address. The nurse hovered nervously near, but did not attempt to silence him. "Going fast," he whispered.

"It will be rest, Charlie-boy," she answered, tears in her eyes.

He smiled, and drifted into that other world so near our own for a few moments. Then she started at Charlotte's name.

"Charlotte," he said in a ghostly whisper, "said she would like a house all green-and pink-with roses--"

Rachael was instantly tense. Ah, to get hold of poor starved little Charlotte, to give her these last precious seconds, to let her know he had thought of her!

"What about Charlotte, dear, dear boy?" she asked eagerly.

"I thought--it would be so pleasant--there--" he said, smiling. He closed his eyes. She heard the little prayer that he had learned in his babyhood for this hour. Then there was silence. Silence.

Silence. Rachael looked fearfully at the nurse. A few minutes later she went to tell his grandmother, who, with two grave sisters sitting beside her, had been lying down since the religious rites of an hour or two ago. Rachael and the smaller, rosy-faced nun helped the stiff, stricken old lady to her feet, and it was with Rachael's arm about her that she went to her grandson's side.

That night old Mrs. Gregory turned to her daughter-in-law and said: "You're good, Rachael. Someone prayed for you long ago; someone gave you goodness. Don't forget--if you ever need--to turn to prayer. I don't ask you to do any more. It was for James to make his sons Christians, and James did not do so. But promise me something, Rachael: if James--hurts you, if he fails you--promise me that you will forgive him!"

"I promise," Rachael said huskily, her heart beating quick with vague fright. Mrs. Gregory was in her deep armchair, she looked old and broken to-night, far older than she would look a few days later when she lay in her coffin. Rachael had brought her a cup of hot bouillon, and had knelt, daughter fashion, to see that she drank it, and now the thin old hand clutched her shoulder, and the eager old eyes were close to her face.

"I have made mistakes, I have had every sorrow a woman can know," said old Mrs. Gregory, "but prayer has never failed me, and when I go, I believe I will not be afraid!" "I have made mistakes, too," Rachael said, strangely stirred, "and for the boys' sake, for Warren's sake, I want to be-- wise!"

The thin old hand patted hers. Old Mrs. Gregory lay with closed eyes, no flicker of life in her parchment-colored face. "Pray about it!" she said in a whisper. She patted Rachael's hands for another moment, but she did not speak again.

At the funeral, kneeling by Warren's side in the great cathedral, her pale face more lovely than ever in a setting of fresh black, Rachael tried for the first time in her life to pray.

They were rich beyond any dream or need now. Rachael could hardly have believed that so great a change in her fortune could make so little change in her feeling. A sudden wave of untimely heat smote the city, and it was hastily decided that the boys and their mother must get to the shore, leaving all the details of settling his mother's estate to Warren. In the autumn Rachael would make those changes in the old house of which she had dreamed so many years ago. Warren was not to work too hard, and was to come to them for every week-end.

He took them down himself in the car, Rachael beside him on the front seat, her baby in her arms, Martin and Mary, with Jim, in the tonneau. Home Dunes had been opened and aired; luncheon was waiting when they got there. Rachael felt triumphant, powerful. Between their mourning and Warren's unexpected business responsibilities she would have a summer to her liking.

He went away the next day, and Rachael began a series of cheerful letters. She tried not to reproach him when a Saturday night came without bringing him, she schooled herself to read, to take walks, to fight depression and loneliness. She and Alice practised piano duets, studied Italian, made sick calls in the village, and sewed for the babies of dark's Hills and Quaker Bridge. About twice a month, usually together, the two went up to the city for a day's shopping. Then George and Warren met them, and they dined and perhaps went to the theatre together. It was on one of these occasions that Rachael learned that Magsie Clay was in town.

"Working hard--too hard," said Warren in response to her questions. "She's rehearsing already for October."

"Warren! In all this heat?"

"Yes, and she looks pulled down, poor kid!"

"You've seen her, then?"

"Oh, I see her now and then. Betty Bowditch had her to dinner, and now and then she and I go to tea, and she tells me about her troubles, her young men, and the other women in the play!"

"I wonder if she wouldn't come down to us for a week?" Rachael said pleasantly. Warren brightened enthusiastically. A little ocean air would do Magsie worlds of good.

Magsie, lunching with Rachael at Rachael's club the following week, was prettily appreciative.

"I would just love to come!" she said gratefully. "I'll bring my bathing suit, and live in the water! But, Rachael, it can only be from Friday night until Monday morning. Perhaps Greg will run me down in the car, and bring me up again?"

"What else would I do?" Warren said, smiling.

Rachael fixed the date. On the following Friday night she met Warren and Magsie at the gate, at the end of the long run. Warren was quite his old, delightful self; the boys, perfection. Alice gave a dinner party, and Alice's brother did not miss the opportunity of a flirtation with Magsie. The visit, for everyone but Rachael, was a great success.

The little actress and Rachael's husband were on friendly, even intimate, terms; Magsie showed Warren a letter, Warren murmured advice; Magsie reached a confident little brown hand to him from the raft; Warren said, "Be careful, dear!" when she sprang up to leap from the car. Well, said Rachael bravely, no harm in that! Warren was just the big, sweet, simple person to be flattered by Magsie's affection. How could she help liking him?

She went to the gate again, on Monday morning this time, to say good-bye. Magsie was tucked in trimly in Rachael's place beside Rachael's husband; her gold hair glinted under a smart little hat; gloves, silk stockings, and gown were all of the becoming creamy tan she wore so much.

"Saturday night?" Rachael said to Warren.

"Possibly not, dear. I can tell better later in the week."

"You don't know how we slaves envy you, Rachael!" Magsie said. "When Greg and I are gasping away in some roof-garden, having our mild little iced teas, we'll think of you down here on the glorious ocean!"

"We're a mutual consolation league!" Warren said with an appreciative laugh.

"He laughs," Magsie said, "but, honestly, I don't know where I'd be without Greg. You don't know how kind he is to me, Rachael!"

"He's kind to everyone," Rachael smiled.

"I don't have to TELL you how much I've enjoyed this!" Magsie added gratefully.

"Do it any other time you can!" Rachael waved them out of sight. She stood at the gate, in the fragrant, warm summer morning, for a long time after they were gone.

In the late summer, placidly wasting her days on the sands with the two boys, a new experience befell Rachael. She had hoped, at about the time of Jimmy's third birthday, to present him and his little brother with a sister. Now the hope vanished, and Rachael, awed and sad, set aside a tiny chamber in her heart for the dream, and went on about her life sobered and made thoughtful over the great possibilities that are wrapped in every human birth. Warren had warned her that she must be careful now, and, charmed at his concern for her grief and shock, she rested and saved herself wherever she could.

But autumn came, and winter came, and she did not grow strong. It became generally understood that Mrs. Gregory was not going about this season, and her friends, when they came to call in Washington Square, were apt to find her comfortably established on the wide couch in one of the great rooms that were still unchanged, with a nurse hovering in the background, and the boys playing before the fire. Rachael would send the children away with Mary, ring for tea, and chatter vivaciously with her guests, later retailing all the gossip to Warren when he came to sit beside her. Often she got up and took her place at the table, and once or twice a month, after a quiet day, was tucked into the motor car by the watchful Miss Snow, and went to the theatre or opera, to be brought carefully home again at eleven o'clock, and given into Miss Snow's care again.

She was not at all unhappy, the lessening of social responsibility was a real relief, and Warren's solicitude and sympathy were a tonic of which she drank deep, night and morning. His big warm hands, his smile, the confidence of his voice, these thrilled and rejuvenated her continually.

The boys were a delight to her. In their small rumpled pajamas they came into her room every morning, dewy from sleep, full of delicious plans for the day. Jim was a masterful baby whose continually jerking head was sure to bump his mother if she attempted too much hugging, but dark-eyed, grave little Derry was "cuddly"; he would rest his shining head contentedly for minutes together on his mother's breast, and when she lifted him from his crib late at night for a last kiss, his warm baby arms would circle her neck, and his rich little voice murmur luxuriously, "Hug Derry."

Muffled rosily in gaiters and furs, or running about her room in their white, rosetted slippers, with sturdy arms and knees bare, or angelic in their blue wrappers after the evening bath, they were equally enchanting to their mother.

"It's a marvel to see how you can be so patient!" Warren said one evening when he was dressing for an especially notable dinner, and Rachael, in her big Chinese coat, was watching the process contentedly from the couch in his upstairs sitting-room.

"Well, that's the odd thing about ill health, Greg--you haven't any chance to answer back," she answered thoughtfully. "If money could make me well, or if effort could, I'd get well, of course! But there seem to be times when you simply are SICK. It's an extraordinary experience to me; it's extraordinary to lie here, and think of all the hundreds of thousands of other women who are sick, just simply and quietly laid low with no by-your-leave! Of course, my being ill doesn't make much trouble; the boys are cared for, the house goes on, and I don't suffer! But suppose we were poor, and the children needed me, and you couldn't afford a nurse--then what? For I'd have to collapse and lie here just the same!"

"It's no snap for me," Warren grumbled after a silence. "Gosh! I will be glad when you're well--and when the damn nurse is out of the house!"

"Warren, I thought you liked Miss Snow!"

"Well, I do, I suppose--in a way. But I don't like her for breakfast, lunch, and dinner--so everlastingly sweet and fresh!' I declare I believe my watch is losing time--this is the third time this week I've been late!'"

This was said in exactly Miss Snow's tone, and Rachael laughed.

But when he was gone a deep depression fell upon her. Dear old boy, it was not much of a life for him, going about alone, sitting down to his meals with only a trained nurse for company! Shut away so deliciously from the world with her husband and sons, enjoying the very helplessness that forced her to lean so heavily upon him, she had forgotten how hard it was for Greg!

Yet how could she get well when the stubborn weakness and languor persisted, when her nights were so long and sleepless, her appetite so slight, her strength so quickly exhausted?

"When do you think I will get well, Miss Snow?" she would ask.

"Come, now, we're not going to bother our heads about THAT," Miss Snow would say cheerfully. "Why, you're not sick! You've just got to rest and take care of yourself, that's all! Dear ME, if you were suffering every minute of the time, you might have something to grumble about!"

Doctor Valentine was equally unsatisfactory, although Rachael loved the simple, homely man so much that she could not be vexed by his kindly vagueness:

"These things are slow to fight, Rachael," said George Valentine. "Alice had just such a fight years ago. When the human machinery runs down, there's nothing for it but patience! You did too much last winter, nursing the baby until you left for California, and then only the hot summer between that and September! Just go slow!"

Perhaps once a month Magsie came in to see Rachael, ready to pour tea, to flirt with any casual caller, or to tickle the roaring baby with the little fox head on her muff. She had been playing in a minor part in a successful production. Among all the callers who came and went perhaps Magsie was the most at home in the Gregory house--a harmless little affectionate creature, unimportant, but always welcome.

Slowly health and strength came back, and one by one Rachael took up the dropped threads of her life. The early spring found her apparently herself again, but there was a touch of gray here and there in her dark hair, and Elinor and Judy told each other that her spirits were not the same.

They did not know what Rachael knew, that there was a change in Warren, so puzzling, so disquieting, that his wife's convalescence was delayed by many a wakeful hour and many a burst of secret tears on his account. She could not even analyze it, much less was she fit to battle with it with her old splendid strength and sanity.

His general attitude toward her, in these days, was one of paternal and brisk kindliness. He liked her new gown, he didn't care much for that hat, she didn't look awfully well, better telephone old George, it wouldn't do to have her sick again! Yes, he was going out, unless she wanted him for something? She was reminded hideously of her old days with Clarence.

Shaken and weak still, she fought gallantly against the pain and bewilderment of the new problem. She invited the persons he liked to the house, she effaced her own claim, she tried to get him to talk of his cases. Sometimes, as the spring ripened, she planned whole days with him in the car. They would go up to Ossining and see the Perrys, or they would go to Jersey and spend the day with Doctor Cheseborough.

Perhaps Warren accepted these suggestions, and they had a cloudless day. Or when Sunday morning came, and the boys, coated and capped, were eager to start, he might evade them.

"I wonder if you'll feel badly, Petty, if I don't go?"

"Oh, WARREN!"

"Well, my dear, I've got some work to do. I ought to look up that meningitis case--the Italian child. Louise'll give me a bite of lunch--"

"But, dearest, that spoils our day!" Rachael would fling her wraps down, and face him ruefully. "How can I go alone! I don't want to. And it's SUCH a day, and the babies are so sweet--"

"There's no reason why you and the children shouldn't go." She had come to know that mild, almost reproachful, tone.

"Oh, but Warren, that spoils it all!"

"I'm sorry!"

Rachael would shut her lips firmly over protest. At best she might wring from him a reluctant change of mind and an annoyed offer of company which she must from sheer pride decline. At worst she would be treated with a dignified silence--the peevish and exacting woman who could not understand.

So she would go slowly down to the car, to Mary beaming beside Martin in the front seat, to the delicious boys tumbling about in the back, eager for Mother. With one on each side of her, a retaining hand on the little gaiters, she would wave the attentive husband and father an amiable farewell. The motor car would wheel about in the bare May sunshine, the river would be a ripple of dancing blue waves, morning riders would canter on the bridle-path, and white-frocked babies toddle along the paths. Such a morning for a ride, if only Warren were there! But Rachael would try to enjoy her run, and would eat Mrs. Perry's or Mrs. Cheseborough's fried chicken and home-made ices with gracious enthusiasm; everyone was quite ready to excuse Warren; his beautiful wife was the more popular of the two.

He was always noticeably affectionate when they got home. Rachael, her color bright from sun and wind, would entertain him with a spirited account of the day while she dressed.

"I wish I'd gone with you; I will next time!" he invariably said.

On the next Sunday she might try another experience. No plans to-day. The initiative should be left to him. Breakfast would drag along until after ten o'clock, and Mary would appear with a low question. Were the boys to go out to the Park? Rachael would pause, undecided. Well, yes, Mary might take them, but bring them in early, in case Doctor Gregory wished to take them somewhere.

And ten minutes later he might jump up briskly. Well! how about a little run up to Pelham Manor, wonderful morning--could she go as she was? Rachael would beg for ten minutes; she might come downstairs in seven to find him wavering.

"Would you mind if we made it a pretty short run, dear, and then if I dropped you here and went on down to the hospital for a little while?"

"Why, Warren, it was your suggestion, dear! Why take a drive at all if you don't feel like it!"

"Oh, it's not that--I'm quite willing to. Where are the kids?"

"Mary took them out. They've got to be back for naps at half-past eleven, you see."

"I see." He would look at his watch. "Well, I'll tell you what I think I'll do. I'll change and shave now--" A pause. His voice would drop vaguely. "What would YOU like to do?" he might suggest amiably.

Such a conversation, so lacking in his old definite briskness where their holidays were concerned, would daunt Rachael with a sense of utter forlornness. Sometimes she offered a plan, but it was invariably rejected. There were friends who would have been delighted at an unexpected lunch call from the Gregorys, but Warren yawned and shuddered negatives when she mentioned their names. In the end, he would go off to the hospital for an hour or two, and later would telephone to his wife to explain a longer absence: he had met some of the boys at the club and they were rather urging him to stay to lunch; he couldn't very well decline.

"Would you like to have me come down and join you anywhere later?" his wife might ask in the latter case.

"No, thank you, no. I may come straight home after lunch, and in that case I'd cross you. Boys all right?"

"Lovely." Rachael would sit at the telephone desk, after she had hung up the receiver, wrapped in bitter thought, a bewildered pain at her heart. She never doubted him; to-morrow good, old, homely, trustworthy George Valentine, whose wife and children were visiting Alice's mother in Boston, would speak of the bridge game at the club. But with his wife waiting for him at home, his wife who lived all the six days of the week waiting for this seventh day, why did he need the society of his men friends?

A commonplace retaliation might have suggested itself to her, but there was no fighting instinct in Rachael now. She did not want to pique him, to goad him, to flirt with him. He should be hers honorably and openly, without devices, without intrigue. Stirred to the deeps of her being by wifehood and motherhood, by her passionate love for her husband and children, it was a humiliating thought that she must coquette with and flatter other men. As a matter of fact, she found it difficult to talk with any interest of anything except Warren, his work and his plans, of Jimmy and Derry, and perhaps of Home Dunes. If it were a matter of necessity she might always turn to the new plays and books, the opera of the season, or the bill for tenement requirements or juvenile delinquents, but mere personalities and intrigue she knew no more. These matters were all of secondary interest to her now; it seemed to Rachael that the time had come when mere personalities, when bridge and cocktails and dancing and half-true scandals were not satisfying.

"Warren," she said one evening when the move to Home Dunes was near, "should you be sorry if I began to go regularly to church again?"

"No," he said indifferently, giving her rather a surprised glance over his book. "Churchgoing coming in again?"

"It's not that," Rachael said, smiling over a little sense of pain, "but I--I like it. I want the boys to think that their mother goes to church and prays-- and I really want to do it myself!"

He smiled, as always a little intolerant of what sounded like sentiment.

"Oh, come, my dear! Long before the boys are old enough to remember it you'll have given it up again!"

"I hope not," Rachael said, sighing. "I wish I had never stopped. I wish I were one of these mild, nice, village women who put out clean stockings for the children every Saturday night, and clean shirts and ginghams, and lead them all into a pew Sunday morning, and teach them the Golden Rule, and to honor their father and their mother, and all the rest of it!"

"And what do you think you would gain by that?" Warren asked.

"Oh, I would gain--security," Rachael said vaguely, but with a suspicion of tears in her eyes. "I would have something to--to stand upon, to be guided by. There is a purity, an austerity, about that old church-going, loving-God-and-your-neighbor ideal. Truth and simplicity and integrity and uprightness--my old great-grandmother used to use those words, but one doesn't ever hear them any more! Everything's half black and half white nowadays; we're all as good or as bad as we happen to be born. There's no more discipline, no more self-denial, no more development of character! I want to--to hold on to something, now that forces I can't control are coming into my life."

"What do you mean by forces you can't control?" he asked with a sort of annoyed interest.

"Love, Warren," she answered quickly. "Love for you and the boys, and fear for you and the boys. Love always brings fear. And illness--I never thought of it before I was ill. And jealousy--"

"What have you got to be jealous of?" he asked, somewhat gruffly, as she paused.

"Your work," Rachael said simply; "everything that keeps you away from me!"

"And you think going to Saint Luke's every Sunday morning at eleven o'clock, and listening to Billy Graves, will fix it all up?" he smiled not unkindly. But as she did not answer his smile, and as the tears he disliked came into her eyes, his tone changed. "Now I'll tell you what's the matter with you, my dear," he said with a brisk kindliness that cut her far more just then than severity would have done, "you're all wound up in self-analysis and psychologic self-consciousness, and you're spinning round and round in your own entity like a kitten chasing her tail. It's a perfectly recognizable phase of a sort of minor hysteria that often gets hold of women, and curiously enough, it usually comes about five or six years after marriage. We doctors meet it over and over again. 'But, Doctor, I'm so nervous and excited all the time, and I don't sleep! I worry so--and much as I love my husband, I just can't help worrying!'"

Looking up and toward his wife as she sat opposite him in the lamplight, Warren Gregory found no smile on the beautiful face. Rachael's hurt was deeper than her pride; she looked stricken.

"Don't put yourself in their class, my dear!" her husband said leniently. "You need some country air. You'll get down to Clark's Hills in a week or two and blow some of these notions away. Meanwhile, why don't you run down to the club every morning, and play a good smashing game of squash, and take a plunge. Put yourself through a little training!" He reopened his book.

Rachael did not answer. Presently glancing at her he saw that she was reading, too.

CHAPTER V

That his overtired nerves and her exhausted soul and body would have recovered balance in time, did not occur to Rachael. She suffered with all the intensity of a strongly passionate nature. Warren had changed to her; that was the terrible fact. She went about stunned and sick, neglecting her meals, forgetting her tonic, refusing the distractions that would have been the best thing possible for her. Little things troubled her; she said to herself bitterly that everything, anything, caused irritation between herself and Warren now. Sometimes the atmosphere brightened for a few days, then the old hopeless tugging at cross purposes began again.

"You're sick, Rachael, and you don't know it!" said Magsie Clay breezily. June was coming in, and Magsie was leaving town for the Villalonga camp. She told Rachael that she was "crazy" about Kent Parmalee, and Rachael's feeling of amazement that Magsie Clay could aspire to a Parmalee was softened by an odd sensation of relief at hearing Magsie's plans--a relief she did not analyze.

"I believe I am sick!" Rachael agreed. "I shall be glad to get down to the shore next week." She told Warren of Magsie's admission that night.

"Kent! She wouldn't look at him!" Warren said comfortably.

"It would be a brilliant match for her," Rachael countered quietly.

She saw that she had antagonized him, but he did not speak again. One of their unhappy silences fell.

Home Dunes, as always, restored health and color magically. Rachael felt more like herself after the first night's sleep on the breezy porch, the first invigorating dip in the ocean. She began to enjoy her meals again, she began to look carefully to her appearance. Presently she was laughing, singing, bubbling with life and energy. Alice, watching her, rejoiced and marvelled at her recovery. Rachael's beauty, her old definite self-reliance, came back in a flood. She fairly radiated charm, glowing as she held George and Alice under the spell of her voice, the spell of her happy planning. Her letters to Warren were in the old, tender, vivacious strain. She was interested in everything, delighted with everything in Clark's Hills. She begged him for news; Vivian had a baby? And Kent Parmalee was engaged to Eliza Bowditch--what did Magsie's say? And did he miss her? The minute she got home she was going to talk to him about having a big porch built on, outside the nursery, and at the back of the house; what about it? Then the children could sleep out all the year through. George and Alice positively stated that they were going around the world in two years, and if they did, why couldn't the Gregorys go, too?

"You're wonderful!" said Alice one day. "You're not the same woman you were last winter!"

"I was ill last winter, woman! And never so ill as when they all thought I was entirely cured! Besides--" Rachael looked down at her tanned arm and slender brown fingers marking grooves in the sand. "Besides, it's partly-- bluff, Alice," she confessed. "I'm fighting myself these days. I don't want to think that we--Greg and I--can't go back, can't be to each other--what we were!"

What an April creature she was, thought Alice, seeing that tears were close to the averted eyes, and hearing the tremble in Rachael's voice.

"Goose!" she said tenderly. "You were a nervous wreck last year, and Warren was working far too hard! Make haste slowly, Rachael."

"But it's three weeks since he was here," Rachael said in a low voice. "I don't understand it, that's all!"

"Nor I--nor he!" Alice said, smiling.

"Next week!" Rachael predicted bravely. And a second later she had sprung up from the sand and was swimming through the surf as if she swam from her own intolerable thoughts.

The next week-end would bring him she always told herself, and usually after two or three empty Sundays there would come a happy one, with the new car which was built like a projectile, purring in the road, George and Alice shouting greetings as they came in the gate, Louise excitedly attempting to outdo herself on the dinner, and the sunburned noisy babies shrieking themselves hoarse as they romped with their father.

To be held tight in his arms, to get his first big kiss, to come into the house still clinging to him, was bliss to Rachael now. But as the summer wore away she noticed that in a few hours the joy of homecoming would fade for him, he would become fitfully talkative, moodily silent, he would wonder why the Valentines were always late, and ask his wife patiently if she would please not hum, his head ached--

"Dearest! Why didn't you say so!"

"I don't know. It's been aching all day!"

"And you let those great boys climb all over you!"

"Oh, that's all right."

"Would you like a nap, Warren, or would you like to go over to the beach, just you and me, and have a swim?"

"No, thank you. I may run the car into Katchogue"--Katchogue, seven miles away, was the site of the nearest garage--"and have that fellow look at my magneto. She didn't act awfully well coming down!"

"Would you like me to go with you, Warren?"

"Love it, my dear, but I have to take Pierre. He's got twice the sense I have about it!"

And again a sense of heaviness, of helplessness, would fall upon Rachael, so that on Sunday afternoon it was almost a relief to have him go away.

"Well," she would say in the nursery again, after the good-byes, kissing the fat little shoulder of Gerald Fairfax Gregory where the old baby white ran into the new boyish tan, "we will not be introspective and imaginative, and cry for the moon. We will take off our boys' little old, hot rumply shirts, and put them into their nice cool nighties, and be glad that we have everything in the world--almost! Get me your Peter Rabbit Book, Jimmy, and get up here on my other arm. Everybody hasn't the same way of showing love, and the main thing is to be grateful that the love is there. Daddy loves his boys, and his home, and his boys' mother, only it doesn't always occur to him that--"

"Are you talking for me, or for you, Mother?" Jimmy would sometimes ask, after puzzled and attentive listening.

"For me, this time, but now I'll talk for you!" Rachael satisfied her hungry heart with their kisses, and was never so happy as when both fat little bodies were in her arms. She grudged every month that carried them away from babyhood, and one day Alice Valentine found her looking at a book of old photographs with an expression of actual sadness on her face.

"Look at Jim, Alice, that second summer--before Derry was born! Wasn't he the dearest little fatty, tumbling all over the place!"

"Rachael, don't speak as if the child was dead!" Alice laughed.

"Well, one loses them almost as completely," Rachael said, smiling. "Jim is such a great big, brown, mischievous creature now, and to think that my Derry is nearly two!"

"Think of me, with Mary fifteen!" Mrs. Valentine countered, "and just as baby-hungry as ever! But I shall have to do nothing but chaperon now, for a few years, and wait for the grandchildren."

"I shouldn't mind getting old, Alice," Rachael said, "if I were like you; you're so temperate and unselfish and sweet that no one could help loving you! Besides, you don't sit around worrying about what people think, you just go on cutting out cookies, and putting buttons on gingham dresses, and let other people do the worrying!"

And suddenly, to the other woman's concern, she burst into bitter crying, and covered her face with her hands.

"I'm so frightened, Alice!" sobbed Rachael. "I don't know what's the matter with me, but I FEEL--I feel that something is all wrong! I don't seem to have any HOLD on Warren any more--you can't explain such things--but I'm--"

She got to her feet, a splendid figure of tragedy, and walked blindly to the end of the long porch, where she stood staring down at the heaving, sun-flooded expanse of the blue sea, and at the roofs of little Quaker Bridge beyond the bar. Lazy waves were creaming, in great interlocked circles, on the white beach, the air was as clear as crystal on the cloudless September morning. Not a breath of wind stirred the tufted grass on the dunes; down by the weather-blown bath-houses a dozen children, her own among them, were shouting and splashing in the spreading shallows.

Alice Valentine, her plain, sweet face a picture of sympathy, sat dumb and unmoving. In her own heart she felt that Rachael's was a terrible situation. What WAS the matter with Warren Gregory, anyway, wondered Alice; he had a beautiful wife, and beautiful children, and if George, with all his summer substituting and hospital work, could come to his family, as he did come every Friday night, it was upon no claim of hard work that Warren could remain away. As a matter of fact, Alice knew it was not for work that he stayed, for George, the least critical of friends, had once or twice told her of yachting parties in which Warren had participated--men's parties, of which Rachael perhaps might not have disapproved, but of which Rachael certainly did not know. George had told her vaguely that Greg liked to play golf on Saturday afternoons, and sleep late on Sunday, and seemed to feel it more of a rest than coming down to the shore.

"I am a fool to break down this way," said Rachael, interrupting her guest's musings to come back to her chair, and showing a composed face despite her red eyes, "but my--my heart is heavy to-day!" Something in the simple dignity of the words brought the tears to Alice's eyes. She held out her hand and Rachael took it and clung to it, as she went on: "I had a birthday yesterday--and Warren forgot it!"

"They all do that!" Alice said cheerfully. "George never remembers mine!"

"But Warren always has before," Rachael said, smiling sadly, "and--and it came to me last night--I didn't sleep very well--that I am thirty-four, and--and I have given him all I have!"

Again tears threatened her self-control, but she fought them resolutely, and in a moment was herself again.

"You love too hard, my dear woman," Alice Valentine remonstrated affectionately; "nothing is worse than extremes in anything. Say to yourself, like a sensible girl, that you have a good husband, and let it go at that! Be as cool and cheerful with Warren as if he were--George, for instance, and try to interest yourself in something entirely outside your own home. I wonder if perhaps this place isn't a little lonely for you? Why don't you try Bar Harbor or one of the mountain places next year, and go about among people, and entertain a little more?"

"But, Alice, people BORE me so--I've had so much of it, and it's always the same thing!"

"I know; I hate it, too. But there are funny phases in marriage, Rachael, and one has to take them as they come. Warren might like it."

Rachael pondered. Elinor Pomeroy and the Villalongas, the Whittakers and Stokes and Parmalees again! Noise and hurry, and dancing and smoking and drinking again! She sighed.

"I believe I'll suggest it to Warren, Alice. Then if he's keen for it, we'll do it next year."

"I would." Mrs. Valentine rose, and looked toward the beach with an idea of locating Martha and Katrina before sending for them. "Isn't it almost lunch time?" she asked, adding in a matter-of-fact tone: "Don't worry any more, Rachael; it's largely a bad habit. Just look the whole thing in the face, and map it out like a campaign. 'The way to begin living the ideal life is to begin,' my father used to say!"

This talk, and others like it, had the effect of bracing Rachael to fresh endurance and of spurring her to fresh courage for the few days that its effect lasted. But sooner or later her bravery would die away, and an increasing discouragement possess her. Lying in her bare, airy bedroom at night, with sombre eyes staring at the arch of stars above the moving sea, an almost unbearable loneliness would fall upon soul and body; she needed Warren, she said to herself, often with bitter tears. Warren, splashing in his bath, scattering wet towels and discarded garments so royally about the place; Warren, in a discursive mood, regarding some operation as he stropped his razor; Warren's old, half-unthinking "you look sweet, dear," when, fresh and dainty, his wife was ready to go downstairs--for these and a thousand other memories of him she yearned with an aching desire that racked her like a bodily pain.

"Oh, it isn't right for him to torture me so!" she would whisper to herself. "It isn't right!"

October found them all back in the city, an apparently united and devoted family again. Rachael entered with great zest into the delayed matter of redecorating and refurnishing the old home on Washington Square, finding the dignified house--Warren's birthplace--more and more to her liking as modern enamel fixtures went into the bathrooms, simple modern hangings let sunshine and air in at the long-darkened windows, and rich tapestry papers and Oriental rugs subdued the effect of severe cream woodwork and colonial mantels.

She found Warren singularly unenthusiastic about it, almost ungracious when he answered her questions or decided for her any detail. But Rachael was firmly resolved to ignore his moods, and went blithely about her business, displaying an indifference--or an assumed indifference--that was evidently somewhat puzzling to Warren and to all her household. She equipped the boys in dark-blue coats and squirrel-skin caps for the winter, marvelling a little sadly that their father did not seem to see the charms so evident to all the world. A rosier, gayer, more sturdy pair of devoted little brothers never stamped through snowy parks, or came chattering in for chops and baked potatoes. Every woman in the neighborhood, every policeman, knew Jim and Derry Gregory; their morning walks were so many separate little adventures in popularity. But Warren, beyond paternal greetings at breakfast, and an occasional perfunctory query as to their health, made no attempt to enter into their lives. They were still too small to interest their father except as good and satisfactory babies.

One bitter December day the thunderbolt fell. Rachael felt that she had always known it, that she had been sitting in this hideous hotel dining-room for years watching Warren--and Margaret Clay.

There was a bitter taste of salt water in her mouth, there was a hideous drumming at her heart. She felt sick and cold from her bewildered brain down to her very feet. When one felt like this--one fainted.

But Rachael did not faint, although it was by sheer power of will that she held her reeling senses. No scene--no, there mustn't be a scene--for

Jimmy's sake, for Derry's sake, no scene. She was here, in the Waldorf Grill, of course. She had been--what had she been doing? She had been--she came downtown after breakfast--of course, shopping. Shopping for the children's Christmas. They were to have coasters--they were old enough for coasters-- she must go on this quiet way, thinking of the children--five was old enough for coasters--and Jim always looked out for Derry.

She couldn't go out. They hadn't seen her; they wouldn't see her, here in this corner. But she dared not stand up and pass them again. Warren--and Magsie. Warren--and Magsie. Oh, God--God--God--what should she do-- she was going to faint again.

Here was her shopping list, a little wet and crumpled because she had put her glove on the snowy handle of the motor-car door. Mary had said that it would be a white Christmas--how could Mary tell?--this was only the eighteenth, only the eighteenth--ridiculous to be panting this way, like a runner. Nothing was going to hurt her--

"Anything--anything!" she said to the waiter, with dry, bloodless lips, and a ghastly attempt at a smile. "Yes, that will do. Thank you, yes, I suppose so. Yes, if you will. Thank you. That will do nicely."

And now she must be quiet. That was the main thing now. They must not see her. She had been shopping, and now she was having her lunch in the Grill. If she could only breathe a little less violently--but she seemed to have no control over her heaving breast, she could not even close her mouth. Nobody suspected anything, and if she could but control herself, nobody would, she told herself desperately.

She never knew that the silent, gray-haired waiter recognized her, and recognized both the man and woman who sat only thirty feet away. She had not ordered coffee, but he brought her a smoking pot. It was not the first time he had encountered the situation. Rachael drank the vivifying fluid, and her nerves responded at once.

She sat up, set her lips firmly, forced herself to dispose of gloves and napkin in the usual way. Her breath was coming more evenly--so much was gained. As for this deadly cold and quivering sensation of nausea, that was no more than fatigue and the frightfully cold wind.

So it was Magsie. Rachael had not been seven years a wife to misread Warren's eyes as he looked at the girl. No woman could misread their attitude together, an attitude of wonderful, sweet familiarity with each other's likes and dislikes under all its thrilling newness. Rachael had seen him turn that very glance, that smiling-eyed yet serious look--

Oh, God! it could not be that he had come to care for Magsie! Her hard-won calm was shattered in a second, she was panting and quivering again. Her husband, her own big, tender, clever Warren--but he was hers, and the boys--he was HERS! Her husband--and this other woman was looking at him with all her soul in her eyes, this other woman cared--all the world might see how she cared for him--and was loved in return!

What had she been hearing, lately, of Magsie? Rachael began dizzily to recall what she could. Magsie had been "on the road," she had had a small part in an unsuccessful play early in the winter. Rachael had been for some reason unable to see it, but she had sent Magsie flowers, and--she remembered now--Warren had represented himself as having looked in on the play with some friends, one evening, and as having found it pretty poor stuff. So little had Magsie and Magsie's affairs seemed to matter, then, that Rachael could not even remember the name of the play, nor of hearing it discussed. The world in general had not seemed inclined to make much of the professional advent of Miss Margaret Clay, and presently the play closed, and Warren, in answer to a careless question from Rachael, had said that they would probably take it on the road until spring.

And then, some weeks ago, she had asked about Magsie again, and Warren had said: "I believe she's in town. Somebody told me the other day that she was to have a part in one of Bowman's things this winter."

"It's amazing to me that Magsie doesn't get ahead faster," Rachael had mused. No more was said.

And how pretty she was, how young she was, Rachael thought now, with a stabbing pain at her heart. How earnestly they were talking--no ordinary conversation. Presently tears were in the little actress's eyes; she had no handkerchief, but Warren had. He gave it to her, and she surreptitiously wiped her eyes, and smiled at him, like a pretty child, in her furs.

Rachael felt actually sick with shock. She felt as if some vital cord in her anatomy had been snapped, and as if she could never control these heavy languid limbs of hers again. Her head ached. A lassitude seemed to possess her. She felt cold, and old, and helpless in the face of so much youth and beauty.

Magsie--and Warren. She must accustom herself to the thought. They cared for each other. They cared--Rachael's heart seemed to shut with an icy spasm, she felt herself choking and shut her eyes.

Well, what could they do--at worst? Could Magsie go out now, and get into the Gregory motor car, and say, "Home, Martin!" to the man? Could Magsie run up the steps of the Washington Square house, gather the cream of the day's news from the butler in a breath, and, flinging off furs and wraps, catch the two glorious boys to her heart?

No! However the situation developed, Rachael was still the wife. Rachael held the advantage, and whatever poor Magsie's influence was, it could be but temporary, it must be unrecognized and unapproved by the world.

Slowly self-control came back, the dizziness subsided, the room sank and settled into its usual aspect. It was hideous, but it was a fact, she must face it--she must face it. There was an honorable way, and a dignified way, and that must be her way. No one must know.

Presently the table near her was empty, and she began to breathe more naturally. She pondered so deeply that for a long time the room was forgotten, and the moving crowd shifted about her unseen. Then abstractedly she rose, and went slowly out to the waiting car. She carried a heart of lead.

"I've kept you waiting, Martin?"

Martin merely touched his hat. It was four o'clock.

And so Rachael found herself facing an unbelievable situation. To love, and to know herself unloved, was a cold, dull misery that clung like a weight to her heart. Her thoughts stumbled in a close, hot fog; from sheer weariness she abandoned them again and again.

She had never been a reasonable woman, but she forced herself to be reasonable now. Logic and philosophy had never been her natural defences, but she brought logic and philosophy to bear upon this hideous circumstance. She did not waste time and tears upon a futile "Why?" It was too late now to question; the fact spoke for itself. Warren's senses were wrapped in the charms of another woman. His own devoted and still young and beautiful wife was not the first devoted and young and beautiful woman to have her claim displaced.

For days after the episode in the Waldorf lunch-room she moved like a conspirator, watching, thinking. Warren had never seemed more considerate of her happiness, more satisfied with life. He was full of agreeable chatter at breakfast, interested in her plans, amused at the boys. He did not come home for luncheon, but usually ran up the steps at five o'clock, and was reading or dressing when Rachael wandered into his room to greet him after the day. He never kissed her now, or touched her hand even by chance; she was reminded, in his general aspect, of those occasions when the delicious Derry wandered out from the nursery, evading the nap which was his duty, but full of the airy conversation and small endearments that only a child on sufferance knows.

Rachael tried in vain to understand the affair; what evil genius possessed Warren; what possessed Magsie? She tried to think kindly of Magsie; poor child, she had had no ugly intention, she was simply spoiled, simply an egotist undeveloped in brain and soul!

But--Warren! Well, Warren's soft, simple heart had been touched by all that endearing kittenish confidence, by Magsie's belief that he was the richest and cleverest and most powerful of men.

So they were meeting for lunch, for tea--where else? What did they talk about, what did they plan or hope or expect? Through all her hot impatience Rachael believed that she could trust them both, in the graver sense. Warren was as unlikely to take advantage of Magsie's youthful innocence as Magsie was to definitely commit herself to a reckless course.

But what then? Absurd, preposterous as it was, it was not all a joke. It had already shut the sun from all Rachael's sky. What was it doing to Warren--to Magsie? With Rachael in a cold and dangerous mood, Warren evasive, unresponsive, troubled, what was Magsie feeling and thinking?

Proudly, and with a bitter pain at her heart, Rachael went through her empty days. Her household affairs ran as if by magic; never was there a more successful conspiracy for one man's comfort than that organized by Rachael and her maids. For the first time since their marriage she and Warren were occupying separate rooms now, but Rachael made it a special charge to go in and out of his room constantly when he was there. She would come in with his mail and his newspaper at nine o'clock, full of cheerful solicitude, or follow him in for the half-hour just before dinner, chatting with apparent ease of heart while he dressed.

Only apparent ease of heart, however, for Warren's invariable courtesy and sweetness filled his wife with sick apprehension. Ah, for the old good hours when he scolded and argued, protested and laughed over the developments of the day. Sometimes, nowadays, he hardly heard her, despite his bright, interested smile. Once he had commented upon her gown the instant she came into the room; now he never seemed to see her at all; as a matter of fact, their eyes never met.

In February he told her suddenly that Margaret Clay was to open in another fortnight at the Lyric, in a new play by Gideon Barrett, called "The Bad Little Lady."

"At the Lyric!" Rachael said in a rush of something almost like joy that they could speak of Magsie at last, "and one of Barrett's! Well, Magsie is coming on! What part does she take?"

"The lead--the title part--Patricia Something-or-other, I believe."

"The LEAD! At the Lyric--why, isn't that an astonishing compliment to Magsie!"

Warren looked for his paper-cutter, cut a page, and shrugged his shoulders without glancing up from his book.

"Well, yes, I suppose it is. But of course she's gone steadily ahead."

"But I thought she wasn't so successful last winter, Warren?"

"I don't know," he said politely, wearily, uninterestedly.

"How did you hear this, Warren?" his wife asked, with a deceitful air of innocence.

"Met her," he answered briefly.

"Well, we must see the play," Rachael said briskly. For some reason her heart was lighter than it had been for weeks. This was something definite and in the open at last after all these days of blundering in the dark. "We could take a box, couldn't we, and ask George and Alice?" she added. Warren's expression was that of a boy whose way with his first sweetheart is too suddenly favored by parents and guardians, and Rachael could have laughed at his face.

"Well," he said without enthusiasm. A week later he told her that he had secured the box, but suggested that someone else than the Valentines be asked, Elinor and Peter, for instance.

"You and George aren't quite as good friends as you were, are you?" Rachael said, gravely.

"Quite," Warren said with his bright, deceptive smile and his usual averted glance. "Ask anyone you please--it was merely a suggestion!"

Rachael asked Peter and Elinor, and gave them a delicious dinner before the play. She looked her loveliest, a little fuller in figure than she had been seven years before, and with gray here and there in her rich hair, but still a beautiful and winning presence, and still with something of youth in her spontaneous, quick speech and ready laughter. Warren was, as always, the attentive host, but Rachael noticed that he was abstracted and nervous to-night, and wondered, with a chill at her heart, if Magsie's new venture meant so much to him as his manner implied.

It was an early dinner, and they reached the theatre before the curtain rose.

"It looks like a good house," said Rachael, settling herself comfortably.

"You can't tell anything by this," Warren said, quickly; "it's a first night and papered."

"Aren't you smart with your professional terms?" Elinor Pomeroy laughed, dropping the lorgnette through which she had been idly studying the house. "What _I_'D like to know," she added interestedly, "what _I_'D like to know is, who's doing this for Magsie Clay? Vera Villalonga says she knows, but I don't believe it. Magsie's a little nobody, she has no special talent, and here she is leading in a Barrett play--"

Peter Pomeroy's foot here pressed lightly against Rachael's; a hint, Rachael instantly suspected, that was intended for his wife.

"Now I think Magsie's as straight as a string," the unconscious Mrs. Pomeroy went on, "but she must have a rich beau up her sleeve, and the question is, who is he? I don't--"

But here, it was evident, Peter's second appeal to his wife's discretion was felt, and it suddenly arrested her flow of eloquence.

"--I don't doubt," floundered Elinor, "that--that is--and of course Magsie IS a talented creature, so that naturally--naturally--some girl makes a hit every year, and why shouldn't it be Magsie? Which is right, Peter, 'why shouldn't it be she' or 'why shouldn't it be her?' I never know," she finished somewhat incoherently.

"I should think any investment in Magsie would be perfectly safe," said Rachael's delightful voice. And boldly she added: "Do you know who is backing this, Warren?"

"To a certain extent--I am," Warren said, after an imperceptible pause. To Peter he added, in a lower voice, the voice in which men discuss business matters: "It was a question of the whole deal falling through--I think she'll make good--this fellow Barrett--"

Rachael began to chat with Elinor, but there was bitterness in her soul. She had leaped into the breach, she had saved the situation, at least before Elinor and Peter. But it was not fair--not fair for Warren to have been deep in this affair with Magsie, with never a word to his wife! She--Rachael-- would have been all interest, all sympathy. There was no reason between civilized human beings why this eternal question of sex should debar men and women from common ambitions and common interests! Let Warren admire Magsie if he wanted to do so, let him buy her her play, and stand between her and financial responsibility, jet him admire her--yes, even love her, in his generous, big-brotherly way! But why shut out of this new interest the kindly cooperation of his devoted wife, who had never failed him, who had borne him sons, who had given him the whole of her passionate heart in the full glory of youth, and in health, and in sickness, when it came, had turned to him for all the happiness of her life!

The play began, and presently the house was applauding the entrance of Miss Margaret Clay. She came down a wide, light-flooded stairway, and in her childish white gown and flower-wreathed shepherdess hat looked about sixteen. "How young she is!" Rachael thought with a pang. Her voice was young, too, the fact being that Magsie was frightened, and that Nature was helping her play her first big ingenue part.

Rachael glanced in the darkness at Warren. He had not joined in the applause, nor did his handsome face express any pleasure. He was leaning forward, his hands locked and hanging between his knees, his eyes riveted on the little white figure that was moving and talking down there in the bright bath of light beyond the footlights.

Despite all reason, despite her desperate effort at self-control, Rachael felt an agony of pure jealousy seize her. In an absolute passion of envy she looked down at Magsie Clay. The young, flower-crowned head, the slender, slippered feet, the youthful and appealing voice--what weapons had she against these? And beyond these was the additional lure--as old as the theatre itself--of the fascinating profession: the work that is like play, the rouge and curls, the loves and rages so openly assumed yet so strangely and stirringly effective! Rachael had gowns a thousand times handsomer than these youthful muslins and embroideries; Rachael's own home was a setting far more beautiful than any that could be simulated within the limits of a stage; if Magsie was a successful ingenue, Rachael might have been called a natural queen of tragedy and of comedy! And yet--

And yet, it was because she, too, saw the charm and came under the spell, that Rachael suffered to-night. If she could have laughed it to scorn, could have admired the surface prettiness, and congratulated Magsie upon the almost perfect illusion, then she would have had the most effective of all medicines with which to cure Warren's midsummer madness.

But it seemed to Rachael, stunned with the terrible force of jealousy, that Magsie was the great star of the stage, that there never had been such a play and such a leading lady. It seemed to her that not only to-night's triumph, but a thousand other triumphs were before her, not only the admiration of these twelve or fifteen hundred persons, but that of thousands more! Magsie would be a rage! Magsie's young favors would be sought far and wide. Magsie's summer home, Magsie's winter apartments, Magsie's clothes and fads, these would belong to the adoring public of the most warmhearted and impressionable city in the world! Rachael saw it all coming with perhaps more certainty than did even the little actress behind the footlights.

"Cute play, but I don't think much of Magsie!" Elinor Pomeroy said frankly. Elinor Vanderwall would not have been so impolitic. But Rachael felt that she would have liked to kiss her guest.

"I think Magsie is rather good," she said deliberately.

"Nothing like praising the girl with faint damns!" Peter Pomeroy chuckled.

"Well, what do you think, Peter?" his hostess asked.

"I--oh, Lord! I don't see a play once a year," he said, with the manner, if not the actual presence, of a yawn. "I think it's rather good. I'll tell you what, Greg, I don't see you losing any money on it," he added, with interest; "it'll run; the matinee girls will come!"

"Magsie'd kill you for that," Elinor said.

"I don't suppose we could see Magsie, Warren, after this is over?" Rachael asked to make him speak.

"What did you say, dear?" He brought his gaze from a general study of the house to a point only a few inches out of range of her own. "No, I hardly think so," he answered when she had repeated her question. "She's probably excited and tired."

"You wouldn't mind my sending a line down by the boy?" Rachael persisted.

"Well, I don't think I'd do that--" He hesitated.

"Oh, I'm strong for it!" Elinor said vivaciously. "It'll cheer Magsie up. She's probably scared blue, and even I can see that this isn't making much of a hit!"

The note was accordingly scribbled and dispatched; Rachael's heart was singing because Warren had not denied Elinor's comment upon the success of the play. The leading man, a popular and prominent actor, was disturbingly good, and there was the part of an Irish maid, a comedy part, so well filled by some hitherto unknown young actress that it might really influence the run of the play; but still, there was a consoling indication already in the air that Margaret Clay's talent was somewhat too slight to sustain a leading woman.

At eleven it was over, and if Rachael had had to endure the comment that the second act was "the best yet," there was the panacea, immediately to follow, that the end of the play was "pretty flat."

Presently they all filed back to the dark, windy stage, and joined Magsie in her dressing-room. She was glowing, excited, eager for praise. Never was a young and lovely woman more confident of her charm than Magsie to-night. A flushed self-satisfaction was present on her face during every second of the ten minutes she gave them; her laughter was self-conscious, her smile full of artless gratification; she could not speak to any member of the little group unless the attention of everyone present was riveted upon her.

A callow youth, evidently her adorer, was awaiting her. She spoke slightingly of Bryan Masters, the leading man.

"He's charming, Rachael," said Magsie, smiling her bored young smile, with deliciously red lips, as she was buttoned into a long fur coat, "but--he wants to impose on the fact that--well, that I have arrived, if you know what I mean? As everyone knows, his day is pretty well over. Now you think I'm conceited, don't you, Greg. Oh, I like him, and he does do it rather well, don't you think? But Richie"--Richie was the escorting young man--"Richie and I tease him by breaking into French now and then, don't we?" laughed Magsie.

Sauntering out from the stage entrance with her friends, Miss Clay was the cynosure of all eyes, and knew it; part of the audience still waited for the tedious line of limousines to disperse. She could not move her bright glance to Warren's without encountering the admiring looks of men and women all about her; she could not but hear their whispers: "There, there she is-- that's Miss Clay now!" Richie, introduced as Mr. Gardiner, muttered that his car was somewhere; it proved to be a handsome car with a chauffeur. Magsie raised her bright face pleadingly to Warren's as she took his hands for goodbye.

"Say you were proud of me, Warren?"

He laughed, his indulgent glance flashing to Elinor and to Rachael, as one who invited their admiration of an attractive child, before he looked down at her again.

"Proud of you! Why, I'm as happy as you are about it!"

"You know," Magsie said to Elinor naively, still holding Warren's hands, "he's helped me--tremendously. He's been just--an absolute angel to me!" And real and becoming tears came suddenly to her eyes; she dropped Warren's hands to find a filmy little handkerchief. A second later her smile flashed out again. "You don't mind his being kind to me, do you, Rachael?" she asked childishly.

Rachael's mouth was dry, she felt that her smile was hideous.

"Why should I, Magsie?" she asked a little huskily, "He's kind to everyone!"

A moment later the Gregorys and their guests were in the car whirling toward the Pomeroy home and supper. It was more than an hour later that Rachael and her husband were alone, and then she only said mildly:

"I wish you had let me know you were helping Magsie, so--so conspicuously, Warren. One hates to be taken unawares that way."

"She asked me to keep the thing confidential," he answered with his baffling simplicity. "She had this good chance, but she couldn't quite swing it. I had no idea that you would care, one way or the other."

"Well, she ought to be launched now," Rachael said. She hated to talk of Magsie, especially in his company, where she could do nothing but praise, but she could somehow find it difficult to speak of anything else tonight.

"Cunning little thing, there she was, holding on to my hands, as innocently as a child!" Warren said with a musing smile. "She's a funny girl--all fire and ice, as she says herself!"

Rachael smothered a scornful interjection. Let Magsie employ the arts of a schoolgirl if she would, but at least let the great Doctor Gregory perceive their absurdity!

"Young Mr. Richie Gardiner seemed louche" she observed after a silence which Warren seemed willing indefinitely to prolong.

"H'm!" Warren gave a short, contented laugh.

"He's crazy about her, but of course to her he's only a kid," he volunteered. "She's funny about that, too. She's emotional, of course, full of genius, and full of temperament. She says she needs a safety-valve, and Gardner is her safety-valve. She says she can sputter and rage and laugh, and he just listens and quiets her down. To-night she called him her 'bread-and-butter'--did you hear her?"

"I wonder what she considers you--her champagne?" Rachael asked with a poor assumption of amusement.

But Warren was too absorbed in his own thoughts to notice it.

"It's curious how I do inspire and encourage her," he admitted. "She needs that sort of thing. She's always up in the clouds or down in the dumps."

"Do you see her often, Warren?" Rachael asked with deadly calm.

"I've seen her pretty regularly since this thing began," he answered absently, still too much wrapped in the memories of the evening to suspect his wife's emotion. Rachael did not speak again.

CHAPTER VI

Only Miss Margaret Clay perused the papers on the following morning with an avidity to equal that of Mrs. Warren Gregory. Magsie read hungrily for praise, Rachael was as eager to discover blame. The actress, lying in her soft bed, wrapped in embroidered silk, and sleepily conscious that she was wakening to fame and fortune, gave, it is probable, only an occasional fleeting thought to her benefactor's wife, but Rachael, crisp and trim over her breakfast, thought of nothing but Magsie while she read.

Praise--and praise--and praise. But there was blame, too; there was even sharply contemptuous criticism. On the whole, Rachael had almost as much satisfaction from her morning's reading as Magsie did. The three most influential papers did not comment upon Miss Clay's acting at all. In two more, little Miss Elsie Eaton and Bryan Masters shared the honors. The Sun remarked frankly that Miss Clay's amateurish acting, her baby lisp, her utter unacquaintance with whatever made for dramatic art, would undoubtedly insure the play a long run. Rachael knew that Warren would see all these papers, but she cut out all the pleasanter reviews and put them on his dresser.

"Did you see these?" she asked him at six o'clock.

"I glanced at some of them. You've not got The Sun here?"

"No--that was a mean one," Rachael said sweetly. "I thought it might distress you, as it probably did Magsie."

"I saw it," he said, evidently with no thought of her feeling in the matter. "Lord, no one minds what The Sun thinks!"

"She's really scored a success," said Rachael reluctantly. Warren did not answer.

For the next three evenings he did not come home to dinner, nor until late at night. Rachael bore it with dignity, but her heart was sick within her. She must simply play the waiting game, as many a better woman had before her, but she would punish Warren Gregory for this some day!

She dressed herself charmingly every evening, and dined alone, with a book. Sometimes the old butler saw her look off from the page, and saw her breast rise on a quick, rebellious breath; and old Mary could have told of the hours her mistress spent in the nursery, sitting silent in the darkness by the sleeping boys, but both these old servants were loyalty's self, and even Rachael never suspected their realization of the situation and their resentment. To Vera, to Elinor, even to Alice Valentine, she said never a word. She had discussed Clarence Breckenridge easily enough seven years before, but she could not criticise Warren Gregory to anyone.

On the fourth evening, when they were to dine with friends, Warren reached home in time to dress, and duly accompanied his wife to the affair. He complained of a headache after dinner, and they went home at about half-past ten. Rachael felt his constraint in the car, and for very shame could not make it hard for him when he suggested that he should go downtown again, to look in at the club.

"But is this right, is it fair?" she asked herself sombrely while she was slowly disrobing. "Could I treat him so? Of course I could not! Why, I have never even looked at a man since our very wedding day--never wanted to. And I will be reasonable now. I will be reasonable, but he tries me hard--he makes it hard!"

She put her face in her hands and began to cry. Warren was deluded and under a temporary spell, but still her dear and good and handsome husband, her dearest companion and confidant. And she missed him.

Oh, to have him back again, in the old way, so infinitely dear and interested, so quick with laughter, so vigorous with comment, so unsparing where he blamed! To have him come and kiss the white parting of her hair once more as she sat waiting for him at the breakfast table, turn to her in the car with his quick "Happy?" once more, hold her tight once more against his warm heart!

How unlike him it was, how contemptible it was, this playing with the glorious thing that had been their love! For the first time in her life Rachael could have played the virago, could have raged and stamped, could have made him absolutely afraid to misuse her so. He did not deserve such consideration, he should not be treated so gently.

While she sat alone, in the long evenings, she tried to follow him in her thoughts. He was somewhere in the big, warm, dark theatre, watching the little pool of brightness in which Magsie moved, listening to the crisp, raw freshness of Magsie's voice. Night after night he must sit there, drinking in her beauty and charm, torturing himself with the thought of her inaccessibility.

It seemed strange to Rachael that this world-old tragedy should come into her life with all the stinging novelty of a calamity. People and press talked about a murder, about an earthquake, about a fire. Yet what was death or ruin or flames beside the horror of knowing love to be outgrown, of living beside this empty mask and shell of a man whose mind and soul were in bondage elsewhere? Rachael came to know love as a power, and herself a victim of that power abused.

Slowly resentment began to find room in her heart. It was all so childish, so futile, so unnecessary! A prominent surgeon, the husband of a devoted wife, the father of two splendid sons, thus flinging pride and sanity to the wind, thus being caught in the lightly flung net of an ordinary, pretty little actress, the daughter of a domestic servant and a soldier in the ranks! And what was to be the outcome? Rachael mused sombrely. Was Warren to tire simply of his folly, Magsie to carelessly fill his place in the ranks of her admirers, Rachael to gracefully forgive and forget?

It was an unpalatable role, yet she saw no other open to her. What was to be gained by coldness, by anger, by controversy? Was a man capable of Warren's curious infatuation to be merely scolded and punished like a boy? She was helpless and she knew it. Until he actually transgressed against their love, she could make no move. Even when he did, or if he did, her only recourse was the hated one of a public scandal: accusations, recriminations.

She began to understand his nature as she had not understood it in all these years. Bits of his mother's brief comment upon him came back to her; uncomprehensible when she first heard them, they were curiously illuminating now. He had been a naturally good boy, awkward, silent, conscientious; turning toward integrity as normally as many of his companions turned toward vice. Despite his natural shyness, his diffidence of manner, he had been strong himself and had scorned weakness in anyone; upright, he needed little guiding. The praise of servants and of his mother's friends had been quite frankly his; even his severe mother and father had been able to find little fault in the boy. But they had early learned that when a minor correction was demanded by their first-born's character, it was almost impossible to effect it. His standard of behavior was high, fortunately, for it was also unalterable. There was no hope of their grafting upon his conscience any new roots. James knew right from wrong with infallible instinct; he was not often wrong, but when he was, no outside criticism affected him. As a baby, he would defend his rare misdeeds, as a boy, he was never thrashed, because there was always some good reason for what he did. He had been misinformed, he certainly understood the other fellows to say this; he certainly never heard the teacher forbid that; handsome, reasonable, self-respecting, he won approval on all sides, and because of this mysterious predisposition toward what was right and just, came safely to the years when he was his own master and could live unchallenged by the high moral standard he set himself.

Some of this Rachael began to perceive. It was a key to his conduct now. He respected Magsie, he admired her; there was no reason why he should not indulge his admiration. No unspoken criticism from his wife could affect him, because he had seen the whole situation clearly and had decided what was seemly and safe in the matter. Criticism only brought a resentful, dull red color to Warren Gregory's face, and confirmed him more stubbornly in the course he was pursuing. He could even enjoy a certain martyr-like satisfaction under undeserved censure, all censure being equally incomprehensible and undeserved. Rachael had once seen in this quality a certain godlike supremacy, a bigness, and splendidness of vision that rose above the ordinary standards of ordinary men; now it filled her with uneasiness.

"Well," she thought, with a certain desperate philosophy, "in a certain number of months or years this will all be over, and I must simply endure it until that time comes. Life is full of trouble, anyway!"

Life was full of trouble; she saw it on all sides. But what trivial matters they were, after all, that troubled Elinor and Vera and Judy Moran! Vera was eternally rushing into fresh, furious hospitalities, welcoming hordes of men and women she scarcely knew into her house; chattering, laughing, drinking; flattering the debutantes, screaming at the telephone, standing patient hours under the dressmaker's hands; never rested, never satisfied, never stopping to think. Judy Moran's trouble was that she was too fat; nothing else really penetrated the shell of her indolent good nature. Kenneth might be politely dropped from the family firm, her husband might die and be laid away, her brother-in-law commence an ugly suit for the reclamation of certain jewels and silver tableware, but all these things meant far less to Mrs. Moran than the unflattering truths her bedroom scales told her every morning. She had reached the age of fifty without ever acquiring sufficient self-control to rid herself of the surplus forty pounds, yet she never buttered a muffin at breakfast time, or crushed a French pastry with her fork at noon, without an inward protest. She spent large sums of money for corsets and gowns that would disguise her immense weight rather than deny herself one cup of creamed-and-sugared tea or one box of chocolates. And she suffered whenever a casual photograph, or an unexpected glimpse of herself in a mirror, brought to her notice afresh the dreadful two hundred and twenty pounds.

And Elinor had her absurd and unnecessary troubles, rich man's wife as she was now, and firmly established in the social group upon whose outskirts she had lingered so long. The single state of her four sisters was a constant annoyance to her, especially as Peter was not fond of the girls, and liked to allude to them as "spinsters" and "old maids," and to ask more entertaining and younger women to the house. Elinor had never wanted a child, but in the third or fourth year of her marriage she had begun to perceive that it might be wise to give her worldly old husband an heir, much better that, at any cost, than to encourage his fondness for Barbara Oliphant's boy, his namesake nephew, who was an officious, self-satisfied little lad of twelve. But Nature refused to cooperate in Elinor's maternal plans and Peter Junior did not make his appearance at the big house on the Avenue. Elinor grew yearly noisier, more reckless, more shallow; she rushed about excitedly from place to place, sometimes with Peter, sometimes with one of her sisters; not happy in either case, but much given to quarrelsome questioning of life. It was not that she could not get what she wanted so much as that she did not know her own mind and heart. Whatever was momentarily tiresome or distasteful must be pushed out of her path, and as almost every friend and every human experience came sooner or later into this category, Elinor found herself stranded in the very centre of life.

Alice had her troubles, too, but when her thoughts came to Alice, Rachael found a certain envy in her heart. Ah, those were the troubles she could have welcomed; she could have cried with sheer joy at the thought that her life might some day slip into the same groove as Alice's life. Rachael loved the atmosphere of the big, shabby house now; it was the only place to which she really cared to go. There was in Alice Valentine's character something simple, direct, and high-principled that communicated itself to everybody and everything in her household. A small girl in her nursery might show symptoms of diphtheria, a broken tile on the roof might deluge the bedroom ceilings, an old cook leave suddenly, or a heavy rain fall upon a Sunday predestined for picknicking, but Alice Valentine, plain, slow of speech, and slow of thought, went her serene way, nursing, consoling, repairing, readjusting.

She had her cares about George, but they were not like Rachael's cares for Warren. Alice knew him to be none too strong, easily tired, often discouraged. His professional successes were many, but there were times when the collapse of a tiny child in a free hospital could blot from George's simple, big, tender heart the memory of a dozen achievements. The wife, deep in the claims of her four growing children, sometimes longed to put her arms about him, to run away with him to some quiet land of sunshine and palms, some lazy curve of white beach where he could rest and sleep, and drift back to his old splendid energy and strength. She longed to cook for him the old dishes he had loved in the early days of their marriage, to read to him, to let the world forget them while they forgot the world.

Instead, a hundred claims kept them here in the current of affairs. Mary was a tall, sweet, gracious girl of sixteen now, like her father, a pretty edition of his red hair and long-featured clever face. Mary must go on with her music, must be put through the lessoning and grooming of a gentlewoman, and take her place in the dancing class that would be the Junior Cotillion in a year or two. Alice Valentine was not a worldly woman, but she knew it would be sheer cruelty to let her daughter grow up a stranger in her own world, different in speech and dress and manner from all the other girls and boys. So Mary went to little dances at the Royces' and the Bowditches', and walked home from her riding lesson with little Billy Parmalee or Frank Whittaker, or with Florence Haviland and Bobby Oliphant. And Alice watched her gowns, and her hair, and her pretty young teeth only a little less carefully than she listened to her confidences, questioned her about persons and things, and looked for inaccuracies in her speech.

George Junior was a care, too, in these days at the non-committal, unenthusiastic age of fourteen, when all the vices in the world, finger on lip, form a bright escort for waking or sleeping hours, and the tenderest and most tactful of maternal questions slips from the shell of boyish silence and gruffness unanswered. Full of apprehension and eagerness, Alice watched her only son; she could not give him every hour of her busy days; she would have given him every instant if she could. He was a good boy, but he was human. Dressed for dinner and the theatre, his mother would look into the children's sitting-room to find Mary reading, George reading, Martha, very conscious of being there on sufferance, also reading virtuously and attentively.

"Good-night, my darlings! You're going to bed promptly at nine, aren't you, Mary--and Gogo, too? You know we were all late last night," Alice would say, coming in.

"I am!" Mary would give her mother her sunny smile. "Leslie Perry is going to be here to-morrow night, anyway, and we're going to Thomas Prince's skating party in the afternoon, aren't we, Mother?"

"Thomas Prince, the big boob!" Gogo might comment without bitterness.

"He's not a big boob, either, is he, Mother?" Mary was swift in defence. "He's not nearly such a boob as Tubby Butler or Sam Moulton!"

"Gosh, that's right--knock Tubby!" Gogo would mumble.

"Oh, my darling boy, and my darling girl!" Alice, full of affection and distress, would look from one to the other. Gogo, standing near his mother, usually had a request.

"They're all over at Sam's to-night. Gosh! they're going to have fun!"

"Father said 'NOT again this week,'" Mary might chant.

"Mary!" Alice's reproachful look would silence her daughter; she would put an arm about her son.

"What is it to-night, dear?"

"Oh, nothing much!" Gogo would fling up his dark head impatiently.

"Just Tubby and Sam?"

"I guess so," gruffly.

"But Daddy feels--" Alice would stop short in perplexity. Why shouldn't he go? She had known Mrs. Moulton from the days when they both were brides, the Moultons' house was near, and it was dull for Gogo here, under the sitting-room lamp. If he had only been as contented as Mary, who, with a good time to remember from yesterday, and another to look forward to to-morrow, was perfectly happy to-night. But boys were different. Sam was a trustworthy little fellow, but Alice did not so much like Tubby Butler. And George did not like to have Gogo away from the house at night. She would smile into the boy's gloomy eyes.

"Couldn't you just read to-night, my son, or perhaps Mary would play rum with you? Wouldn't that be better, and a long night's sleep, than going over to Sam's EVERY night?"

But she would leave a disappointed and sullen boy behind her; his disgusted face would haunt her throughout the entire evening.

Martha was not so much a problem, and little Katharine was still baby enough to be a joy to the whole house. But between the children's meals, their shoes and hats and lessons, Alice was a busy woman, and she realized that her responsibilities must increase rather than lessen in the next few years. When Mary was married, and Gogo finishing college, and Martha ready to be entertained and chaperoned by her big sister, then she and George might take Kittiwake and run away; but not now.

Rachael formed the habit of calling at the Valentine house through the wet winds of March and April, coming in upon Alice at all hours, sometimes with the boys, sometimes alone. Alice, in her quiet way, was ready to open her heart completely to her brilliant friend. Rachael spoke of all topics except one to Alice. They discussed houses and maids, the children, books and plays and plans for the summer, birth and death, the approaching responsibility of the vote, philosophies and religions, saints and sages. And the day came when Rachael spoke of Warren and of Margaret Clay.

It was a quiet, wet spring afternoon, a day when the coming of green leaves could be actually felt in the softened air. The two women were upstairs in Alice's white and blue sitting-room enjoying a wood fire. Jim and Derry were in the playroom with Kittiwake; the house was silent, so silent that they could hear the drumming of rain on the leads, and the lazy purr of the fire.

Alice was first incredulous, and then stunned at the story.

Rachael told all she knew, the change in her husband, the opening night of "The Bad Little Lady," her lonely dinners and evenings, and Magsie's complacent attitude of possession.

"Well," said Alice, who had been an absorbed and astounded listener, when she finished, "I confess I don't understand it! If Warren Gregory is making a fool of himself over Margaret Clay, no one is going to be as much ashamed as he is when he is over it. I think with you," Alice added, much in earnest, "that as far as any actual infidelity goes, neither one would be CAPABLE of it! Magsie's a selfish little featherhead, but she has her own advantage too close at heart, and Warren, no matter what preposterous theory he has to explain his interest in Magsie, isn't going to actually do anything that would put him in the wrong!" She paused, but Rachael did not speak, and something in her aspect, as she sat steadily watching the fire, smote Alice to the heart. "I have never been so shocked and so disappointed in my life!" Alice went on, "I can't YET believe it! The only thing you can do is keep quiet and dignified, and wait for the whole thing to wear itself out. This explains the change between George and Warren. I knew George suspected something from the way he tried to shut me up when I saw Warren the other night at the theatre."

"Now that I've talked about it," Rachael smiled, "I believe I feel better!" And presently she dried her eyes, and even laughed at herself a little as she and Alice fell to talking of other things. When Rachael, a boy in each hand, said good-bye, and went out into the pale, late afternoon sunshine that followed the rain, Alice accompanied her to the door, and stood for a moment with her at the top of the street steps.

"You're so lovely, Rachael," said her friend affectionately. "It doesn't seem right to have anything ever trouble anyone so pretty!"

Rachael only smiled doubtfully in answer, but Derry and Jim talked all the way home, their mother listening in silence. She found their conversation infinitely more amusing when uninfluenced by her. Both were naturally observant, Jim logical and reasonable, Derry always misled by his fancy and his dreams. When Tim was a lion, he was a lion who lived in the Gregory nursery, sat in the chairs that belonged to the Gregory children, and preyed upon their toys, as toys. But Derry was a beast of another calibre. The polished nursery floor was the still water of jungle pools, and the cribs were trees which a hideous and ferocious beast, radically differing in every way from little Gerald Gregory, climbed at will. Jim was a lion who liked to be interrupted by grown-ups, who was laughing at his make-believe all the time, but Derry was so frightfully in earnest as to often terrify himself, and almost always impress his brother, with his roarings and ravaging.

To-day their conversation ran along pleasantly; they were companionable little brothers, and only unmanageable when separated.

"All the men walking home will get their feet horrid an' wet," said Jim, "and then the ladies will scold 'em!"

"This would be a great, big ocean for a fairy," Derry commented, flicking a wide puddle with a well-protected little foot. "Jim," he added in an anxious undertone, "could a fairy drown?"

"Not if he had his swimming belt on," Jim said hardily.

"All the fairies have to take little white rose leaves, and make themselves swimming belts," Derry said dreamily, "'r else their mothers won't let them go swimming, will they, Mother?"

They did not wait for her answer, and Rachael was free to return to her own thoughts. But the interruption roused her, and she watched the little pair with pleasure as they trotted before her on the drying sidewalks. Derry was blond and Jim dark, yet they looked alike, both with Rachael's dark, expressive eyes, and with their father's handsome mouth and sudden, appealing smile. But Rachael fancied that her oldest son was most like his father in type, and found it hard to be as stern with Jim as she was with the impulsive reckless, eager Derry, whose faults were more apt to be her own.

To-night she went with them to the nursery, where their little table was already set for supper and their small white beds already neatly turned down.

"Mother's going to give us our baths!" shouted Jim. Both boys looked at her eagerly; Rachael smiled doubtfully.

"Mother's afraid that she will have to dress, to meet Daddy downtown," she began regretfully, when old Mary interposed respectfully:

"Excuse me, Mrs. Gregory. But Dennison took a message from Doctor this afternoon. I happen to know it because Louise asked me if I didn't think she had better order dinner for you. Doctor has been called to Albany on a case, and was to let you know when to expect him."

"Goody--goody--good-good!" shouted Jim, and Derry joined in with a triumphant shriek, and clasped his arms tightly about his mother's knees. Rachael had turned a little pale, but she kissed both boys, and only left them long enough to change her gown to something loose and comfortable.

Then she came back to the nursery, and there were baths, and games, and suppers, and then stories and prayers before the fire, Mary and Rachael laughing over the fluffy heads, revelling in the beauty of the little bodies.

When they were in bed she went down to a solitary dinner, and, as she ate it, her thoughts went back to other solitary dinners years ago. Utter discouragement and something like a great, all-enveloping fear possessed her. She was afraid of life. She had dented her armor, broken her steel, she had been flung back and worsted in the fight.

What was the secret, then, Rachael asked the fire, if youth and beauty and high hopes and great love failed like so many straws? Why was Alice contented, and she, Rachael, torn by a thousand conflicting hopes and fears? Why was it, that with all her cleverness, and all her beauty, the woman who had been Rachael Fairfax, and Rachael Breckenridge, and Rachael Gregory, had never yet felt sure of joy, had never dared lay hands upon it boldly, and know it to be her own, had trembled, and apprehended, and distrusted where women of infinitely lesser gifts had been able to enter into the kingdom with such utter certainty and serenity?

Sitting through the long evening by the fire, in the drowsy silence of the big drawing-room, Rachael felt her eyes grow heavy. Who was unhappy, who was happy--what was all life about anyway--Dennison and old Mary came in at eleven, and looked at her for a long five minutes. Their eyes said a great many things, although neither spoke aloud. The fire had burned low, the light of a shaded lamp fell softly on the sleeping woman's face. There was a little frown between the beautiful brows, and once she sighed lightly, like a child.

The man stepped softly back into the hall, and Mary touched her mistress.

"Mrs. Gregory, you've dropped off to sleep!"

Rachael roused, looked up, smiling bewilderedly. Her look seemed to search the shadows beyond the old woman's form. Slowly the new look of strain and sorrow came back into her eyes.

"Why, so I did!" she said, getting to her feet. "I think I'll go upstairs. Any message from Doctor Gregory?"

"No message, Mrs. Gregory."

"Thank you, Mary, good-night!" Rachael went slowly out through the dimly lighted arch of the hall doorway, and slowly upstairs. She deliberately passed the nursery door. Her heart was too full to risk a visit to the boys tonight. She lighted her room and sank dazedly into a chair.

"I dreamed that we were just married, and in the old studio," she said, half aloud. "I dreamed I had the old-feeling again, of being so sure, and so beloved! I thought Warren had come home early and had brought me violets!"

CHAPTER VII

A day later Dennison brought up the card of Miss Margaret Clay. Rachael turned it slowly in her hands, pondering, with a quickened heartbeat and a fluctuating color. Magsie had been often a guest in Rachael's house a year ago, but she had not been to see Rachael for a long time now. They were to meet, they were to talk alone together--what about? There was nothing about which Rachael Gregory cared to talk to Margaret Clay.

A certain chilliness and trembling smote Rachael, and she sat down. She wished she had been out. It would be simple enough to send down a message to that effect, of course, but that was not the same thing. That would be evading the issue, whereas, had she been out, she could not have held herself responsible for missing Magsie.

Well, the girl was in the neighborhood, of course, and had simply come in to say now do you do? But it would mean evasions, and affectations, and insincerities to talk with Magsie; it would mean lying, unless there must be an open breach. Rachael found herself in a state of actual dread of the encounter, and to end it, impatient at anything so absurd, she asked Dennison to bring the young lady at once to her own sitting-room.

This was the transformed apartment that had been old Mrs. Gregory's, running straight across the bedroom floor, and commanding from four wide windows a glimpse of the old square, now brave in new feathery green. Rachael had replaced its dull red rep with modern tapestries, had had it papered in peacock and gray, had covered the old, dark woodwork with cream-colored enamel and replaced the black marble mantel with a simply carved one of white stone. The chairs here were all comfortable now; Rachael's book lay on a magazine-littered table, a dozen tiny, leather-cased animals, cows, horses, and sheep, were stabled on the hearth, and the spring sunlight poured in through fragile curtains of crisp net. Over the fireplace the great oil portrait of Warren Gregory smiled down, a younger Warren, but hardly more handsome than he was to-day. A pastel of the boys' lovely heads hung opposite it, between two windows, and photographs of Jim and Derry and their father were everywhere: on the desk, on the little grand piano, under the table lamp. This was Rachael's own domain, and in asking Magsie to come here she consciously chose the environment in which she would feel most at ease.

Upstairs came the light, tripping feet. "In here?" said the fresh, confident voice. Magsie came in.

Rachael met her at the door, and the two women shook hands. Magsie hardly glanced at her hostess, her dancing scrutiny swept the room and settled on Warren's portrait.

She looked her prettiest, Rachael decided miserably. She was all in white: white shoes, white stockings, the smartest of little white suits, a white hat half hiding her heavy masses of trimly banded golden hair. If her hard winter had tired Magsie--"The Bad Little Lady" was approaching the end of its run--she did not show it. But there was some new quality in her face, some quality almost wistful, almost anxious, that made its appeal even to Warren Gregory's wife.

"This is nice of you, Magsie," Rachael said, watching her closely, and conscious still of that absurd flutter at her heart. Both women had seated themselves, now Rachael reached for the silk-lined basket where she kept a little pretence of needlework, and began to sew. There were several squares of dark rich silks in the basket, and their touch seemed to give her confidence.

"What are you making?" said Magsie with a rather touching pretence at interest. Rachael began to perceive that Magsie was ill at ease, too. She knew the girl well enough to know that nothing but her own affairs interested her; it was not like Magsie to ask seriously about another woman's sewing.

"Warren likes silk handkerchiefs," explained Rachael, all the capable wife, "and those I make are much prettier than those he can find in the shops. So I pick up pieces of silk, from time to time, and keep him supplied."

"He always has beautiful handkerchiefs," said Magsie rather faintly. "I remember, years ago, when I was with Mrs. Torrence, thinking that Greg always looked so--so carefully groomed."

"A doctor has to be," Rachael answered sensibly. There were no girlish vapors or uncertainties about her manner; she had been the man's wife for nearly seven years; she was in his house; she need not fear Magsie Clay.

"I suppose so," Magsie said vaguely.

"What are your plans, Magsie?" Rachael asked kindly, as she threaded a needle.

"We close on the eighteenth," Magsie announced.

"Yes, so I noticed." Rachael had looked for this news every week since the run of the play began. "Well, that was a successful engagement, wasn't it?" she asked. It began to be rather a satisfaction to Rachael to find herself at such close quarters at last. What a harmless little thing this dreaded opponent was, after all!

"Yes, they were delighted," Magsie responded still in such a lackadaisical, toneless, and dreary manner that Rachael glanced at her in surprise. Magsie's eyes were full of tears.

"Why, what's the matter, my dear child?" she asked, feeling more sure of herself every instant.

Her guest took a little handkerchief from her pretty white leather purse, and touched her bright brown eyes with it lightly.

"I'll tell you, Rachael," said she, with an evident effort at brightness and naturalness, "I came here to see you about something to-day, but I--I don't quite know how to begin. Only, whatever you think about it, I want you to remember that your opinion is what counts; you're the one person who-- who can really advise me, and--and perhaps help me and other people out of a difficulty."

Rachael looked at her with a twinge of inward distaste. This rather dramatic start did not promise well; she was to be treated to some youthful heroics. Instantly the hope came to her that Magsie had some new admirer, someone she would really consider as a husband, and wanted to make of Rachael an advocate with Warren, who, in his present absurd state of infatuation, might not find such a situation to his taste.

"I want to put to you the case of a friend of mine," Magsie said presently, "a girl who, like myself, is on the stage." Rachael wondered if the girl really hoped to say anything convincing under so thin a disguise, but said nothing herself, and Magsie went on: "She's pretty, and young--" Her tone wavered. "We've had a nice company all winter," she remarked lamely.

This was beginning to be rather absurd. Rachael, quite at ease, raised mildly interrogatory eyes to Magsie.

"You'll go on with your work, now that you've begun so well, won't you?" she asked casually.

"W--w--well, I suppose so," Magsie answered dubiously, flushing a sudden red. "I--don't know what I shall do!"

"But surely you've had an unusually encouraging beginning?" pursued Rachael comfortably.

"Oh, yes, there's no doubt about that, at least!" Magsie said. About what was there doubt, then? Rachael wondered.

She deliberately allowed a little silence to follow this remark, smiling, as if at her own thoughts, as she sewed. The younger woman's gaze roved restlessly about the room, she leaned from her chair to take a framed photograph of the boys from a low bookcase, and studied it with evidently forced attention.

"They're stunning!" she said in an undertone as she laid it aside.

"They're good little boys," their mother said contentedly. "I know that the queerest persons in the world, about eating and drinking, are actresses, Magsie," she added, smiling, "so I don't know whether to offer you tea, or hot soup, or an egg beaten up in milk, or what! We had a pianist here about a year ago, and--"

"Oh, nothing, nothing, thank you, Rachael!" Magsie said eagerly and nervously. "I couldn't--"

"The boys may be in soon," Rachael remarked, choosing to ignore her guest's rather unexpected emotion.

This seemed to spur Magsie suddenly into speech. She glanced at the tall old moonfaced clock that was slowly ticking near the door, as if to estimate the time left her, and sat suddenly erect on the edge of her chair.

"I mustn't stay,'" she said breathlessly. "I--I have to be back at the theatre at seven, and I ought to go home first for a few minutes. My girl--she's just a Swedish woman that I picked up by chance--worries about me as if she were my mother, unless I come in and rest, and take an eggnog, or something." She rallied her forces with a quite visible effort. "It was just this, Rachael," said Magsie, looking at the fire, and twisting her white gloves in desperate embarrassment, "I know you've always liked me, you've always been so kind to me, and I can only hope that you'll forgive me if what I say sounds strange to you. I thought I could come here and say it, but--I've always been a little bit afraid of you, Rachael--and I"--Magsie laughed nervously--"and I'm scared to death now!" she said simply.

Something natural, unaffected, and direct in her usually self-conscious and artificial manner struck Rachael with a vague sense of uneasiness. Magsie certainly did not seem to be acting now; there were real tears in her pretty eyes, and a genuine break in her young voice.

"I'm going straight ahead," she said rapidly, "because I've been getting up my courage this whole week to come and see you, and now, while Greg is in Albany, I can't put it off any longer. He doesn't know it, of course, and, although I know I'm putting myself entirely at your mercy, Rachael, I believe you'll never tell him if I ask you not to!"

"I don't understand," Rachael said slowly.

"I've been thinking it all out," Magsie went on, "and this is the conclusion--at least, this is what I've thought! You have always had everything, Rachael. You've always been so beautiful, and so much admired. You loved Clarence, and married him--oh, don't think I'm rude, Rachael," the girl pleaded eagerly, as Rachael voiced an inarticulate protest, "because I'm so desperately in earnest, and s-s-so desperately unhappy!" Her voice broke on a rush of tears, but she commanded it, and hurried on. "You've always been fortunate, not like other women, who had to be second best, but ALWAYS the cleverest, and ALWAYS the handsomest! I remember, when I heard you were to marry Greg, I was just sick with misery for two or three days! I had seen him a few weeks before in Paris, but he said nothing of it, didn't even mention you. Don't think I was jealous, Rachael--it wasn't that. But it seemed to me that you had everything! First the position of marrying a Breckenridge, then to step straight into Greg's life. You'll never know how I--how I singled you out to watch--"

"Just as I have singled you out this horrible winter," Rachael said to herself, in strange pain and bewilderment at heart. Magsie watched her hopefully, but Rachael did not speak, and the girl went on:

"When I came to America I thought of you, and I listened to what everyone said of you. You had a splendid boy, named for Greg, and then another boy; you were richer and happier and more admired than ever! And Rachael--I know you'll forgive me--you were so much FINER than ever-- when I met you I saw that. I couldn't dislike you, I couldn't do anything but admire, with all the others. I remember at Leila's wedding, when you wore dark blue and furs, and you looked so lovely! And then I met Greg again. And truly, truly, Rachael, I never dreamed of this then!"

"Dreamed of what?" Rachael said with dry lips. The girl's voice, the darkening room, the dull, fluttering flames of the dying fire, seemed all like some oppressive dream.

"Dreamed--" Magsie's voice sank. Her eyes closed, she put one hand over her heart, and pressed it there. "Then came my plan to go on the stage," she said, taking up her story, "and one day, when I was especially blue, I met Greg. We had tea together. I've never forgotten one instant of that day! He tried to telephone you, but couldn't get you; we just talked like any friends. But he promised to help me, he was so interested, and I was homesick for Paris, and ready to die in this awful city! After that you gave me a dinner, and then we had theatricals, and then Bowman placed me, and I had to go on the road. But I saw Greg two or three times, and one day--one day last winter"--again her voice faltered, as if she found the memories too poignant for speech--"we drove in the Park," she said dreamily; "and then Greg saw how it was."

Rachael sat silent, stunned.

"Oh, Rachael," the girl said passionately. "Don't think I didn't fight it! I thought of you, I tried to think for us all. I said we would never see each other again, and I went away--you know that! For months after that day in the Park we hardly saw each other. And then, last summer, we met again. And he talked to me so wonderfully, Rachael, about making the best of it, about being good friends anyway--and I've lived on that! But I can't live on that forever, Rachael."

"You've been seeing each other?" Rachael asked stupidly.

"Oh, every day! At tea, you know, or sometimes especially before you came back, at dinner. And, Rachael, nobody will ever know what it's done for me! Greg's managed all my business, and whenever I was utterly discouraged and tired he had the kindest way of saying: 'Never mind, Magsie, I'm tired and discouraged, too!'" Magsie's face glowed happily at the memory of it. "I know I'm not worthy of Greg's friendship," she said eagerly. "And all the time I've thought of you, Rachael, as having the first right, as being far, far above me in everything! But--I'm telling you everything, you see--" Magsie interrupted herself to explain.

"Go on!" Rachael urged, clearing her throat.

"Well, it's not much. But a week or two ago Greg was talking to me about your being eager to get the boys into the country early this year. He looked awfully tired that afternoon, and he said that he thought he would close this house, and live at the club this summer, and he said 'That means you have a dinner date every night, Magsie!' And suddenly, Rachael--I don't know what came over me, but I burst out crying"--Magsie's eyes filled now as she thought of it--"and I said, 'Oh, Greg, we need each other! Why can't we belong to each other! You love me and I love you; why can't we give up our work and the city and everything else, and just be happy!'"

"And what did--Warren say?" Rachael asked in a whisper.

"Oh, Rachael! That's what I've been remembering ever since!" Magsie said. "That's what made me want to come to you; I KNEW you would understand! You're so good; you want people to be happy," said Magsie, fighting tears again and trying to smile. "You have everything: your sons, your position, your beauty--everything! I'm--I'm different from some women, Rachael. I can't just run away with him. There is an honorable and a right way to do it, and I want to ask you if you'll let us take that way!"

"An honorable way?" Rachael echoed in an unnatural voice.

"Well--" Magsie widened innocent eyes. "Nobody has ever blamed YOU for taking it, Rachael!" she said simply. "And nobody ever blamed Clarence, with Paula!"

Rachael, looking fixedly at her, sat as if turned to stone.

"You are brave, Magsie, to come and tell me this," she said at last quietly.

"You are kind to listen to me," Magsie answered with disarming sincerity. "I know it is a strange thing to do." She laughed nervously. "Of course, I know THAT!" she added. "But it came to me that I would the other day. Greg and I were talking about dreams, you know--things we wanted to do. And we talked about going away to some beach, and swimming, and moonlight, and just rest--and quiet--"

"I see," Rachael said.

"Greg said, 'This is only a dream, Magsie, and we mustn't let ourselves dream!'" Magsie went on. "But--but sometimes dreams come true, don't they?"

She stopped. There was an unearthly silence in the room.

"I've tried to fight it, and I cannot," Magsie presently said in a small, tired voice; "it comes between me and everything I do. I'm not a great actress--I know that. I don't even want to be any more. I want to go away where no one will ever see me or hear of me again. I've heard of this--feeling"--she sent Rachael a brave if rather uncertain smile--"but I never believed in it before! I never believed that when--when you care"--Rachael was grateful to be spared the great word--"you can't live or breathe or think anything"-- again there was an evasion--"but the one thing!"

And with a long, tired sigh, again she relapsed into silence. Rachael could find nothing to say.

"Honestly, HONESTLY," the younger woman presently added, "you mustn't think that either one of us saw this coming! We were simply carried away. It was only this year, only a few months ago, that I began to think that perhaps--perhaps if you understood, you would set--Greg free. You want to live just for the boys, you love the country, and books, and a few friends. Your life would go on, Rachael, just as it has, only he would be happy, and I would be happy. Oh, my God," said Magsie, with quivering lips and brimming eyes, "how happy I would be!"

Rachael looked at her in impassive silence.

"At all events," the visitor said more composedly, "I have been planning for a week to come to you, Rachael, and have this talk. I may have done more harm than good--I don't know; but from the instant I thought of it I have simply been drawn, as if I were under a spell. I haven't said what I meant to, I know that. I haven't said"--her smile was wistful and young and sweet, as, rising from her chair, she stood looking down at Rachael--"how badly I feel that it--it happens so," said Magsie. "But you know how deeply I've always admired you! It must seem strange to you that I would come to you about it. But Ruskin, wasn't it, and Wagner--didn't they do something like this? I knew, even if things were changed between you and Greg, that you would be big enough and good enough to help us all to find the--the solution, if there is one!"

Rachael stood up, too, so near her guest that she could put one hand on Magsie's shoulder. The girl looked up at her with the faith of a distressed child.

"I'm glad you did come, Magsie," said Rachael painfully, "although I never dreamed, until this afternoon, that--this--could possibly have been in Warren's thoughts. You speak of--divorce, quite naturally, as of course anyone may, to me. But I never had thought of it. It's a sad tangle, whatever comes of it, and perhaps you're right in feeling that we had better face it, and try to find the solution, if, as you say, there is one."

And Rachael, breathing a little hard, stood looking down at Magsie with something so benign, so tragic, and so heroic in her beautiful face that the younger woman was a little awed, even a little puzzled, where she had been so sure. She would have liked to put her arms about her hostess's neck, and to seal their extraordinary treaty with a kiss, but she knew better. As well attempt to kiss the vision of a ministering angel. Rachael, one arm on Magsie's shoulder, her whole figure and her face expressing painful indecision, had never seemed so remote, so goddesslike.

"And--and you won't tell him of this?" faltered Magsie.

"Ah--you must leave that to me," Rachael said with a sad smile.

For a few seconds longer they looked at each other. Then Rachael dropped her arm, and Magsie moved a little. The visitor knew that another sentence must be in farewell, but she felt strangely awkward, curiously young and crude. Rachael, except for the falling of her arm, was motionless. Her eyes were far away, she seemed utterly unconscious of herself and her surroundings. Magsie wanted to think of one more thing to say, one clinching sentence, but everything seemed to be said. Something of the other woman's weariness and coldness of spirit seemed to communicate itself to her; she felt tired and desolate. It seemed a small and insignificant matter that she had had her momentous talk with Rachael, and had succeeded in her venture. Love was failing her, life was failing.

"I hope--I haven't distressed you--too awfully, Rachael," Magsie faltered. She had not thought of herself, a few hours ago, as distressing Rachael at all. She had thought that Rachael might be scornful, might be cold, might overwhelm her with her magnificence of manner, and shame her for her daring. She had come in on a sudden impulse, and had had no time for any thought but that her revelation would be exciting and dramatic and astonishing. She was sincerely anxious to have Warren freed, but not so swept away by emotion that she could not appreciate this lovely setting and her own picturesque position in the eyes of her beautiful rival.

"Oh, no!" Rachael answered, perfunctorily polite, and with her eyes still fixed darkly on space. And as if half to herself, she added, in a breathless, level undertone:

"It all rests with Warren!"

Presently Magsie breathed a faint "Good-bye," following it with an almost inaudible murmur that Dennison would let her out. Then the white figure was gone from the gloom of the room, and Rachael was alone.

For a time she was so dazed, so emotionally exhausted by the event of the last hour, that she stood on, fixed, unseeing, one hand pressed against her side as if she stopped with it the mouth of a wound. Occasionally she drew a long, sharp breath as the dying sometimes breathe.

"It all rests with Warren," she said presently, half-aloud, and in a toneless, passive voice. And slowly she turned and slowly went to the window.

The room was dark, but twilight lingered in the old square, and home-going men and women were filing across it. The babies and their nurses were gone now, there were only lounging men on the benches. Lumbering green omnibuses rocked their way through the great stone arch, and toward the south, over the crowded foreign quarter, the pink of street lamps was beginning to battle with the warm purple and blue that still hung in the evening sky. The season had been long delayed, but now there was a rustle of green against the network of boughs; a few warm days would bring the tulips and the fruit blossoms.

What a sweet, good, natural world it was in which to be happy! With its wheeling motor cars, its lovers seated in high security for the long omnibus ride, its laborers pleasantly ready for the home table and the day's domestic news! The chattering little Jewish girls from one of the uptown department stores were gay with shrilly voiced plans; the driver, riding lazily home on a pile of empty bags, had no quarrel with the world; the smooth-haired, unhatted Italian women from the Ghetto, with shawls wrapped over their full breasts, and serene black-eyed babies toddling beside them, were placidly content with the run of their days. It remained for the beautiful woman in the drawing-room to look with melancholy eyes upon the springtime, and tear out her heart in an agony no human power could cure.

"It all rests with Warren," Rachael said. Magsie was nothing, she was nothing; the world, the boys, were nothing. It was for Warren to hold their destinies in his hands and decide for them all. No use in raging, in reasoning, in arguing. No use in setting forth the facts, the palpable right and wrong. No use in bitterly asking the unanswering heavens if this were right and just, this system that could allow any young girl to feel any married man, any father, her natural prey. She had come to love Warren just as in a few years she might come to love someone else. That was all permissible; regrettable perhaps for Warren's wife, an unmistakable calamity for Warren's boys, but, from Magsie's standpoint, comprehensible and acceptable. If Warren were free, Magsie was well within her rights; if he were not, Rachael was the last woman in the world to dispute it.

After a while Rachael began to move mechanically about the room. She sat down at her desk and wrote a few checks; the boys little first dancing lessons must be paid for, the man who mended the clock, the woman who had put all her linen in order. She wrote briskly, reaching quickly for envelopes and stamps, and, when she had finished, closed the desk with her usual neatness. She telephoned the kitchen; had she told Louise that Doctor Gregory might come home at midnight? He might be at home for breakfast. Then she glanced about the quiet room, and went softly out, through the inner door, to her own bedroom adjoining. She walked on little usual errands between bureau and wardrobe, steadily proceeding with the changing of her gown. Once she stopped short, in the centre of the floor, and stood musing for a few silent minutes, then she said, aloud and lightly:

"Poor Magsie--it's all so absurd!"

If for a few seconds her thoughts wandered, they always came swiftly back. Magsie and Warren had fallen in love with each other--wanted to marry each other. Rachael tried to marshal her whirling thoughts; there must be simple reason somewhere in this chaotic matter. She had the desperate sensation of a mad-woman trying to prove herself sane. Were they all crazy, to have got themselves into this hideous fix? What was definite, what facts had they upon which to build their surmises?

Warren was her husband, that was one fact; Warren loved her, that was another. They had lived together for nearly eight years, planned together, they knew each other now, heart and soul. And there were two sons. These being facts for Rachael, what facts had Magsie? Rachael's heart rose on a wild rush of confidence. Magsie had no basis for her pretension. Magsie was young, and she had madly and blindly fallen in love. There was her single claim: she loved. Rachael could not doubt it after that hour in the sitting-room. But what pitiable folly! To love and to admit love for another woman's husband!

Thinking, thinking, thinking, Rachael lay awake all night. She composed herself a hundred times for sleep, and a hundred times sleep evaded her. Magsie--Warren--Rachael. Their names swept round and round in her tired brain. She was talking to Magsie, so eloquently and kindly; she was talking to Warren. Warren was shocked at the mere thought of her suspicions, had seen nothing, had suspected nothing, couldn't believe that Rachael could be so foolish! Warren's arms were about her, he was going to take her and the boys away. This was a bad atmosphere for wives, this diseased and abnormal city, Warren said. She was buying steamer coats for Derry and Jim--

Magsie! Again the girl's tense, excited face rose before Rachael's fevered memory. "You mustn't think either one of us saw this coming!"

Rachael rose on her elbow, shook her pillows, flashed a night-light on her watch. Quarter to three. It was a rather dismal hour, she thought, not near enough either midnight or morning. Tossing so long, she would be sleepless all night now.

Well, what was marriage anyway? Was there never a time of serenity, of surety? Was any pretty, irresponsible young woman free to set her heart upon another woman's husband, the father of another woman's children? Rachael suddenly thought of Clarence. How different the whole thing had seemed then! Clarence's pride, Clarence's child, had they been so hurt as her pride and her children were to be hurt now?

She must not allow herself to be so easily frightened. She had been thinking too many months of the one thing; she could not see it fairly. Why, Magsie had been infinitely more dangerous in the early days of her success; there was nothing to fear from the simple, apprehensive Magsie of this afternoon! The only sensible thing was to stop thinking of it, and to go to sleep. But Rachael felt sick and frightened, experienced sensations of faintness, sensations like hunger. Her eyes seemed painfully open, she could not shut them. Her breath came fitfully. She sighed, turned on her side. She would count one hundred, breathing deep and with closed eyes. "Sixteen, seventeen!" Rachael sat suddenly erect, and looked at her watch again. Twenty-two minutes past three.

Morning broke with wind and rain; the new leaves in the square were tossing wildly; sleet struck noisily against the windows. Rachael, waking exhausted, after not more than an hour's sleep, went through the process of dressing in a weary daze. The boys, as was usual, came in during the hour, full of fresh conversation and eager to discuss plans for the day. Jim tied strings from knob to knob of her bureau drawers, Derry amused himself by dashing a chain of glass beads against the foot of the bed until the links gave and the tiny balls rolled in every direction over the floor.

"Never mind," Rachael consoled the discomfited junior, "Pauline will come in and pick them all up. Mother doesn't care!"

Derry, however, howled on unconsoled, and Rachael, stopping, half-dressed, to take him in her arms, mused while she kissed him over the tiny sorrow that could so convulse him. Was she no more than a howling baby robbed of a toy? Nothing could be more real than Derry's sense of loss, no human being could weep more desolately or more unreasonably. Were her love and her life no more than a string of baubles, scattered and flung about by some irresponsible hand? Was nothing real except the great moving sea and the arch of stars above the spring nights? Life and death, and laughter and tears, how unimportant they were! Eight years ago she had felt herself to be unhappy; now she knew that in those days she had known neither sorrow nor joy. Since then, what an ecstasy of fulfilled desire had been hers! She had lived upon the heights, she had tasted the fullest and the sweetest of human emotions. What other woman--Cleopatra, Helen, all the great queens of countries and of art--had known more exquisite delight than hers had been in those first days when she had waited for Warren to come to her with violets?

The morning went on like an ugly dream. At nine o'clock Rachael sent down an untouched breakfast tray. Mary took the boys out into the struggling sunshine. The house was still.

Rachael lay on her wide couch, staring wretchedly into space. Her head ached. The moonfaced clock struck a slow ten, the hall clock downstairs following it with a brisk silver chime. Vendors in the square called their wares; the first carts of potted spring flowers were going their rounds.

Shortly after ten o'clock she heard Warren run upstairs and into his room. She could hear his voice at the telephone; he wanted the hospital-- Doctor Gregory wished to speak to Miss Moore.

Miss Moore? Doctor Gregory would be there at eleven ... please have everything ready. Miss Moore, who was a veteran nurse and a privileged character, asked some question as to the Albany case; Warren wearily answered that the patient had not rallied; it was too bad--too bad.

Once it would have been Rachael's delight to soothe him, to give him the strong coffee he needed before eleven o'clock, to ask about the poor Albany man. Now she hardly heard him. Beginning to tremble, she sat up, her heart beating fast.

"Warren!" she called in a shaken voice.

He came to her door immediately, and they faced each other, his perfunctory greeting arrested by her look.

"Warren," said Rachael with a desperate effort at control, "I want you to tell me about--about you and Magsie Clay."

Instantly his face darkened. He gazed back at her steadily, narrowing his eyes.

"What about it?" he asked sharply.

Rachael knew that she was growing angry against her passionate resolution to keep the conversation in her own hands.

"Magsie came to see me yesterday," she said, panting.

Had she touched him? She could not tell. There was no wavering in his impassive face.

"What about it?" he asked again after a silence.

His wife pushed the rich, tumbled hair from her face with a wild gesture, as if she fought for air.

"What about it?" she echoed, in a constrained tone, still with that quickened shallow breath. "Do you think it is CUSTOMARY for a girl to come to a man's wife, and tell her that she cares for him? Do you think it is CUSTOMARY for a man to have tea every day with a young actress who admits she is in love with him--"

"I don't know what you're talking about!" Warren said, his face a dull red.

"Do you mean to tell me that you don't know that Margaret Clay cares for you," Rachael asked in rising anger, "and that you have never told her you care for her--that you and she have never talked about it, have never wished that you were free to belong to each other!"

"You will make yourself ill!" Warren said quietly, watching her.

His tone brought Rachael abruptly to her senses. Fury and accusation were not her best defence. With Warren calm and dignified she would only hurt her claim by this course. In a second she was herself again, her breath grew normal, she straightened her hair, and with a brief shrug walked slowly from the room into her own sitting-room adjoining. Following her, Warren found her looking down at the square from the window.

"If you are implying anything against Magsie, you are merely making yourself ridiculous, Rachael," he said nervously. "Neither Magsie nor I have forgotten your claim for a single instant. If she came here and talked to you, she did so absolutely without my knowledge."

"She said so," Rachael admitted, heart and mind in a whirl.

"From a sense of protection--for her," Warren went on, "I did NOT tell you how much we have come to mean to each other. I am extremely--unwilling--to discuss it now. There is nothing to be said, as far as I am concerned. It is better not to discuss it; we shall not agree. That Magsie could come here and talk to you surprises me. I naturally don't know what she said, or what impression she gave you. I would only remind you that she is young--and unhappy." He glanced at the morning paper he carried in his hand with an air of casual interest, and added in a moderate undertone, "It's an unhappy business!"

Rachael stood as if she had been shot through the heart--motionless, dumb. She felt the inward physical convulsion that might have followed an actual shot. Her heart seemed to be struggling under a choking flood, and black circles moved before her eyes.

Watching her, Warren presently began to enlarge upon the subject. His tone was that of frank and unashamed, if regretful, narrative. Rachael perceived, with utter stupefaction, that although he was sorry, and even angry at being drawn into this talk, he was far from being confused or ashamed.

"I am sorry for this, Rachael," he began in the logical tone she knew so well. "I think, frankly, that Magsie made a mistake in coming to you. The situation isn't of my making. Magsie, being a woman, being impulsive and impatient, has taken the law into her own hands." He shrugged. "She may have been wise, or unwise, I can't tell!"

He paused, but Rachael did not speak or stir.

Warren had rolled up the paper, and now, in his pacing, reaching the end of the room, he turned, and, thrusting it into his armpit, came back with folded arms.

"Now that this thing has come up," he said in a practical tone, "it is a great satisfaction to me to realize how reasonable a woman you are. I want you to know just how this whole thing happened. Magsie has always been a most attractive girl to me. I remember her in Paris, years ago, young, and with a pretty little way of turning her head, and effective eyes."

"I know all this, Warren!" Rachael said wearily.

"I know you do. But let me recapitulate it," he said, resuming in a businesslike voice: "When I met her at Hoyt's wedding I knew right away that we had a personality to deal with--something rare! I remember thinking then that it would be interesting to see whom she cared for, what that volcanic little heart would be in love--Time went on; we saw more of her. I met her, now and then, we had the theatricals, and the California trip. One day, that fall, in the Park, I took her for a drive, innocently enough, nothing prearranged. And I remember asking if any lucky man had made an impression upon her."

Warren smiled, his eyes absent. Rachael's look of superb scorn was wasted.

"It came to me in a flash," he went on, "that Magsie had come to care for me. Poor little Magsie, she hadn't meant to, she hadn't seen it coming. I remember her looking up at me--she didn't have to say a word. 'I'm sorry, Magsie,' I said. That was all. The touching thing was that even in that trouble she turned to me. We talked it over, I took her back to her hotel, and very simply she said, 'Kiss me, once, Greg, and I'll be good!' After that I didn't see her for a long, long time.

"It seemed to me a sacred charge--you can see that. I couldn't doubt it, the evidence was right there before my eyes, and thinking it over, I couldn't be much surprised. We were in the fix, and of course there was nothing to be done. She went away and that was the end of it, then. But when I saw her again last winter the whole miserable business came up. The rest, of course, she told you. She is unhappy and rebellious, or she would never have dared to come to you! I can't understand her doing so, now, for Magsie is a good little sport, Rachael; she knows you have the right of way. The affair has always been with that understanding. However much I feel for Magsie, and regret the whole thing--why, I am not a cad!" He struck her to her heart with his friendly smile. "You brought the subject up; I don't care to discuss it," he said. "I don't question your actions, and all I ask is that you will not question mine!"

"Perhaps--the world--may some day question them, Warren!" Rachael tried to speak quietly, but she was beginning to be frightened at her own violence. She shook with actual chill, her mouth was dry and her cheeks blazing.

"The world?" He shrugged. "I can hardly see that it is the world's business that you go your way and I go mine!" he said reasonably. He glanced at his watch. "Perhaps you will be so good as to say no more about it?" he suggested. "I have no time, now, anyway. Marriage--"

"Warren!" Rachael interrupted hoarsely. She stopped.

"Marriage," he went on, "never stands still! A man and woman are growing nearer together hourly, or they are growing apart. There is no need, between reasonable beings, for recriminations and bitterness. A man is only a man, after all, and if I have been carried off my feet by Magsie--as I admit I have been--why, such things have happened before! When she and my wife--who might have protected my dignity--meet to discuss the question of their feelings, and their rights, then I confess that I am beyond my depth."

He took a deep chair and sat back, his knees crossed, his elbow on the chair arm, his chin resting on his hand, as one conscious of scoring a point.

"And what about the boys' feelings and rights?" Rachael said in a low, tense tone.

"There you are!" Warren exclaimed. "It's all absurd on the face of it--the whole tangle!"

His wife looked at him in grave, dispassionate scrutiny. Of what was he made, this handsome, well-groomed man of forty-eight? What fatal infection had poisoned heart and brain? She saw him this morning as a stranger, and as a most repellent stranger.

"But it is a tangle in which one still sees right and wrong, Warren," she said, desperately struggling for calm. "Human relationships can't be discussed as if they were the moves on a chess-board. I make no claim for myself--the time has gone by when I could do so--but there is honor and decency in the world, there is simple uprightness! Your attentions, as a married man, can only do Magsie harm, and your daring"--suddenly she began restlessly to pace the floor as he had done--"your daring in coming here to me, to tell me that any other woman has a claim on you," she said, beginning to breathe violently, "only shows me how blind, how drugged you are with--I don't know what to call it--with your own utter lawlessness! What right has Margaret Clay compared to MY right? Are my claims, and my sons' claims, to be swept aside because a little idle girl of Magsie's age chooses to flirt with my husband? What is marriage, anyway--what is parenthood? Are you mad, Warren, that you can come here to our home and talk of 'tangles'--and rights? Do you think I am going to argue it with you, going to belittle my own position by admitting, for one second, that it is open to question?"

She flashed him one blazing look, then resumed her walking and her angry rush of words.

"Why, if some four-year-old child came in here and began to contend for Derry's place," Rachael asked passionately, "how long would we seriously consider his right? If I must dispute the title of Magsie Clay this year, why not of Jennie Jones next year, of Polly Smith the year after that? If--"

"Now you are talking recklessly," Warren Gregory said quietly, "and you have entirely lost sight of the point at issue. Nobody is attempting a controversy with you."

The cool, analytical voice robbed Rachael of all her fire. She sat down, and was silent.

"What you say is quite true," pursued Warren, "and of course, if a woman chooses to stand on her RIGHTS--if it becomes a question of legal obligation--"

"Warren! When was our marriage that?"

"I don't say it was that! I am protesting because YOU talk of rights and titles. I only say that if the problem has come down to a mere question of what is LEGAL, why, that in itself is a confession of failure!"

"Failure!" she echoed with white lips.

"I am not speaking of ourselves, I tell you!" he said, annoyed. "But can any sane person in these days deny that when a man and woman no longer pull together in double harness, our world accepts an honorable change?"

Rachael was silent. These had been her words eight years ago.

"They may have reasons for not making that change," Warren went on logically; "they may prefer to go on, as thousands of people do, to present a perfectly smooth exterior to the world. But don't be so unfair as to assume that what hundreds of good and reputable men and women are doing every day is essentially wrong!"

"You know that you may say this--to me, Warren," she said with a leaden heart.

"Anybody may say it to anybody!" he answered irritably. "Tying a man and a woman together doesn't necessarily make them--"

She interrupted with a quick, breathless, "WARREN!"

"Well!" Again he shrugged his shoulders and again glanced at his watch. "It seems to me that you shouldn't have spoken of the matter if you were not prepared to discuss it!" he said.

Rachael felt the room whirling. She could neither see nor feel anything now but the fury that possessed her. Perhaps twice in her life before, never with him, had she so given way to anger.

"_I_ shouldn't have spoken of it, Warren!" she echoed. "I should have borne it, and smiled, and said nothing! Perhaps I should! Perhaps some women would have done that--"

"Rachael!" he interrupted quickly. But she swept down his words in the wild tide of her own.

"Warren!" she said with deadly decision, "I'm not that sort of woman. You've had your fun--now it's my turn! Now it's my turn!" Rachael repeated in a voiceless undertone as she rapidly paced the room. "Now you can turn to the world, and SEE what the world thinks! Let them know how often you and Magsie have been together, let them know that she came here to ask me to set you free, and then see what the general verdict is! I'm not going to hush this up, to refrain from discussing it because you don't care to, because it hurts your feelings! It SHALL be discussed, and you shall be free! You shall be free, and if you choose to put Magsie Clay here in my place, you may do so!"

"Rachael!" he said angrily. And he caught her thin wrists in his hands.

"Don't touch me!" she said, wrenching herself free. "Don't touch me, you cruel and wicked and heartless--! Go to Magsie! Tell her that I sent you to her! Take your hands off me, Warren--"

Standing back, discomfited, he attempted reason.

"Rachael! Don't talk so! I don't know what to make of you! Why, I never saw you like this. I never heard you--"

The door of her room closed behind her. She was gone. A long silence fell in the troubled room where their voices had warred so lately.

Warren looked at his watch, looked at her door. Then he went out the other door, and downstairs, and out of the house. Rachael heard him go. She was still breathing fast, still blind to everything but her own fury. She would punish him, she would punish him. He should have his verdict from the world he trusted so serenely; he should have his Magsie.

The clocks struck eleven: first the slow clock in her sitting-room, then the quick silvery echo from downstairs. Rachael glanced about nervously. The Bank--the boys' lunches--the trunks--

She went downstairs. In the little breakfast-room off the big dining-room the array of Warren's breakfast waited. Old Mary, with the boys, had just come in the side door.

"Mary," Rachael said quickly, "I want you to help me. Pack some clothes for the boys and me, and give them some luncheon. We are going down to Clark's Hills on the two o'clock train--"

"My God! Mrs. Gregory, you look very bad, my dear!" said Mary.

The unconscious endearment, the shock and concern visible on Mary's homely, honest face were too much for Rachael. Her face changed to ivory, she put one hand to her throat, and her lips quivered.

"Help me--some coffee--Mary!" she whispered. "I think--I'm dying!"

BOOK III

CHAPTER I

Warren went to the hospital and performed his operation. It was a long, hard strain for all concerned, and the nurses told each other afterward that you could see Doctor Gregory's heart was in it, he looked as bad as the child's father and mother did. It was after one o'clock when the surgeons got out of their white gowns, and Warren was in the cold, watery sunlight of the street before he realized that he had had nothing to eat since his dinner in Albany last night.

He looked about vaguely; there were plenty of places all about where he could get a meal. He saw Magsie--

Magsie often drove about in hansom-cabs--they were one of her delights; and more than once of late she had come to meet Warren at some hospital, or even to pick him up at the club. But this was the first time that she had done so without prearrangement.

She leaned out of the cab, a picture of youth and beauty, and waved a white glove. How did she know he was in here? she echoed his question. He had written her from Albany that he would operate at Doctor Berry's hospital this morning she reminded him. And where was he going now?

"I'm awfully worried this morning, honey-girl," said Warren, "and I can't stop to play with nice little Magsies in new blue dresses! My head is blazing, and I believe I'll go home--"

"When did you get in, and where did you have breakfast?" she asked with pretty concern. "Greg, you've not had any? Oh, I believe he hasn't had any! And it's after one, and you've been operating! Get STRAIGHT in--"

"No, dear!" he smiled as she moved to one side of the seat, and packed her thin skirts neatly under her, "not to-day! I'll--"

"Warren Gregory!" said Magsie sternly, "you get right straight in here, and come and have your breakfast! Now, what's nearest? The Biltmore!" She poked the upper door with her slim umbrella. "To the Biltmore!" commanded Magsie.

At a quiet table Warren had coffee and eggs and toast, and more coffee, and finally his cigar. The color came back into his face, and he looked less tired.

Magsie was a rather simple little soul under her casing of Parisian veneer, and was often innocently surprised at the potency of her own charm. That men, big men and wise men, were inclined to take her artful artlessness at its surface value was a continual revelation to her. Like Rachael, she had gone to bed the night before in a profoundly thoughtful frame of mind, a little apprehensive as to Warren's view of her call, and uneasy as to the state in which she had left his wife. But, unlike Rachael, Magsie had not been wakeful long. The consideration of other people's attitudes never troubled her for more than a few consecutive minutes. She had been genuinely stirred by her talk that afternoon, and was honestly determined to become Mrs. Warren Gregory; but these feelings did not prevent her from looking back, with thrilled complacence, to the scene in Rachael's sitting-room, and from remembering that it was a dramatic and heroic thing for a slender, pretty girl in white to go to a man's wife and plead for her love. "No harm done, anyway!" Magsie had reflected drowsily, drifting off to sleep; and she had awakened conscious of no emotion stronger than a mild trepidation at the possibility of Warren's wrath.

Dainty and sweet, she came to meet him halfway, and now sat congratulating herself that he was soothed, fed, and placidly smoking before their conversation reached deep channels.

"Greg, dear, I've got a horrible confession to make!" began Magsie when this propitious moment arrived.

"You mean your call on Rachael?" he asked quickly, the shadow coming back to his eyes. "Why did you do it?"

Magsie was conscious of being frightened.

"Was she surprised, Greg?"

"I don't know that she was surprised. Of course she was angry."

"Well," Magsie said, widening her childish eyes, "didn't you EXPECT her to be angry?"

"I didn't expect her to take any attitude whatever," Warren said with a look half puzzled and half reproving.

"Greg!" Magsie was quite honestly astonished. "What did you expect her to do? Give you a divorce without any feeling whatever?"

There was no misunderstanding her. For a full minute Warren stared at her in silence. In that minute he remembered some of his recent talks with Magsie, some of his notes and presents, he remembered the plan that involved a desert island, sea-bathing, moonlight, and solitude.

"I think, if you had been listening to us," Magsie went on, as he did not answer, "you could not have objected to one word I said! And Rachael was lovely, Greg. She told me she would not contest it--"

"She told you THAT?"

"Well, she said several times that it must be as you decide." Magsie dimpled demurely. "And I was--nice, too!" she asserted youthfully. "I didn't tell her about this--and this!" and with one movement of her pretty hand Magsie indicated the big emerald on her ring finger and the heavy bracelet of mesh gold about her wrist. Suddenly her face brightened, and with an eager movement she leaned across the narrow table, and caught his hand in both her own. "Ah, Greg," she said tenderly, "does it seem true, that after all these months of talking, and hoping, you and I are going to belong to each other?"

"But I have no idea that Rachael is seriously considering a divorce," Warren said slowly. "Why should she? She has no cause!"

"She thinks she has!" Magsie said triumphantly.

"She isn't the sort of woman to think things without reason," Warren said.

"She doesn't have to think," Magsie assured him with the same air of satisfaction; "she knows! Everyone knows how much you and I have been together: everyone knows that you backed 'The Bad Little Lady'--"

"Everyone has no right to draw conclusions from that!" Warren said.

Magsie shrugged her shoulders.

"And what do we care, Greg? I don't care what the world thinks as long as I have you! Let them have the letters, let them buzz--we'll be miles away, and we won't care! And in a year or two, Greg, we'll come back, and they'll all flock about us--you'll see! That's the advantage of a name like the Gregory name! Why, who among them all dropped Clarence on Paula's account, or Rachael on Clarence's?"

"Your going to see her has certainly--complicated things," Warren said reflectively.

"On the contrary," Magsie said confidently, "it has cleared things up. It had to come, Greg; every time you and I talked about it we brought the inevitable nearer! Why, you weren't ever at home. Could that have gone on forever? You had no home, no wife, no freedom. I was simply getting sick of the whole thing! Now at least we're all open and aboveboard; all we've got to do is quietly set the wheels in motion!"

"Well, I'll tell you what must be the first step, Magsie," Warren said after thought; "I'm going home now to see Rachael. I'll talk the whole thing over with her. Then I'll come to see you."

"Positively?" asked Magsie.

"Positively."

"You won't just telephone that you're delayed, Greg, and leave me to wonder and worry?" the girl asked wistfully. "I'll wait until any hour!" He looked at her kindly, with a gentleness of aspect new in their relationship.

"No, dear. It's nearly three now. I'll come take you to tea at, say, half-past four. I am operating again to-night, at nine, and SOME TIME I've got to get in a bath and some sleep. But there'll be time for tea."

Magsie chattered gayly, but Warren was almost silent as they gathered together their belongings, and went out to the street. He called her another cab and beckoned to the man who was waiting with his own car.

"In a few months, perhaps," said Magsie at parting, "when he's all tired and cross, I'll make him coffee AT HOME, and see that he gets his rest and quiet whenever he needs it!"

She did not like his answer.

"Rachael's a wonder at that sort of thing," he said. Magsie had not heard him speak so of his wife for months. "In fact, she spoils me," he added.

"Spoils you by leaving you alone in this hot town for six months out of every year?" Magsie laughed lightly. "Good-bye, dear! At half-past four?"

But even while he nodded Warren Gregory was resolving, in his soul, that he must never see Magsie Clay again. His world was strange and alarming; was falling to pieces about him. He was thirsting for Rachael: her voice, her reproaches, her forgiveness. In seven minutes he would be at home talking to his wife--

Dennison reported, with an impassive face, that Mrs. Gregory had left two hours ago with the children. He believed that they were gone to the Long Island house, sir. Warren, stupefied, went slowly upstairs to have the news confirmed by Pauline. Mrs. Gregory had taken Mary and Millie, sir. And there was a note.

Of course there was a note. To emotion like Rachael's emotion silence was the only unthinkable thing. She had planned a dozen notes, written perhaps five. The one she left was brief:

MY DEAR WARREN: I am leaving with the children for Clark's Hills. You will know best what steps to take in the matter of the freedom you desire. I will cooperate in any way. I have written Magsie that I will not contest your divorce. If for any reason you come to Clark's Hills, I will of course be obliged to see you. I ask you not to come. Please spare me another such talk as ours this morning. I have plenty of money.

Always faithfully, R. G.

Warren read it, and stood in the middle of her bedroom with the sheet crushed in his hand. Pauline had put the empty room in order--in terrible and desolate order. Usually there were flowers in the jars and glass bowls, a doll's chair by the bed, and a woolly animal seated in the chair; a dainty litter of lace scattered on Rachael's sewing-table. Usually she was there when he came in tired, to look up beautiful and concerned: "Something to eat, dear, or are you going to lie down?"

Standing here with the note that ended it all in his hand, he wondered if he was the same man who had so often met that inquiry with an impatient: "Just please don't bother me, dear!" Who had met the succeeding question with, "I don't know whether I shall dine here or not!"

It was half-past three. In an hour he would see Magsie.

In that hour Magsie had received Rachael's note, and her heart sang. For the first time, in what she would have described as this "funny, mixed-up business," she began seriously to contemplate her elevation to the dignity of Warren Gregory's wife. Rachael's note was capable of only one interpretation: she would no longer stand in their way. She was taking the boys to the country, and had given Warren the definite assurance of her agreement to his divorce. If necessary, on condition that her claim to the children was granted, she would establish her residence in some Western city, and proceed with the legal steps from there.

Magsie was frightened, excited, and thrilled all at once. She felt as if she had set some enormous machinery in motion, and was not quite sure of how it might be controlled. But on the whole, complacency underlay all other emotions. She was going to be married to the richest and nicest and most important man of her acquaintance!

At heart, however, her manner belied her; Magsie had little self-confidence. She lived in a French girl's terror that youth would leave her before she had time to make a good match. If nobody knew better than Magsie that she was pretty, also nobody knew better that she was not clever. Men tired of her dimples and giggles and round eyes. Bryan Masters admired her, to be sure, but then Bryan Masters was also a divorced man, and an actor whose popularity was already on the wane. Richie Gardiner admired her in his pathetic, hopeless way, and Richie was young and rich. But Magsie shuddered away from Richie's coughing and fainting; his tonics and his diet had no place in her robust and joyous scheme of life. Besides, all Magsie's world would envy her capture of Greg; he belonged to New York. And Richie's father had been a miner, and his mother was "impossible!"

Magsie dressed exquisitely for the tea; it seemed to her that she had never been so pleasantly excited in her life. She felt a part of the humming, crowded city, the spring wind and the uncertain sky. Life was thrilling and surprising.

Half-past four o'clock came, and Warren came. They were in Magsie's little apartment now, and she could go into his arms. Warren was rather quiet as they went out to tea, but Magsie did not notice it.

As a matter of fact, the man was bewildered; he was tired and worried about his work; but that was the least of it. He could not believe that the day's dazing and flying memories were real--the Albany train, Rachael's room, the hospital, Magsie and the Biltmore breakfast-room, Rachael's room again, and now again Magsie.

Were the lawsuits about which one read in the papers based on no more than this? Apparently not. Magsie seemed perfectly confident of the outcome; Rachael had not shown any doubt. One woman had practically presented him to the other; the law was to be consulted.

The law? How would those letters of Magsie's read if the law got hold of them? His memory flew from note to note. These hastily scratched words would be flung to the wind of gossip, that wind that blew so merrily among the houses where he was known. He had called Magsie his "wonder-child" and his "good little bad girl!" He had given her rings and sashes and a gold purse and a hat and white fox furs--any one gift he had made her was innocent enough in itself! But taken with all the others--

Magsie was in high feather; some tiresome preliminaries, and the day was won! She had not planned so definite a campaign, but it was all coming about in a fashion that more than fulfilled her plans. So, said Magsie to herself, stirring her tea, that was to be her fate: Paris, America, the stage, and then a rich marriage? Well, so be it. She could not complain.

"Greg," she said a dozen times, "isn't it all like a dream?"

To Warren Gregory, as he walked down the street after leaving her at the theatre, it was indeed like a dream, a frightful dream. He could hardly credit his senses, hardly believe that all these horrible things were true, that Rachael knew all about Magsie, and that Magsie was quietly thinking of divorce and marriage! Rachael, in such a rage, rushing away with the boys--why, he had made no secret of his admiration for Magsie from Rachael, he had often talked to her enthusiastically of Magsie! And here she was furiously offering him his freedom.

Well, what had he done after all? What a preposterous fuss about nothing. His thoughts were checked and chilled by the memory of letters that Magsie had. Magsie could prove nothing by those letters--

But what a fool they would make him! Warren Gregory remembered the case of a dignified college professor whose private correspondence had recently been given to the press, and he felt a cool shudder run down his spine. Rachael, reading those letters! It was unthinkable! She and the world would think him a fool! It came to him suddenly that she and the world would be right. He was a fool, and it was a fool's paradise in which he had been wandering: to take his wife and home and sons for granted, and to spend all his leisure at the feet of a calculating little girl like Magsie!

"What did you expect her to do?" Magsie had asked. What would any sane man expect her to do? Smile with him at the new favorite's charms, and take up her life in loneliness and neglect?

And now, Rachael was gone, and he stood promised to Magsie. So much was clear. Rachael would fight for her divorce. Magsie would fight for her husband.

"Oh, my God, how did we ever get into this sickening, sickening mess?" Warren said out loud in his misery.

He had not dined, he did not think of dinner as he paced the windy, cool city streets hour after hour. Nine struck, and he hailed a cab, and went to the hospital, moving through his work like a man in a dream. The woman whose life he chanced to save throughout all her days would say she had had a lovely doctor. Warren hardly saw her. He thought only of Magsie, Magsie who had in her possession a number of compromising letters, every one sillier than the last--Magsie, who expected him to divorce his wife and marry her. He was in such a state of terror that he could not think. Every instant brought more disquiet to his thoughts; he felt as if, when he stepped out into the street again, the newsboys might be calling his divorce, as if honor and safety and happiness were gone forever.

He did not see Magsie again that night, but walked and walked, entering his house sick and haggard, and sleeping the hours restlessly away.

At nine o'clock the next morning he went to the telephone, and called the Valentine house. Doctor Valentine was not at home, he was informed. Was Mrs. Valentine there? Would she speak to Doctor Gregory?

A long pause. Then the maid's pleasant impersonal voice again. Mrs. Valentine begged Doctor Gregory to excuse her.

Warren felt as if he had been struck in the face. Under the eyes of irreproachable and voiceless servants he moved about his silent house. The hush of death seemed to him to lie heavy in the lovely rooms that had been Rachael's delight, and over the city that was just breaking into the green of spring. He dressed, and left directions with unusual sternness; he would be at the hospital, or the club, if he was wanted. He would come home to dinner at seven.

"Mrs. Gregory may be back in a day or so, Pauline," he said. "I wish you'd keep her rooms in order--flowers, and all that."

"Yes, sir," Pauline said respectfully. "Excuse me, Doctor--" she added.

"Well?" said Warren as she paused.

"Excuse me, Doctor, but I telephoned Mrs. Prince yesterday, as Mrs. Gregory suggested," Pauline went on timidly, "and she would be glad to have me come at any time, sir."

Warren's expression did not change.

"You mean that Mrs. Gregory dismissed you?" he suggested.

"Yes, sir!" said Pauline with a sniff. "She paid me for--"

"Then I should make an arrangement with Mrs. Prince, by all means!" Warren said evenly. But a deathlike terror convulsed his heart. Rachael had burned her bridges!

He sent Magsie a note and flowers. He was "troubled by unexpected developments," he said, and too busy to see her to-day, but he would see her to-morrow.

CHAPTER II

Magsie had awakened to a sense of pleasure impending. It was many months since she had felt so important and so sure of herself. Her self-esteem had received more than one blow of late. Bowman had attempted to persuade her to take "The Bad Little Lady" on the road; Magsie had indignantly declined. He had then offered her a poor part in a summer farce; about this Magsie had not yet made up her mind.

Now, she said to herself, reading Warren's note over her late breakfast tray, perhaps she might treat Mr. Bowman to the snubbing she had long been anxious to give him. Perhaps she might spend the summer quietly, inconspicuously, somewhere, placidly awaiting the hour when she would come out gloriously before the world as Warren Gregory's wife. Not at all a bad prospect for the daughter of old Mrs. Torrence's companion and housekeeper.

A caller was announced and was admitted, a thin, restless woman who looked thirty-five despite or perhaps because of the rouge on her sunken cheeks and the smart gown she wore. The years had not treated Carol Pickering kindly: she was an embittered, dissatisfied woman now, noisily interested in the stage as a possible escape from matrimony for herself, and hence interested in Magsie, with whom she had lately formed a sort of suspicious and resentful intimacy.

Joe Pickering had entirely justified in eight years the misgivings felt toward him by everyone who had Carol Breckenridge's interests at heart. His wife had come to him rich, and a few hours after their wedding her father's death had more than doubled the fortune left her by her grandmother. But it would be a sturdy legacy indeed that might hope to resist such inroads as the aimless and ill-matched young couple made upon it from their first day together.

Idly acquiring, idly losing, being cheated and robbed on all sides, they drifted through an unhappy and exciting year or two, finally investing much of their money in bonds, and a handsome residue in that favorite dream of such young wasters: the breeding of horses for the polo market. "What if we lose it all--which we won't--we've still got the bonds!" Joe Pickering, leaden pockets under his eyes, his weak lips hanging loose, had said with his unsteady laugh. What inevitably followed, and what he had not foreseen, was that he should lose more than half the bonds, too. They were seriously crippled now, and began to quarrel, to hate each other for a greater part of the time; and their little son's handsome dark eyes fell on some sad scenes. But now, in the child's sixth year, they were still together, still appearing in public, and still, in that mysterious way known only to their type, rushing about on motor parties, buying champagne, and entertaining after a fashion in their cramped but pretentious apartment.

Of late Billy had been seriously considering the stage. She was but twenty-six, after all, and she still had a girl's thirst for admiration and for excitement. She had called on Magsie, entertained the young actress, and the two had discovered a certain affinity. Magsie was delighted to see her now. They greeted each other affectionately, and Magsie, sending out her tray, settled herself comfortably in her pillows, and took the interested Carol entirely into her confidence, with the single reservation of Warren Gregory's name.

"Handsome, and rich as Croesus, and his wife would divorce him, and belongs to one of the best families," summarized Billy. "Why, I think you would be a fool to do anything else!"

"S'pose I would," dimpled Magsie in interesting embarrassment.

"Have a heart, and tell me who it is," teased Carol, slipping her foot from her low shoe to study a hole in the heel of her silk stocking.

"Oh, I couldn't!" Magsie protested.

"Well, I shall guess, if I can," the other woman warned her. And presently she added: "I'll tell you what, if you do give it up, I'm going straight to Bowman, and ask for your place in your new show! There's nothing about it that I couldn't do, and I believe he might give me a chance! I'll tell you what: you wait until the last moment before you tell him, and then he can't be prepared in advance. And I'll risk having Jacqueline make me a couple of gowns, and be all ready to jump in. I'll learn the part, too," said Billy kindling; "you'll coach me in it, won't you?"

"Of course I will!" Magsie agreed, but she did not say it heartily. The conversation was not extremely pleasing to Magsie at the moment. She loved Warren, of course, but it was certainly a good deal to resign, even to marry a Gregory of New York! Why, here was Billy, who had been a rich man's daughter, and had married the man of her choice, and had a nice child, mad to step into her shoes!

And it was a painful reflection that probably Billy could do it. Billy was smart, she had a dash and finish about her that might well catch a manager's eye, and more than that, it was a rather poor part. It was no such part as Magsie had had in "The Bad Little Lady." There was a comedian in this cast, and a matinee idol for a leading man, and Magsie must content herself with a part and a salary much smaller than was given to either of these.

She thought of Warren, and also fleetingly of Bryan Masters, and even of Richie Gardiner, and decided that it was a bitter and empty world, and she wished she had never been born. Bowman would be smart enough to see that he need pay Billy almost no salary, that she might be a discovery--the discovery for which all managers are always so pathetically on the alert, and that in case the play failed--Magsie was sure, this morning, that it would be the flattest failure ever seen on Broadway--he would have no irate leading lady to pacify; Billy would be only too grateful for the opportunity to try and fail.

"Farce is the most difficult thing in the world to play," she said, now clinging desperately to her little distinction.

"Oh, I know that!" Billy answered absently. She would have a smart apartment on the Drive, and dear little old Breck should drive with her in the Park, and go to the smartest boys' school in the country--

"And of course, I may not marry!" said Magsie.

Carol hardly heard her. She was looking about the comfortable hotel apartment, all in a pretty disorder now, with Magsie's various possessions scattered about. There were pictures of actors on the mantel, heavily autographed, and flowers thrust carelessly into vases. There was a great sheaf of Killarney roses; the envelope that had held a card still dangled from their stems. Carol would have given a great deal to know whose card had been torn from it, and whose name was ringing just now in Magsie's brain. She even cared enough to tentatively interrogate Anna, Magsie's faithful Swedish woman.

"Well, perhaps we shall have a change here, Anna?" Billy said brightly but cautiously, when she was in the hall. She wondered whether the woman would let her slip a bill into her hand.

"Maybe," said Anna impassively.

"How shall you like keeping house for a man and wife?" Billy pursued.

"Aye do that bayfore," remarked Anna, responsive to this kindly interest; "aye ban hahr savan yahre, now, en des country."

"And do you like Miss Clay's young man?" Billy said boldly. But at this shift of topic the light faded from Anna's infantile blue eyes, and a wary look replaced it.

"She got more as one feller," she remarked discouragingly. Billy, outfaced, departed, feeling rather contemptible as she walked down the street. Joe was at home; she had left him in bed when she left the house at ten o'clock, and little Breck had been rather listlessly chatting with the colored boy in the elevator, and had begged his mother to take him downtown. Billy was really sorry for the little boy, but she did not know what to do about it; she wondered what other women did with little lonely boys of six. If she went home, it would not materially better the situation; the cook was cross to-day anyway, and would be crosser if Joe shouted for his breakfast in his usual ungracious manner. She could not go to Jacqueline and talk dresses unless she was willing to pay something on the last bill.

Billy thought of the bank, as she always did think of the bank, when her reflections reached this point. There were the bonds, not as many as they had been, but still fine, salable bonds. She could pay the cook, pay the dressmaker, take Breck home a game, look at hats, spend the day in exactly the manner that pleased her best. She had promised Joe that they would discuss the sale of the next one together when they had sold the last bond, a month ago, and avoid it if possible. But what difference did one make?--a paltry fifty dollars a year! Perhaps it would be possible not to tell Joe--

Billy looked in her purse. She had a dollar bill and fifty cents, more than enough to take her to the bank in appropriate style. She signalled a taxicab.

Magsie did not see Warren the next day, but they had tea and a talk on the day following. She told him gayly that he needed cheering, and presently took him into Tiffany's, where Warren found himself buying her a coveted emerald. Somehow during the afternoon he found himself talking and planning as if they really loved each other, and really were to be married. But it was an unsatisfactory hour. Magsie was excited and nervous, and was rather relieved than otherwise that her interviews with her admirer were necessarily short. As a matter of fact, the undisciplined little creature was overtired and unreasonable. She would have given her whole future for a quiet week in bed, with frivolous novels to read, and Anna to spoil her, no captious manager to please, no exhausting performances to madden her with a sense of her own and other people's imperfections, and no Warren to worry her with his long face.

Added to Magsie's trials, in this dreadful week, was an interview with the imposing mother of young Richie Gardiner, a handsome, florid lady, who had inherited a large fortune from the miner husband whose fortunes she had gallantly shared through some extraordinary adventures in Nome. Mrs. Gardiner idolized her son; she was not inclined to be generous to the little flippant actress who had broken his heart. Richie would not go to the healing desert, he would not go to any place out of sound of Miss Clay's voice, out of the light of Miss Clay's eyes. Mrs. Gardiner had no objection to Magsie's person, nor to her profession, the fact being that her own origin had been even more humble than that of Miss Clay, but she wanted the treasure of her boy's love to be appreciated; she had been envying, since the hour of his birth, the woman who should win Richie's love.

Stout, overdressed, deep-voiced, she came to see the actress, and they both cried; Magsie said that she was sorry--she was so bitterly sorry--but, yes, there was someone else. Mrs. Gardiner shrugged philosophically, wiped her eyes, drew a deep breath. No help for it! Presently she heavily departed; her solid weight, her tinkling spangles, and her rainbow plumes vanished into the limousine, and she was whirled away.

Magsie sighed; these complications were romantic. What could one do?

CHAPTER III

Silent, abstracted, unsmiling, Rachael got through the days. She ate what Mary put before her, slept fairly well, answered the puzzled boys the second time they addressed her. She buckled sandals, read fairy tales, brushed the unruly heads, and listened to the wavering prayers day after day. Her eyes were strained, her usually quick, definite motions curiously uncertain; otherwise there was little change.

Alice, in spite of her husband's half protest, went down to Clark's Hills, deciding in the first hour that the worst of the matter was all over and Rachael quite herself, gradually becoming doubtful, and returning home in despair. Her tearful account took George down to the country house a week later.

Rachael met them; they dined with her. She was interested about the Valentine children, interested in their summer plans. She laughed as she quoted Derry's latest ventures with words. She walked to her gate to wave them good-bye on Monday morning, and told Alice that she was counting the days until the big family came down. But George and Alice were heavy hearted as they drove away.

"What IS it?" asked Alice, anxious eyes upon her husband's kind, homely face. "She's like a person recovering from a blow. She's not sick; but, George, she isn't well!"

"No, she's not well," George agreed soberly. "Bad glitter in her eyes, and I don't like that calm for fiery Rachael! Well, you'll be down here in a week or two--"

"Last week," Alice said not for the first time, "she only spoke of--of the trouble, you know--once. We were just going out to dinner, and she turned to me, and said: 'I didn't like my bargain eight years ago, Alice, and I tore my contract to pieces! Now I'll pay for it.'"

"And you said?"

"I said, 'Oh, nonsense, Rachael. Don't be morbid! There's no parallel between the cases!'"

"H'm!" The doctor was silent for a long time. "I don't know what Greg's doing," he added after thought.

"The question is, what is Magsie doing?" said Alice.

"In my opinion, Rachael's simply blown up," George submitted.

"Magsie told her they had talked of marriage!" Alice countered. George gave an incredulous snort.

"Well, then, Magsie lied," he said firmly.

"She really isn't the lying type, George. And there's no question that Greg and she did see each other every day, and that he wrote her letters and gave her presents!" Alice finished rather timidly, for her husband's face was a thunder-cloud. The old car flew along at thirty-five miles an hour.

"Damn FOOL!" George presently muttered. Alice glanced at him in sympathetic concern.

"George, why don't you see him?"

George preserved a stern silence for perhaps two flying minutes, then he sighed.

"Oh, he'll come to me fast enough when he needs me! Lord, I've pulled old Greg out of trouble before." His whole face grew tender as he added: "You know Greg is a genius, Alice; he's not like other men!"

"I should hope he wasn't!" said Alice with spirit.

"We--ll!" She was sorry for her vehemence when George merely shook his head and ended the conversation on the monosyllable. After a while she attempted to reopen the subject.

"If geniuses can act that way, I'd rather have our girls marry grocers!"

The girls' father smiled absently.

"Oh, well, of course!" he conceded.

"Greg is no more a genius than you are, George," argued Alice.

"Oh, Alice, Alice!" he protested, really distressed, "don't ever let anyone hear you say that! Why, that only shows that you don't know what Greg is. Lord, the man seems to have an absolute instinct for bones; he'll take a chance when not one of the rest will! No, you mark my words, Alice, Greg has let Magsie Clay make a fool of him; he's been overtired and nervous-- we've all seen that--but he's as innocent of any actual harm in this thing as our Gogo!"

"Innocent!" sniffed Alice. "He'll break Rachael's heart with his innocence, and then he'll marry Magsie Clay--you'll see!"

"He'll come to me to get him out of it within the month--you'll see!" George retorted.

"He'll keep out of your way!" Alice predicted confidently. "I know Greg. He has to be perfect or nothing."

But it was only ten days later that Warren Gregory walked up the steps of the Valentine house at about ten o'clock on a silent, hazy morning. George had not yet left the house for the day. The drawing-room furniture was swathed in linen covers, and a collection of golf irons, fishing rods, canoe paddles, and tennis rackets crowded the hallway. The young Valentines were departing for the country to-morrow, and their excited voices echoed from above stairs.

Warren had supposed them already gone. Rachael was alone, then, he reflected, alone in that desolate little country village! He nodded to the maid, and asked in a guarded tone for Doctor Valentine. A moment later George Valentine came into the drawing-room, and the two men exchanged a look strange to their twenty years of affectionate intercourse. Warren attempted mere cold dignity; he was on the defensive, and he knew it. George's look verged on contempt, thinly veiled by a polite interest in his visitor's errand.

"George," said Warren suddenly, when he had asked for Alice and the children, and an awkward silence had made itself felt; "George, I'm in trouble. I--I wonder if you can help me out?"

He could hardly have made a more fortunate beginning; halting as the words were, and miserable as was the look that accompanied them, both rang true to the older man, and went straight to his heart.

"I'm sorry to hear it," George said.

Warren folded his arms, and regarded his friend steadily across them.

"You know Rachael has left me, George?" he began.

"I--well, yes, Alice went down there first, and then I went down," George said. "We only came back ten days ago." There was another brief silence.

"She--she hasn't any cause for this, you know, George," Warren said, ending it, after watching the other man hopefully for further suggestion.

"Hasn't, huh?" George asked thoughtfully, hopefully.

"No, she hasn't!" Warren reiterated, gaining confidence. "I've been a fool, I admit that, but Rachael has no cause to go off at half-cock, this way!"

"What d'you mean by that?" George asked flatly. "What do you mean--you've been a fool?"

"I've been a fool about Magsie Clay," Warren admitted, "and Rachael learned about it, that's all. My Lord! there never was an instant in my life when I took it seriously, I give you my word, George!"

"Well, if Rachael takes it seriously, and Magsie takes it seriously, you may find yourself beginning to take it seriously, too," George said with a dull man's simple evasion of confusing elements.

"Rachael may get her divorce," Warren said desperately. "I can't help that, I suppose. I've got a letter from her here--she left it. I don't know what she thinks! But I'll never marry Margaret Clay--that much is settled. I'll leave town--my work's ended, I might as well be dead. God knows I wish I were!"

"Just how far have you gone with Magsie?" George interrupted quietly.

"Why, nothing at all!" Warren said. "Flowers, handbags, things like that! I've kissed her, but I swear Rachael never gave me any reason to think she'd mind that."

"How often have you seen her?" George asked in a somewhat relieved tone. "Have you seen her once a week?"

"Oh, yes! I say frankly that this was a--a flirtation, George. I've seen her pretty nearly every day---"

"But she hasn't got any letters--nothing like that?"

Warren's confident expression changed.

"Well, yes, she has some letters. I--damn it! I am a fool, George! I swear I wrote them just as I might to anybody. I--I knew it mattered to her, you know, and that she looked for them. I don't know how they'd read!"

George was silent, scowling, and Warren said, "Damn it!" again nervously, before the other man said:

"What do you think she will do?"

"I don't know, George," Warren said honestly.

"Could you--buy her off?" George presently asked after thought.

"Magsie? Never! She's not that type. She's one of ourselves as to that, George. It was that that made me like Magsie--she's a lady, you know. She thinks she's in love; she wants to be married. And if Rachael divorces me, what else can I do?"

"Rachael wants the divorce for the boys," George said. "She told Alice so. She said that except for that, nothing on earth would have made her consider it. But she doesn't want you and Magsie Clay to have any hold over her sons--and can you blame her? She's been dragged through all this once. You might have thought of that!"

"Oh, my God!" Warren said, stopping by the mantel, and putting his face in his hands.

"Well, what did you think would happen?" George asked as Magsie had asked.

Then for perhaps two long minutes there was absolute silence, while Warren remained motionless, and George, in great distress, rubbed his upstanding hair.

"George, what shall I do?" Warren burst out at length.

"Why, now I'll tell you," the older man said in a tone that carried exquisite balm to his listener. "Alice and I have talked this over, of course, and this seems to me to be the only way out: we know you, old man--that's what hurts. Alice and I know exactly what has got you into this thing. You're too easy, Warren. You think because you mean honorably by Magsie Clay, and amuse yourself by being generous to her, that Magsie means honorably by you. You've got a high standard of morals, Greg, but where they differ from the common standards you fail. If the world is going to put a certain construction upon your attentions to an actress, it doesn't matter what private construction you happen to put upon them! Wake up, and realize what a fool you are to try to buck the conventions! What you need is to study other people's morals, not to be eternally justifying and analyzing your own. I don't know how you'll come out of this thing. Upon my word, it's the worst mess we ever got into since you misquoted Professor Diggs and he sued you. Remember that?"

"Oh, George--my God--how you stood by me then," Warren said. "Get me out of this, and I'll believe that there never was a friend like you in the world! I don't know what I ever did to have you and Alice stand by me--"

"Alice isn't standing by you to any conspicuous extent," George Valentine said smilingly, "although, last night, when she was putting the girls to bed, she put her arms about Martha, and said, 'George, she wouldn't be here to-day if Greg hadn't taken the chance and cut that thing out of her throat!' At which, of course," Doctor Valentine added with his boyish smile, "Martha's dad had to wipe his eyes, and Martha's mother began to cry!"

And again he frankly wiped his eyes.

"However, the thing is this," he presently resumed, "if you could buy off Magsie--simply tell her frankly that you've been a fool, that you don't want to go on with it--no, eh?" A little discouraged by Warren's dubious shake of the head, he went on to the next suggestion. "Well, then, if you can't--tell her that there cannot be any talk at present of a legal separation, and that you are going away. Would you have the nerve to do that? Tell her that you'll be back in eight months or a year. But of course the best thing would be to buy her off, or call it off in some way, and then write Rachael fully, frankly--tell her the whole thing, ask her to wait at least one year, and then let you see her--"

Warren could see himself writing this letter, could even see himself walking into the dear old sitting-room at Home Dunes.

"I might see Magsie," he said after thought, "and ask her what she would take in place of what she wants. It's just possible, but I don't believe she would---"

"Well, what could she do if you simply called the whole thing off?" George asked. "Hang it! it's a beastly thing to do, but if she wants money, you've got it, and you've done her no harm, though nobody'll believe that."

"She'll take the heartbroken attitude," Warren said slowly. "She'll say that she trusted me, that she can't believe me, and so on."

"Well, you can stand that. Just set your jaw, and think of Rachael, and go through with it once and for all."

"Yes, but then if she should turn to Rachael again?"

"Ah, well, she mustn't do that. Let her think that, after the year, you'll come to a fresh understanding rather than let her fight. And meanwhile, if I were you, I would write Rachael a long letter and make a clean breast. Alice and the girls go down to-morrow; they'll keep me in touch. How about coming in here for a bachelor dinner Friday? Then we can talk developments."

"George, you certainly are a generous loyal friend!" Warren Gregory said, a dry huskiness in his voice as he wrung the other's hand in good-bye.

George went upstairs to tell the interested and excited and encouraged Alice about their talk, and Alice laughed and cried with-pleasure, confident that everything would come out well now, and grateful beyond words that Greg was showing so humbled and penitent a spirit.

"Leave Rachael to me!" Alice said exultingly. "How we'll all laugh at this nonsense some day!"

Even Warren Gregory, walking down the street, was conscious of new hope and confidence. He was not thinking of Magsie to-day, but of Rachael, the most superb and splendid figure of womanhood that had ever come into his life. How she had raged at him in that last memorable talk; how vital, how vigorous she was, uncompromising, direct, courageous! And as a swimmer, who miles away from shore in the cruel shifting green water, might think with aching longing of the quiet home garden, the kitchen with its glowing fire and gleaming pottery, the pleasant homely routine of uneventful days, and wonder that he had ever found safety and comfort anything less than a miracle, Warren thought of the wife he had sacrificed, the children and home that had been his, unchallenged and undisputed, only a few months before. He knew just where he had failed his wife. He felt to-day that to comfort her again, to take her to dinner again, violets on her breast, and to see her loosen her veil, and lay aside her gloves with those little gestures so familiar and so infinitely dear would be heaven, no less! What comradeship they had had, they two, what theatre trips, what summer days in the car, what communion over the first baby's downy head, what conferences over the new papers and cretonnes for Home Dunes!

Girded by these and a hundred other sacred memories he went to Magsie, who was busy, the maid told him, with her hairdresser. But she presently came out to him, wrapped snugly in a magnificent embroidered kimono, and with her masses of bright hair, almost dry, hanging about her lovely little face. She had never in all their intercourse shown him quite this touch of intimacy before, and he felt with a little wince of his heart that it was a sign of her approaching possession.

"Greg, dear," said Magsie seating herself on the arm of his chair, and resting her soft little person against him, "I've been thinking about you, and about the wonderful, WONDERFUL way that all our troubles have come out! If anyone had told us, two months ago, that Rachael would set you free, and that all this would have happened, we wouldn't have believed it, would we? I watched you walking down the street yesterday afternoon, and, oh, Greg, I hope I'm going to be a good wife to you; I hope I'm going to make up to you for all the misery you've had to bear!"

This was not the opening sentence Warren was expecting. Magsie had been petulant the day before, and had pettishly declared that she would not wait a year for any man in the world. Warren had at once seized the opening to say that he would not hold her to anything against her will, to be answered by a burst of tears, and an entreaty not to be "so mean." Then Magsie had to be soothed, and they had gone to tea as a part of that familiar process. But to-day her mood was different; she was full of youthful enthusiasm for the future.

"You know I love Rachael, Greg, and of course she is a most exceptional woman," bubbled Magsie happily, "but she doesn't appreciate the fact that you're a genius--you're not a little everyday husband, to be held to her ideas of what's done and what isn't done! Big men are a law unto themselves. If Rachael wants to hang over babies' cribs, and scare you to death every time Jim sneezes--"

Warren listened no further. His mind went astray on a memory of the night Jim was feverish, a memory of Rachael in her trailing dull-blue robe, with her thick braids hanging over her shoulders. He remembered that Jim was promised the circus if he would take his medicine; and how Rachael, with smiling lips and anxious eyes, had described the big lions and the elephants for the little restless potentate----

"--because I've had enough of Bowman, and enough of this city, and all I ask is to run away with you, and never think of rehearsals and routes and all the rest of it in my life again!" Magsie was saying. Presently she seemed to notice his silence, for she asked abruptly: "Where's Rachael?"

Warren roused himself from deep thought.

"At the Long Island house; at Clark's Hills."

"Oh!" Magsie, who was now seated opposite him, clasped her hands girlishly about her knees. "What is the plan, Greg?" she asked vivaciously.

"Her plan?" Warren said clearing his throat.

"Our plan!" Magsie amended contentedly. And she summarized the case briskly: "Rachael consents to a divorce, we know that. I am not going on with Bowman, I've decided that. Now what?" She eyed his brooding face curiously. "What shall I do, Greg? I suppose we oughtn't to see each other as we did last summer? If Rachael goes West--and I suppose she will--shall I go up to the Villalongas'? They're terribly nice to me; and I think Vera suspects---"

"What makes you think she does?" Warren asked, feeling as if a hot, dry wind suddenly smote his skin.

"Because she's so nice to me!" Magsie answered triumphantly. "Rachael's been just a little snippy to Vera," she confided further, "or Vera thinks she has. She's not been up there for ages! I could tell Vera---"

Warren's power of reasoning was dissipated in an absolute panic. But George had primed him for this talk. He assumed an air of business.

"There are several things to think of, Magsie," he said briskly, "before we can go farther. In the first place, you must spend the summer comfortably. I've arranged for that--"

He handed her a small yellow bank-book. Magsie glanced at it; glanced at him.

"Oh, Greg, dear, you're too generous!"

"I'm not generous at all," he answered with an honest flush. "I know what I am now, Magsie, I'm a cad."

"Who says you're a cad?" Magsie demanded indignantly.

"I say so!" he answered. "Any man is a cad who gets two women into a mess like this!"

"Greg, dear, you shan't say so!" Her slender arms were about his neck.

"Well--" He disengaged the arms, and went on with his planning. "George Valentine is going to see Rachael," he proceeded.

"About the divorce?" said Magsie with a nod.

"About the whole thing. And George thinks I had better go away."

"Where?" demanded Magsie.

"Oh, travelling somewhere."

"Rio?" dimpled Magsie. "You know you have always had a sneaking desire to see Rio."

Warren smiled mechanically. It had been Rachael's favorite dream "when the boys are big enough!" His sons--were they bathing this minute, or eagerly emptying their blue porridge bowls?

"Magsie, dear," he said slowly, "it's a miserable business--this. I'm as sorry as I can be about it. But the truth is that George wants me to get away only until he and Alice can get Rachael into a mood where she'll forgive me. They see this whole crazy thing as it really is, dear. I'm not a young man, Magsie, I'm nearly fifty. I have no business to think of anything but my own wife and my work and my children--Don't look so, Magsie," he broke off to say; "I only blame myself! I have loved you--I do love you--but it's only a man's love for a sweet little amusing friend. Can't we--can't we stop it right here? You do what you please; draw on me for twice that, for ten times that; have a long, restful summer, and then come back in the fall as if this was all a dream---"

Magsie had been watching him steadily during this speech, a long speech for him. At first she had been obviously puzzled, then astonished, now she was angry. She had grown pale, her pretty childish mouth was a little open, her breath coming fast. For a full minute, as his voice halted, there was silence.

"Then--then you didn't mean all you said?" Magsie demanded stormily, after the pause. "You didn't mean that you--cared? You didn't mean the letters, and the presents, and the talks we've had? You knew I was in earnest, but you were just fooling!" Sheer excitement and fury kept her panting for a moment, then she went on: "But I think I know who's done this, Greg!" she said viciously; "it's Mrs. Valentine. She and her husband have been talking to you; they've done it. She's persuaded you that you never were in earnest with me!" Magsie ran across the room, flung open the little desk that stood there, and tore the rubber band from a package of letters. "You take her one of these!" she said, half sobbing. "Ask her if that means anything! Greg, dear!" she interrupted herself to say in a child's reproachful tone, "didn't you mean it?" And with her soft hair floating, and her figure youthful under the simple lines of her Oriental robe, she came to stand close beside him, her mood suddenly changed. "Don't you love me any more, Greg?" said she.

"Love you!" he countered with a rueful laugh, "that's the trouble."

She linked her soft little hands in his, raised reproachful eyes.

"But you don't love me enough to stand by me, now that Rachael is so cross?" she asked artlessly. "Oh, Greg, I will wait years and years for you!"

Warren's expression was of wretchedness; he managed a smile.

"It's only that I hate to let you in for it all, dear. And let her in for it. I feel as if we hadn't thought it out--quite enough," he said.

"What does it let Rachael in for?" she asked quickly. "Here's her letter, Greg--I'll read it to you! Rachael doesn't mind."

"Well--it will be horrible for you," he submitted in a troubled tone. "Horrible for us both."

"You mean your work can't spare you?" she asked with a shrewd look.

"No!" He shrugged wearily. "No. The truth is, I want to get away," he said in an undertone.

"Ah, well!" Magsie understood that. "Of course you want to get away from the fuss and the talk, Greg," she said eagerly. "I think we all ought to get away: Rachael to Long Island, I to Vera, you anywhere! We can't possibly be married for months---" Suddenly her voice sank, she dropped his hands, and locked her smooth little arms about his neck. "But I'll be waiting for you, and you for me, Greg," she whispered. "Isn't it all settled now, isn't it only a question of all the bother, lawyers and arrangements, before you and I belong to each other as we've always dreamed we might?"

He looked down gravely, almost sadly, and yet with tenderness, upon the eager face. He had always found her lovable, endearing, and sweet; even out of this hideous smoke and flame she emerged all charming and all desirable. He tightened his arms about the thinly wrapped little figure.

"Yes. I think it's all settled now, Magsie!" he said.

"Well, then!" She sealed it with one of her quick little kisses. "Now sit down and read a magazine, Greg," she said happily, "and in ten minutes you'll see me in my new hat, all ready to go to lunch!"

CHAPTER IV

The blue tides rose and fell at Clark's Hills, the summer sun shone healingly down upon Rachael's sick heart and soul. Day after day she took her bare-headed, sandalled boys to the white beach, and lay in the warm sands, with the tonic Atlantic breezes blowing over her. Space and warmth and silence were all about; the incoming breakers moved steadily in, and shrank back in a tumble of foam and blue water; gulls dipped and wheeled in the spray. As far as her dreaming eyes could reach, up the beach and down, there was the same bath of warm color, blue sea melting into blue sky, white sand mingling with yellow dunes, until all colors, in the distance, swam in a haze of dull gold.

Now and then, when even the shore was hot, the boys elected to spend their afternoon by the bay on the other side of the village. Here there was much small traffic in dingies and dories and lobster-pots; the slower tides rocked the little craft at the moorings, and sent bright swinging light against the weather-worn planks under the pier. Rachael smiled when she saw Derry's little dark head confidently resting against the flowing, milky beard of old Cap'n Jessup, or heard the bronzed lean younger men shout to her older son, as to an equal, "Pitch us that painter, will ye, Jim!"

She spoke infrequently but quietly of Warren to Alice. The older woman discovered, with a pang of dismay, that Rachael's attitude was fixed beyond appeal. There was such a thing as divorce, established and approved; she, Rachael, had availed herself of its advantages; now it was Warren's turn.

Rachael would live for her sons. They must of course be her own. She would take them away to some other atmosphere: "England, I think," she told Alice. "That's my mother country, you know, and children lead a sane, balanced life there."

"I will be everything to them until they are--say, ten and twelve," she added on another day, "and then they will begin to turn toward their father. Of course I can't blame him to them, Alice. And some day they will come to believe that it is all their mother's fault--that's the way with children! And so I'll pay again."

"Dearest girl, you're morbid!" Alice said, not knowing whether to laugh or cry.

"No, I mean it, I truly mean that! It is disillusioning for young boys to learn that their father and mother were not self-controlled, normal persons, able to bear the little pricks of life, but that our history has been public gossip for years, that two separate divorces are in their immediate history!"

"Rachael, don't talk so recklessly!"

Rachael smiled sadly.

"Well, perhaps I can be a good mother to them, even if they don't idealize me!" she mused.

"I have come to this conclusion," she told

Alice one day, about a fortnight later, "while civilization is as it is, divorce is wrong. No matter what the circumstances are, no matter where the right and wrong lie, divorce is wrong."

"I suppose there are cases of drink or infidelity--" Alice submitted mildly.

"Then it's the drink, or the infidelity that should be changed!" Rachael answered inflexibly. "It's the one vow we take with God as witness; and no blessing ever follows a broken vow!"

"I think myself that there are not many marriages that couldn't be successes!" Alice said thoughtfully.

"Separation, if you like!" Rachael conceded with something of her old bright energy. "Change and absence, for weeks and months, but not divorce. Paula Verlaine should never have divorced Clarence; she made a worse match, if that was possible, and involved three other small lives in the general discomfort. And I never should have married Clarence, because I didn't love him. I didn't want children then; I never felt that the arrangement was permanent; but having married him, I should have stayed by him. I know the mood in which Clarence took his own life; he never loved me as he did Bill, but he wouldn't have done it if I had been there!"

"I cannot consider Clarence Breckenridge a loss to society," Alice said.

"I might have made Clarence a man who would have been a loss to society," Rachael mused. "He was proud; loved to be praised. And he loved children; one or two babies in the nursery would have put Billy in second place. But he bored me, and I simply wouldn't go on being bored. So that if I had had a little more courage, or a little more prudence in the first place, Billy, Clarence, perhaps Charlotte and Charlie, Greg, Deny, Jim, Joe Pickering, and Billy might all have been happier, to say nothing of the general example to society."

"I hear that Billy is unhappy enough now," Alice said, pleased at Rachael's unusual vivacity. "Isabella Haviland told my Mary that Cousin Billy was talking about divorce."

"From Joe?--is that so?" Rachael looked up interestedly. "I hadn't heard it, and somehow I don't believe it! They have a curious affinity through all their adventures. Poor little Bill, it hasn't been much of a life!"

"They say she is going on the stage," Alice pursued, "which seems a pity, especially for the child's sake. He's an attractive boy; we saw him with her at Atlantic City last winter--one of those wonderfully dressed, patient, pathetic children, always with the grown-ups! The little chap must have a rather queer life of it drifting about from hotel to hotel. They're hard up, and I believe most of the shops and hotels have actually black-listed them. He would seem to be the sort of man who cannot hold on to anything, and, of course, there's the drinking! She's not the girl to save him. She drinks rather recklessly herself; it's a part of her pose."

"I wonder if she would let the youngster come down here and scramble about with my boys?" Rachael said unexpectedly. She had not seriously thought of it; the suggestion came idly. But instantly it took definite hold. "I wonder if she would?" she added with more animation than she had shown for some time. "I would love to have him, and of course the boys would go wild with joy! I would be so glad to do poor old Billy a good turn. She and I were always friends, and had some queer times together. And more than that"--Rachael's eyes darkened--"I believe that if I had had the right influence over her she never would have married Joe. I regarded the whole thing too lightly; I could have tried, in a different way, to prevent it, at least. I am certainly going to write her, and ask for little Breckenridge. It would be something to do for Clarence, too," Rachael added in a low tone, and as if half to herself, "and for many long years I have felt that I would be glad to do something for him! To have his grandson here--doesn't it seem odd?-and perhaps to lend Billy a hand; it seems almost like an answer to prayer! He can sleep on the porch, between the boys, and if he has some old clothes, and a bathing suit--"

"MY DEAR BILLY," she wrote that night, "I have heard one or two hints of late that you have a good many things in your life just now that make for worry, and am writing to know if my boys and I may borrow your small son for a few weeks or a month, so that one small complication of a summer in the city will be spared you. We are down here on Long Island on a strip of high land that runs between the beautiful bay and the very ocean, and when Jim and Derry are not in the one they are apt to be in the other. It will be a great joy to them to have a guest, and a delight to me to take good care of your boy. I think he will enjoy it, and it will certainly do him good.

"I often think of you with great affection, and hope that life is treating you kindly. Sometimes I fancy that my old influence might have been better for you than it was, but life is mistakes, after all, and paying for them, and doing better next time.

"Always affectionately yours, RACHAEL."

Three days elapsed after this letter was dispatched, and Rachael had time to wonder with a little chill if she had been too cordial to Billy, and if Billy were laughing her cool little laugh at her one-time step-mother's hospitality and moralizing.

But as a matter of fact, the invitation could not have been more happily timed for young Mrs. Pickering. Billy, without any further notice to Magsie, had been to see Magsie's manager, coolly betraying her friend's marriage plans, pledging the angry and bewildered Bowman to secrecy, and applying for the position on her own account in the course of one brief visit.

Bowman would not commit himself to engaging Billy, but he was infinitely obliged to her for the news of Magsie, and told her so frankly.

It was when she returned home from this call, and hot and weary, was trying to break an absolute promise to the boy, involving the Zoo and ice-cream, that Rachael's letter arrived.

Billy read it through, sat thinking hard, and presently read it again. The softest expression her rather hard young face ever knew came over it as she sat there. This was terribly decent of Rachael, thought Billy. She must be the busiest and happiest woman in the world, and yet her heart had gone out to little Breck. The last line, however, meant more than all the rest, just now, to Billy Pickering. She was impressionable, and not given to finding out the truths of life for herself. Rachael's opinions she had always respected. And now Rachael admitted that life was all mistakes, and added that heartening line about paying for them, and doing better.

"'Cause I am so hot--and I never had any lunch--and you said you would!" fretted the little boy, flinging himself against her, and sending a wave of heat through her clothing as he did so.

"Listen, Breck," she said suddenly, catching him lightly in her arm, and smiling down at him, "would you like to go down and stay with the Gregory boys?"

"I don't know 'em," said Breck doubtfully.

"Down on the ocean shore," Billy went on, "where you could go in bathing every day, and roll in the surf, and picnic, and sleep out of doors!"

"Did they ask me?" he demanded excitedly.

"Their mother did, and she says that you can stay as long as you're a good boy, down there where it's nice and cool, digging in the sand, and going bare foot--"

"I'll be the best boy you ever saw!" Breck sputtered eagerly. "I'll work for her, and I'll make the other kids work for her--she'll tell you she never saw such a good boy! And I'll write you letters--"

"You won't have to work, old man!" Billy felt strangely stirred as she kissed him. She watched him as he rushed away to break the news of his departure to the stolid Swedish girl in the kitchen and the colored boy at the elevator. He jerked his little bureau open, and began to scramble among his clothes; he selected a toy for Jim and a toy for Derry, and his mother noticed that they were his dearest toys. She took him downtown and bought him a bathing suit, and sandals, and new pajamas, and his breathless delight, as he assured sympathetic clerks that he was going down to the shore, made her realize what a lonely, uncomfortable little fellow he had been all these months. He could hardly eat his supper that night, and had to be punished before he would even attempt to go to sleep, and the next morning he waked his mother at six, and fairly danced with impatience and anxiety as the last preparations were made.

Billy took him down to Clark's Hills herself. She had not notified Rachael, or answered her in any way, never questioning that Rachael would know her invitation to be accepted. But from the big terminal station she did send a wire, and Rachael and the boys met her after the hot trip.

"Billy, it was good of you to come," Rachael said, kissing her quite naturally as they met.

"I never thought of doing anything else," Billy said, breathing the fresh salt air with obvious pleasure. "I had no idea that it was such a trip. But he was an angel--look at them now, aren't they cute together?"

Rachael's boys had taken eager possession of their guest; the three were fast making friends as they trotted along together toward the old motor car that Rachael ran herself.

"It's a joy to them," their mother said. "Get in here next to me, Bill; I'm not going even to look at you until I get you home. Did you ever see the water look so delicious? We'll all go down for a dip pretty soon. I live so simply here that I'm entirely out of the way of entertaining a guest, but now that you're here, you must stay and have a little rest yourself!"

"Oh, thank you, but--" Billy began in perfunctory regret. Her tone changed: "I should love to!" she said honestly.

Rachael laughed. "So funny to hear your old voice, Bill, and your old expressions."

"I was just thinking that you've not changed much, Rachael."

"I? Oh, but I've gray hair! Getting old fast, Billum."

"And how's Greg?" Billy did not understand the sudden shadow that fell across Rachael's face, but she saw it, and wondered.

"Very well, my dear."

"Does he get down here often? It's a hard trip."

"He always comes in his car. They make it in--I don't know-- something like two hours and ten minutes, I think. This is my house, with all its hydrangeas in full bloom. Yes, isn't it nice? And here's Mary for Breckenridge's bag."

Rachael had got out of the car, and now she gave Billy's boy her hand, and stood ready to help him down.

"Well, Breck," said she, "do you think you are going to like my house, and my little boys? Will you give Aunt Rachael a kiss?"

Billy said nothing as the child embraced his new-found relative heartily, nor when Rachael took her upstairs to show her the third hammock between the other two, and herself invested the visitor in blue overalls and a wide hat. But late that evening, after a silence, she said suddenly:

"You're more charming than ever, Rachael; you're one of the sweetest women I ever saw!"

"Thank you!" Rachael said with a little note of real pleasure under her laugh.

"You've grown so gentle, and good," said Billy a little awkwardly. "Perhaps it's just because you're so sweet to Breck, and because you have such a nice way with children, but I--I am ever and ever so grateful to you! I've often thought of you, all this time, and of the old days, and been glad that so much happiness of every sort has come to you. At first I felt dreadfully--at that time, you know--"

She stopped and faltered, but Rachael looked at her kindly. They were sitting on the wide porch, under the velvet-black arch of the starry sky, and watching the occasional twinkle of lights on the dark surface of the bay.

"You may say anything you like to me, Billy," Rachael said.

"Well, it was only--you know how I loved him--" Billy said quickly. "I've so often thought that perhaps you were the only person who knew what it all meant to me. I only thought he would be angry for a while. I thought then that Joe would surely win him. And afterward, I thought I would go crazy, thinking of him sitting there in the club. I had failed him, you know! I've never talked about it. I guess I'm all tired out from the trip down."

It was clumsily expressed; the words came as if every one were wrung from the jealous silence of the long years, but presently Billy was beside Rachael's chair, kneeling on the floor, and their arms were about each other.

"I killed him!" sobbed Billy. "He spoke of me the last of all. He said to Berry Stokes that he--he loved me. And he had a little old picture of me--you remember the one in the daisy frame?--over his heart. Oh, Daddy, Daddy!--always so good to me!"

"No, Bill, you mustn't say that you killed him," Rachael said, turning pale. "If you were to blame, I was, too, and your grandmother, and all of us who made him what he was. I didn't love him when I married him, and he was the sort of man who has to be loved; he knew he wasn't big, and admirable, and strong, but many a man like Clancy has been made so, been made worth while, by having a woman believe in him. I never believed in him for one second, and he knew it. I despised him, and where he sputtered and stammered and raged, I was cool and quiet, and smiling at him. It isn't right for human beings to feel that way, I see it now. I see now that love--love is the lubricant everywhere in the world, Bill. One needn't be a fool and be stepped upon; one has rights; but if loving enough goes into everything, why, it's bound to come out right."

"Oh, I do believe it!" said Billy fervently, kneeling on the floor at Rachael's feet, her wet, earnest eyes on Rachael's face, her arms crossed on the older woman's knees.

"I believe," Rachael said, "that in those seven years I might have won your father to something better if I had cared. He wasn't a hard man, just desperately weak. I've thought of it so often, of late, Bill. There might have been children. Clancy had a funny little pathetic fondness for babies. And he was a loving sort of person---"

"Ah, wasn't he?" Billy's eyes brimmed again. "Always that to me. But not to you, Rachael, and little cat that I was--I knew it. But you see I had no particular reverence for marriage, either. How should I? Why, my own mother and my half-sisters--hideous girls, they are, too--were pointed out to me in Rome a year ago. I didn't know them! I could have made your life much easier, Rachael. I wish I had. I was thinking that this afternoon when Breck was letting you carry him out into deep water, clinging to you so cunningly. He is a cute little kid, isn't he? And he'll love you to death! He's a great kisser."

"He's a great darling," smiled Rachael, "and all small boys I adore. He'll begin to put on weight in no time. And--I was thinking, Bill--he would have reconciled Clancy to you and Joe, perhaps; one can't tell! If I had not left him, Clarence might have been living to-day, that I know. He only--did what he did in one of those desperate lonely times he used to dread so."

"Ah, but he was terrible to you, Rachael!" Billy said generously. "You deserved happiness if anyone ever did!" Again she did not understand Rachael's sharp sigh, nor the little silence that followed it. Their talk ran on quite naturally to other topics: they discussed all the men and women of that old world they both had known, the changes, the newcomers, and the empty places. Mrs. Barker Emory had been much taken up by Mary Moulton, and was a recognized leader at Belvedere Bay now; Straker Thomas was in a sanitarium; old Lady Torrence was dead; Marian Cowles had snatched George Pomeroy away from one of the Vanderwall girls at the last second; Thomas Prince was paralyzed; Agnes Chase had married a Denver man whom nobody knew; the Parker Hoyts had a delicate little baby at last; Vivian Sartoris had left her husband, nobody knew why. Billy was quite her old self as she retailed these items and many more for Rachael's benefit.

But Rachael saw that the years had made a sad change in her before the three days' visit was over. Poor little, impudent, audacious Billy was gone forever--Billy, who had always been so exquisite in dress, so prettily conspicuous on the floor of the ballroom, so superbly self-conscious in her yachting gear, her riding-clothes, her smart little tennis costumes! She was but a shadow of her old self now. The smart hats, the silk stockings, the severely trim frocks were still hers, but the old delicious youth, her roses, her limpid gaze, the velvety curve of throat and cheek, these were gone. Billy had been spirited, now she was noisy. She had been amusingly precocious, now she was assuming an innocence, a naivete, that were no longer hers, had never been natural to her at any time. She had always been coolly indifferent to the lives of other men and women. Now she was embittered as to her own destiny, and full of ugly and eager gossip concerning everyone she knew.

She chanced upon the name of Magsie Clay, little dreaming how straight the blow went to Rachael's heart, but had excellent reasons of her own for not expressing the belief that Magsie would soon leave the stage, and so gave no hint of Magsie's rich and mysterious lover. She did tell Rachael that she herself meant to go on the stage, but imparted no details as to her hopes for doing so.

"Just how much money is left, Billy?" Rachael presently felt herself justified in asking.

"Oh, well"--Billy had always hated statistics--"we sold the Belvedere Bay place last year, you know, but it was a perfect wreck, and the Moultons said they had to put seventeen thousand dollars into repairs, but I don't believe it, and that money, and some other things, were put into the bank. Joe was just making a scene about it--we have to draw now and then--we sank I don't know what into those awful ponies, and we still have that place--it's a lovely house, but it doesn't rent. It's too far away. The kid adores it of course, but it's too far away, it gives me the creeps. It's just going to wreck, too. Joe says sometimes that he's going to raise chickens there. I see him!" Billy scowled, but as Rachael did not speak, she presently came back to the topic. "But just how much of my money is left, I don't know. There are two houses in East One Hundredth--way over by the river. Daddy took them for some sort of debt."

Rachael remembered them perfectly. But she could not revert to the days when she was Clarence's wife without a pang, and so let the allusion go.

"Why he took them I don't know," Billy resumed, "ten flats, and all empty. They say it would cost us ten thousand dollars to get them into shape. They're mortgaged, anyway."

"But Billy, wouldn't that bring you in a fair income, in itself, if it was once filled?"

"My dear, perhaps it would. But do you think you could get Joe Pickering to do it? As long as the money in the bank lasts--I forget what it is, several thousand, more than twenty, I think--we'll go along as we are. Joe has a half-interest in a patent, anyway, some sort of curtain-pole; it's always going to make us a fortune!"

"But, Billy, if you and the boy took a little place somewhere, and you had one good maid--up there on the pony farm, for instance--surely it would be saner, surely it would be wiser, than trying to think of the stage now with him on your hands!"

"Except that I would simply die!" Billy said. "I love the city, and the excitement of not knowing what will turn up. And if Joe would behave himself, and if I should make a hit, why, we'll be all right."

A queer, hectic, unsatisfying life it must be, Rachael thought, saying good-bye to her guest a day or two later. Dressing, rouging, lacing, pinning on her outrageously expensive hats, jerking on her extravagant white gloves, drinking, rushing, screaming with laughter, screaming with anger, Billy was one of that large class of women that the big city breeds, and that cannot live elsewhere than in the big city. She would ride in a thousand taxicabs, worrying as she watched the metre; she would drink a thousand glasses of champagne, wondering anxiously if Joe were to pay for it; she would gossip of a dozen successful actresses without the self-control to work for one-tenth of their success, and she would move through all the life of the theatres and hotels without ever having her place among them, and her share of their little glory. And almost as reckless in action as she was in speech, she would cling to the brink of the conventions, never quite a good woman, never quite anything else, a fond and loyal if a foolish and selfish mother, some day noisily informing her admirers that she actually had a boy in college, and enjoying their flattering disbelief. And so would disappear the last of the handsome fortune that poor Clarence's father had bequeathed to him, and Clarence's grandson must fight his way with no better start than his grandfather had had financially, and with an infinitely less useful brain and less reliable pair of hands. Billy might be widowed or freed in some less unexceptionable way, and then Billy would marry again, and it would be a queer marriage; Rachael could read her fate in her character.

She wondered, walking slowly the short mile that lay between her house and the station, when Billy was gone, just how a discerning eye might read her own fate in her own character. Just what did the confused mixture of good motives and bad motives, erratic unselfishnesses and even more erratic weaknesses that was Rachael, deserve of Fate? She had bought some knowledge, but it had been dearly bought; she had bought some goodness, but at what a cost of pain!

"I don't believe that Warren ever did one-tenth the silly things we suspected him of!" Alice exclaimed one day. "I believe he was just an utter fool, and Magsie took advantage of it!"

Rachael did not answer, but there was no brightening of her sombre look. Her eyes, grave and sad, held for Alice no hope that she had come, as George and Alice had come, to a softer view of Warren's offence.

"I see him always as he was that last horrible morning," she said to Alice. "And I pray that I will never look upon his face again!" And when presently Alice hinted that George was receiving an occasional letter from Warren, Rachael turned pale.

"Don't quote it to me, Alice," she said gently; "don't ask me to hear it. It's all over. I haven't a heart any more, just a void and a pain. You only hurt me--I can't ever be different. You and George love me, I know that. Don't drive me away. Don't ever feel that it will be different from what it is now. I--I wish him no ill, God knows, but--I can't. It wouldn't be happiness for me or for him. Please, PLEASE--!"

Alice, in tears, could only give her her way.

CHAPTER V

Upon the discontented musings of Miss Margaret Clay one hot September morning came Mrs. Joseph Pickering, very charming in coffee-colored madras, with an exquisite heron cockade upon her narrow tan hat. Magsie was up, but not dressed, and was not ill pleased to have company. Her private as well as professional affairs were causing her much dissatisfaction of late, and she was at the moment in the act of addressing a letter to Warren, now on the ocean, from whom she had only this morning had an extremely disquieting letter.

Warren had come to see her the day before sailing, and with a grave determination new to their intercourse, had repeated several unpalatable truths. Rachael, on second thoughts, he told her, had absolutely refused him a divorce.

"But she can't do that! She wrote me herself--" Magsie had begun in anger. His distressed voice interrupted her.

"She's acting for the boys, Magsie. And she's right."

"Right!" The little actress turned pale as the full significance of his words and tone dawned upon her. "But--but what do you mean! What about ME?"

To this Warren had only answered with an exquisitely uncomfortable look and the simple phrase, "Magsie, I'm sorry."

"You mean that you're not going to MAKE her keep her word?"

And again she had put an imperative little hand upon his arm, sure of her power to win him ultimately. Days afterward the angry blood came into her face when she remembered his kind, his almost fatherly, smile, as he dislodged the hand.

"Magsie, I'm sorry. You can't despise me as I despise myself, dear. I'm ashamed. Some day, perhaps, there'll be something I can do for you, and then you'll see by the way I do it that I want with all my heart to make it up to you. But I'm going away now, Magsie, and we mustn't see each other any more."

Magsie, repulsed, had flung herself the length of the little room.

"You DARE tell me that, Greg?"

"I'm sorry, Magsie!"

"Sorry!" Her tone was vitriol. "Why, but I've got your letters. I've got your own words! Everyone knows-the whole world knows! Can you deny that you gave me this?--and this? Can you deny--"

"No, I'm not denying anything, Magsie. Except--that I never meant to hurt you. And I hope there was some happiness in it for you as there was for me."

Magsie had dropped into a chair with her back to him.

"I've made you cross," she said penitently, "and you're punishing me! Was it my seeing Richie, Greg? You know I never cared---"

"Don't take that tone," he said.

Her color flamed again, and she set her little teeth. He saw her breast rise and fall.

"Don't think you can do this, Greg," she said with icy viciousness. "Don't delude yourself! I can punish you, and I will. Alice and George Valentine can fix it all up to suit themselves, but they don't know me! You've said your say now, and I've listened. Very well!"

"Magsie," he said almost pleadingly, interrupting the hard little voice, "can't you see what a mistake it's all been?"

She looked at him with eyes suddenly flooded with tears.

"M-m-mistake to s-s-say we loved each other, Greg?"

The man did not answer. Presently Magsie began to speak in a sad, low tone.

"You can go now if you want to, Greg. I'm not going to try to hold you. But I know you'll come back to me to-morrow, and tell me it was all just the trouble other people tried to make between us--it wasn't really you, the man I love!"

"I'll write you," he said after a silence. And from the doorway he added, "Good-bye." Magsie did not turn or speak; she could not believe her ears when she heard the door softly close.

Next day brought her only a letter from the steamer, a letter reiterating his good-byes, and asking her again to forgive him. Magsie read it in stupefaction. He was gone, and she had lost him!

The first panic of surprise gave way to more reasonable thinking. There were ways of bringing him back; there were arguments that might persuade Rachael to adhere to her original resolution. It could not be dropped so easily. Magsie began to wonder what a lawyer might advise. Billy came in upon her irresolute musing.

"Hello, dearie! But I'm interrupting---" said Billy.

"Oh, hello, darling! No, indeed you're not," Magsie said, tearing up an envelope lazily. "I was trying to write a letter, but I have to think it over before it goes."

"I should think you could write a letter to your beau with your eyes shut," Billy said. "You've had practice enough! I know you're busy, but I won't interrupt you long. Upon my word, I had a hard enough time getting to you. There was no boy at the lift, and only a dear old Irish girl mopping up the floors. We had a long heart-to-heart talk, and I gave her a dollar."

"A dollar! I'll have to move-you're raising the price of living!" said Magsie. "She's the janitor's wife, and they're rich already. What possessed you?"

"Well, she unpinned her skirts and went after the boy," Billy said idly, "and it was the only thing I had." She was trying quietly to see the name on the envelope Magsie had destroyed, but being unsuccessful, she went on more briskly, "How is the beau, by the way?"

"I wish I had never seen the man!" Magsie said, glad to talk of him. "His wife is raising the roof now---"

"I thought she would!" Billy said wisely. "I didn't see any woman, especially if she's not young, giving all that up without a fight! You know I said so."

"I know you did," said Magsie ruefully. "But I don't see what she can do!"

"Well, she can refuse to give him his divorce, can't she?" Billy said sensibly.

"But CAN she?" Magsie was obviously not sure.

"Of course she can!"

"But she doesn't want him. I went to see her--"

"Went to see her? For heaven's sake, what did you do that for?"

"Because I cared for him," Magsie said, coloring.

"For heaven's sake! You had your nerve! And what sort of a person is she?"

"Oh, beautiful! I knew her before. And she said that she would not interfere. She was as willing as he was; then---"

"But now she's changed her mind?"

"Apparently." Magsie scowled into space.

"Well, what does HE say?" Billy asked after a pause.

"Why, he can't--or he seems to think he can't--force her."

"Well, I don't know that he can--here. There are states--"

"Yes, I know, but we're here in New York," Magsie said briefly. A second later she sat up, suddenly energetic and definite in voice and manner. "But there ARE ways of forcing her, as she will soon see," said Magsie in a venomous voice. "I have his letters. I could put the whole thing into a lawyer's hands. There's such a thing as-as a breach of promise suit--"

"Not with a married man," Billy interrupted. Magsie halted, a little dashed.

"How do you know?" she demanded.

"You'd have to show you had been injured--and you've known all along he was married," Billy said.

"Well"--Magsie was scarlet with anger--"I could make him sorry, don't worry about that!" she said childishly.

"Of course, if his wife DID consent, and then changed her mind, and you sent his letters to her," Billy said after cogitation. "It might--he may have glossed it all over, to her, you know."

"Exactly!" Magsie said triumphantly. "I knew there was a way! She's a sensitive woman, too. You know you can't go as far as you like with a girl, Billy," she went on argumentatively, "without paying for it somehow!"

"Make him pay!" said the practical Billy.

"I don't want--just money," Magsie said discontentedly. "I want--I don't want to be interfered with. I believe I shall do just that," she went on with a brightening eye. "I'll write him---"

"Tell him. Ever so much more effective than writing!" Billy suggested.

"Tell him then," Magsie did not mean to betray his identity if she could help it, "that I really will send these things on to his wife--that's just what I'll do!"

"Are there children?" asked Billy.

"Two--girls," Magsie said with barely perceptible hesitation.

"Grown?" pursued the visitor.

"Ye-es, I believe so." Magsie was too clever to multiply unnecessary untruths. She began to dress.

"What are you doing this afternoon?" asked Billy. "I have the Butlers' car for the day. Joe brought it into town to be fixed, and can't drive it out until tomorrow. We might do something. It's a gorgeous car."

"I'm not doing one thing in the world. Where's Joe?"

"Joe Pickering?" asked Billy. "Oh, he's gone off with some men for some golf and poker. We might find someone, and go on a party. Where could we go--Long Beach? It's going to be stifling hot."

"Stay and have lunch with me," said Magsie.

"I can't to-day. I'm lunching with a theatrical man at Sherry's. I tell you I'm in deadly earnest. I'm going to break in! Suppose I come here for you at just three. Meanwhile, you think up someone. How about Bryan Masters?"

Magsie made a face.

"Well," said Billy, departing, "you think of someone, and I will. Perhaps the Royces would go--a nice little early party. The worst of it is, no one's in town!"

She ran downstairs and jumped into the beautiful car.

"Sherry's, please, Hungerford," said Billy easily. "And then you might get your lunch, and come for me sharp at half-past two."

The man touched his hat. Billy leaned back against the rich leather upholstery luxuriously; she was absolutely content. Joe was quiet and away, dear little old Breck was in seventh heaven down on the cool seashore, and there was a prospect of a party to-night. As they rolled smoothly downtown the passing throng might well have envied the complacent little figure in coffee-colored madras with the big heron feather in her hat.

When Billy was gone, Magsie, with a thoughtful face and compressed lips, took two packages of letters from her desk and wrapped them for posting. She fell into deep musing for a few minutes before she wrote Rachael's name on the wrapper, but after that she dressed with her usual care, and carried the package to the elevator boy for mailing. As she came back to her rooms a caller was announced and followed her name into Magsie's apartment almost immediately. Magsie, with a pang of consternation, found herself facing Richie Gardiner's mother.

Anna would never have permitted this, was Magsie's first resentful thought, but Anna was on a vacation, and the elevator boy could not be expected to discriminate.

"Good morning, Mrs. Gardiner," said Magsie; "you'll excuse my dressing all over the place, but I have no maid this week. How's Richie?"

Mrs. Gardiner was oblivious of anything amiss. She sat down, first removing a filmy scarf of Magsie's from a chair, and smiled, the little muscle-twitching smile of a person in pain, as if she hardly heard Magsie's easy talk.

"He doesn't seem to get better, Miss Clay," said she, almost snorting in her violent effort to breathe quietly. "Doctor doesn't say he gets worse, but of course he don't fool me--I know my boy's pretty sick."

The agony of helpless motherhood was not all lost upon Magsie, even though it was displayed by a large, plain woman in preposterous clothes, strangely introduced into her pretty rooms, and a most incongruous figure there.

"What a SHAME!" she said warmly.

"It's a shame to anyone that knew Rich as I did a few years ago," his mother said. "There wasn't a brighter nor a hardier child. It wasn't until we came to this city that he begun to give way--and what wonder? It'd kill a horse to live in this place. I wish to God that I had got him out of it when he had that first spell. I may be--I don't know, but I may be too late now." Tears came to her eyes, the hard tears of a proud and suffering woman. She took out a folded handkerchief and pressed it unashamedly to her eyes. "But he wouldn't go," she resumed, clearing her throat. "He was going to stay here, live or die. And Miss Clay, YOU know why!" She stopped short, a terrible look upon Magsie.

"I?" faltered Magsie, coloring, and feeling as if she would cry herself.

"You kept him," said his mother. "He hung round you like a bee round a rose--poor, sick boy that he was! He's losing sleep now because he can't get you out of his thoughts."

She stopped again, and Magsie hung her head.

"I'm sorry," she said slowly. And with the childish words came childish tears. "I'm awfully sorry, Mrs. Gardiner," stammered Magsie. "I know--I've known all along--how Richie feels to me. I suppose I could have stopped him, got him to go away, perhaps, in time. But--but I've been unhappy myself, Mrs. Gardiner. A person--I love has been cruel to me. I don't know what I'm going to do. I worry and worry!" Magsie was frankly crying now. "I wish there was something I could do for Richie, but I can't tell him I care!" she sobbed.

Both women sat in miserable silence for a moment, then Richard Gardiner's mother said: "It wouldn't do you any harm to just--if you would--to just see him, would it? Don't say anything about this other man. Could you do that? Couldn't you let him think that maybe if he went away and came back all well you'd--you might--there might be some chance for him? Doctor says he's got to go away AT ONCE if he's going to get well."

The anguish in her voice and manner reached Magsie at last. There was nothing cruel about the little actress, however sordid her ambitions and however selfish her plans.

"Could you get him away, now?" she said almost timidly. "Is he strong enough to go?"

"That's what Doctor says; he ought to go away TO-DAY, but--but he won't lissen to me," his mother answered with trembling lips. "He's all I have. I just live for Rich. I loved his father, and when Dick was killed I had only him."

"I'll go see him," said Magsie in sudden generous impulse. "I'll tell him to take care of himself. It's simply wicked of him to throw his life away like this."

"Miss Clay," said Mrs. Gardiner with a break in her strong, deep voice, "if you do that--may the Lord send you the happiness you give my boy!" She began to cry again.

"Why, Mrs. Gardiner," said Magsie in a hurt, childish voice, "I LIKE Richie!"

"Well, he likes you all right," said his mother on a long, quivering breath. With big, coarse, tender fingers she helped Magsie with the last hooks and bands of her toilette. "If you ain't as pretty and dainty as a little wax doll!" she observed admiringly. Magsie merely sighed in answer. Wax dolls had their troubles!

But she liked the doglike devotion of Richie's big mother, and the beautiful car--Richie's car. Perhaps the hurt to her heart and her pride had altered Magsie's sense of values. At all events, she did not even shrink from Richie to-day.

She sat down beside the white bed, beside the bony form that the counterpane revealed in outline, and smiled at Richie's dark, thin eager face and sunken, adoring eyes. She laid her warm, plump little hand between his long, thin fingers. After a while the nurse timidly suggested the detested milk; Richie drank it dutifully for Magsie.

They were left together in the cool, airy, orderly room, and in low, confidential tones they talked. Magsie was well aware that the big doctors themselves would not interrupt this talk, that the nurses and the mother were keeping guard outside the door. Richie was conscious of nothing but Magsie.

In this hour the girl thought of the stormy years that were past and the stormy future. She had played her last card in the game for Warren Gregory's love. The letters, without an additional word, were gone to Rachael. If Rachael chose to use them against Warren, then the road for Magsie, if long, was unobstructed. But suppose Rachael, with that baffling superiority of hers, decided not to use them?

Magsie had seriously considered and seriously abandoned the idea of holding out several letters from the packages, but the letters, as legal documents, had no value to anyone but Rachael. If Rachael chose to forgive and ignore the writing of them, they were so much waste paper, and Magsie had no more hold over Warren than any other young woman of his acquaintance.

But Magsie was more or less committed to a complete change. The break with Bowman could not be avoided without great awkwardness now. She despised herself for having so simply accepted a bank account from Warren, yet what else could she do? Magsie had wanted money all her life, and when that money was gone---Richie was falling into a doze, his hand still tightly clasping hers. She slipped to her knees beside the bed, and as he lazily opened his eyes she gave him a smile that turned the room to Heaven for him. When a nurse peeped cautiously in, a warning nod from Magsie sent the surprised and delighted woman away again with the great news. Mr. Gardiner was asleep!

The clock struck twelve, struck one, still Magsie knelt by the bedside, watching the sleeping face. Outside the city was silent under the summer sun. In the great hospital feet cheeped along wide corridors, now and then a door was opened or closed. There was no other sound.

Magsie eyed her charge affectionately. When he had come to her dressing-room in former days trying to ignore his cough, trying to take her about and to order her suppers as the other men did, he had been vaguely irritating; but here in this plain little bed, so boyish, so dependent, so appreciative, he seemed more attractive than he ever had before. Whatever there was maternal in Magsie rose to meet his need. She could not but be impressed by the royal solicitude that surrounded the heir to the "Little Dick Mine." Mrs. Richard Gardiner would be something of a personage, thought Magsie dreamily. He might not live long!

Of course, that was calculating and despicable; she was not the woman to marry where she did not love! But then she really did love Richie in a way. And Richie loved her--no question of that! Loved her more than Warren did for all his letters and gifts, she decided resentfully.

When Richie wakened, bewildered, at one o'clock, Magsie was still there. She insisted that he drink more milk before a word was said. Then they talked again, Magsie in a new mood of reluctance and gentleness, Richie half wild with rising hope and joy.

"And you would want me to marry you, feeling this way?" Magsie faltered.

"Oh, Magsie!" he whispered.

A tear fell on the thin hand that Magsie was patting. Through dazzled eyes she saw the future: reckless buying of gowns--brief and few farewells--the private car, the adoring invalid, the great sunny West with its forests and beaches, the plain gold ring on her little hand. In the whole concerned group--doctor, nurse, valet, mother, maid--young Mrs. Gardiner would be supreme! She saw herself flitting about a California bungalow, lending her young strength to Richie's increasing strength in the sunwashed, health-giving air.

She put her arms about him, laid her rosy cheek against his pale one.

"And you really want me to go out," Magsie began, smiling through tears, "and get a nice special license and a nice little plain gold ring and come back here with a nice kind clergyman, and say 'I will'---"

But at this her tears again interrupted her, and Richard, clinging desperately to her hand, could not speak either for tears. His mother who had silently entered the room on Magsie's last words suddenly put her fat arms about her and gave her the great motherly embrace for which, without knowing it, she had hungered for years, and they all fell to planning.

Richard could help only with an occasional assent. There was nothing to which he would not consent now. They would be married as soon as Magsie and his mother could get back with the necessities. And then would he drink his milk, good boy--and go straight to sleep, good boy. Then to-morrow he should be helped into the softest motor car procurable for money, and into the private car that his mother and Magsie meant to engage, by hook or crook, to-night. In six days they would be watching the blue Pacific, and in three weeks Richie should be sleeping out of doors and coming downstairs to meals. He had only to obey his mother; he had only to obey his wife. Magsie kissed him good-bye tenderly before leaving him for the hour's absence. Her heart was twisting little tendrils about him already. He was a sweet, patient dear, she told his mother, and he would simply have to get well!

"God above bless and reward you, Margaret!" was all Mrs. Gardiner could say, but Magsie never tired of hearing it.

When the two women went down the hospital steps they found Billy Pickering, in her large red car, eying them reproachfully from the curb.

"This is a nice way to act!" Billy began. "Your janitor's wife said you had come here. I've got two men--" Magsie's expression stopped her.

"This is Mr. Gardiner's mother, Billy," Magsie said solemnly. "The doctors agree that he must not stand this climate another day. He had another sinking spell yesterday, and he--he mustn't have another! I am going with them to California--"

"You ARE?" Billy ejaculated in amazement. Magsie bridled in becoming importance.

"It is all very sudden," she said with the weary, patient smile of the invalid's wife, "but he won't go without me." And then, as Mrs. Gardiner began to give directions to the driver of her own car, which was waiting, she went on inconsequentially, and in a low and troubled undertone, "I didn't know what to do. Do--do you think I'm a fool, Billy?"

"But what'll the other man say?" demanded Billy.

Magsie, leaning against the door of the car, rubbed the polished wood with a filmy handkerchief.

"He won't know," she said.

"Won't know? But what will you tell him?"

"Oh, he's not here. He won't be back for ever so long. And--and Richie can't live--they all say that. So if I come back before he does, what earthly difference can it make to him that I was married to Richie?"

"MARRIED!" For once in her life Billy was completely at a loss. "But are you going to MARRY him?"

Magsie gave her a solemn look, and nodded gravely. "He loves me," she said in a soft injured tone, "and I mean to take as good care of him as the best wife in the world could! I'm sick of the stage, and if anything happens with--the other, I shan't have to worry--about money, I mean. I'm not a fool, Billy. I can't let a chance like this slip. Of course I wouldn't do it if I didn't like him and like his mother, too. And I'll bet he will get well, and I'll never come back to New York! Of course this is all a secret. We're going right down to the City Hall for the license now, and the ring---There are a lot of clothes I've got to buy immediately--"

"Why don't you let me run you about?" suggested Billy. "I don't have to meet the men until six--I'll have to round up another girl, too; but I'd love to. Let Mama go back to Mr. Gardiner!"

"Oh, I couldn't," Magsie said, quite the dutiful daughter. "She's a wonderful person; she's arranging for our own private car, and a cook, and I may take Anna if I can get her!"

"All righto!" agreed Billy.

A rather speculative look came into her face as the other car whirled away. She suddenly gave directions to the driver.

"Drive to Miss Clay's apartment, where you picked me up this morning, Hungerford!" she said quickly. "I--I think I left something there--gloves--"

"I wonder if you would let me into Miss Clay's apartment?" she said to the beaming janitor's wife fifteen minutes later. "Miss Clay isn't here, and I left my gloves in her rooms."

Something in Magsie's manner had made her feel that Magsie had good reason for keeping the name of her admirer hid. Billy had felt for weeks that she would know the name if Magsie ever divulged it. And this morning she had noticed the admission that the wronged wife was a beautiful woman--and the hesitation with which Magsie had answered "Two girls." Then Magsie had said that she would "write him," not at all the natural thing to do to a man one was sure to see, and Rachael had said that Warren was away! But most significant of all was her answer to Billy's question as to whether the children were grown. Magsie had admitted that she knew the wife, had "known her before," and yet she pretended not to know whether or not the children were grown. Billy had had just a fleeting idea of Warren Gregory before that, but this particular term confirmed the suspicion suddenly.

So while Magsie was getting her marriage license, Billy was in Magsie's apartment turning over the contents of her wastepaper basket in feverish haste. The envelope was ruined, it had been crushed while wet; a name had been barely started anyway. But here was the precious scrap of commencement, "My dearest Greg--"

Billy was almost terrified by the discovery. There it was, in irrefutable black and white. She stuffed it back into the basket, and left the house like a thief, panting for the open air. A suspicion only ten minutes before, now she felt as if no other fact on earth had ever so fully possessed her. For an hour she drove about in a daze. Then she went home, and sat down at her desk, and wrote the following letter:

"Mv DEAR RACHAEL: The letter with the darling little 'B' came yesterday. I think he is cute to learn to write his own letter so quickly. Tell him that mother is proud of him for picking so many blackberries, and will love the jam. It is as hot as fire here, and the park has that steamy smell that a hothouse has. I have been driving about in Joe Butler's car all afternoon. We are going to Long Beach to-night.

"Rachael--Magsie Clay and a man named Richard Gardiner were married this afternoon. He is an invalid or something; he is at St. Luke's Hospital, and she and his mother are going to take him to California at once. What do you know about that? Of course this is a secret, and for Heaven's sake, if you tell anybody this, don't say I gave it away.

"If Magsie Clay should send you a bunch of letters, she will just do it to be a devil, and I want to ask you to burn them up before you read them. You know how you talked to me about divorce, Rachael! What you don't know can't hurt you. Don't please Magsie Clay to the extent of doing exactly what she wants you to do. If anyone you love has been a fool, why, it is certainly hard to understand how they could, but you stand by what you said to me the other day, and forget it.

"I feel as if I was breaking into your own affairs. I hope you won't care, and that I'm not all in the dark about this--" "Affectionately, BILLY."

CHAPTER VI

This letter, creased from constant reading, Rachael showed to George Valentine a week later. The doctor, who had spent the week-end with his family at Clark's Hills, was in his car and running past the gate of Home Dunes on his way back to town when Rachael stopped him. She looked her composed and dignified self in her striped blue linen and deep-brimmed hat, but the man's trained look found the circles about her wonderful eyes, and he detected signs of utter weariness in her voice.

"Read this, George," said she, resting against the door of his car, and opening the letter before him. "This came from Billy--Mrs. Pickering, you know--several days ago."

George read the document through twice, then raised questioning eyes to hers, and made the mouth of a whistler.

"What do you think?" Rachael questioned in her turn.

"Lord! I don't know what to think," said George. "Do you suppose this can be true?"

Rachael sighed wearily, staring down the road under the warming leaves of the maples into a far vista of bare dunes in thinning September sunshine.

"It might be, I suppose. You can see that Billy believes it," she said.

"Sure, she believes it," George agreed. "At least, we can find out. But I don't understand it!"

"Understand it?" she echoed in rich scorn. "Who understands anything of the whole miserable business? Do I? Does Warren, do you suppose?"

"No, of course nobody does," George said hastily in distress. He regarded the paper almost balefully. "This is the deuce of a thing!" he said. "If she didn't care for him any more than that, what's all the fuss about? I don't believe the threat about sending his letters, anyway!" he added hardily.

"Oh, that was true enough," Rachael said lifelessly. "They came."

George gave her an alarmed glance, but did not speak.

"A great package of them came," Rachael added dully. "I didn't open it. I had a fire that morning, and I simply set it on the fire." Her voice sank, her eyes, brooding and sombre, were far away. "But I watched it burning, George," she said in a low, absent tone, "and I saw his handwriting--how well I know it--Warren's writing, on dozens and dozens of letters--there must have been a hundred! To think of it--to think of it!"

Her voice was like some living thing writhing in anguish. George could think of nothing to say. He looked about helplessly, buttoned a glove button briskly, folded the letter, and made some work of putting it away in an inside pocket.

"Well," Rachael said, straightening up suddenly, and with resolute courage returning to her manner and voice, "you'll have, somebody look it up, will you, George?"

"You may depend upon it-immediately," George said huskily. "It--of course it will make an immense difference," he added, in his anxiety to be reassuring saying exactly the wrong thing.

Rachael was pale.

"I don't know how anything can make a great difference now, George," she answered slowly. "The thing remains--a fact. Of course this ends, in one way, the sordid side, the fear of publicity, of notoriety. But that wasn't the phase of it that ever counted with me. This will probably hurt Warren--"

"Oh, Rachael, dear old girl, don't talk that way!" George protested. "You can't believe that Warren will feel anything but a--a most unbelievable relief! We all know that. He's not the first man who let a pretty face drive him crazy when he was working himself to death." George was studying her as he spoke, with all his honest heart in his look, but Rachael merely shook her head forlornly.

"Perhaps I don't understand men," she said with a mildness that George found infinitely more disturbing than any fury would have been.

"Well, I'll look up records at the City Hall," he said after a pause. "That's the first thing to do. And then I'll let you know. Boys well this morning?"

"Lovely," Rachael smiled. "My trio goes fishing to-day, packing its lunch itself, and asking no feminine assistance. The lunch will be eaten by ten o'clock, and the boys home at half-past ten, thinking it is almost sundown. They only go as far as the cove, where the men are working, and we can see the tops of their heads from the upstairs' porch, so Mary and I won't feel entirely unprotected. I'm to lunch with Alice, so my day is nicely planned!"

The bright look did not deceive him, nor the reassuring tone. But George Valentine's friendship was more easily displayed by deeds than words, and now, with an affectionate pat for her hand, he touched his starter, and the car leaped upon its way. Just four hours later he telephoned Alice that the wedding license of Margaret Rose Clay and Richard Gardiner had indeed been issued a week before, and that Magsie was not to be found at her apartment, which was to be sublet at the janitor's discretion; that Bowman's secretary reported the absence of Miss Clay from the city, and the uncertainty of her appearing in any of Mr. Bowman's productions that winter, and that at the hospital a confident inquiry for "Mr. and Mrs. Gardiner" had resulted in the discreet reply that "the parties" had left for California. George, with what was for him a rare flash of imagination, had casually inquired as to the name of the clergyman who had performed the ceremony, being answered dispassionately that the person at the other end of the telephone "didn't know."

"George, you are an absolute WONDER!" said Alice's proud voice, faintly echoed from Clark's Hills. "Now, shall you cable--anybody--you know who I mean?"

"I have," answered the efficient George, "already."

"Oh, George! And what will he do?"

"Well, eventually, he'll come back."

"Do you THINK so? I don't!"

"Well, anyway, we'll see."

"And you're an angel," said Mrs. Valentine, finishing the conversation.

Ten days later Warren Gregory walked into George Valentine's office, and the two men gripped hands without speaking. That Warren had left for America the day George's cable reached him there was no need to say. That he was a man almost sick with empty days and brooding nights there was no need to say. George was shocked in the first instant of meeting, and found himself, as they talked together, increasingly shocked at the other's aspect.

Warren was thin, his hair actually showed more gray, there were deep lines about his mouth. But it was not only that; his eyes had a tired and haunted look that George found sad to see, his voice had lost its old confident ring, and he seemed weary and shaken. He asked for Alice and the children, and for Rachael and the boys.

"Rachael's well," George said. "She looks--well, she shows what she's been through; but she's very handsome. And the boys are fine. We had the whole crowd down as far as Shark Light for a picnic last Sunday. Rachael has little Breck Pickering down there now; he's a nice little chap, younger than our Katrina--Jim's age. The youngster is in paradise, sure enough, and putting on weight at a great rate."

"I didn't know he was there," Warren said slowly. "Like her--to take him in. I wish I had been there--Sunday. I wish to the Lord that it was all a horrible dream!"

He stopped and sat silent, looking gloomily at the floor, his whole figure, George thought, indicating a broken and shamed spirit.

"Well, Magsie's settled, at least," said George after a silence.

"Yes. That wasn't what counted, though," Warren said, as Rachael had said. "She is settled without my moving; there's no way in which I can ever make Rachael feel that I would have moved." Again his voice sank into silence, but presently he roused himself. "I've come back to work, George," he said with a quiet decision of manner that George found new and admirable. "That's all I can do now. If she ever forgives me--but she's not the kind that forgives. She's not weak--Rachael. But anyway, I can work. I'll go to the old house, for the present, and get things in order. And you drop a hint to Alice, when she talks to Rachael, that I've not got anything to say. I'll not annoy her."

George's heart ached for him as Warren suddenly covered his face with his hands. Warren had always been the adored younger brother to him, Warren's wonderful fingers over the surgical table, a miracle that gave their owner the right to claim whatever human weaknesses and failings he might, as a balance. George had never thought him perfect, as so much of the world thought him; to George, Warren had always been a little more than perfect, a machine of inspired surgery, underbalanced in many ways that in this one supreme way he might be more than human. George had to struggle for what he achieved; Warren achieved by divine right. The women were in the right of it now, George conceded, they had the argument. But of course they didn't understand--a thing like that had nothing to do with Warren's wife; Rachael wasn't brought into the question at all. And Lord! when all was said and done Warren was Warren, and professionally the biggest figure in George's world.

"I don't suppose you feel like taking Hudson's work?" said George now. "He's crazy to get away, and he was telling me yesterday that he didn't see himself breaking out of it. Mrs. Hudson wants to go to her own people, in Montreal, and I suppose Jack would be glad to go, too."

"Take it in a minute!" Warren said, his whole expression changing. "Of course I'll take it. I'm going to spend this afternoon getting things into shape at the house, and I think I'll drop round at the hospital about five. But I can start right in to-morrow."

"It isn't too much?" George asked affectionately.

"Too much? It's the only thing that will save my reason, I think," Warren answered, and after that George said no more.

The two men lunched together, and dined together, five times a week, with a curious change from old times: it was Warren who listened, and George who did the talking now. They talked of cases chiefly, for Warren was working day and night, and thought of little else than his work; but once or twice, as September waned, and October moved toward its close, there burst from him an occasional inquiry as to his wife.

"Will she ever forgive me, George?" Warren asked one cool autumn dawning when the two men were walking away from the hospital under the fading stars. Warren had commenced an operation just before midnight, it was only concluded now, and George, who had remained beside him for sheer admiration of his daring and his skill, had suggested that they walk for a while, and shake off the atmosphere of ether and of pain.

"It's a time like this I miss her," Warren said. "I took it all for granted, then. But after such a night as this, when I would go home in those first years, and creep into bed, she was never too sleepy to rouse and ask me how the case went, she never failed to see that the house was quiet the next morning, and she'd bring in my tray herself--Lord, a woman like that, waiting on me!"

George shook his head but did not speak. They walked an echoing block or two in silence.

"George, I need my wife," Warren said then. "There isn't an hour of my life that some phase of our life together doesn't come back to me and wring my heart. I don't want anything else--our sons, our fireside, our interests together. I've heard her voice ever since. And I'm changed, George, not in what I always believed, because I know right from wrong, and always have, but I don't believe in myself any more. I want my kids to be taught laws--not their own laws. I want to go on my knees to my girl---"

His voice thickened suddenly, and they walked on with no attempt on either side to end the silence for a long time. The city streets were wet from a rain, but day was breaking in hopeful pearl and rose.

"I can say this," said George at last: "I believe that she needs you as much as you do her. But Rachael's proud--"

"Ah, yes, she's that!" Warren said eagerly as he paused.

"And Warren, she has been dragged through the muck during the last few years," George resumed in a mildly expostulatory tone.

"Oh, I know it!" Warren answered, stricken.

"She hates coarseness," pursued George, "she hates weakness. I believe that if ever a divorce was justified in this world, hers was. But to have you come back at her, to have Magsie Clay break in on her, and begin to yap breezily about divorce, and how prevalent it is, and what a solution it is, why, of course it was enough to break her heart!"

"Don't!" Warren said thickly, quickening his pace, as if to walk away from his own insufferable thoughts.

For many days they did not speak of Rachael again; indeed George felt that there was nothing further to say. He feared in his own heart that nothing would ever bring about a change in her feeling, or rather, that the change that had been taking place in her for so many weeks was one that would be lasting, that Rachael was an altered woman.

Alice believed this, too, and Rachael believed it most of all. Indeed, over Rachael's torn and shaken spirit there had fallen of late a peace and a sense of security that she had never before known in her life. She tried not to think of Warren any more, or at least to think of him as he had been in the happy days when they had been all in all to each other. If other thoughts would creep in, and her heart grow hot and bitter within her at the memory of her wrongs, she resolutely fought for composure; no matter now what he had been or done, that life was dead. She had her boys, the sunsets and sunrises, the mellowing beauty of the year. She had her books, and above all her memories. And in these memories she found much to blame in herself, but much to pity, too. A rudderless little bark, she had been set adrift in so inviting, so welcoming a sea twenty years ago! She had known that she was beautiful, and that she must marry--what else? What more serious thought ever flitted through the brain of little Rachael Fairfax than that it was a delicious adventure to face life in a rough blue coat and feathered hat, and steer her wild little sails straight into the heart of the great waters?

She would have broken Stephen's heart; but Stephen was dead. She had seized upon Clarence with never a thought of what she was to give him, with never a prayer as to her fitness to be his wife, nor his fitness to be the father of her children. She had laughed at self-sacrifice, laughed at endurance, laughed at married love--these things were only words to her.

And when she had tugged with all her might at the problem before her, and tried, with her pitiable, untrained strength to force what she wished from Fate, then she had flung the whole thing aside, and rushed on to new experiments--and to new failures.

Always on the surface, always thinking of the impression she made on the watching men and women about her, what a life it had been! She had never known who made Clarence's money, what his own father had been like, what the forces were that had formed him, and had made him what he was. He did not please her, that began and ended the story. He had presently flung himself into eternity with as little heed as she had cast herself into her new life.

Ah, but there had been a difference there! She had loved there, and been awakened by great love. Her child's crumpled, rosy foot had come to mean more to her than all the world had meant before. The smile, or the frown, in her husband's eyes had been her sunshine or her storm. Through love she had come to know the brimming life of the world, the pathos, the comedy that is ready to spill itself over every humble window-sill, the joy that some woman's heart feels whenever the piping cry of the new-born sounds in a darkened room, the sorrow held by every shabby white hearse that winds its way through a hot and unnoticing street. She had clung to husband and sons with the tigerish tenacity that is the rightful dower of wife and mother; she had thought the world well lost in holding them.

And then the sordid, selfish past rose like an ugly mist before her, and she found at her lips the bitter cup she had filled herself. She was not so safe now, behind her barrier of love, but that the terrible machinery she had set in motion might bring its grinding wheels to bear upon the lives she guarded. She had flung her solemn promise aside, once; what defence could she make for a second solemn promise now? The world, divorce mad, spun blindly on, and the echo of her own complacent "one in twelve" came faintly, sickly back to her after the happy years.

"Divorce has actually no place in our laws, it isn't either wrong or right," Rachael said one autumn day when they were walking slowly to the beach. Over their heads the trees were turning scarlet; the days were still soft and warm, but twilight fell earlier now, and in the air at morning and evening was the intoxicating sharpness, the thin blue and clear steel color that mark the dying summer. Alice's three younger children were in school, and the family came to Clark's Hills only for the week-ends, but Rachael and her boys stayed on and on, enjoying the rare warmth and beauty of the Indian Summer, and comfortable in the old house that had weathered fifty autumns and would weather fifty more.

"In some states it is absolutely illegal," Rachael continued, "in others, it's permissible. In some it is a real source of revenue. Now fancy treating any other offence that way! Imagine states in which stealing was only a regrettable incident, or where murder was tolerated! In South Carolina you cannot get a divorce on any grounds! In Washington the courts can give it to you for any cause they consider sufficient. There was a case: a man and his wife obtained a divorce and both remarried. Now they find they are both bigamists, because it was shown that the wife went West, with her husband's knowledge and consent, to establish her residence there for the explicit purpose of getting a divorce. It was well-established law that if a husband or wife seek the jurisdiction of another state for the sole object of obtaining a divorce, without any real intent of living there, making their home there, goes, in other words, just for divorce purposes, then the decree having been fraudulently obtained will not be recognized anywhere!"

"But thousands do it, Rachael."

"But thousands don't seem to realize--I never did before--that that is illegal. You can't deliberately move to Reno or Seattle or San Francisco for such a purpose. All marriages following a divorce procured under these conditions are illegal. Besides this, the divorce laws as they exist in Washington, California, or Nevada are not recognized by other states, and so because a couple are separated upon the grounds of cruelty or incompatibility in some Western state, they are still legally man and wife in New York or Massachusetts. All sorts of hideous complications are going on: blackmail and perjury!"

"I wonder why divorce laws are so little understood?" Alice mused.

"Because divorce is an abnormal thing. You can't make it right, and of course we are a long way from making it wrong. But that is what it is coming to, I believe. Divorce will be against the law some day! No divorce on ANY GROUNDS! It cannot be reconciled to law; it defies law. Right on the face of it, it is breaking a contract. Are any other contracts to be broken with public approval? We will see the return of the old, simple law, then we will wonder at ourselves! I am not a woman who takes naturally to public work--I wish I were. But perhaps some day I can strike the system a blow. It is women like me who understand, and who will help to end it."

"It is only the worth-while women who do understand," said Alice. "You are the marble worth cutting. Life is a series of phases; we are none of us the same from year to year. You are not the same girl that you were when you married Clarence Breckenridge--"

"What a different woman!" Rachael said under her breath.

"Well," said Alice then a little frightened, "why won't you think that perhaps Warren might have changed, too; that whatever Warren has done, it was done more like--like the little boy who has never had his fling, who gets dizzy with his own freedom, and does something foolish without analyzing just what he is doing?"

"But Warren, after all, isn't a child!" Rachael said sadly.

"But Warren is in some ways; that's just it," Alice said eagerly. "He has always been singularly--well, unbalanced, in some ways. Don't you know there was always a sort of simplicity, a sort of bright innocence about Warren? He believed whatever anybody said until you laughed at him; he took every one of his friends on his own valuation. It's only where his work is concerned that you ever see Warren positive, and dictatorial, and keen--"

Rachael's eyes had filled with tears.

"But he isn't the man I loved, and married," she said slowly. "I thought he was a sort of god--he could do no wrong for me!"

"Yes, but that isn't the way to feel toward anybody," persisted Alice. "No man is a god, no man is perfect. You're not perfect yourself; I'm not. Can't you just say to yourself that human beings are faulty--it may be your form of it to get dignified and sulk, and Warren's to wander off dreamily into curious paths--but that's life, Rachael, that's 'better or worse,' isn't it?"

"It isn't a question of my holding out for a mere theory, Alice," Rachael said after a while; "I'm not saying that I'm all in the right, and that I will never see Warren again until he admits it, and everyone admits it--that isn't what I want. But it's just that I'm dead, so far as that old feeling is concerned. It is as if a child saw his mother suddenly turn into a fiend, and do some hideously cruel act; no amount of cool reason could ever convince that child again that his mother was sweet and good."

"But as you get older," Alice smiled, "you differentiate between good and good, and you see grades in evil, too. Everything isn't all good or all bad, like the heroes and the villains of the old plays. If Warren had done a 'hideously cruel' thing deliberately, that would be one thing; what he has done is quite another. The God who made us put sex into the world, Warren didn't; and Warren only committed, in his--what is it?--forty-eighth year one of the follies that most boys dispose of in their teens. Be generous, Rachael, and forgive him. Give him another trial!"

"How CAN I forgive him?" Rachael said, badly shaken, and through tears. "No, no, no, I couldn't! I never can."

They had reached the beach now, and could see the children, in their blue field coats, following the curving reaches of the incoming waves. The fresh roar of the breakers filled a silence, gulls piped their wistful little cry as they circled high in the blue air. Old Captain Semple, in his rickety one-seated buggy, drove up the beach, the water rising in the wheel-tracks. The children gathered about him; it was one of their excitements to see the Captain wash his carriage, and the old mare splash in the shallow water. Alice seated herself on a great log, worn silver from the sea, and half buried in the white sand, but Rachael remained standing, the sweet October wind whipping against her strong and splendid figure, her beautiful eyes looking far out to sea.

"You two have no quarrel," the older woman added mildly. "You and Warren were rarely companionable. I used to say to George that you were almost TOO congenial, too sensitive to each other's moods. Warren knew that you idolized him, Rachael, and consequently, when criticism came, when he felt that you of all persons were misjudging him, why, he simply flung up his head like a horse, and bolted!"

"Misjudging?" Rachael said quickly, half turning her head, and bringing her eyes from the far horizon to rest upon Alice's face. The children had seen them now, and were running toward them, and Alice did not attempt to answer. She sighed, and shrugged her shoulders.

A dead horseshoe crab on the sands deflected the course of the racing children, except Derry, who pursued his panting way, and as Rachael sat down on the log, cast himself, radiant and breathless, into her arms. She caught the child to her heart passionately. He had always been closer to her than even the splendid first-born because of the giddy little head that was always getting him into troubles, and the reckless little feet that never chose a sensible course. Derry was always being rescued from deep water, always leaping blindly from high places and saved by the narrowest possible chance, always getting his soft mop of hair inextricably tangled in the steering-gear of Rachael's car, or his foot hopelessly twisted in the innocent-looking bars of his own bed, always eating mysterious berries, or tasting dangerous medicines, always ready to laugh deeply and deliciously at his own crimes. Jim assumed a protective attitude toward him, chuckling at his predicaments, advising him, and even gallantly assuming the blame for his worst misdeeds. Rachael imagined them in boarding-school some day; in college; Jim the student, dragged from his books and window-seat to go to the rescue of the unfortunate but fascinating junior. Jim said he was going to write books; Derry was going--her heart contracted whenever he said it--was going to be a doctor, and Dad would show him what to do!

Ah, how proud Warren might have been of them, she thought, walking home to-day, a sandy hand in each of hers, Derry hopping on one foot, twisting, and leaping; Jim leaning affectionately against her, and holding forth as to the proper method of washing wagons! What man would not have been proud of this pair, enchanting in faded galatea now, soon to be introduced to linen knickerbockers, busy with their first toiling capitals now, some day to be growling Latin verbs. They would be interested in the Zoo this winter, and then in skating, and then in football--Warren loved football. He had thrown it all away!

Widowed in spirit, still Rachael was continually reminded that she was not actually widowed, and in the hurt that came to her, even in these first months, she found a chilling premonition of the years to come. Warmhearted Vera Villalonga wrote impulsively from the large establishment at Lakewood that she had acquired for the early winter. She had heard that Rachael and Greg weren't exactly hitting it off--hoped to the Lord it wasn't true--anyway, Rachael had been perfectly horrible about seeing her old friends; couldn't she come at once to Vera, lots of the old crowd were there, and spend a month? Mrs. Barker Emery, meeting Rachael on one of the rare occasions when Rachael went into the city, asked pleasantly for the boys, and pleasantly did not ask for Warren. Belvedere Bay was gayer than ever this year, Mrs. Emory said; did Rachael know that the Duchess of Exton was visiting Mary Moulton--such a dear! Georgiana Vanderwall, visiting the Thomases at Easthampton, motored over one day to spend a sympathetic half morning with Rachael, pressing that lady's unresponsive hand with her own large, capable one, and murmuring that of course--one heard--that the Bishop of course felt dreadfully--they only hoped--both such dear sweet people--

Rachael felt as if she would like to take a bath after this well-meant visitation. A day or two later she had a letter from Florence, who said that "someone" had told her that the Gregorys might not be planning to keep their wonderful cook this winter. If that was true, would Rachael be so awfully good as to ask her to go see Mrs. Haviland?

"The pack," Rachael said to Alice, "is ready to run again!"

CHAPTER VII

November turned chilly, and in its second week there was even a flutter of snow at Clark's Hills. Rachael did not dislike it, and it was a huge adventure to the boys. Nevertheless, she began to feel that a longer stay down on the bleak coast might be unwise. The old house, for all its purring furnace and double windows, was draughty enough to admit icy little fingers of the outside air, here and there, and the village, getting under storm shutters and closing up this wing or that room for the winter, was so businesslike in its preparations as to fill Rachael's heart with mild misgivings.

Alice still brought her brood down for the week-ends, and it was on one of these that Rachael suddenly decided to move. The two women discussed it, Rachael finally agreeing to go to the Valentines' for a week before going on to Boston--or it might be Washington or Philadelphia--any other city than the one in which she might encounter the boys' father. Alice had never won her to promise a visit before, and although Rachael's confidence in her--for Rachael neither extracted a promise from Alice as to any possible encounter with Warren, nor reminded her friend that she placed herself entirely at Alice's mercy--rather disconcerted Alice, she had a simple woman's strong faith in coincidence, and she felt, she told George, that the Lord would not let this opportunity for a reconciliation go by. Mrs. Valentine had seen Warren Gregory now, more than once, and far more potent than any argument that he might have made was his silence, his most unexpected and unnatural silence. There was no explanation; indeed Warren had little to say on any subject in these days. He liked to come now and then, in the evening, to the Valentine house, but he would not dine there, and confined his remarks almost entirely to answers to George. Physically, Alice thought him shockingly changed.

"He is simply broken," she said to George, in something like fright. "I didn't know human beings could change that way. Warren--who used to be so positive! Why, he's almost timid!"

She did not tell Rachael this, and George insisted that, while Rachael and the boys were at the house, Warren must be warned to keep away; so that Alice had frail enough material with which to build her dreams. Nevertheless, she dreamed.

It was finally arranged that Rachael and little Jim should go up to town on a certain Monday with Alice; that Rachael should make various engagements then, as to storage, packing, and such matters as the care of the piano and the car, for the winter. Then Jim, for the first time in his life, would stay away from his mother overnight with Aunt Alice, Rachael returning to Clark's Hills to bring Mary and Derry up the next day in the car. Jim was to go to the dentist, and to get shoes; there were several excellent reasons why it seemed wise to have him await his mother and brother in town rather than make the long trip twice in one day. Mary smuggled Derry out of sight when the Monday morning came, and Rachael and her oldest son went away with the Valentines in the car.

It was a fresh, sweet morning in the early winter, and both women, furred to the eyes, enjoyed the trip. The children, snuggled in between them, chattered of their own affairs, and Rachael interrupted her inexhaustible talk with Alice only to ask a question of the driver now and then.

"I shall have to bring my own car over this road to-morrow, Kane," she explained. "I have never been at the wheel myself before in all the times I have done it."

"Mar-r-tin does be knowin' every step of the way," suggested Kane.

"But Martin hasn't been with me this summer," the lady smiled.

"I thought I saw him runnin' the docther's car yesterda' week," mused Kane who was a privileged character. "Well,'tis not hard, Mrs. Gregory. The whole place is plasthered wid posts. But the thing of it is, ma'am," he added, after a moment, turning back toward her without taking his eyes from the road, "there does be a big storm blowin' up. Look there, far over there, how black it is."

"But that won't break to-day?" Rachael said uneasily, thinking of Derry.

"Well, it may not--that's thrue. But these roads will be in a grand mess if we have anny more rain--that's a fact for ye," Kane persisted.

"Then don't come until Wednesday," suggested Alice.

"Oh, Alice, but I'll be so frantic to see my boy!"

"Twenty-four hours more, you goose!" Alice laughed. Rachael laughed, too, and took several surreptitious kisses from the back of Jimmy's neck as a fortification against the coming separation.

Indeed, she found it unbelievably hard to leave him, trotting happily upstairs with his beloved Katharine, and to go about her day's business anticipating the long trip back to Home Dunes without him. However, there were not many hours to spare, and Rachael had much to do. She set herself systematically to work.

By one o'clock everything was done, with an hour to spare for train time. But she had foolishly omitted luncheon, and felt tired and dizzy. She turned toward a downtown lunchroom, and was held at the crossing of Fifth Avenue and one of the thirties idly watching the crowd of cars that delayed her when she saw Warren in his car.

He was on the cross street, and so also stopped, but he did not see her. Martin was at the wheel, Warren buttoned to the neck in a gray coat, his hat well down over his eyes, alone in the back seat. He was staring steadily, yet with unseeing eyes, before him, and Rachael felt a sense of almost sickening shock at the sight of his altered face. Warren, looking tired and depressed, looking discouraged, and with some new look of diffidence and hurt, besides all these, in his face! Warren old! Warren OLD!

Rachael felt as if she should faint. She was rooted where she stood. Fifth Avenue pushed gayly and busily by her under the leaden sky. Furred old ladies, furred little girls, messenger boys and club men, jostling, gossiping, planning. Only she stood still. And after a while she looked again where Warren had been. He was gone. But had he seen her? her heart asked itself with wild clamor. Had he seen her?

She began to walk rapidly and blindly, conscious of taking a general direction toward the Terminal Station, but so vague as to her course that she presently looked bewilderedly about to find that she was in Eighth Avenue and that, standing absolutely still again, and held by thought, she was being curiously regarded by a policeman. She gave the man a dazed and sickly smile.

"I am afraid I am a little out of my way," she stammered. "I am going to the station."

He pointed out the direction, and she thanked him, and blindly went on her way. But her heart was tearing like a living thing in her breast, and she walked like a wounded creature that leaves a trail of life blood.

Oh, she was his wife--his wife--his wife! She belonged there, in that empty seat beside him, with her shoulder against that gray overcoat! What was she doing in this desolate street of little shops, faint and heartsick and alone! Oh, for the security of that familiar car again! How often she had sat beside him, arrested by the traffic, content to placidly watch the shifting crowd, to wait for the shrill little whistle that gave them the right of way! If she were there now, where might they be going? Perhaps to a concert, perhaps to look at a picture in some gallery, but first of all certainly to lunch. His first question would be: "Had your lunch?" and his answer only a satisfied nod. But he would direct Martin to the first place that suggested itself to him as being suitable for Rachael's meal. And he would order it, no trouble was too much for her; nothing too good for his wife.

She was not beside him. She was still drifting along this hideous street, battling with faintness and headache, and never, perhaps, to see her husband again. One of her sons was in the city, another miles away, To her horror she felt herself beginning to cry. She quickened her pace, and reckless of the waiter's concern, entered the station restaurant and ordered herself a lunch. But when it came she could not eat it, and she was presently in the train, without a book or magazine, still fasting except for a hurried half cup of tea, and every instant less and less able to resist the corning flood of her tears.

All the long trip home she wept, quietly and steadily, one arm on the window sill, a hand pressed against her face. There were few other passengers in the train, which was too hot. The winter twilight shut down early, and at last the storm broke; not violently, but with a stern and steady persistence. The windows ran rain, and were blurred with steam, the darkening landscape swept by under a deluge. When the train stopped at a station, a rush of wet air, mingled with the odors of mackintoshes and the wet leather of motor cars, came in. Rachael would look out to see meetings, lanterns and raincoats, umbrellas dripping over eager, rosy faces.

She would be glad to get home, she said to herself, to her snuggly little comforting Derry. They would not attempt to make the move to-morrow--that was absurd. It had been far too much of a trip to-day, and Alice had advised her against it. But it had not sounded so formidable. To start at seven, be in town at ten, after the brisk run, and take the afternoon train home--this was no such strain, as they had planned it. But it had proved to be a frightful strain. Leaving Jim, and then catching that heart-rending glimpse of the changed Warren--Warren looking like a hurt child who must bear a punishment without understanding it.

"Oh, what are we thinking about, to act in this crazy manner!" Rachael asked herself desperately. "He loves me, and I--I've always loved him. Other people may misjudge him, but I know! He's horrified and shamed and sorry. He's suffering as much as I am. What fools--what utter FOOLS we are!"

And suddenly--it was nearly six o'clock now, and they were within a few minutes of Clark's Hills--she stopped crying, and began to plan a letter that should end the whole terrible episode.

"Your stop Quaker Bridge?" asked the conductor, coming in, and beginning to shift the seats briskly on their iron pivots, as one who expected a large crowd to accompany him on the run back.

"Clark's Hills," Rachael said, noticing that she was alone in the train.

"Don't know as we can get over the Bar," the man said cheerily.

"Looks as if we were going to try it!" Rachael answered with equal aplomb as the train ran through Quaker Bridge without stopping, and went on with only slightly decreased speed. And a moment later she began to gather her possessions together, and the conductor remarked amiably: "Here we are! But she surely is raining," he added. "Well, we've only got to run back as far as the car barn--that's Seawall--to-night. My folks live there."

Rachael did not mind the rain. She would be at home in five minutes. She climbed into a closed surrey, smelling strongly of leather and horses, and asked the driver pleasantly how early the rain had commenced. He evidently did not hear her, at all events made no answer, and she did not speak again.

"Where's my Derry?" Rachael's voice rang strong and happy through the house. "Mary--Mary!" she added, stopping, rather puzzled, in the hall. "Where is he?"

How did it come to her, by what degrees? How does such news tell itself, from the first little chill, that is not quite fear, to the full thundering avalanche of utter horror? Rachael never remembered afterward, never tried to remember. The moment remained the blackest of all her life. It was not the subtly changed atmosphere of the house, not Mary's tear-swollen face, as she appeared, silent, at the top of the stairs; not Millie, who came ashen-faced and panting from the kitchen; not the sudden, weary little moan that floated softly through the hallway--no one of all these things.

Yet Rachael knew--Derry was dying. She needed not to know how or why. Her furs fell where she stood, her hat was gone, she had flown upstairs as swiftly as light. She knew the door, she knew what she would see. She went down on her knees beside him.

Her little gallant, reckless, shouting Derry! Her warm, beautiful boy, changed in these few hours to this crushed and moaning little being, this cruelly crumpled and tortured little wreck of all that had been gay and sound and confident babyhood!

In that first moment at his side it had seemed to Rachael that she must die, too, of sheer agony of spirit. She put her beautiful head down against the brown little limp hand upon which a rusty stain was drying, and she could have wailed aloud in the bitter rebellion of her soul. Not Derry, not Derry, so small and innocent and confiding--her own child, her own flesh and blood, the fibre of her being! Trusting them, obeying them, and betrayed--brought to this!

At her first look she had thought the child dead; now, as she drew back from him, and caught her self-control with a quivering breath, and wrung her hands together in desperate effort to hold back a scream, she found it in her heart to wish he were. His little face was black from a great bruise that spread from temple to chin, his mouth cut and swollen, his eyes half shut. His body was doubled where it lay, a great bubble of blood moved with his breath. He breathed lightly and faintly, with an occasional deep gasp that invariably brought the long, heart-sickening moan. They had taken off part of his clothes, his shoes and stockings, but he still wore his Holland suit, and the dark-blue woolen coat had only been partly removed.

Rachael, ashen-faced, rose from her knees, and faced Mary and Millie. With bitter tears the story was told. He had been playing, as usual, in the barn, and Mary had been swinging him. Not high, nothing like as high as Jimmie went. And Millie came out to say that their dinner was ready, and all of a sudden he called out that he could swing without holding on, and put both his hands up in the air. And then Mary saw him fall, the board of the swing falling, too, and striking him as he fell, and his face dashing against the old mill-wheel that stood by the door. And he had not spoken since.

His arm had hung down loose-like, as Mary carried him in, and Millie had run for the doctor. But Doctor Peet wouldn't be back until seven, and the girls had dared do no more than wash off his face a little and try to make him comfortable. "I wish the Lord had called me before the day came," said Mary, "me, that would have died for him--for any of you!"

"I know that, Mary," Rachael said. "It would have happened as easily with me. We all know what you have been to the boys, Mary. But you mustn't cry so hard. I need you. I am going to drive him into town."

"Oh, my God, in this storm?" exclaimed Millie.

"There's nothing else to do," Rachael said. "He may die on the way, but his mother will do what she can. I couldn't have Doctor Peet, kind as he is. Doctor Gregory--his father--will know. It's nearly seven now. We must start as fast as we can. You'll have to pin something all about the back seat, Mary, and line it with comforters. We'll put his mattress on the seat--you'll make it snug, won't you?--and you'll sit on the floor there, and steady him all you can, for I'll have to drive. We ought to be there by midnight, even in the storm."

"I'll fix it," Mary said, with one great sob, and immediately, to Rachael's great relief, she was her practical self.

"And I want some coffee, Millie," she said, "strong; I'm not hungry, but if you have something ready, I'll eat what I can. Did Ruddy come up and get the car to-day, for oil and gas, and so on?"

"He did," said Millie, eager to be helpful.

"That's a blessing." Rachael turned to look at the little figure on the bed. Her heart contracted with a freezing spasm of terror whenever her eyes even moved in that direction.

But there was plenty to do. She got herself into dry, warm clothes. She leaned over her little charge, straightening and adjusting as best she could, shifting the little body as gently as was possible to the smaller mattress, covering it warmly but lightly. As she did so she wondered which one of those long, moaning breaths would be the last; when would little Derry straighten himself--and lie still?

No time to think of that. She tied on her hat and veil, and went out to look at the car. The rear seat was lined with pillows, the curtain drawn. She had matches, her electric flashlight, her road maps, a flask of brandy--what else?

Millie had run for neighbors, and the chains were finally adjusted. The car had been made ready for the run, and was in good shape.

The big shadowy barn that was the garage was full of dancing shapes in the lantern-light. The rain splashed and spattered incessantly outside; a black sky seemed to have closed down just over their heads. She was in a fever to get away.

Slowly the dazzling headlights moved in the pitchy blackness, the wheels grated but held their own. The car came to the side door, and the little mattress came out, and the muffled shape that was Mary got in beside it. Then there was buttoning of storm curtains by willing hands, and many a whispered good wish to Rachael as she slipped in under the wheel. Millie was beside her, at the last moment, begging to be of some use if she might.

"There's just this, Mrs. Gregory," said Ruddy Simms nervously, when the engine was humming, and, Rachael's gloved hand racing the accelerator, "they say the tide's making fast in all this rain! I don't know how you'll do at the Bar. She's ugly a night, like this; what with the bay eating one side, and the sea breaking over the other!"

"Thank you," Rachael said, not hearing him. "God bless you! Good-bye!"

She released the clutch. The big car leaped forward, into the darkness. The clock before her eyes said thirty-five minutes past seven. Rain beat against the heavy cloth of the curtains, water swished and splashed under the wheels, and above the purring of the engine they could hear the clinking fall of the chains. There was no other sound except when Derry caught a moaning breath.

Clark's Hills passed in blackness, the road dropped down toward the Bar. Rachael could feel that Mary, in the back seat, was praying, and that Millie was praying beside her. Her own heart rose on a wild and desperate prayer. If they could cross this narrow strip between the bay and the ocean, then whatever the fortune of the road, she could meet it. Telephones, at least, were on the other side, resources of all sorts. But to be stopped here!

The look of the Bar, when they reached it, struck chill even to Rachael's heart. In the clear tunnels of light flung from the car lamps it seemed all a moving level of restless water smitten under sheets of rain. Anything more desperate than an effort to find the little belt of safety in this trackless spread of merciless seas it would be hard to imagine. At an ordinary high tide the Bar was but a few inches above the sea; now, with a wind blowing, a heavy rain falling, and the tide almost at the full, no road whatever was visible. It was there, the friendly road that Rachael and the hot and sandy boys had tramped a hundred times, but even she could not believe it, now, so utterly impassable did the shifting surface appear.

But she gallantly put the car straight into the heart of it, moving as slowly as the engine permitted, and sending quick, apprehensive glances into the darkness as she went.

"At the worst, we can back out of this, Millie," said she.

"Of course we can," Millie said, suppressing frightened tears with some courage.

The water was washing roughly against the running boards; to an onlooker the car would have had the appearance of being afloat, hub-deep, at sea.

Slowly, slowly, slowly they were still moving. The car stopped short. The engine was dead. Rachael touched her starter, touched it again and again. No use. The car had stopped. The rain struck in noisy sheets against the curtains. The sea gurgled and rushed about them. Derry moaned softly.

And now the full madness of the attempted expedition struck her for the first time. She had never thought that, at worst, she could not go back. What now? Should they stand here on the shifting sand of the Bar until the tide fell--it was not yet full. Rachael felt her heart beating quick with terror. It began to seem like a feverish dream.

Neither maid spoke, perhaps neither one realized the full extent of the calamity. With the confidence of those who do not understand the workings of a car, they waited to have it start again.

But both girls screamed when suddenly a new voice was heard. Rachael, starting nervously as a man's figure came about the car out of the black night, in the next second saw, with a great rush of relief, that it was Ruddy Simms. He was a mighty fellow, devoted to the Gregorys. He proceeded rather awkwardly to explain that he hadn't liked to think of their trying to cross the Bar, and so had come with them on the running board.

"Oh, Ruddy, how grateful I am to you!" Rachael said. "Perhaps you can go back and get us a tow? What can we do?"

"Stuck?" asked Ruddy, wading as unconcernedly about the car as if the sun were shining on the scene.

"No, I don't think so, not yet. But I can feel the road under us giving already. And I've killed my engine!"

Ruddy deliberated.

"Won't start, eh?"

"She simply WON'T!"

"Ain't got a crank, have ye?"

Rachael stared.

"Why, yes, we have, under my seat here. But is there a chance that she might start on cranking?" she said eagerly.

"Dun't know," Ruddy said non-committally.

Rachael was instantly on her feet, and after some groping and adjusting, the cranking was attempted. Failure. Ruddy went bravely at it again. Failure. Again Rachael touched the starter.

"No use!" she said with a sinking heart.

But Ruddy was bred of sea-folk who do not expect quick results. He tugged away again vigorously, and again after that. And suddenly--the most delicious sound that Rachael's ears had ever heard--there was the sucking and plunging that meant success. The car panted like a giant revived, and Ruddy stood back in the merciless green light and sent Rachael a smile. His homely face, running rain, looked at her as bright as an angel's.

"Dun't know as I'd stand there, s'deep in my tracks!" shouted Ruddy.

Gingerly, timidly, she pushed the car on some ten feet. "What I's thinking," suggested Ruddy then, coming to put his face in close to hers, and shouting over the noise of wind and water, "is this: if I was to walk ahead of ye, kinder feeling for the road with my feet, then you could come after, d'ye see?"

"Oh, Ruddy, do you think we can make it, then?" Rachael's face was wet with tears.

"Dun't know," he said. He took off his immense boots and gray socks, and rolled up his wet trousers, the better to feel every inch of rise or fall in the ground beneath his feet, and Millie held these for him as if it were a sacred charge.

And then, with the full light of the lamps illumining his big figure, and with the water rushing and gurgling about them, and the rain pouring down as if it were an actual deluge, they made the crossing at Clark's Bar. The shifting water almost blinded Rachael sometimes, and sometimes it seemed as if any way but the way that Ruddy's waving arms indicated was the right one; as if to follow him were utter madness. The water spouted up through the clutch, and once again the engine stopped, and long moments went by before it would respond to the crank again. But Rachael pushed slowly on. She was not thinking now, she was conscious of no feeling but that there was an opposite shore, and she must reach it.

And presently it rose before them. The road ran gradually upward, a shallow sheet of running water covering it, but firm, hard roadway discernible nevertheless. Rachael stopped the car, and Ruddy came again and put his face close to hers, through the curtains.

"Now ye've got straight road, Mrs. Gregory, and I hope to the good Lord you'll have a good run. Thank ye, Millie--much obliged!"

"Ruddy!" said Rachael passionately, her wet gloves holding his big, hairy hands tight. "I'll never forget this! If he has a chance to live at all, this is his chance, and you've given it to him! God bless you, a thousand times!"

"That's all right," said Ruddy, terribly embarrassed. "You've always been awful good to my folks. I'm glad we done it! Good-night!" Then Ruddy had turned back for the walk home in the streaming blackness, and Rachael, drawing a deep breath, was on her way again. She stopped only for a quick question to Mary.

"No change?"

"Just the same."

The wet miles flew by; rain beat untiringly against the curtains, slished in two great feathers of water from under the rushing wheels. Rachael watched her speedometer; twenty-five--twenty-eight--thirty--they could not do better than that in this weather. And they had a hundred miles to go.

But that hundred was only eighty-six now, only eighty. Villages flew by, and men came out and stood on the dripping porches of crossroad stores to marvel as the long scream of Rachael's horn cut through the night air. Twenty minutes past eight o'clock--eight minutes of nine o'clock. The little villages began to grow dark.

There was nothing to pass on the road; so much was gain. Except in the villages, and once or twice where a slow, rattling wagon was plodding along on the wet mirror-like asphalt, Rachael might make her own speed. The road lay straight, and was an exceptionally good road, even in this weather. She need hardly pause for signboards. The rain still fell in sheets. Seventy-two miles to go.

"How is he, Mary?"

"The same, Mrs. Gregory. Except that he gives a little groan now and then--when it shakes him!"

"My boy! But not sleeping?" "Oh, no, Mrs. Gregory. He just lies quiet like."

"God bless him!" Rachael said under her breath. Aloud she said: "Millie, couldn't you lean over, and watch him a few minutes, and see what you think?"

Then they were flying on again. Rachael began to wonder just how long the run was. They always carelessly called it "a hundred miles." But was it really a hundred and two, or ninety-eight? What a difference two or three miles would make to-night! She fell into a nervous shiver; suppose they reached the bridge, and then Mary should touch her arm. "He doesn't look right, Mrs. Gregory!" Suppose that for the little boy that they finally carried into New York there was no longer any hope. Her little Derry--

The child that might have been the joy of a happy home, that might have grown to a dignified inheritance of the love and tenderness that had been between his father and mother. Robbed in his babyhood, taken away from the father he adored, and now--this! Sixty-one miles to go.

"Detour to New York." The sign, with all its hideous import, rose before her suddenly. No help for it; she must lose one or two, perhaps a dozen miles, she must give up the good road for a bad one. She must lose her way, too, perhaps. Had Kane gone over this road yesterday? It was much farther on that she had spoken to Kane. Perhaps he had, but she could not remember, doubt made every foot of the way terrible to Rachael. She could only plunge on, over rocks, over bumps, into mud-holes. She could only blindly take what seemed of two turnings the one most probably right.

"Oh--Mother!" The little wail came from Derry. Rachael, her heart turned to ice, slowed down--stopped and leaned into the half darkness in the back of the car. The child's lovely eyes were opened. Rachael could barely see his white face.

"My darling!" she said.

"Will you not--bump me so, Mother?" the little boy whispered.

"I will try not to, my heart!" Rachael, wild with terror, looked to Mary's face. Was he dying, now and here?

"Oh Moth--it hurts so!"

"Does it, my darling?"

He drowsed again. Rachael turned back to her wheel. They must go more slowly now, at any cost.

The road was terrible, in parts, after the hours of heavy rain, it seemed almost impassable. Rachael pushed on. Presently they were back in the main road again, and could make better time. Of the hundred miles only fifty remained. But that meant nothing now. How much time had she lost in that frightful bypath? Rachael's face was dripping with rain, rain had trickled under her clothing at neck and wrists. Through her raincoat the breast of her gown was soaking, and her feet ached with the strain of controlling the heavy car. Water came in long runnels through the wind-shield, and struck her knees; she had turned her dress back, her thin silk petticoat was soaked, and the muscles of knees and ankles were cold and sore. But she felt these things not at all. Her eyes burned ahead, into the darkness, she heard nothing but the occasional fluttering moan from Derry; she thought nothing but that she might be too late--too late--too late!

At the first town of any size she stopped, a telegram to George taking shape in her mind. But the wires here were down, as they had been farther down the Island. The rain was thinning, but the wind was rising every second, and as she rushed on she saw that in many places the lights on the road were out; all the Island lay battered and bruised under the storm.

Slowly as they seemed to creep, yet the miles were going by. Freeport--Lynbrook--Jamaica--like a woman in a dream she reached the bridge and a moment later looked down upon the long belt of lights winking in the rain that was New York.

And here, on the very apex of the bridge, came the most heart-rending moment of the run, for the little boy began to cough, and for two or three frightful minutes the women hung over him, speechless with terror, and knowing that at any second the exhausted little body might succumb to the strain. Blindly, as with a long, choked cry he sank back again, Rachael went back to her wheel. Third Avenue--Fifth Avenue--Forty-second Street tore by; they were running straight down toward Washington Arch as the clocks everywhere struck midnight. The wide street was deserted in the rain, it shone like a mirror, reflecting long pendants of light.

They were turning the corner; she was out of the car, and had glanced at the familiar old house. Wet, exhausted, fired by a passion that made her feel curiously light and sure, Rachael put her arms about her child, and carried him up the steps. Mary had preceded her, the door was opened; a dazed and frightened maid was looking at her.

Then she was crossing the familiar hall; lights were in the library, and Warren in the library, somebody with him, but Rachael only caught a glimpse of the old familiar attitude: he was sitting in a straight-backed chair, his legs crossed, and one firm hand grasping a silk-clad ankle as he intently listened to whatever was being said.

"Warren!" she said in a voice that those who heard it remembered all their lives. "It's Derry! He's hurt--he's dying, I think! Can you--can you save him?" And with a great burst of tears she gave up the child.

"My God--what is it!" said Warren Gregory on his feet, and with Derry in his arms, even as he spoke. For a second the tableau held: Rachael, agonized, her beautiful face colorless, and dripping with rain, her husband staring at her as if he could not credit his senses, the child's limp body in his arms, yet not quite freed from hers. In the background were the whitefaced servants and the gray-headed doctor upon whose conversation the newcomers had so abruptly broken.

"We've just brought him up from Clark's Hills!" Rachael said.

"From Clark's Hills--YOU!"

His look, the dear familiar look of solicitude and concern, tore her to the soul.

"There was nothing else to do!" she faltered.

"But--you drove up to-night?"

"Since seven."

He looked at her, and Rachael felt the look sink into her soul like rain into parched land.

"And you came straight to me!" His voice sank. "Rachael," he said, "I will save him for you if I can!"

And instantly there began such activities in the old house as perhaps even its dignified century of living had never known. Rachael, hungry through these terrible hours of suspense for just the wild rush and hurry, watched her husband as if she had never seen him before. Presently lights blazed from cellar to attic, maids flew in every direction, fires were lighted, the moving of heavy furniture shook the floors. Derry, the little unconscious cause of it all, lay quiet, with Mary watching him.

New York had been asleep; it was awakened now. Motor cars wheeled into the Gregorys' street; Mrs. Gregory herself answered the door. Here was the nurse, efficient, yet sympathetic, too, with her paraphernalia and her assistants. Yes, she had been able to get it, Doctor Gregory. Yes, Doctor, she had that. Here was the man from the drug store--that was all right, Doctor, that was what he expected, being waked up in the night; thank you, Doctor. And here was George Valentine, too much absorbed in the business in hand to say more than an affectionate "Hello" to Rachael. But with George was Alice, white-faced but smiling, and little sleepy Jimmy, who was to be smuggled immediately into bed.

"I thought you'd rather have him here," said Alice.

Rachael knew why. Rachael knew what doctors said to each other, when they gathered, and used those quick, low monosyllables. She knew why Miss Redding was speeding the arrangements for the improvised operating-room with such desperate hurry. She knew why one of these assisting doctors was delegated to do nothing but sit beside Derry, watching the little hurt breast rise and fall, watching the bubble of blood form and break on the swollen mouth.

Warren had told her to get into dry clothing, and then to take a stimulant, and have something to eat. And eager to save him what she could, she was warm and dry now. She sat in Derry's room, and presently, when they came to stand beside him, Warren and George, they found her agonized eyes, bright with questions, facing them. But she knew better than to speak.

Neither man spoke for a few dreadful moments. Warren looked at the child without a flicker of change in his impassive look; George bit his lip, and almost imperceptibly shook his head. And in their faces Rachael read the death of her last faint hope.

"We don't dare anesthetize him until we know just the lie of those broken ribs," said Warren gravely to his wife, "and yet the little chap is so exhausted that the strain of trying to touch it may--may be too much for him. There's no time for an X-ray. Some of these fellows think it is too great a risk. I believe it may be done. If there are internal injuries, we can't hope to--" He paused. "But otherwise, I believe--"

Again his voice dropped. He stood looking at the little boy with eyes that were not a surgeon's now; all a father's.

"Good little chap," he said softly. "Do you remember how he used to watch Jim, through the bars of his crib, when he was about eight months old, and laugh as if Jim was the funniest thing in the world?"

Rachael looked up and nodded with brimming eyes. She could not speak.

They carried Derry away, and Rachael followed them up to the head of the stairway outside of the operating-room, and sat there, her hands locked in her lap, her head resting against the wall. Alice dared not join her, she kept her seat by the library fire, and with one hand pressed tight against her eyes, tried to pray.

Rachael did not pray. She was unable even to think clearly. Visions drifted through her tired brain, the panorama of the long day and night swept by unceasingly. She was in Eighth Avenue again, she was in the hot train, with the rain beating against the windows, and tears running down her hot cheeks. She was entering the house--"Where's my boy?" And then she was driving the car through that cruel world of water and wind. She would have saved him if she could! She had done her share. Instantly, unflinchingly, she had torn through blackness and storm; a battered ship beating somehow toward the familiar harbor. Now he must be saved. Rachael knew that madness would come upon her if these hideous hours were only working toward the moment when she would know that she had been too late. For the rest of her life she would only review them: the Bar, the wet roads, the detour, and the frightful seconds on the bridge. There had been something expiatory, something symbolic in this mad adventure, this flight through the night. The fires that had been burning in her heart for the past terrible hours were purged, she must be changed forevermore after to-night. But for the new birth, Derry must not be the price! The strain had been too great, the delicate machinery of her brain would give, she could not take up life again, having lost him--and lost him in this way--

They were torturing him; the child's cry of utter agony reached her where she sat. It came to her, in a flash, that Warren had said there might be no merciful chloroform. Cold water broke out on her forehead, she covered her ears with her hands, her breath coming wild and deep. Derry!

"Oh, no--Daddy! Oh, no, Daddy! Oh, Mother--Mother--!"

"Oh, my God! this is not right," Rachael said half aloud. "Oh, take him, take him, but don't let him suffer so!"

She was writhing as if the suffering were her own. For perhaps five horrible moments the house rang, then there was sudden silence.

"Now he is dead," Rachael said in the same quiet, half-audible tone. "I am glad. He will never know what pain is again. Five perfect little years, with never one instant that was not sweet and good. Gerald Fairfax Gregory--five years old. One sees it in the papers almost every day. But who thinks what it means? Just the mother, who remembers the first cry, and the little crumpled flannel wrappers, and the little hand crawling up her breast. He walked so much sooner than Jim did, but of course he was lighter. And how he would throw things out of windows--the camera that hit the postman! Oh, my God!"

For the anguished screaming had recommenced, and the child wanted his mother.

Rachael bore it for endless, agonizing minutes. Presently Alice, white-faced, was kneeling on the step below her, and their wet hands were clasped.

"Dearest, why do you sit here!"

"Oh, Alice, could I get Warren, do you think? They mustn't--it's too cruel! He's only a baby, he doesn't understand! Better a thousand times to let him go--tell them so! Get George--tell him I say so!"

"Rachael, it's terrible," said Alice, who was crying hard, "b-b-but they must think there is a chance, dear. We couldn't interrupt them now. He would see you--there, he's quiet again. That may be all!"

But it was not the end for many hours. The women on the stairs, and the sobbing maids in the diningroom, hoped and despaired, and grew faint and sick themselves as the merciless work went on. Once George came out of the room for a few minutes, with a face flaked with white, and his surgeon's gown crumpled, wet with water and stained here and there a terrible red. He did not speak to either woman, and in answer to Alice's breath of interrogation merely shook his head.

At four o'clock Warren himself came to the door. Rachael sprang to her feet, was close to him in a second. The sight of him, his gown, his hands, his dreadful face, turned Alice faint, but Rachael's voice was steady.

"What is it?"

"We are nearly done. Nearly done," Warren said. "I can't tell yet--nobody can. But I must finish it. Do you think you could--he keeps asking for you. I am sorry to ask you--"

"Hold him?" Rachael's voice of agony said. "Yes, I could do that. I--I have been wanting to!"

"No--there is no necessity for that. He is on the table. But if he could see you. It is the very end of our work," he answered. "It may be that he can't-- you must be ready for that."

"I am ready," she said.

A second later she was in the room with the child. She saw nothing but Derry, his little body beneath the sheet rigidly strapped to the table. The group gave place, and Rachael stood beside him. His beautiful baby eyes, wild with terror and agony, found her; she bent over him, and laid her fingers on his wet little forehead. He wanted his mother to take him away, he had been calling her--hadn't she heard him? Please, please, not to let anyone touch him again!

Rachael summoned a desperate courage. She spoke to him, she could even smile. Did he remember the swing--yes, but he didn't remember Mother bringing him all the way up, so that Daddy and Uncle George--

His brave eyes were fixed on hers. He was trying to remember, trying to answer her smile, trying to think of other things than the recommencing pain.

No use. The hoarse, terrible little screams began again. His little hand writhed in hers.

"Mother--PLEASE--will you make them stop?"

Rachael was breathing deep, her own forehead was wet. She knew the child's strength was gone.

"Just a little more, dearest," she said, white lipped; eyes full of agonized appeal turned to George.

"Doctor--" One of the nurses, her hand on his pulse, said softly. George Valentine looked up.

Rachael's apprehensive glance questioned them both. But Warren Gregory did not falter, did not even glance away from his own hands.

Then it was over. The tension in the room broke suddenly, the atmosphere changed, although there was not an audible breath. The nurses moved swiftly and surely, needing no instructions. George lifted Derry's little hand from Rachael's, and put one arm about her. Warren put down his instrument, and bent, his face a mask of anxiety, over the child. Derry was breathing--no more. But on the bloodless face that Warren raised there was the light of hope.

"I believe he will make it, George," he said. "I think we have saved him for you, Rachael! No--no--leave him where he is, Miss Moore. Get a flat pillow under his head if you can. Cover him up. I'm going to stay here."

"Wouldn't he be more comfortable in his bed?" Rachael's shaken voice asked in a low tone. She was conscious only that she must not faint now.

"He would be, of course. But it may be just by that fraction of energy that he is hanging on. Brave little chap, he has been helping us just as if he knew--"

But this Rachael could not endure. Her whole body shook, the room rocked before her eyes. She had strength to reach the hall, saw Alice standing white and tense, at the top of the stairs--then it was all darkness.

It seemed hours later, though it was only minutes, that Rachael came dreamily to consciousness in her own old room, on her own bed. Her idly moving eyes found the shaded lamp, found Alice sitting beside her. Alice's hand lay over her own. For a long time they did not speak.

A perfect circle of shadow was flung on the high ceiling from the lamp. Outside of the shadow were the familiar window draperies, the white mantel with its old candlesticks, the exquisite crayon portrait of Jim at three, and Derry a delicious eighteen-months-old. There was the white bowl that had always been filled with violets, empty now. And there were the low bookcases where a few special favorites were kept, and the quaint old mahogany sewing-table that had been old Mrs. Gregory's as a bride.

Rachael was exhausted in every fibre of body and soul, consecutive thought was impossible now; her aching head defied the effort, but lying here, in this dim light, there came to her a vision of the years that might be. If she were ever rested again, if little Derry were again his sunny, resolute self, if Warren and she were reunited, then what an ideal of fine and simple and unselfish living would be hers! How she would cling to honor and truth and goodness, how she would fortify herself against the pitfalls dug by her own impulsiveness. She and Warren had everything in life worth while, it was not for them to throw their gifts away. Their home should be the source of help to other homes, their sons should some day go out into the world equipped with wisdom, disciplined and self-controlled, ready to meet life far more bravely than ever their mother had.

There was a low voice at her door. Alice was gone, and Warren was kneeling beside her. And as she laid one tired arm about his neck, in the dear familiar fashion of the past, and as their eyes met, Rachael felt that all her life had been a preparation for this exquisite minute.

"I thought you would like to know that he is sleeping, and we have moved him," Warren said. "In three days you will have him roaring to get up."

Tears brimmed Rachael's eyes.

"You saved him," she whispered.

"YOU saved him; George says so, too. If that fellow down there had given him chloroform, there would have been no chance. Our only hope was to relieve that pressure on his heart, and take the risk of it being too much for him. He's as strong as a bull. But it was a fight! And no one but a woman would have rushed him up here in the rain."

Rachael's eyes were streaming. She could not speak. She clung to her husband's hand for a moment or two of silence.

"And now, I want to speak to you," Warren said, ending it. "I have nothing to say in excuse. I know--I shall know all my life, what I have done. It is like a bad dream."

His uncertain voice stopped. Husband and wife looked full at each other, both breathing quickly, both faces drawn and tense.

"But, Rachael," Warren went on, "I think, if you knew how I have suffered, that you would--that some day, you would forgive me. I was never happy. Never anything but troubled and excited and confused. But for the last few months, in this empty house, seeing other men with their wives, and thinking what a wife you were--It has been like finding my sight--like coming out of a fever--" He paused. Rachael did not speak.

"I know what I deserve at your hands," Warren said. "Nobody--nobody--not old George, not anyone--can think of me with the contempt and the detestation with which I think of myself! It has changed me. I will never--I can never, hold up my head again. But, Rachael, you loved me once, and I made you happy--you've not forgotten that! Give me another chance. Let me show you how I love you, how bitterly sorry I am that I ever caused you one moment of pain! Don't leave me alone. Don't let me feel that between you and me, as the years go by, there is going to be a widening gulf. You don't know what the loneliness means to me! You don't know how I miss my wife every time I sit down to dinner, every time I climb into the car. I think of the years to come--of what they might have been, of what they will be without you! And I can't bear it. Why, to go down with you and the boys to Clark's Hills, to tell you about my work, to take you to dinner again--my God! it seems to me like Heaven now, and I look back a few years, when it was all mine, and wonder if I have been sane, wonder if too much work, and all the other responsibilities, of the boys, and Mother's death, and the estate, and poor little Charlie, whether I really wasn't a little twisted mentally!"

Rachael tightened her arms about his neck, pressed her wet face to his.

"Sweetheart," said her wonderful voice, a mere tired essence of a voice now, "if there is anything to forgive, I am so glad to forgive it! You are mine, and I am yours. Please God we will never be parted again!"

And then for a long time there was silence in the room, while husband and wife clung together, and the hurt of the long months was cured, and dissolved, and gone forever. What Warren felt, Rachael could only know from his tears, and his passionate kisses, and the grip of his arms. For herself, she felt that she might gladly die, being so held against his heart, feeling through her entire being the rising flood of satisfied love that is life and breath to such a nature as hers.

"I am changed," said Warren after long moments; "you will see it, for I see it myself. I can see now what my mother meant, years ago, when she talked to me about myself. And I am older, Rachael."

"I am not younger," Rachael said, smiling. "And I think I am changed, too. All the pressure, all the nervous worry of the last few years, seem to be gone. Washed away, perhaps, by tears--there have been tears enough! But somehow--somehow I am confident, Warren, as I never was before, that happiness is ahead. Somehow I feel sure that you and I have won to happiness, now, won to sureness. With each other, and the boys, and books and music, and Home Dunes, the years to come seem all bright. After all, we are young to have learned how to live!"

And again she drew his face down to hers.

Alice did not come back again, but Mary came in with a cup of smoking soup. Mrs. Valentine had taken the doctor home, but they would be back later on. It was after six, and Doctor Gregory said Mrs. Gregory was to drink this, and try to get some sleep. But first Mary and Rachael must talk over the terrible and wonderful night, and Rachael must creep down the hall, to smile at the nurse, who sat by the heavily sleeping Derry.

Then she slept, for hours and hours, while the winter sun smiled down on the bare trees in the square and women in furs and babies in woolens walked and chattered on the leaf-strewn paths.

Such a sleep and such a waking are memorable in a lifetime. Rachael woke, smiling and refreshed, in a radiant world. Afternoon sunshine was streaming in at her windows, she felt rested, deliciously ready for life again.

To bathe, to dress with the chatting Jimmy tying strings to her dressing-table, to have the maids quietly and cheerfully coming and going in the old way; this in itself was delight. But when she tiptoed into Derry's room, and found hope and confidence there, found the blue eyes wide open, under the bandage, and heard the enchanting little voice announce, "I had hot milk, Mother," Rachael felt that her cup of joy was brimming.

He had fallen out of the swing, Derry told her, and Dad had hurted him, and Jimmy added sensationally that Derry had broken his leg!

"But just the same, we wanted our Daddy the moment we woke up this morning," Miss Moore smiled, "and we managed to hold up one arm to welcome him, and it was Daddy that held the glass of milk, wasn't it, Gerald?"

"She calls me Gerald because she doesn't know me very well," said Derry in a tactful aside, and Rachael, not daring to laugh for fear of beginning to cry, could only kiss the brown hand, and devour, with tear-dazzled eyes, the eager face.

Then she and Jimmy went down to have a meal that was like breakfast and luncheon and tea in one, with Warren. And to Rachael, thinking of all their happy meals together, since honeymoon days, this seemed the best of all. The afternoon light in the breakfast-room, the maids so poorly concealing their delight in this turn of events, little Jim so pleased at finding a meal served at this unusual hour, and his parents seemingly disposed to let him eat anything and everything, and Warren, tired--so strangely gray--and yet utterly content and at peace; these made the hour memorably happy; a forerunner of other happy hours to come.

"It seems to me that there never was such a bright sunshine, and never such a nice little third person, and never such coffee, and such happiness!" said Rachael, her eyes reflecting something of the placid winter day; soul and body wrapped in peace. "Yesterday--only yesterday, I was wretched beyond all believing! To-day I think I have had the best hours of my life!"

"It is always going to be this way for you, Rachael," her husband said, "my life is going to be one long effort to keep you absolutely happy. You will never grieve on my account again!"

"Say rather," she said seriously, "that we know each other, and ourselves, now. Say that I will never demand utter perfection of you, or you of me. But, Warren--Warren--as long as we love each other--"

He had come around the table to her side, and was kneeling with his arms about her, and Rachael locked her hands about his neck. He was tired, he had had no sleep after the difficult night, and he seemed to her strangely broken, strangely her own. Rachael felt that he had never been so infinitely dear, so much hers to protect and save. The wonder of marriage came to her, the miracle of love rooted too deep for disturbance, of love fed on faults as well as virtues; so light a tie in the beginning, so powerful a bond as the years go by.

"As long as we love each other!" she said, smiling through tears, her eyes piercing him to the very soul.

He did not speak, and so for a moment they remained motionless, looking at each other. But when she released him, with one of her quick, shy kisses, he knew that the heart of Rachael was satisfied.